D0357397

Title:	Never Been Kissed
Author:	Timothy Janovsky
Agent:	Kevin O'Connor
	O'Connor Literary Agency
Publication date:	May 3, 2022
Category:	Romance
Format:	Trade Paperback Original
ISBN:	978-1-7282-5058-8
Price:	$14.99 U.S.
Pages:	288 pages

This book represents the final manuscript being distributed for prepublication review. Typographical and layout errors are not intended to be present in the final book at release. It is not intended for sale and should not be purchased from any site or vendor. If this book did reach you through a vendor or through a purchase, please notify the publisher.

Please send all reviews or mentions of this book to the Sourcebooks marketing department:
marketing@sourcebooks.com

For sales inquires, please contact
sales@sourcebooks.com

For librarian and educator resources, visit:
sourcebooks.com/library

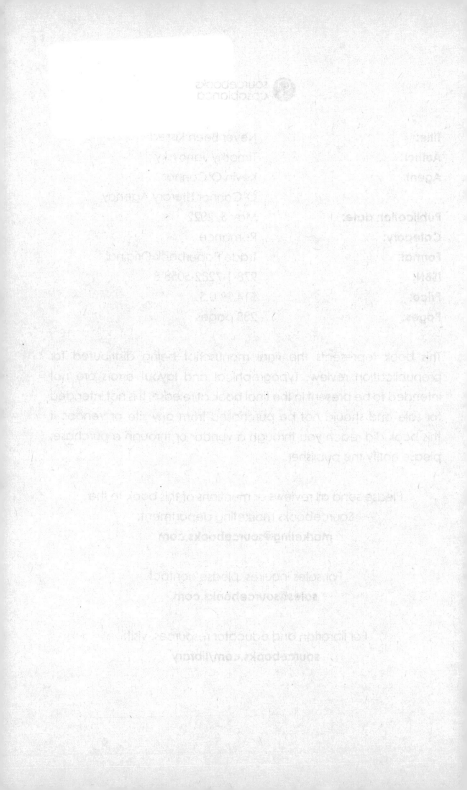

Title:	Never Been Kissed
Author:	Timothy Janovsky
Agent:	Kevin O'Connor
	KO Connor Literary Agency
Publication date:	May 3, 2022
Category:	Romance
Format:	Trade Paperback Original
ISBN:	978-1-7282-5058-8
Price:	$14.99 U.S.
Pages:	288 pages

This book represents the final material being distributed for prepublication review. Typographical and layout errors are not intended to be present in the final book. Please do not quote without checking your copy against the finished book. This book is for sale and should not be published. This advance copy it for sale and should not be published. This advance copy is not for sale and should not be published. This material, if resold, placed online or distributed through a vendor or through a purchase, please notify the publisher.

Please send all reviews or mentions of this book to the Sourcebooks marketing department.
marketing@sourcebooks.com

For sales inquiries, please contact:
sales@sourcebooks.com

For librarian and educator resources, visit:
sourcebooks.com/library

NEVER BEEN Kissed

TIMOTHY JANOVSKY

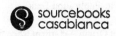

sourcebooks
casablanca

Copyright © 2022 by Timothy Janovsky
Cover and internal design © 2022 by Sourcebooks
Cover art by Monique Aimee

Sourcebooks and the colophon are registered trademarks of Sourcebooks.

All rights reserved. No part of this book may be reproduced in any form or by
any electronic or mechanical means including information storage and retrieval
systems—except in the case of brief quotations embodied in critical articles or
reviews—without permission in writing from its publisher, Sourcebooks.

The characters and events portrayed in this book are fictitious or
are used fictitiously. Any similarity to real persons, living or dead,
is purely coincidental and not intended by the author.

All brand names and product names used in this book are trademarks,
registered trademarks, or trade names of their respective holders.
Sourcebooks is not associated with any product or vendor in this book.

Published by Sourcebooks Casablanca, an imprint of Sourcebooks
P.O. Box 4410, Naperville, Illinois 60567–4410
(630) 961-3900
sourcebooks.com

[Library of Congress Cataloging-in-Publication Data]

Printed and bound in [Country of Origin—confirm when printer is selected].
XX 10 9 8 7 6 5 4 3 2 1

For my parents, Theresa and John.

"You can't meet someone until you've become what you're becoming."

—Nora Ephron

Chapter 1

Every perfect first kiss has three key elements:

✓ The right place—the senior prom, the lookout of a fairy-tale castle, the bed of a pickup truck on a beautifully starry night.

✓ The right moment—just as the Fourth of July fireworks build to a crescendo, during a moonlit slow dance, right after that first emotional "I love you."

✓ The right person—a young Leonardo DiCaprio (no exceptions).

If you're lucky, you get all three. But if you're me, you get a hole-in-the-wall gay club practically vibrating to "Let's Hear It for the Boy" and a prima-donna drag queen named Goldie Prawn.

"What do y'all say? Should I give this cutie a birthday smooch?" Goldie asks the boisterous crowd gathered around the small, scuffed-up stage. Raised drinks dot the air in answer. I try to push them all down with the power of my mind. Now would be the perfect moment for surprise telekinetic powers to kick in.

Goldie turns toward me with clear intent. Her tall, blond wig of curls is dangerously close to toppling off her round, perfectly beat face. If I was a prankster who relished the spotlight, I might take this opportunity to tap it off and get a laugh, play it up as a bit we rehearsed beforehand, all to avoid the incoming kiss.

But, alas, I'm not a prankster. I'm something worse. I'm a scared, freshly twenty-two-year-old boy standing onstage in front of a bunch of strangers on his birthday, horrified at the thought of having a flippant first kiss.

This isn't how it was supposed to happen.

"Kiss! Kiss! Kiss!" the horde chants as if kisses were nothing more than free samples given out at Costco.

Kisses, to me at least, are sacred. They have weight. They *mean something.*

Anxiety-induced panic punches me in the gut. I don't want to let everyone down or ruin the fun. Maybe I can pretend this one doesn't count? I'll wipe it from my record later.

I'm always waffling on this. The peer pressure to get my first kiss over with is at an all-time high right now, making me feel smaller than small.

"Kiss! Kiss! Kiss!" The chants grow louder.

Just as I'm about to let those painted puckered lips collide with my own, I...

I...

I whip my head away. Miss Prawn catches my cheek, and the crowd of rowdy queers boos with wild abandon.

I flush hot, shrink down, and attempt to shrug it off.

The power of teleportation? No? Okay, fine. Being a mere mortal seriously sucks sometimes.

"Oh, honey, what, did you think my kiss was going to turn you into a frog?" Goldie asks. "That's *princesses*. I'm a *queen!*" An Alice in Wonderland "Off with her head!" sound bite rings out, as if this had all been planned. "Oh my word, Paul in the DJ booth is at the top of his game tonight!"

"Always the best for you, Goldie." Paul's disembodied voice booms through the place.

Goldie showboats a second before swiveling back to me. "Anywho, since you're an adorable little cupcake and it's your birthday, I'm gonna let it slide!" She flashes me a vicious side-eye before turning all her attention back to the crowd. "All right, y'all, let's hear it for the boy!"

As the dance floor morphs back into a sea of raging, writhing bodies, lights low and inhibitions lower, my best friends, Avery and Mateo, march me off the stage and into the nearby bathroom. It's their fault I was up there in the first place. Well, them and the homemade Birthday Babe sash I'm wearing over my snug, sporty, going-out tank top.

"WTH! Why didn't you kiss her?" Avery asks. Her glittery, *Euphoria*-inspired eye makeup glimmers in the flickering half-light over the sludgy sink.

"Shut up, Aves. You know why he didn't kiss her," Mateo says. "The reason is stupid, but even a stupid reason is a reason."

"It's not stupid," I protest. "It's romantic. There's a difference."

"Romance and stupidity are synonymous," says a bald man in a leather harness taking a leak at the nearby urinal. It's hard to avoid the sudden overwhelming sound and unpleasant aroma of the steady stream of beer-produced piss.

"Thanks for your input," I say.

"Happy birthday, though," Studded Harness says.

Mateo laughs. "You're twenty-two now, babe. Don't you think it's time to give up on the perfect-kiss-before-the-credits and finally settle?"

"'Settle' is not in my vocabulary." I didn't settle for my second-choice college. I didn't settle for assistant manager at Wiley's Drive-In, my glorious, film-laden summer job for the past seven years. I don't even settle for Pepsi when I ask for Coke. Giving up on my perfect first kiss isn't exactly an option for me.

"Wren, some of us sucked it up, settled, and survived," Avery says. "You remember how my first kiss with Caleb went?"

"As if I could ever forget that vivid description of your ex-boyfriend's chalupa breath. Not every conversation is a creative writing assignment, okay?"

Avery knocks me in the arm and then melts into my side. She's the perfect height to tuck her head into the crook of my neck when she's wearing her strappy heels. Her thick, curly brunette mane falls onto my face and into my open, unsuspecting mouth. *Blegh.*

"I'm merely saying you can't control everything." She sighs. "That, and you have a weird obsession with first kisses for someone who's never had one."

"I think Wren supersedes obsession," Mateo says. He's produced a Sharpie from his pocket and is inking his name and number onto the bathroom mirror, which is more phone book than looking glass at this point. He's all about that cosmic connection, letting the universe work its magic to land him his lover of the month. The apps don't do it for him these days. I wish I could be that carefree with my fate.

"I have a vision for my first kiss, okay? What's wrong with that? People moodboard their weddings. What's the difference?" I sound petulant, arms folded across my chest.

"The difference," Mateo snaps, pointing the uncapped pen in my face, "is that you don't need a gold band and a seven-tiered cake to suck face! Geez, you gotta let life be life."

"That's radically profound," Studded Harness says.

I jump, having forgotten we aren't alone. "I'm sorry. What are you still doing here?"

"You're kinda blocking the sink..."

"Oh." I shuffle away. "Sorry."

The reflective floor and neon-green walls have begun to give me a headache. Though that may be the many, many mixed drinks I consumed this evening to ring in my twenty-second like it's nobody's business. But I guess that was my mistake. It's never nobody's business when it's my business. My business is always my friends' business.

I suppose I shouldn't be hard-pressed over harmless meddling in my love life, but they have to face the facts: there isn't one viable, eligible suitor around. Not one I'd want to suck face—like Mateo so eloquently put it—with, anyway.

I tell them I'm tired and ready to call the rideshare. Mateo dots the *i*'s in his last name with stars before we beeline out of the bathroom. I avoid making eye contact with Goldie, who's holding court near the bar. Onstage, she may have been gracious, but hell knows no fury like a drag queen scorned.

On our way out, at Avery's behest, we snag stamps on the backs of our hands.

"You coming back tonight?" Stacia, the door girl, asks Avery in a husky voice. She's a butch dreamboat in a black faux-leather jacket covered in snaps over a weathered, patterned button-down. She cradles Avery's right hand as she blots the blue ink from her pad. Tonight, the image etched into her wooden block is a winged hippo with the neck of a giraffe and the tail of a tiger.

Avery is always (*always*) wondering where Stacia gets these from because, naturally, that's how she admits she has a crush—by talking about one minute detail until Mateo and I tell her to shut up already. Lovingly, of course.

Avery is caught off guard by the question, but manages to say, "Uh, probably not. It's late. Why do you ask?"

"I ask"—Stacia stops midsentence to blow a bit on the back of Avery's hand, setting the image onto her skin—"because every time you're in here, you swing by for my stamp and then scamper off into the night, never to be seen from again." She boldly edges Avery a little closer. "If you're looking for an excuse to talk to me, you could just come say hi next time. It gets lonely up here when all the fun is out on the dance floor."

Avery stammers, on the verge of flirtation overload, so Mateo swoops in and saves the day. "I'll be sure my friend here takes the note. Have a good night." He ushers a tongue-tied Avery out into the alley before she can make a fool of herself, and I follow close behind. The streetlamp shows her cheeks are still burning bright from the exchange.

Jealousy, that unwelcome freshman at a seniors-only party, loudly makes himself known to me. It's been so long since I've felt the unwavering heat of flirty banter, interminable eye contact, and touches that last a hair too long. I'm happy for Aves—I am—but damn, do I miss it. Just because I still haven't been kissed doesn't mean I don't want all of, well, *that*.

The black sedan pulls up within minutes. Rashan, one of our favorite townies, is a career driver, and we always make sure to text him before we get on the app. If we're going to support a company with questionable business ethics, we at least want to leave Rashan a big tip for his killer playlists and the plethora of phone chargers snaking out the back of his center console.

Over the sound of the new Ariana Grande, he says, "Happy birthday,

Wren! How does it feel to be twenty-two? I remember those days." His voice sounds longing as he turns the heat on partial blast. The three of us are wearing more stray strands of metallic confetti than articles of clothing at this point, so it's much appreciated in the nighttime chill.

"Aren't you only twenty-six?" Mateo asks.

"Youth escaped me centuries ago," Rashan says. The rigidity of the Pennsylvania city blocks gives way to residential homes and then the Rosevale College campus. Rashan's blinker ticks on before he adds, "Getting lucky tonight?"

I know this question is directed at me, the birthday boy who should be bouncing up and down for birthday sex, but there's a big wad of spit sitting in my throat stopping my answer. Which is good because I never know how to answer that question anyway.

"For Wren, getting lucky means Barbra Streisand's directorial catalog was just added to the Criterion Collection," Avery groans, like she doesn't love a good drinking game set to *Yentl*. She knows all the words to "Papa, Can You Hear Me?" and not just because her father is a Reform Jewish rabbi. "He's the grandpa of our group."

"Yup, he's an old soul who takes it slow. Soooooo slow that he's never even been kissed," Mateo says. He gets mouthy when he's drunk.

"If you're looking to fix that, I've got lips, you've got lips, we could smush 'em together," Rashan offers. As far as I know, Rashan is a solid zero on the Kinsey scale, and, frankly, he could use some of our tip money to invest in a collection of ChapStick. So, I'll politely pass.

"I'm flattered," I say, "really. But, I'm saving myself for something special."

"You do realize how sad that sounds, right?" Mateo asks.

"I'm with him on this one," Avery adds.

"I don't know. I think it's kinda sweet," Rashan counters. As if to prove he's on my side, Rashan brings the car to a screeching stop outside of our apartment building, and both of my friends' heads go crashing into the front seats.

"Ouch!" they cry in unison.

"Sorry, lead foot!" he says, not sounding particularly sorry at all.

Booting up my own best sorry-not-sorry attitude, I just adjust my Birthday Babe sash before smugly unbuckling the seat belt this *grandpa* had been smart enough to put on.

"Serves you both right," I say with a satisfied smile before sauntering inside for some much-needed rest.

Chapter 2

The B in the silver 3B on our blue apartment door is hanging on by a single slender nail. Right now, I can't help but feel like I'm that B, a bad bitch seconds away from free fall. What's going to push me over the edge?

We always say we're going to fix the B, but never get around to it. Oh well. It's only been six months. I think it adds character to our otherwise identical, college-approved living arrangements. Off-campus housing is hard to come by and even harder to keep cute. Besides, those letters birthed our group chat name—The 3Bee Gees, appropriate mainly because our favorite song to take tequila shots to is "Stayin' Alive."

Ha, ha, ha, haaaaa.

I stumble into the dark when the door opens. Avery struggles to get her key out of the lock. Nobody is willing to face the harsh fluorescent lights that have surely been here since the seventies—mostly because we always end up looking like drowned rats when we return home from a night at the club. I flop down first onto the purple and green eyesore of a futon that the previous tenants left behind. I need to rest my eyes, my feet, my everything.

I'm about to doze off in what can only be described as a post-disco-disco nap when the singing starts.

"Happy birthday to you…"

Mateo and Avery are carrying in a plate of chocolate-covered cannolis from my favorite bakery. They've stuck a small smattering of lit candles into the cream. The glow illuminates the lower halves of my friends' faces, making them look like the phantoms of could-have-beens past—not that I'm still obsessing over all that or anything. (Except I totally am.)

I can't figure out why it's bugging me so much tonight. Falling behind everyone has never really bothered me, especially since most of my high school friends were straight, and straight people exist on a completely different relationship timeline than LGBTQ people do. Doesn't that grant me some leeway?

Though, in all honesty, there might be some truth mixed in with the earlier taunting. This is the first night in a long time I begin to wonder if maybe it's finally my moment to do something about my kisslessness.

My anxiety reminds me that I'm not getting any younger. Twenty-two is halfway to forty-four, and forty-four is halfway to eighty-eight, and if I'm one-fourth of the way to being nearly ninety, it might be time to put these lips to the test. Use them the way God intended. Even if some people believe God intended for them only to be used in monogamous, heterosexual matrimony.

If I squint, the flecks of birthday candle flame before me look like bulbs on a fancy movie-theater marquee. One that reads:

Wren's Super Queer Kiss-Before-the-Credits Quest Starring Wren Roland, Directed by Wren Roland, Written by Wren Roland, Produced by Wren Roland... Now presented in Cinemascope!

I must admit, it has a nice ring to it. And if the universe won't orchestrate the first kiss of my dreams, then maybe it's time I write it into existence for myself.

I'll get my friends off my back and my first kiss off my coming-of-age checklist. *On my own terms.* A win-win.

So, after a slightly off-key but still totally well-meaning song, I make a wish that this will be the summer I stop standing behind the sound stage of my life and start acting like a protagonist for once.

A post-Hays Code protagonist, that is.

As Mateo divvies up the cannolis, Avery asks, "What'd'ya wish for?"

"More phallic desserts, I bet," Mateo jokes.

"Can't I enjoy a baked good without the Freudian psychoanalysis? Besides, I can't tell you what I wished for or it won't come true." I devour my first bite of creamy, crunchy Italian goodness. Phallic or not, they're too delicious to waste.

"Come on, you can't be that superstitious. What if we can help you make that wish come true? What if the universe put us, your friggin' fabulous best friends, here to be your WGGs?" Avery loves speaking in cheeky acronyms and has moved into the sage-advice phase of her comedown, which I love, but would never admit.

"Uh, let me guess, walrus golfing groupies?" I say with equal cheekiness.

"Wish-granting guides, duh!" she chimes back.

"Being a wish-granting guide sounds like a lot of work," Mateo whines. "Can't I just plant one on you and call it a night?"

My heart catches, but only for a second. "No, thanks. I'm good."

I reach for the glass of water Avery set out for me so I can swallow both the crusted cannoli bits and my battered pride. Freshman year, I thought about kissing Mateo. A lot. This was before I was out, but after he and I became assigned roommates turned close friends.

Now, we're in too deep, and he knows too much. The allure is gone. And that's fine. Honestly, it is. Except I still have an email drafted to him in a special folder on my Google account. It's my Pre-Coming-Out-Almost-Kisses folder (covertly titled, Do Not Look Here! It's Tentacle Porn!)

It's the place I'd poured all my misplaced feelings before I knew I was queer. Before I stopped, dropped, and rolled out of the closet as "gay." If that's even still how I identify.

There are four total messages sitting unsent in that folder. I haven't even thought about it in half a year.

"Isn't there anyone we went to high school with that you'd want to kiss?" Avery asks, aimlessly scrolling through her socials, cannoli crumbs still collected on her chest.

Two names from yesteryear flash through my mind on that marquee from before, but I ignore them. Or, try to ignore them. But try as I might, one name grows bigger and brighter the more I try to switch off the screen.

"Wait!" Avery shouts as if she can see those flashing lights. "What about Derick? I know you're a geezer who doesn't really do social media anymore, but I saw he came out sophomore year of college. You were obsessed with him back in the day. Do you think he'll be home for the summer?"

Derick Haverford. His senior picture, in his purple and black cap and gown, appears on a fake pinup movie poster below the marquee. The picture is the same one I mooned over under my comforter by phone flashlight the summer after graduation. The one I drew dainty hearts around in red pen before that epic night of our almost-kiss-gone-wrong. Lovesick doesn't even begin to describe what I was for him.

I'm sure he'll be home, considering his dad is an investor and part owner of Any Weather Transportation Group, the company that oversees the commercial bus lines to and from Philadelphia and New York City. If you commute for work or travel for pleasure from our county, you're familiar with the Any Weather Transportation Group and the face of the freshly graying man on all the local ads.

I wonder if that's what Derick will look like all grown up and filled out.

I wonder if he ever thinks of me, too.

"He ghosted me, remember?" Is it still considered ghosting if you're only friends who almost kissed once? Maybe that's ghouling or zombieing or poltergeisting. Whichever one terrorizes the most and yells *boo!* the least.

"Oh." Avery twirls a strand of her hair and doesn't meet my eyes. "Right."

"Ghosting should be punishable by death," Mateo says, tapping on his phone at hyperspeed. He looks up to catch our matching concerned expressions. "What? Ick. Fine. At least a public flogging."

"A public flogging? You'd like that, wouldn't you?" Avery teases. Mateo is a proud kinkster, and we love him for it.

As much as I wish I could punish Derick for throwing away an amazing year of friendship for a rotating cast of frat boys, allowing our bond to become emotional bondage, there's not much I can do about it. It is what it is. I'm destined to be his maybe. He's destined to be my almost.

"Derick's in the past." I sigh with finality. "Maybe I'll meet someone at the drive-in. That's sort of always been the fantasy. Hitting it off with a movie buff who has the same taste as I do. I mean, that place is my only hope, really. I'll be chained to Wiley's all summer. I'm doing everything in my power to make sure it stays open." My boss, Earl, would never admit that the drive-in is suffering financial hardship, but with a new streaming service dropping every second, how could it not be? "I'd like to keep a steady paycheck. My student loans aren't going to pay themselves."

"I know you just got promoted, but you aren't thinking about staying there after this summer, are you? We're going to be adults who need, like, adult jobs."

"How astute." I roll my eyes at Avery. "And how is Wiley's not, like, an adult job?"

She shrugs, nestling herself farther into the pillows on the futon. "I just mean, obviously, I don't want it to have to close or anything. We've worked there together since high school. It's our special place. I'll do whatever I can to make this season great, but I'm going to be job hunting for full-time work ASAP. Earl doesn't pay that well."

"He doesn't?" Mateo pipes up. "How did I let you two talk me into working there again?"

"Like your Rosevale summer-stock theater salary was going to be so much better?" Avery shoots back. After a disastrous casting snafu where Mateo was passed over for the role of Bobby in *Company*, he faced a real Sophie's choice between bussing tables at his parents' Filipino fusion restaurant in Brooklyn or joining us in the land of summertime cinema to make some money.

"At least I'd get paid in applause there."

Avery flicks a crumb in his direction.

I don't care to consider what Avery was suggesting. The thought of leaving Wiley's has me in hives. It's embedded in my DNA. It's the reason I became a film studies major. Most humans are sixty percent water, but I swear I'm sixty percent fountain soda at this point.

"It's time for me to retire," I say. I can't sit still with the uncertain feelings any longer. "Good night, my darlings."

"Bedtime already?" Avery asks with an exaggerated sigh. She knows I'm faking tired.

Mateo jumps up, phone clutched in his amber manicure. "Looks like my night is just beginning."

He flips the screen toward us. I guess the club bathroom worked its wonders. A handsome, Black, round-faced boy with a shaved head who I recognize as a junior in the Women and Gender Studies department has sent a selfie to Mateo's cell with a text reading:

I dunno who u r, but I like ur confident mirror game

It's not a Shakespearean sonnet, but I can tell, to Mateo, it's as good as gold.

His fingers fly across the screen. "I'm meeting him in the library gardens in ten."

The library gardens are the only place on campus that aren't regularly patrolled by campus safety, and if you move to the right spot, you can't be seen by the security cameras. On any given weekend night, there are at least eight couples in the early stages of a hookup milling about the rosebushes and wooden arches.

If it weren't already painfully obvious, I've never been. And never will be. I've never really had a desire to.

"Can you believe the mirror worked? The mirror never works," Mateo swoons.

"The magic of PYOT," Avery says, poking me pointedly in the pec. "Putting. Yourself. Out. There."

"As much as I'd love to PMOT with a PYT and receive some TLC, all my attempts at love have been DOA," I mutter, besting Avery at her own game.

"Well, make like a celebrity in their Notes app and CTN!" That's Avery-speak for *Change the narrative.*

"One more for the road," Mateo says, taking down our handle of vanilla vodka from its perch on top of the yellowing fridge. I'm still fuzzy from the vodka crans at the club, but I claim the shot glass I got abroad on my trip to Dublin, covered in cartoon donkeys. Mateo's a heavy pourer, but he's also a frequent spiller. I'll only end up with three-quarters of a shot, max. I'll be fine.

"Happy birthday, babe. May twenty-two be the year of you!"

"Did you just come up with that?" Avery asks, shocked.

"You're not the only poet and you know it!" Mateo juts out a hip, strikes a pose.

We bring our shot glasses together.

In unison, we say our bawdy Irish toast, "Here's to you, here's to me, the best of friends we'll always be. But if we ever disagree, then fuck you. Here's to me!"

That swig of alcoholic heaven goes down with a sharp, rancorous sting. There's a new, clear ringing in my ears, bells signaling the start of something. But what exactly?

"Later, babes." Mateo grabs his keys, his jacket, and his student ID lanyard. The door thumps closed behind him.

Avery's back to scrolling, so I slink, even tipsier, into my room. My twinkle lights are still on, illuminating my movie posters from *Casablanca* to *The Wizard of Oz*. I even have some newer ones like *Lady Bird* and *Moonlight*. I usually feel right at home amid my movie memorabilia, but for some reason, tonight, on the other side of twenty-two, I suddenly feel unmoored.

I think it's all this discussion of my stunted romantic life and my hazy, half-formed quest. That thought alone sends me skidding over to my laptop where I unlock my tentacle-porn folder. Before I know it, I'm cooing over every word and line of sappy prose I put down on electronic paper for first kisses that never were.

Dear Derick...

Dear Mateo...

Dear Cole...

Dear Alfie...

Do you remember that night we...

If my dad had just shown up five minutes later...

I've known since Halloween...

The longer I read and reread, the heavier my eyelids grow and the more the words slide together. Despite the blue light of my laptop being a supposed stimulant, I find my brain failing and my head slumping. That's when a drunken idea pops up like a comic strip bubble: *Send them. I dare you.*

It's a bad idea in more ways than one, but a protagonist on a kiss quest needs a costar, right? My mind doesn't register what my fingers are doing. After about an hour, lost in my feels, I pull off my Warby Parker knockoff glasses, lay my head down, and pass out to a soft, sweet chorus of *whooshes*.

Chapter 3

The morning sun mars my dreamful sleep. In all the chaos and cannolis, I never closed my blinds. When I open my eyes, I realize I never even made it to my bed. I've got squares impressed into the left side of my face from my laptop keyboard.

I sip from a Rosevale College water bottle like a wayward traveler lost in the desert. It does nothing to mitigate the feeling of cotton balls in my mouth, reminding me of when I got my two impacted wisdom teeth removed. Only this time I'm not under the influence of fun anesthetics.

The pounding in my head plays on as I get up. If death came by delivery app, I'd place a request right away: one large order of eternal sleep, hold the stomach nausea.

At least it's Saturday. I have exams to study for and papers to write and group presentations to plan for but...*I have nowhere to be.*

My muscles instantly relax at the prospect of a self-care day before the triathlon that is finals week. I slip an old-timey VHS tape out of my impressive collection and let Nora Ephron nurse me back to health.

I curl into the fetal position on my twin bed and groan, setting the remote down at my side. There's no better way to cure a hangover than to listen to Tom Hanks waxing poetic about pencil bouquets. The movie projects itself onto the inside of my eyelids. I've seen it enough times to know it shot by shot. The autumnal colors come to me with little effort.

A notification ding intermingles with the Cranberries crooning over the fabulous Upper West Side montage. Maybe it's Professor Tanson looking to schedule our end-of-semester meeting. She's my film studies advisor and the head of the department. If I don't email her back within ten minutes of receipt, she will inevitably lose track of my response in the mess of her ever-flooding inbox, so I slog over to my laptop, covered in vinyl stickers of Greta Gerwig and Noah Baumbach to see what she needs.

The email banner scrolls across the top, and when I click into it, I'm confused by an address I haven't seen in a long time.

FROM: Derick.Haverford.Photo@gmail.com

TO: RolandOnTheRiver14@gmail.com

SUBJECT: Re: Tonight at the Drive-In

Hey stranger,
   Long time, no talk.
   Wow...I did NOT expect to wake up to this.

No.

Nonononononono.

Memories from last night harpoon me to the chair. My jaw locks and my pulse quickens. *Please* tell me time travel is still in the cards for my impending secret superpower...

Panicking, I launch a Google search and attempt to figure out how to unsend an email. An already-received email. An already-read email. An already replied-to email.

This is what happens when you hit the vodka a little too hard. This is what happens when your best friends chastise you for being a stupid romantic. This is what happens when you take that extra shot despite your hurting heart, desperate to catch back up to the crowd you call your peers.

I think I might throw up. I slam the laptop shut and bolt for our shared bathroom, racing past Avery in the living room. She's conked out on the futon, snuggling our favorite *Twinks and Otters and Bears, Oh my!* pillow. Mateo, thankfully, is nowhere in sight.

Hanging my head in the chiffon-yellow toilet, I dry heave for a few minutes, but my body won't expel anything—not the alcohol, not our pregame munchies, not even my mushy ball of mashed-up feelings. Instead, I slump down on the cold, white tile, open my phone, and read on:

I'm thinking maybe you sent this to me by accident. Totally cool if you did. No worries.

No worries? I'm 110 percent worries and angst and idiocy.

From the floor, I reach blindly onto the cluttered sink counter and pull a tiny paper cup from its sleeve. I flip on the faucet, letting the cold water run over the back of my hand. It's the first nice feeling I've had all morning.

As soon as I take a calming sip, a loud voice rings out from the front doorway. "Baaaaaaabes, I'm hooooooooome!" It's very Ricky Ricardo, but the audience laughter isn't for Mateo's flamboyant entrance. It's all mocking me, the boy stuffing chocolates into his mouth as the conveyor belt of his love life speeds up and out of control.

I do a spit take into the toilet as I remember: *Mateo got one of those emails.*

When Mateo, Avery, and I all moved into 3B at the start of junior year, I should've deleted the email. The feelings had faded by then. Our almost-kiss at the Pride House basement beach bash, wearing matching Hawaiian shirts and leis, was a thing of the past. The door to something more was shut and sealed ages ago.

Now, I crawl to the actual door, slam it shut, and lock it. I know I can't hide in here forever. To seem less unstable, I run the shower but never get in. There's a worsening feeling that says no matter how much lavender-scented body scrub I use, I'll never know calm again.

"Wren?" Avery's groggy question comes from the other side of the door. "Are you doing that thing where you pretend to be showering to avoid us?"

"He's definitely avoiding me. Look at this," Mateo says in what he thinks is a whisper but is actually a stage whisper that whips right through the thin door.

Mustering up all my strength, I jerk the door open and snatch Mateo's phone out from between them. Neither has enough time to blink or react. I'm running into the living room where I jump onto the futon, frantically finding the buttons to delete the evidence of my emotional downfall.

One click is all it takes for the email to self-destruct. *Whew.* I can breathe again.

Mateo and Avery stand at the inlet to the hallway looking both mighty confused and confusingly parental. Disappointment looms in the air. I hand the phone back, but my peace of mind is still nowhere to be found.

"Are you done acting like one of those aggressive rescue dogs who just needs a patient owner with lots of treats to learn to love again?" Avery asks, hands on hips.

Mateo unlocks his phone again. "Do you think he'll bite me if I tell him that Gmail stores your trash for thirty days?" I groan with great volume. "Also, like I wasn't gonna take a screenshot?" He's glaring at me now.

I lie down in defeat, folding my arms over my chest to protect myself from the onslaught. I probably look like the corpse of a boy who once had starry-eyed prospects, but now has nothing. Here lies Wren Roland, beloved son, tolerable brother, loyal friend, and hopeless romantic (heavy on the hopeless).

Mateo and Avery kneel around the coffee table, which is covered in our plentiful cacti friends. Mortification crackles in my chest until I feel ready to fizzle out entirely.

"Just spitballing here, but does this have something to do with the long-winded, partially confusing, entirely embarrassing but semisweet email about our almost-kiss that I received last night while I was making out with Brandon?" Mateo asks. I don't even need to look to know his eyebrows are doing a provocative dance.

"*Oof.* I totally forgot you two almost kissed," Avery says, amused. "I'd kill to visit the parallel universe where that happened. I bet you two dated for, I don't know, three months and then broke up over something stupid like which Lady Gaga album is the best…"

"*Born This Way.*"

"*A Star is Born* soundtrack."

Mateo gasps. "You're clearly in a crisis, so I'm going to pretend you didn't say that." Disdain seeps from every syllable.

"If you're not ready to talk about it, we get it," Avery says.

I'm pretty sure I'll never be able to talk about the fact that in my drunken spiral of sadness, I sent four boys four different emails they were never meant to lay eyes on. I thought coming out was going to be the biggest life-altering event I could handle this year, but, somehow, this overrules even that. I'm going to be picking up the pieces of this forever. Mateo is never going to let me live it down. Who knows what else Derick said in response. And I can only hope and pray the other emails failed to send.

"Forget that noise. Stop stalling and spill, babe," Mateo demands.

My mind is in ruins. The aftershocks are still reverberating through my sternum. I have no idea what those emails mean, or why I sent them. Sure, I was sad and drunk and annoyingly nostalgic, but that doesn't explain why I didn't immediately send follow-ups reading: *Sorry! I got hacked! LOL LMAO Hahahahaahaha. Send me bitcoin.*

Wait. Is it too late to do that?

"It's an old email," I mutter, fiddling with a stray thread on the armrest. I decide not to mention the others. Not now anyway.

"No duh. I figured as much. But, why now? Why'd you send it now?" he asks.

"I didn't mean to…" It sounds pathetic. I can make up a billion excuses, but it doesn't refute the fact that somewhere in my subconscious I *wanted* to send them. Maybe I just wanted the attention, the possibility. I don't know.

Or, maybe, I thought this was the first step on my kiss quest. Reel in the almosts and turn them into actuals. There's a twisted sort of logic there.

"Didn't mean to or regretted it after?" he asks.

"Ugh." I press the heels of my hands into my eye sockets.

"Babe," Mateo says, reaching a hand across the table and finding my shoulder. "I'm not judging you. I'm trying to get to the bottom of why you're acting so weird."

I'm acting so weird because I came out as "gay" to my family approximately five months ago and something about it still doesn't feel quite right. The word *queer* feels better in my body, more encompassing of me, but I'm not sure I'm ready to say that out loud or what that means. I can't just come out all over again. When you add together the email fiasco and our impending graduation, acting weird feels warranted. Earned, even.

"Are you okay?" Avery asks after some serious silence.

It's a great question. One I can't answer until I get this fire under control. So instead I get up and fumble for my lanyard on the hook by the door. I stuff my feet into sneakers and my arms into a denim jacket I've yet to wear this spring. Without my bag or my books or my laptop, I tell them I need to go study, get some air, be alone. Like the supportive best friends they've been all along, they let me claim my space.

I don't let the *thud* of the door closing behind me make me feel any worse. I'm on a mission to take back my dignity.

♡

B-level of the library is where I go to be alone. The ambient hushed chatter and tapping of nails across keyboards meld together to make an in-person ASMR video performed in surround sound only for me.

I feel safe and serene here. It's nothing like the dead silence of C-level where Avery gives even the quietest of coughers a dirty look. Nor is it boisterous like A-level where Mateo and his fellow theater majors do readings of Tennessee Williams plays at full volume with questionable southern drawls.

My cozy little B-level corner is sequestered away from the world and, more importantly, my apartment mates. The email blast from the past is something I need to settle alone. At least right now. They wouldn't understand the haplessness lodged in my chest cavity. That's why I'm here, logged in to one of the school computers, taking in Derick's response.

I hold my breath and click into the email.

FROM: Derick.Haverford.Photo@gmail.com
TO: RolandOnTheRiver14@gmail.com
SUBJECT: Re: Tonight at the Drive-In

Hey stranger,
    Long time, no talk.
    Wow…I did NOT expect to wake up to this.
    I'm thinking maybe you sent this to me by accident. Totally cool if you did. No worries.

I exhale. Okay, so my eyes didn't deceive me before. It's not a string of sparkly heart emojis and a marriage proposal, but that's not the end of the world, right? He's flattered. Confused. Embarrassed, maybe. But, he's cool with me baring my soul in such an unfiltered manner. He's not sending screenshots to all his friends and laughing behind my back.

I hope.

I remember that night. Mostly. You and all our friends. When the show started, we could see so many stars from the truck bed. The pillows, the blankets, the string lights. It was all beautiful.

Beautiful. The sense memory sends a chill up my spine. It was the summer before we left for college. Limitless in so many ways.

I borrowed Dad's pickup truck, Earl let me off for a night, and a bunch of us piled in to see the latest release.

While the movie wasn't anything to alert the critics about, I didn't care. I spent the night half-snuggled up against Derick, sharing a blanket (stolen from my sister's room) and a complimentary bucket of popcorn from the snack shack.

Since all nine of our friends couldn't ride into the lot in my dad's truck, some of them had to drive themselves and park their cars in the overflow off to the side, facing away from the screen. When they joined us, we laughed and snacked and snapped selfies, and the future felt far away. Something to worry about tomorrow.

But, as the night wore on, part of the group began to head out for curfews.

It was the last time we all got to chill before college happened. Was it just me, or did it feel kind of bittersweet?

For me, the sweet outweighed the bitter.

Eventually, it was just Derick and me. Kind of. Avery had dozed off nearby in a pile of pillows. With our popcorn depleted, during the second movie (which was somehow snoozier than the first) I thought I felt Derick's hand brush mine under the blanket.

Our eyes met like a big, romantic movie B-plot. We were parked far enough toward the back of the half-empty lot, so I knew nobody would see. And if I'd had the balls, I might've taken the risk and leaned over. Heart hammering in my ears, I could have sworn Derick was. But, right as it seemed like our sheer hormonal will would pull us in, Avery woke up with a ferocious start, forcing us both to shoot back into platonic place.

"What did I miss?" she asked, reaching for the Twizzlers in our laps.

The moment was decimated. When I got home that night, I cried while I wrote his email.

Anyway, please don't hate me, but I don't really remember that particular part. Not that way, at least. I had a lot going on. It was late. And, well, I hope this doesn't hurt your feelings, but I didn't think of you like that.

Wow. His hope is ill-timed. My feelings are dashed. And, damn, now I'm crying in the middle of the library. Not that this would be the first time that's happened, but it sure is the most devastating.

I didn't think of anyone like that, really. I didn't let myself. It was complicated. My sexuality situation was kind of...a mess back then. Don't take it personally.

Don't take it personally? It's bad enough that he ghosted me. Now, he's formally rejected me. In writing. Forever preserved to taint the memory of that one perfect almost-kiss. *This* is why I should learn to leave the love stories for the screen.

A girl two years below me wearing a French braid and a Taylor Swift T-shirt gives me a sympathetic look from across the row of computers and says in the sweetest voice, "It's only finals week. You'll get through it."

If only these tears were over something as stupid and simple as grades. I compose myself enough to thank her before forcing myself to finish reading Derick's upsetting response.

He's signed his email:

See you soon,

Derick (but you already knew that)

See me soon? What could he mean by that?

PS. Happy belated birthday, Wrenji.

Wrenji.

Only he called me that. On his first day of fourth grade at Willow Valley Elementary, he was seated next to me for science class. I was shy and quiet—in some ways I still am—so when he asked what my name was, he heard "Ben" instead of "Wren."

"Does anyone call you Benji?" he'd asked.

"If you mean Wrenji, then sure," I joked back.

He looked at me all confused and then said, "Okay, nice to meet you, Wrenji."

And I was too nervous to ever correct him. Eventually, it just became our thing, and I was okay with that. Right now, I wished he hadn't used it as a weapon of mass emotional destruction.

Before I can even consider writing him back, I distract myself by clicking the link to his professional website, right below his signature. He must run a formal photography business now. Back in the day, he was the Willow Valley yearbook photographer extraordinaire. No photo got into the publication without his express approval. He was a savant for capturing the moment.

Now, it looks like he's branched out into portraiture—headshots for actors and LinkedIn pictures for business professionals. The layout is sleek and the background is a slate gray. His portfolio is impressive. He's even done a few big events, sweet sixteens and bar mitzvahs.

His images have a way of dropping you into a memory you never even had. Obviously, I don't know this middle-aged man lighting a candle with his daughter in the poofy purple gown and tiara, but it feels like I do. That's what's touching about it.

When I click into a separate subfolder, I notice he's even uploaded some of his high school work. I scroll through lacrosse-match pictures and panoramas of senior prom.

In my scrolling, amid the slideshow, I spot a familiar face. Big eyes behind rounded glasses. Unruly hair tamed by plentiful product.

It's me in my navy tuxedo, smiling next to Avery in a lavish hotel ballroom. She's laughing at a joke I made, and I'm holding her exposed upper arm, keeping her upright in her too-high high heels. She ditched them immediately after this was taken for the pair of pink socks she kept in her clutch.

Anger emerges from its shadowy hiding spot, beating my sadness to a pulp.

Why would he post this? If I meant that little to him freshman year of college, over winter break when he went quiet on me, why would he keep up this small sign of what we once were? He dropped out of our group hangs, started spending more time with his brothers who were egging him to rush the Delta Tau Delta chapter at his college. All the men in his family were members, and it was important to them that he kept the Greek-life tradition alive. It was a major concern in his overall college selection process.

Something about him hardened then. He drifted out of our high school chat, and my solo texts were left on read. And now...

Do I email him back? Does he even deserve that? Or is it my turn to sever the tie once more?

The questions taste like the memory of too-sweet candy canes—the ones we gave out when we both volunteered to be elves for the Santa-on-a-firetruck display run by the Willow Valley Fire Department. It was for the community service portion of our peer leadership class. I signed up first and Derick tagged along.

When we arrived at the station together, the chief, with a pillow stuffed up the front of his red suit, handed us two hangers and asked, "Aren't you boys a little big to be elves?"

Turned out, we were. The costumes were both a child's size extra-large, and the sight of Derick in the mandatory striped tights, which looked like second-skin capris on him, made me burst out laughing. But he took it in stride, strutting the streets of Willow Valley in the December cold like he'd never been more comfortable in his life.

Me? I hung behind him and tried to blend into the scenery, pulling the hat down as far as it would go to hide my identity.

Sensing my discomfort, Derick got the driver to play my favorite holiday tune, "White Christmas," from the truck speakers at top volume.

"Sing it with me, Wrenji," he shouted over the music. And before I knew it, the whole block had broken into joyous song. Derick wrapped his sturdy arm around me, pulled me into his side, and together we jigged up the street like real elves on December 26.

When we got back to the station and were alone in the side office once again, I was still shivering like holy hell. Pennsylvania winters are no joke. Right as I was about to change into my oversize woolen sweater, Derick noticed my shivering and offered to share the very last piping hot cup of cocoa with me. I thanked him and brought the cup to my mouth. Before I could sip, he tapped my wrist and whispered, "Careful. Don't burn yourself."

He blew across the top, his breath ghosting over my lips. Suddenly, I was shivering even more than before. And when I drank, realizing my lips were where his lips had been moments ago, I choked.

"You okay?" he asked. I nodded through my coughing fit. "Here." He took the cup and patted my back a few times. When I'd calmed, he held me close, tight. "For warmth," he qualified.

"Yeah," I said, melting like the marshmallows in our cup. "For warmth."

But I knew—or I *thought* I knew—it was for so much more.

I really, sincerely thought maybe we could be *something* more, too. But, it turned out I was wrong all along—not only didn't he need me in his life, but he'd never thought of me in it in the first place.

I rip off the rose-colored glasses of nostalgia, crack my knuckles, and force myself to type back:

You're right. It was an accident. I was drunk. I'm sorry. Please forget this ever happened.

Best,
Wren

I'm about to send but then I add:

PS. Thank you. It's sweet that you remembered.

Click. Boom. Gone.

The kiss quest is officially canceled.

I log out of the computer, discard my latte with its sad, melted whipped-cream topping, and step back out into the May sunshine. Warmth hits my face as I slip off my denim jacket and tie it around my waist.

It's not until I'm halfway back to the apartment that I think with relief: *If the other guys respond, I can handle it. At least the worst is over with.*

Chapter 4

The worst is not over with.

Derick
It's going to be hard to just forget about your email when we're
working together this summer.

That's it. One text is all it took to ruin what should be a momentous
occasion.

The Rosevale College graduation ceremony takes place on the ginormous football field. The turf tickles my toes when I slip my bare feet out
of my black loafers. The day is ungodly hot, and the sun beats down on
everything, not a cloud in sight. Bleachers on both sides are packed with
parents and families, friends and professors. I spot my dad, mom, and
younger sister, Claire, up on the far side, fanning themselves with the card-
stock programs.

It's all pomp and very sweaty circumstance.

After four excruciating years, I expected something a little more than
a faux-leather folder with a piece of paper typed out in Latin inside. I just
hadn't expected that *more* to be Derick's text-delivered bombshell.

Derick was silent all week and randomly, in the middle of my college
graduation, he decides to dig up the distressing hatchet. Next time, I won't
leave a map to where I buried it.

My eyes scan the single sentence repeatedly until the letters blur together into something resembling sense. What does he mean? Earl sent me a list of the new summer recruits. Mateo's was the only name that stood out to me. Had I missed something?

The girl next to me, Gemma Rollind, gives me a look as I stare obsessively at my phone, like *How rude can you be?* But these matters are too pressing to put on pause. Besides, they're still only at the W's, so we're some ways away from standing and throwing our bedazzled caps up in the air for that extraordinary snapshot moment. The kind I'm sure Derick could exquisitely capture with his camera and his eyes closed.

I left my plain black cap blank. No motivational quote or grad school mascot. I'd like to say it was part of my antisocial media stance (also, arts and crafts aren't my forte much to Mom's chagrin), but I just have no idea what's next for me. Beyond this summer at Wiley's, I have no clue what the future holds, and no song lyric or Michelle Obama motivational speech could capture that kind of Gen-Z ennui.

I type back:

What do you mean we'll be working together?

I don't even bother to put my phone away. Compulsively, I open and close various apps to give my fidgeting fingers something to do without drawing too much attention. When the notification dings in, I swear my heart stops.

Derick

I'm the new social-media marketing intern for the summer Didn't Earl tell you?

This. Can't. Be. Happening.

Earl is notorious for forgetting to tell me important information, but this is by far his worst offense. Not that he knows about our history. Nor would he care if he did. I only wish that for once, he'd loop me in on major decisions like I'm an adult and not the brace-faced fifteen-year-old boy he hired back in the day. I'm a manager now. The promotion was formalized with paperwork! I deserve to know these things!

Panic pings up into my throat. If he's making a drastic change like hiring a social-

media marketing intern for the summer, it must mean the lot is doing worse than it was last season. Wiley's can't meet its demise. Not now that I'm finally getting the opportunity I worked so hard for. That fear is strong enough to overwhelm my lingering embarrassment for now.

Are you sure? That doesn't sound like something Earl would do.

He thinks Twitters are for birds and TikToks are for clocks.

Wiley's is my last bit of normalcy. When this ceremony ends, I will be free from the clutches of academia, but I'll also be booted from the only routine I've ever known. School for nine months out of the year, the drive-in for three. It's the only math that computes in my brain.

Derick

More than sure. Haven't you seen the Instagram feed I made already?

I haven't. I went social-media dark after my freshman year of college. One of the many reasons my friends badger me about being a *grandpa* who refuses to get hip.

I'm not the selfie type. I don't duck-face. I don't shirtless shot. I don't ring-light. Call me old-fashioned, but I fight the urge to share as much as possible because my self-conscious nature can't handle having to steal my supply of serotonin from likes and comments.

And maybe a small part of me couldn't handle Derick's nagging presence on every app imaginable. My phone became a torture device each time I opened it, watching his life, in perfect pictures and memes, marching on without me. It was brutal.

The next text that comes in contains a screenshot of Derick's formal offer of employment. Limited pay, minimal hours, but extensive duties pertaining to "building our personal brand." (Not Earl's wording, I'm sure of it. The only branding he knows about is branding livestock.)

Underneath, Derick has attached another photo. It's a selfie.

He's taller (genetically), more handsome (improbably), and at Wiley's (unfortunately).

He's standing in front of the squat, neon-pink snack shack shooting the camera a thumbs-up. His thick hair practically glistens during golden hour. It's my favorite time at the lot, right before the madness of the evening breaks out. It's weird that at one time he was my favorite person, maybe even above Avery, but that era has long since passed. Now, he's the guy who *didn't think of me like that.*

In the end, I miss the cap toss, trapped in the middle of drafting the right response to Derick. Cheers, robust and ecstatic, erupt around me, but I can't quite bring myself to care.

$$\heartsuit$$

"I'm quitting Wiley's," I say to Avery as soon as we sit down. Our parents are paying for a celebratory lunch at a fancy kosher-friendly restaurant with plum-colored chairs and golden accent decor. The real adults are down at the other end of the long rectangular table, chatting about our stellar accomplishments, so they can't hear my firm declaration.

Mateo has his face stuck in his phone, texting Brandon. As Mateo tells it, they didn't even end up having sex that first night. They split a chicken-finger basket from the 24/7 food truck parked by the Student Life Center and discussed Ryan Murphy's oeuvre at length, laughing over their favorite Sarah Paulson characters.

My well-worked-out jealousy keeps coming back for more.

"What? That's so stupid. Don't say that," Avery says. She rips a piece of fresh bread from the basket and dunks it happily in the garnished olive oil in front of us.

"No, I'm serious. I can't go back there."

Avery stops chewing and squints at me. "Is this about what I said about it not being an adult job? Because I didn't mean that for, like, now. I meant that for the future," she says, fiddling with one of her turquoise-beaded boho earrings.

The server begins asking for drink orders. I request a glass of sparking rosé even though the idea of alcohol makes me queasy. I stayed dry all through finals week to keep a clear head and a solid focus. Finish strong, and all that. But, really, alcohol is part of the reason I'm in this mess. Though alcohol is also part of the reason I was forewarned about Derick descending upon the one place I hold dear. So, thanks, alcohol, I guess?

"No, it's because Derick is working at Wiley's now..."

Mateo looks up long enough to utter, "The one from the Polaroids in our freshman dorm?" Derick was featured in more than a few of those photos I displayed on a strand of twine above my bed. I nod heavily. "The Derick who ghosted you? The Derick who you've been pining over forever?" More reluctant nods. "The Derick," Mateo continues, "who's staring at us from across the dining room?"

My head whips around so fast I fear my skull might roll off like a bowling ball. A pair of eyes the color of ocean mist pierce me from two tables away. His large hands are raised, dwarfed utensils standing at attention. The sleeves of his maroon blazer are pushed up and ruffled, and his floral tie is hanging limply from his unbuttoned collar. He's the doodled-upon Composition Book in a family of Moleskines.

A memory vortex opens, and I'm sucked inside.

Derick and I orbited in the same social circle in high school when I wasn't working. I skipped most of the house parties for Wiley's shifts, but daytime trips to the Jersey Shore or afternoon trips to the Willow Valley Mall usually included a cast of nine, with Derick playing the male lead and me playing the mousy wallflower.

Somehow, we always ended up walking just behind the pack, making inside jokes and stealing away for private scavenger hunt games of "who can find the weirdest object." A purse shaped like a banana. A phone case with "Grandma's Got It Going On" above a photoshopped picture of Betty White in a bikini. One time, I even slapped down seven quarters for a water-gun game just to win a stuffed pug the size of a beach umbrella. I won that round. We christened him Mega Pug, stuffed him in the trunk of Derick's shiny two-seater, and wrote up a fake contract for joint custody.

I whisk back to reality when Mateo waves a hand in front of my face.

"It's the same guy," I admit, experiencing a series of heart shocks. The same high-voltage ones that hit me when I saw Derick's name for the first time in my inbox.

Without thinking, I send Derick a small, pathetic wave. He begins to stand, but his father, charting the trajectory of heated eye contact, whispers something acidic that forces Derick back down. Sheepish. The look that follows has half-formed apology written all over it.

The edge of the white linen tablecloth gets balled up in my frustrated fist, nearly sending the full drinks sliding into my lap.

Maybe this is my superpower: electromagnetism. Except instead of supercharged metallic objects, I attract distressing, emotional situations at every turn.

"I sent him a confessional email, too." I let that hang in the air.

"There were other emails?" Avery asks a little too loudly. Our parents' heads snap in our direction. We smile our innocent, still naive enough smiles, so they return to their discussion about tax returns or hot-water heaters or the right brand of kombucha or whatever.

"There were four total. They were my almost-kiss emails. One for each boy I almost had my first with and then, just, didn't." I sip my wine to steel myself. "Mateo and Derick and then Cole, who was president of Film Club when I was a high school freshman, and Alfie, my eighth-grade summer-camp crush. Cole's failed to send, Alfie's is in limbo somewhere, and, well, you know the rest." My tale of woe feels unreal. I'm glad I'm sharing this burden now, though; baring it alone would break me.

"Cole? Really? He was a dick," Avery says.

"He was nice to me."

"Because you worshipped the ground he walked on." She grabs another piece of bread. I wish I could refute the claim, but she's right. Freshman Me was enamored with his knowledge of classic cinema and his arthouse tastes. He was a beanie-wearing, skateboarding marvel. No wonder I organized all the room reservations, booked all the screenings, and took down all the meeting minutes without hesitation.

"Don't throw stones, babe. Who among us has not been crushed by a crush on a fuck boy before?" Mateo gives Avery a wicked look, rich with backstory, before turning back to me. "Anyway, what did Derick say in response to the email?"

I give them the SparkNotes version before adding, "I thought part of our friendship, back in the day, was because we always kind of knew the other was…"

"Baptized in a bathhouse of homosexuality?" Mateo asks.

"Where do you come up with these things?" Avery scrunches her nose at him.

"I like to think it's divine intervention." He does the sign of the cross and then bows his head like the former cherubic altar boy he is.

I crack a laugh. Thank God his stage whisper doesn't travel down the table. The sound of clinking forks covers it up as the platter of fried calamari gets set down. Squid wouldn't sit well with me right now. Rejection and mortification are building a home and garden in my stomach, a new pair of partying permanent residents I'd aggressively like to evict.

Avery rolls her eyes, taking a big glug from her copper Moscow mule mug. I take her cue and allow the bubbles in my sparkling rosé to imbue me with a false sense of lightness.

Across the way, Mr. Haverford rises and heads toward the restrooms. Derick's eyes return to our table in a series of darting glances. The conversation between the rest of his family continues around him, but he doesn't say a word.

Ignore him.

"Maybe I can work at Rosevale for the summer. The film department is always looking for people to digitize the archives," I say, trying to change the subject.

"You can't be for real," Mateo says. I'm a weeping willow bent under his snarky side-eye.

"What am I supposed to do right now?"

He pauses for a second, gears whirring. "Own up to it. Tell him he's an ass for ghosting you. See what happens. Let life be life." It's a repetition of his birthday bathroom advice. I should get that printed on a shot glass for him as a Christmas gift. "Who knows what will happen from there? After all, some of the best apologies end with a kiss."

Mateo's right, yet an apology isn't the *Back to the Future* DeLorean he seems to think it is. It won't allow us to travel through time and space to fix the lost and broken trust. Would I even want to do that, anyway? Derick said in his message he never thought of me like that.

Though, I guess before there were feelings or flirtation, there was friendship. True and strong. If I'm going to work with him all summer, I need some semblance of closure on that.

With his dad safely out of sight, I text Derick on impulse:

Meet me in the gazebo past the veranda

I stand with uncertain legs and excuse myself before the main course arrives. The outside air has cooled off with a steady breeze that ripples the silvery surface of the nearby pond. I march along the uneven stone path toward the gazebo, which is empty. Parking myself on a bench facing the water, I calm myself with a familiar film score that I conjure from memory. Something soft with lots of twinkling, jingling piano. Danny Elfman, maybe.

The song is just about to hit its apex when I hear: "Hi."

Derick is standing over me, raking a hand through his beachy hair. My calm song flips to something sultry with a throbbing bassline. Damn the devious band leader inside my brain.

"Hello." I stand and extend a hand to him as if this is a business meeting and he's just entered my office. He looks at it, unsure, and I retract it right away. "Sorry to disrupt your dinner."

"Sorry for staring. It's just, I mean, you being here caught me by surprise."

"You being here caught *me* by surprise. Shouldn't you be in the Berkshires somewhere getting ready to graduate?" Before we left for college four years ago, we compared academic calendars, swearing we'd meet on breaks to catch up. Hang out. Spend real *time* together.

That never happened.

"I graduated last weekend. Moved back. My brothers all just got off work and flew in or drove into town to celebrate, so that's what we're here doing," he says. "Celebrating."

"Same here. I graduated today. I picked this place because we came here on that date once." My blunder makes me blush. "*Co*-date, I mean."

Co-dates were part of our peer leadership class. As co-leaders for community service projects, Derick and I were required to hang out outside of class and charitable assignments to get to know one another. One night, he suggested this spot for a quick dinner, and even though I could barely afford an appetizer, we chatted through three courses that he charged to his dad's bougie credit card.

"He won't even notice," Derick had said. They're that kind of rich.

Derick doesn't smile at my faux pas. He's nothing but pure earnestness. "If this is about the email… Look, Wrenji, I'm sorry. I…"

I don't know whether he's going to say *I'm sorry I fell out of your life* or *I'm sorry I never felt the same way about you*, and I realize I don't *want* to know. Hearing the words out loud would be so much worse than anything I could imagine. To ward off the upset, my defensiveness rips through to the surface. "What?" I fake a laugh. "It's not about the email. No, I don't care about that." I desperately care about that. "I don't feel that way anymore either." I have no idea how I feel. "That meant nothing." He used to mean everything.

His eyebrows thread together. "It didn't seem like it meant nothing."

I really can't handle being let down gently right now, so I switch tactics. "No, seriously. But I mean, if you want to talk about something, how about you tell me why you ghosted me freshman year?" *Like I wasn't your friend. Like I didn't even matter.* My legs are somehow even wobblier as I stand and cross to the opposite side of the gazebo. The sun hides behind a patch of clouds and the twinkle lights spontaneously come on, casting a romantic glow across our horribly unromantic scene.

He sighs, rubs a hand across his eyes. "Wrenji." There's so much weight I can't even begin to understand embedded in that old nickname.

That year, when his texts grew sparse before I came home for winter break, I thought, "He's busy." When his texts grew monosyllabic leading up to our reunion, I thought, "He's always been brief." Then, on the night of what should've been our first college hang, he stood me up without a word.

I'm both desperate and afraid to hear how he could so easily slip in and out of my life as if I meant nothing, but then—

"Derick?" We turn to see Derick's brother Damien, the former high school baseball team captain turned college championship outfielder with the goatee and long hair to match. "The tiramisu is getting gross and Dad's getting annoyed. Like, he's-threatening-to-leave-without-you-level annoyed. Let's go."

I'm glad he keeps away because, right at that moment, my heart decides to give up, spurring tears to spill out my eyes. Tilting my head away so Derick can't see, I wave a dismissive hand. "Yeah, bye. See you later."

He hesitates, but doesn't say anything else. And soon all I hear are his footfalls crunching back up and into the restaurant.

I take five minutes to myself and then return to the table, doing my best to act like everything is fine. Avery and Mateo give me twin expectant looks, but I ignore them. I ignore Derick and his family across the busy restaurant, even when Derick tries to catch my eye as they eventually get up to leave. After the table is set with entrees and sides, Dad insists on making a toast, a riff on the one he usually gives at his annual New Year's Eve party for the township utilities crew he oversees. I lift my glass, which must be full of cement right now with the amount of effort it takes.

I tune him out until the very end when he says, "To new beginnings!"

The irony is not lost on me.

All the glasses tap together at once.

Clink. Clank. My heart (and summer) is sunk.

Chapter 5

Dr. Tanson is in a meeting.

At least that's what the sign on her office door says.

We had our own 10:32 a.m. meeting scheduled because for some reason she doesn't believe in normal timetables. ("Who gave the intervals of five all the power?" she once yelled at our Queer Cinema class as if we had burdened her with the concept of time.) She also doesn't believe in being punctual, so at 10:40 a.m., I decide to call Earl and follow up about the Derick situation.

The Wiley's Drive-In Instagram account Derick mentioned making in his text popped up in the Suggested For You section on Avery's personal Instagram account right after the lunch that lacerated my already delicate heart. The feed is populated with Boomerangs and Reels of the popcorn machine overflowing and upcoming giveaways. There's a Facebook business page with a few dozen likes and even a TikTok account. Derick is gearing up to get this rebranding off the ground with propellers.

It's nice to see someone taking the initiative, but it's also difficult to swallow that he's the man behind it.

Man. Geez. That's not the way we thought of each other back in high school. I don't know how I feel about how easy it would be to think of him that way now, if I let myself.

Earl picks up right before I'm sent to voicemail. "Kid, how you holding up? Not celebrating too much, I hope." His gruff bass is muffled by the hairs of his unkempt mustache. The crackle I hear isn't a connection issue; it's his scraggly facial hair tickling the receiver.

I skip the pleasantries. "Why didn't you tell me about Derick Haverford?"

I'm standing now, leaving my TCM tote bag with my laptop and bullet journal inside on the seat beside the office door. The atrium of the Media and Communications building is quiet, all marble floors and Grecian pillars. Studious and serious. Collegiate in all the clichéd ways.

The underclassmen left at the end of finals week and all the seniors are set to move out of their campus-owned housing today, but in a stroke of luck, our landlord is letting us stay on through the summer. This season won't be a total wash with my friends by my side. I can avoid my childhood bedroom for a little bit longer while I figure out where I'm going to live next.

"You may be a manager now, but it's still my lot, kid." I hate when Earl takes that paternal tone with me.

I puff out a sigh. "I know, I know. I'm just not sure branching out into social media is the way to drum up business. People like the vintage nature of Wiley's. They don't need all the bells and whistles to get excited about us." Making it too modern might cause it to lose some of its homespun feel. The one Earl's forefathers worked so hard to create. When Earl switched to digital projection and sound equipment when I started there all those years ago—a massive investment that I'm still not sure how he financed—the vibe changed. Even at fifteen, I noticed. Though I had to admit, not many other people did. My argument against advancement may have more to do with my personal feelings than my desire to save Wiley's and preserve all that makes it wonderful. Selfish, I know.

There is a long stretch of silence before Earl says, "Look, kid, the returns aren't great right now, the upkeep is getting more expensive, and we can't compete with the comfort of someone's well-loved couch. Face it, we're a relic." He laughs. "Hell, *I'm* a relic. But I'm not giving up on this place. We've got too much to offer. That's why I agreed to let Derick intern, so he can help bring in a bigger audience."

His reasoning is sound. I want to say I have another solution, but I don't.

"Okay. As long as you know what you're doing."

"I've been running this lot since my dad passed it down to me. I'm almost sixty-eight. I'd like to think I know what I'm doing by now."

I lean up against one of the white columns and catch my breath. Little by little, the lot has had to adapt, sure, but adapting is necessary. Change, however, can be forced. Just like how Derick is being forced back into my life with this new position.

"Fine." I know I'm wasting my breath on a war I shouldn't wage.

"I've got other ideas, too. We're going to bring back the fireworks viewing on the Fourth of July. Maybe we'll do some throwback showings and offer period-specific pricing. Orientation is right around the corner. Bring your big ideas, kid."

"Will do."

Right as we're saying our goodbyes, Dr. Tanson opens her door. She's wearing a jewel-toned blouse that accentuates her dark-brown skin and a matching chunky necklace of intertwined shiny loops. Beside her is Oscar Villanueva, the proud new owner of a Rosevale College honorary degree after a stupendous commencement speech only days ago.

I try not to appear too starstruck. In the film world, he's a big deal.

He's wearing navy slacks and a purple button-down and sports a shaped black beard. In his domineering presence, I must look like a wreck. If I had known I was meeting my idol, I'd have worn a belt, combed my hair, and checked for pit stains.

"My apologies, Wren. Mr. Villanueva and I got lost in conversation. I forgot to check the time," Dr. Tanson says. She turns to address him. "Wren is one of our more advanced film studies students. He did his undergraduate capstone on his hometown of Willow Valley and its connection to the silver screen. Have you heard of Alice Kelly?"

Oscar's tan face brightens with immediate recognition. "Of course. She's a lost icon. I've been looking for information on her 1978 directorial feature debut *Chompin' at the Bit* for ages, but all of my requests for access to the film have been ignored or denied."

Oscar's claim to fame is a well-reviewed book and *Don't You Forget About...Pod*, a podcast dedicated to lost and forgotten films. I'm a big fan of both. He's my Ira Glass. A part of me wonders whether Dr. Tanson deliberately booked our meetings one right after the other as a way to make sure our paths crossed. My research would be right up his alley, and she was always looking for ways to help her students get their big break.

"That's not surprising. Alice Kelly is practically a hermit," I say. I would be one, too, if my fall from grace happened so swiftly from up that high. Alice went from Willow Valley teen voted Most Likely to Make It Big in her 1965 yearbook to being involved in an Oscar-nominated documentary by the time she was twenty-six.

"I figured. Why is it all the greats end up being eccentrics?" Oscar asks with a knowing laugh.

"Alice's film was one of the main subjects of Wren's work. It's quite an impressive piece he wrote, focusing mostly on the single-night structure and the queer undertones. It's amazing what he was able to develop without actually being able to watch the film. I'd be happy to send you some excerpts if that's all right with Wren," Dr. Tanson says in a tone that suggests I have no choice in the matter. What was supposed to be an advisor-student send-off meeting has officially turned into a networking setup.

"Uh, um, sure, yeah, I'd love to share what I have." My tongue is in a sailor's knot.

"Have you been in touch with Alice Kelly at all in your research?" Oscar asks.

I shake my head as my mouth remembers how to form full words again. "I wish. I really could've used a primary source. Again, she's a recluse. Doesn't even do her own grocery shopping. So, I couldn't even orchestrate a run-in. She holes up in her farmhouse on the more rural side of Willow Valley. Not the kind of place you just pop by for a visit."

"That's too bad," he says. "That would make one hell of a podcast episode. Charting her course from student to cameraperson to feature director, weaving in her marriage to Peter Borellio and mentorship with Betsy Palmer." The script outline he's already begun writing practically materializes over his head. "My audience would eat it up."

I wrote the bible on her body of work for a final grade, and even I'm itching to hear what he'd have to say in an episode like that. Film Twitter would be abuzz.

"If you get even a glimpse of *Chompin' at the Bit* or information about her process or frame of mind while making it, I'd love to have you on my show."

My heart picks up impressive speed. Me? On a nationally recognized podcast? Alongside the bestselling author of *Forgotten Films: Hollywood's Rarely Seen Gems*? That kind of platform boost could bolster my credibility, make me more hirable in an already slim market.

But, let's face it. I'm not a well-spoken expert like he is. A BA in film studies and a plucky passion are all I have going for me. Besides, I tried getting to Alice and was led down a path of little return. I can't expect this time to be any different.

Yet, in the back of my mind, I hear Avery's sentiments about getting adult jobs. I didn't want to admit it in the moment, but she was a little right. I can't stay on the Wiley's payroll forever. Not as my only source of income. It barely covers my summer rent, which my parents refused to help with since it's not for school anymore. They wanted me to sublet my room in the apartment and spend the summer with them at their house. As if that wouldn't be totally tragic. Like what happened to Alice back then, except significantly less serious.

"There was supposed to be a hometown premiere of her movie at Wiley's Drive-In, where I work, after the initial New York and LA events. It never happened because of early walkouts and the critics' negative reviews." I'm sure he already knows all of this, but Alice went into hiding after a series of misogynistic pans hit the major publications. Most of them mentioned the laughable zombie makeup and melodramatic plot. Some even went as far as to publicly call into question Alice's sexuality. A blow they never would've dealt to one of her male counterparts.

"I think people are ready to reevaluate her work. I would love to make that premiere finally happen," I say. In fact, that's been one of my dreams ever since I first heard about Alice Kelly. Being able to rewrite history and finally host the premiere that never was…it's the kind of thing that could bring big business to Wiley's. *If* there was actually a way to get my hands on her film.

Oscar's well-groomed eyebrows rise in intrigue.

"You didn't mention that to me," Dr. Tanson scolds.

"Well, right, because I'm not sure it can actually…"

Oscar cuts in, misreading my wistful dreams as actual plans. "When do you think this might take place? August, perhaps? This could be huge. My podcast has been bubbling under the Top 100 lists on all major platforms, and an episode of this magnitude could push me over the top. It's fresh, it's relevant." He scratches his chin in enthusiastic thought. "I could even imagine interest in an Alice Kelly biography."

"For you to write?"

"No," he says as if it's the easiest thing in the world, "for you."

I won't let myself imagine a future where I get to put my film studies degree to use by writing a published book. One that goes out into the world with my name on the cover and a dust jacket with my photo in it. That would be the pinnacle of success.

A daydream drifts through my mind despite my best efforts.

In a professional studio, Derick hoists a camera as I pose for my author photos. "Tilt your head a little to the left," he says, kindly commanding.

When I don't get it right on the second try, he comes over and uses the pads of his fingers to reposition my chin, his thumb accidentally brushing over my bottom lip as our eyes catch.

Dammit, too late. Now, I've pictured it. And I want it. I want it so badly.

The book part. Not the Derick part. The Derick part is off the table. He's made clear more than once that whatever connection I thought we had has been discontinued, and everything I always secretly wanted is out of the question.

But *this*… This feels like the universe giving me exactly what I needed. Forget a kiss quest; I now had a career quest.

In a flurry of excitement, I say, "I'll make it happen." It's a bold claim that I can't substantiate or take back. Avery's right. I need to get a foothold in adulthood sooner rather than later. Book or not, solidifying Oscar as a contact could lead to a film-centric life for me beyond Wiley's. Possibility balloons around me.

"Fantastic. It's been a pleasure meeting you." He checks his Apple Watch. "I have a car waiting for me, but thank you again, Dr. Tanson, for arranging all of this. I've loved my time here on your campus." He fishes into his expensive-looking brown leather wallet marked with a fleur-de-lis and produces a business card. I didn't know people still had these. It's glossy and pointy and professional. "Be in touch should you gather any new intel, and please send me your capstone paper. I'd be thrilled to read it."

I stand there, stupefied. Is this what Mateo meant by letting life be life?

Dr. Tanson ushers me into her spotless, colorful office with a sly smile. We chat for another hour about her sneaky ways, her faith in me, and how much I'm going to miss her sarcastic yet encouraging comments in the margins of my double-spaced papers. I might not miss the stress of academic life, but I will miss the amazing people I met moving through it.

On my walk back to 3B, I pop in my headphones. Despite Derick's abrupt reappearance in my life, I'm going to make the best of this summer. More than that, I'm going to make this *happen*. A big event like Alice's could build buzz and bring in sales. It could be the start of something big for me— something more important than a one-sided love story.

An almost-kiss may have almost killed me then, but I'm stronger now.

At least, I think I am.

I'm going to have to be.

Chapter 6

"Did someone die?" Mateo asks on the drive over to orientation day at the lot.

"No."

"Then why are we listening to funeral dirges?"

Max Richter's finest, postminimalism compositions are pulsating through my car speakers. Film scores keep me level. I need balance before my next run-in with Derick, before I'm thrust into a new position at the drive-in with double the responsibility. This summer is already stacking up like a pile of dirty dishes on the sink edge, dangerously close to teetering over.

Ignoring Mateo's comment, I turn up the volume.

We're all wearing our bright-yellow T-shirts with a pink Wiley's logo on the breast pocket. The word STAFF is stamped on the back in sticky-looking block letters. It's a horrendous uniform no one is happy about.

"Can I crop mine at least?" Mateo had asked before we left.

Avery and I hid all the scissors.

When I step out of the car in the grassy field, I'm hit with the familiar smells of home—fresh-cut grass and cow dander from the massive dairy plant down the road. It's not Yankee Candle fresh, but you get used to it. Willow Valley is a charming sprawl of farmland, decently funded public schools, and a historic main street. It's about a twenty-minute drive from Rosevale, which I chose because it had the best film studies program in the area.

I'm thankful I remembered to put on my work sneakers—the mud-stained, well-worn Nikes—as I approach the concessions shack with its cartoon personified snack foods painted on the outside walls. The sole screen sits on the far side and the other perimeters are fenced and lined with tall, thin trees, which give the space a sense of privacy. The only places where the trees break are at the entrances and one corner of the back where a two-story family home with eggshell shutters can be seen.

That's my childhood home. When I say I grew up at Wiley's Drive-In, I literally mean it. From my second-story bedroom, I could peer into the lot. On nights I couldn't sleep, I'd peek out my window and watch the soundless second feature, movie stars running from swamp monsters, or racing cars, or singing songs in the rain. It was all magical to me, all beautiful.

Of course, some nights, when they showed a family film and the weather was right, my parents would break out the lawn chairs, and me and Claire would race down to the fence with our microwave popcorn and portable radio to soak in the latest blockbuster.

When I got older, the backyard wasn't good enough for me. I'd collect my friends, including Avery, in whichever car my parents would let me borrow. Usually the cobalt-blue, 4x4 pickup truck since it had the most space in the bed for hanging out. We'd ride into the lot with cash to blow on peanut M&M's and slushies.

I'd like to say I chose the reel life, but the reel life chose me. Or, more exactly, Earl Wiley chose me. When I turned fifteen, he demanded my parents let him hire me. I was there almost every weekend anyway. It only made sense, and I wanted the work. So, I elbowed my way up the ranks, and here I am, the new manager, reporting for duty.

Avery and Mateo veer off to join the growing throng of coworkers, chattering together, looking a little nervous. They're about to be indoctrinated into the land of do-you-want-to-make-that-a-combo-for-fifty-cents-more?

Earl stands with his feet spread apart on the mound as I approach. He's waiting for me. In one hand, he twirls a pristine name tag.

"It's like I'm about to be knighted," I joke when I'm within earshot.

"Don't make me do a British accent, kid. It'll end badly for both of us," he says while pinning the pink piece of plastic to my chest. Derick's impending arrival fades away for a moment. Whatever emotional catastrophe may be coming for me can wait. This is a real-life level up finally, *finally* unlocked.

Earl slips a bent envelope from the back pocket of his faded Wranglers and places it in my hand. He's not the sentimental type, and I know this isn't an early paycheck. I'm not stupid enough to think that his cute, vintage drive-in has the kind of bank that lends itself to birthday bonuses or graduation checks.

It doesn't even have the kind of bank to sustain itself through a single season, but that's a problem I might have a solution to now, thanks to Oscar Villanueva.

The card is a dollar-store variant with balloons on the front and a blank inside. In his shaky hand, Earl has written:

Happy Birthdagraduation. I got you a card and a name tag.

Below, he's drawn a big, amorphous arrow to a miniscule PS:

There's a six-pack of cider with your name on it in the concessions fridge, but it's not from me. I'm your boss. That would be unprofessional.

"Thanks, Earl." We're not the hugging type, so we opt for a firm handshake. I hesitate for a moment. On the heels of his generosity, I want to bring up my possible plans. "Hey, do you think we can make some time to talk about doing a special event here in August?"

His bushy eyebrows go up into his receding hairline. "What do you have in mind?"

"Remember how you said to bring my big ideas?" I ask, and he nods. "Well, what about a premiere of Alice Kelly's *Chompin' at the Bit*?"

His eyebrows disappear onto the back of his head, do a one-eighty, and circle back to their rightful place. "Do pigs fly now or something? What makes you think you can make that happen, kid?"

I try appealing to the businessman inside him. He may hide his savvy beneath a disheveled exterior, but he's an industry man with the plentiful credentials and experience to back it up. The drive-in has been in his family since its inception, when it was nothing more than a field behind a historic hotel, a sheet tied to two poles and a rinky-dink projector. Earl never married or had kids, so I know the genetic line stops with him, but that doesn't mean the establishment should cease to exist.

He strikes a thinking pose, forefinger outlining his stubbly chin. "You had trouble getting in touch with Alice for your big college paper. How's it going to be different this time?"

"I have a lead." I nearly spit from the abrupt acidity of lying. I don't make a habit of telling half-truths, but little white ones every now and then seem innocuous enough. If I can make this happen, all will be forgiven. Earl never needs to know that I'm flying by the seat of my pants.

He nods, impressed. "If you say so, kid. I'll consider it. Not sure we have the funds to make it fancy, but come back to me with approval, and I'll see what I can do."

"Thank you. Really." I slip his card into the waistband of my shorts. "You won't regret this."

He cracks a crinkly smile. I shine one right back.

With newfound anticipation flapping through me, I sneak up behind Avery. One tap is all it takes for her to shriek piercingly loud.

"Okay, ILY, but how many times do I need to tell you not to scare me like that?" Her hands hold steady over her heart.

"Remember when we did that special *Friday the 13th* screening two summers ago, and we scrounged up Jason masks just to scare the piss out of this girl?" Youssef, a returner who runs the projection booth, asks. We got Avery good right as she was pouring herself a soda during the slow bout. When we jumped out from the walk-in fridge, she crushed the cup so hard that the Sprite shot up into her face. She was snorting bubbles out of her nose for hours.

"Hardy, har-har. You two think you're the Impractical Jokers, I swear."

Working the drive-in is a lot like going to summer camp, except instead of paying to kayak or do archery, we get paid to watch free movies and goof around in the snack-shack break room. Sometimes we see who can catch the most Skittles in their mouths or we do speed-stacking competitions with the medium-sized drink cups.

Though, I guess now that I'm a manager I can't partake in the minute-to-win-it challenges where the loser is put on trash pickup at the end of the night, grabber tool and all. I need to be overseeing the lot, filling out forms, writing up the schedule. I hope this promotion doesn't end up sucking the fun out of my summer.

Avery must see that dawning realization on my face. "You're not going to be one of those managers who walks around with a stick up his ass, are you? I can't handle another Hank situation. Bad breath, bad BO, and a bad attitude…"

"Wren only has one of those things," Mateo mocks. The group snickers. He's winning their affections already, which is great. I just wish he'd do it without undermining me. Even in a playful way. He goes to flick my name tag but misses and hits my nipple. I go to roughhouse him a bit, the catty play-fighting we do back at the apartment, but I want to set a good example for the newcomers, so I let it roll right off my back. For now.

Creak. Earl revs up the bullhorn and puts his lips to it.

"Gather round, folks. Welcome to orientation day for another season at Wiley's Drive-In. You've heard the phrase 'summer fun in the sun'? Great. We're here to bring the 'summer delight in the night'!" Not a single laugh or hoot can be heard. Earl's deadpan never changes. I think he doesn't want anybody to know he's got a huge, tender heart under that raggedy polo. "Eh-hem, so…we're here to work. Serious work. We're here to bring this community another year of movies and memories. If that doesn't sound up your alley, you can feel free to take a hike now."

Nobody moves a muscle, and I mouth along to the rest of the welcome speech. I've had it memorized for at least three years now. Earl never deviates, probably because public speaking makes him nervous, too. He prefers phone calls with film distributors and local vendors where he can let his business acumen and his love of cinema shine without having to be seen. Earl and I are cut from the same cloth that way—a modest, sturdy denim, perhaps? The pair of jeans you've worn so many times you could never part with even after they don't fit anymore.

"Why don't we get our managers up here to introduce themselves," Earl offers. I join Veronica, a girl a few years older than I am with pink-tipped box braids and a congenial smile. We get along well, and we'll be dividing up duties this season. I've learned a lot from her over the years.

Weirdness worms around inside me as I stand before the group. I'm usually just one of the smiling faces among the crowd. The view from here is frightening. Being in front of big groups has always made me nervous. I want to be a leader, but I'm not quite sure I know how.

Just as Earl is about to hand the megaphone to me, my nerves already shot, a shiny, fancy car barrels into the lot with a booming accelerator and a cloud of smoke.

Earl prompts me to continue, yet I devolve into a fit of embarrassing, phlegmy coughs when the sun spotlights Derick Haverford stepping out of his car.

Derick is wearing designer sunglasses, chinos, and a classic white T-shirt—French-tucked, of course. Like Marlon Brando circa *Streetcar Named Desire* if he shopped at Calvin Klein and met the Fab Five. A DSLR camera bag hangs off one solid shoulder, swinging in counterpoint to his stride. My heart lurches forward as I rock back on my heels.

At the restaurant, he was wearing his family-approved costume, but seeing him now in his old, patented attire flings me back to slamming lockers and high-school hallways. The memory of pushing our graffitied desks together for projects in peer leadership. His closeness always caused goosebumps.

I mutter my name into the mic and pass it along to Veronica, my shining moment dimmed.

I could be brazen over email with the security of the computer screen and a wasting liver between me and emotion, but now, since the restaurant, I'm physically vulnerable. He saw my face. He heard the hurt. He apparently didn't care. That pains me way more than any missed movie marathon ever could.

Earl starts breaking the team up into groups. He's going to send one returner to each station and rotate small groups of the trainees around to get a feel for the full beast.

I'm about to volunteer myself for concessions, Avery's home base—action-loving masochist that she is—but like some cruel joke, Earl makes me stay behind as the rest of the pack ventures out into the expansive field.

"Mr. Haverford, that was quite the entrance. Glad you could make it. Didn't want you to miss all the excitement." Earl motions behind him where mostly teenagers are fiercely focused on proper register etiquette and traffic-control techniques. It's not exactly thrilling stuff.

"Thanks for having me," Derick says. He pulls off his shades and slides one of the arms through the collar of his shirt so they dangle from his neck like a medallion. They make me wonder what happened to the gold crucifix necklace that used to always hang there. The one he'd toy with whenever he was thinking extra hard, taking the chain between his lips to ponder a difficult test question.

Earl turns to me. "Since you and Derick are already well acquainted, I figured you could give him the grand tour. Show him the ropes around here." I'd prefer to show Derick the door. The two of us walking next to each other through the site of what might have been feels oddly intimate and unspeakably one-sided, yet Derick's gazing at me with those blue-gray eyes, and I'm trapped in a gridlock. Which side will win: giddiness or grief?

"He needs the lay of the land so he can go ahead and get started, since he thought our social-media presence was so lacking."

"It was nonexistent," Derick corrects.

"Whatever," Earl grumbles. "Hey! Wren, maybe he can help you out with that project you were yammering on about. Work that out amongst yourselves." Across the lot, two boys begin using the light-up traffic wands as light sabers. "Whoa! Stop that! Don't underestimate the force!" Earl yells, jogging away.

"Let's go," I say curtly.

"What was that?" Derick leans in close enough that I can smell his cedarwood and orange-ginger cologne. For a second, it's senior year again and I'm back outside Ye Olde Bookshop on Halloween night—the chilly eve I fully registered my feelings for him. Right before the start of the his-torical ghost tour, he saw me shivering as usual, undid his Burberry scarf (his Ken doll costume was almost too perfect anyway), and handed it to me with a warm smile. High on his cologne, I barely listened to the petite, brown-skinned girl whose throaty voice echoed eerily through the storied graveyard.

That scarf is still in a special, secret compartment in my closet back in 3B. I silently vow to purge myself of those memories, start the tour, and probably dump the scarf.

Probably.

I shove my hands into my pockets so he doesn't see them shake. He pulls his camera from its pouch. The long Nikon lens catches the sun beams and almost blinds me. He wields it with impressive authority as I gesture toward the main screen with clipped precision. The faster I get through this, the faster we can go our separate ways.

"Sorry we got interrupted the other day," Derick says almost under his breath when I break for a beat. I know he feels the awkward tension in the air as we round the storage shed. His half apology does nothing to diffuse it. "Damien is known for his bad timing. He was born three weeks early during my uncle Leon's wedding. Smack-dab in the middle of the vows, a real Kleenex moment killed by broken water and pained shouting. I was only three, but I remember the ceremony stopping and my aunt fainting and... Wow, sorry. Geez, it seems like all I do is apologize around you lately."

I huff. I don't even mean to huff. It's a reflex that I can't help. There's too much irony that he's apologizing for everything but the obvious. To cover it up, I start to turn away, deliberately lightening my voice as if none of this—including him—means anything to me. "Anyway, so, moving on."

"Please don't do that." The camera falls from his hands in frustration, bouncing against the rigid muscles of his stomach.

I turn back. "Do what? I'm not *doing* anything." I'm being a brat, obviously, but aren't I entitled to? Maybe I'm dismissing him now, but only because he dismissed me back then.

"Wrenji." He sighs. And, dammit, for the second time, I'm all too helpless against that nickname. Left powerless by the exasperated way it floats out of his mouth and swirls into my eardrums. It transports me back to our playground days, to kickball and him never letting me get picked last. I drop the thorny behavior because even now I hate to see him hurt. Even though that sentiment doesn't flow both ways. "I wanted to tell you—"

Again, suddenly, I desperately don't want to hear whatever he has to tell me. I'm afraid it'll hurt too much. "I'm doing my job," I say, cutting him off. "You're doing your job. We both have do those jobs in proximity of one another. Let's not make this any harder than it has to be."

And then, before he can say anything more, I start away. He's quick to follow, calling my name—determined to have this talk—so I detour straight for the snack shack. There are too many prying ears present for either of us to say anything there.

Avery's got the newbies working like a well-oiled machine. Two team up on a step stool filling the soft-serve machine with a giant bag of mix. Another pair are cleaning out the popcorn maker. Avery leans up against the counter, snacking on a pack of Reese's Pieces.

"Hello, Derick. Nice to see you," Avery says with a casual iciness. She had a few choice names for him after I relayed what happened at the restaurant. He doesn't seem to notice her tone, and he greets her with a gregarious smile. We flip up a portion of the chipped teal countertop and pass through to the other side. Mateo is hobbling, holding two heavy soda-syrup refills. It's day one and he's already complaining that his feet hurt.

Derick turns back once to capture the frenzy in a single frame. It wounds me to admit that this will probably look dazzling on our Instagram feed. Not that I'm 100 percent behind it just yet.

I broke my social-media boycott the other day just to inspect his work. The feed is racking up more views and likes than I expected, and we aren't even open for the season yet.

At warp speed, I show him the empty break room with the punch cards and the time clock, the jumbo wall calendar covered in Post-it notes, and the box filled with rolls and rolls of old film posters. We save them all in case we do an encore showing. Most get adopted by me afterward so I can hang them in my room. Even if they're wrinkly and torn at the edges, I don't care. I love them anyway.

"And that's everything. Tell Earl I went to inventory the shed," I say, attempting to extract myself from this moment as efficiently as possible.

He stops me as I start to slip by, his voice low even though we're alone back here. "I really do think we need to talk." When I just look up at him, lips set in a stubborn line, he adds, "Okay. Let's do it the old-fashioned way then.

Two truths and lie. Isn't that how you got all those middle schoolers to open up in our mentoring sessions? You loved those icebreaker games."

"We're college graduates. Our icebreaker days are behind us." My light laugh rings hollow.

"I'll go first," he says, ignoring me. "One: I have three older brothers. Two: I've got an extensive sneaker collection, and I change the pairs out during the day to match my mood. Three: Wren Roland sent me a sweet email that caught me completely off guard and—"

Without letting him finish that sentence, I pull him out of the break room and into a nearby closet, full of popcorn buckets and churro season-ing, to make sure the others can't walk in and witness this. I will not let him undermine my authority like Mateo did, especially not by airing out my lovelorn miscalculation.

Even if he did just say my email was *sweet*. Which is a revelation I'll have to spiral about later.

The whirring of the soda machine and the cheerful chatter from the main room can't be heard from in here. The lone, ancient light bulb buzzes over our heads.

"Can we not talk about the electronic elephant in the room, please?"

"Oh, so now it's an elephant? The other day it didn't matter," he says, folding his arms defiantly across his chest. I take stock of how wide he is. His shoulders practically brush the shelves that bracket us in. "So, which is it?"

"I said drop it."

"I mean the lie. Which one is the lie?" There's a playful softness to his tone, all his vowels elongated.

"It's the brother thing. Damien's younger than you, obviously. You just told that whole story," I state. He nods. "Did I win? Are we done now? Can I get back out there?"

"Not until you play, too. Those were always the rules, right?" He takes a daring step closer. He's a glutton for challenges.

Thrown off-kilter, I rattle off the first three things that come to mind, putting a stop to this ridiculousness. "One: I'm a Gemini, though I'm not sure I believe in astrology. Two: Whenever 'Proud Mary' comes on the radio or a playlist, everyone in my family sings 'rollin' on the river' as 'Roland on the river.' Nobody ever laughs, but we like it. Three: Over winter break, freshman year of college, I was ghosted and stood up by one of my supposed closest friends and I'm not sure I even want to forgive him for it."

My second truth is punctuated by the sound of Mateo shouting from just down the hall, "Be right there!" Scurrying feet fly by as he runs past our closet, and the door I'd left carefully cracked slams shut. I realize I forgot to set the stopper. The hinges are temperamental.

"Shit. Sorry." I turn back to grab the doorknob, but the light bulb flickers once before it gives out and we're plunged into darkness. All my other senses stir to attention. The feeling of Derick's hot breath from across the way floods me with too many unnamable feelings. This is what I get for putting off repairs. And conversations, apparently. "One second."

Simultaneously, we reach out. My hand lands on the slippery doorknob; his hand lands on mine. His palm is huge and a little clammy. The friction from before turns to fission in an instant. The coarse hairs on my arm stand at attention. It's epic and electric in a way I didn't expect.

"Sorry," he mumbles, pulling away.

"You're fine." I shake it off. "You were right. You really are always apologizing around me lately." I'm still salty about the obvious apology yet to be made, even as a small part of me whispers that I'm not being fair—not when I keep trying to block him from saying more, afraid of how it may make me feel.

When I turn the knob, it won't budge. There must be something weighty on the other side of the door that's blocking us in. I remember Mateo moving those Coke syrup boxes and, of course, he would set them down exactly where they shouldn't be. Those things weigh roughly 25 pounds each, and judging from the give, there must be a whole stack of them outside.

I bang and twist and push. Nothing does the trick. Someone got the smart idea to turn on the radio. No one can hear us over the danceable, upbeat pop track that's blaring at a worrying decibel beyond the door.

"I, uh, think we're stuck."

"Stuck? Nah. Let me try." With all the bravado he learned from his brothers, Derick attempts the handle for himself. As my eyes adjust, I can only see the faint outline of him, but he throws his shoulder into the wood like his hulking body is going to help the situation and not just leave him with an injury. After three tries, he says in defeat, "Oh. I guess we are stuck."

"I think I established that already." Machismo is my biggest pet peeve. Switching my brain back to manager mode, I assess the situation. "Someone will realize we're in here and let us out soon." Knowing Mateo, I reconsider. He could be anywhere, doing anything by now if Avery isn't keeping a close, watchful eye on him. "I hope. I *really* hope. But, no need to panic."

"I wasn't panicking."

Oh, right. That's just me. A stifling sweat starts on my brow and grows slicker the longer we're in here. Is the room shrinking or am I just imagining it?

"Everything okay?" he asks. The sound of my own breathing has gotten steadily louder, becoming an added instrument to the song seeping in through the cracks in the doorframe.

I hang my head in my hands. "This is the last thing I needed on my first day as manager. I'm by far the youngest person Earl has hired for this role, and I can't screw it up. Also, just, small spaces…"

There's a throaty sound of understanding from Derick's side of the closet. "This isn't my ideal first day either."

"Why did you even take this job?" I ask. Shouldn't he have secured some bigwig position by now? His school was pretentious and expensive enough to have an alumni network and a career center. Not to mention his father's wealth of contacts.

"Didn't exactly have a choice." His grayish outline dramatically sinks to the floor.

I roll my eyes, though he can't see. "Sorry you're slumming it with us for the summer."

"That came out wrong." He groans, and I don't press it. I'm not the best at communicating my feelings either. "Sit. Make yourself comfortable," he instructs. "We might be here a while."

The panic remounts. "Don't say tha—"

"You're not a Gemini. You're a Taurus," he says, cutting my sentence short.

"Huh?" I maneuver myself down to the floor, knocking our knees only once. A quick bump, and a quicker brush. I ignore the rush of saturated adrenaline it causes.

"That's the lie. You're the bull." Oh, he's trying to distract me. I let him. "Hardworking, compassionate, but because of those horns…stubborn as hell."

Even though it's a dig, I erupt into laughter over how ridiculous this is. How after all this time, we've ended up stuck in a pitch-black closet together.

"Fair."

"Listen, Wrenji." He grows serious, measured. "At the risk of sounding like a broken record, I am so sorry for what happened back—"

Derick gets cut off by Mateo finally moving the soda syrups and abruptly throwing open the closet door. He catches us practically sitting in each other's laps between boxes of paper straws, and he snorts, surprise morphing into amusement. "Earl's looking for you." Mateo's singsong delivery sounds oh so tattletale.

I rush to standing, but it's too late. Earl's behind Mateo looking peeved at the perceived situation. I know how this looks and it's not great. "Wren, what's going on? I told you to show him around, not sit in a dark closet and… We need you at the admission booth."

"Sorry, we got stuck."

Earl raises a callused hand. "No excuses, kid. Get on with it. We don't got all day."

Sufficiently reprimanded, I shuffle, red-faced, out of the closet and past the swarm of newbies who've gathered nearby to listen in.

My head feels full of unpopped kernels, relentlessly rolling around. I shouldn't have let my guard down like that.

As I exit the snack shack, I kick myself for thinking for one second that Derick and I could play it cool as coworkers. We couldn't even hack it as friends, postgrad. He doesn't even want to be here.

An almost-kiss. An almost-apology. I've had enough of Derick Haverford's almosts.

I need to focus on my *actual* job before I *actually* lose it.

Text Message

Derick

Two truths and a lie

Round 2:

1. I found our old collaborative Spotify playlist and listened to it on my run today. It still slaps.
2. We really need to talk. Without getting interrupted this time. I want to make this right.
3. That was my first time coming out of a closet…

And, later:

Hello?

Later still:

Wrenji?

And finally:

Sorry

That was a stupid joke.

Chapter 7

My Chevy takes the rocky driveway in stride. There's something to be said about a sturdy used car that handles well even with a nervous driver behind the wheel. Right now, a microscopic battalion is firing cannons squared at my vital organs. Partially because this is a risky venture and partially because there are texts from Derick burning a hole in my pocket that I can't bring myself to respond to.

I took the leap and decided to show up at Alice Kelly's doorstep. After a disastrous first weekend at the drive-in, I need to bring Earl a win. I'm turning this hot-mess express around at whatever cost.

This is the only way I can get to Alice. Her address is public information. If she asks me to leave, I'll leave. I'm not looking to get arrested for trespassing. Here's hoping she sees the good in me and lets me stay.

The farther I drive, the creepier the scene gets, even though it's broad daylight. I steer my way past empty pastures, hacked-up fences, and abandoned tractors, tipped over, wheels somehow spinning. A stray pitchfork is inexplicably staked into the grass near a turning point.

This is the perfect setup for a modern-day horror movie. Lonely divorcee gets angry, lures young boy into house, keeps him in basement, tortures him in creative ways with kitchen appliances. I'm only assuming here. I don't stomach horror outside Hitchcock and del Toro, and there are no birds or amphibious humanoids in sight, so that's a good sign.

The sheer number of BEWARE OF DOG signs I pass is unnerving, though.

I count seven still standing and one fallen in the road, but I know there's no turning back. There's not enough space to make a U-turn. Besides, I'm on a mission. I put on suit pants for this.

In the distance, a dilapidated farmhouse strikes the sky with a pointed white roof and in-need-of-a-power-wash siding. Its windows form a spooky face on the front exterior. A shiver races through my body.

The overgrown nature of the grass and the hazard of fallen tree branches makes it difficult to decide where to park. There's one lone truck at the base of the stairs, but I'm sure it hasn't been driven in years based on its permanent tire impressions and the weeds snaking through the wheels. I pull up behind it, squeezing between a weather vane that's fallen from the roof and what appears to be a disassembled bike.

I stop at the porch stairs. They are a jumble of loose boards, so I stretch over them with a long stride that almost tears the center seam of my pants. There's no discernable doorbell, so I summon my courage and I knock below the ninth sign reading, CAUTION: Dogs on Premises.

No answer. No barks either. That's odd.

Harder this time, I knock again.

Still no answer.

Carefully, I cross the porch where a rocking chair looks close to crumbling. The curtains are drawn on all the windows, so I can't see inside. I pray these advertised dogs aren't feasting on Alice's festering carcass somewhere beyond the front door.

Just as I'm about to peer around the side, a breeze forces the rocking chair into creaky motion.

"Boo!" comes a witchy voice beneath my shrill scream.

I jump sky-high when I notice an elderly woman with a shock of stringy white hair standing behind the screen door. There's a naughty smile stamped on her face. She wears an oversize cardigan and a pair of round glasses with telescopic lenses.

"Crap, you scared me," I gasp.

"Watch your language, boy! Don't make me clean your mouth out with soap. My eyesight may be going, but my hearing is as sharp as a bat's." She has a smoker's voice, a habit she probably picked up when cigarettes were still Hollywood glamorous. When she pushes the screen aside, I get a good look at her gnarled, long nails. Maybe she is a witch after all, and this is a fairy-tale retelling instead of a horror movie.

She looks nothing like the preened woman with flawless cheekbones featured in her headshot from the seventies, but I recognize her all the same. "Sorry, Ms. Kelly."

A beat passes before she says, "You real estate agents are all the same. A bunch of jumpy Jacks with no good manners."

"Wh-what?" I stammer. I steal a quick glance down at my outfit and realize I do look sort of like a real estate agent—my button-down, my blazer, even though it's now June and I'm sweating, the only bow tie I own with a yellow, buttery popcorn pattern on it. Judging by her glasses, I'm sure she can't make out the details properly.

"You are here to evaluate the house, aren't you?" she asks even as she steps inside, gesturing for me to follow.

I only hesitate a moment. It feels wrong to take advantage of an aging woman with a feigned grasp on memory, yet this is my in. I'm not exploiting her, right? I'm merely bamboozling her into a beneficial situation. A trick that ends in a treat. The treat being her reemergence into film society! I'll just step inside, give her a minute to warm up to me, then come clean and do my best to convince her to give me a chance. Easy.

There's not much house to evaluate anyway. It's in shambles. Each step I take makes me fearful I might fall through the floorboards.

I shuffle around behind her. She doesn't close or lock the door, and it feels rude to bring it up, so I gently press it back into place while she's busy flitting down the hall. There's a TV in another room somewhere playing a rerun of *The Mary Tyler Moore Show*. I can tell by Rhoda's nasally voice and the memorable laugh track.

I nearly knock my head on a piece of loose molding when she leads me into the kitchen. The linoleum floors are scratched and the cabinets have fared no better. Alice doesn't seem to mind any of this as she opens one with an unfastened handle and turns the stove-top knob three times before the burner lights. I don't know whether to sit or stand, so I end up leaning against a nearby counter.

"You have a lovely…"

"Don't lie, boy. Flattery is for fools," she says. I think about the prepared speech I had for her. It's almost all complimentary regarding how ahead of her time she was. This woman seems like she'd spit right in my face if I said any of that stuff to her. "Sit down. Stop making me nervous."

I heed her demand. The table is an artifact of another time, a silver rim with a pale-pink top. Somehow, this is the one object that looks kept beyond reason. There's a stack of coasters in the center, and napkins sit in a decorative holster. She places chipped saucers at two spots with dainty, doll-like cups on them.

"I hope you like decaf because that's all I've got."

"Decaf is great. Thanks." The bag itself takes up half the cup, leaving very little room for hot water. It's clear she's not used to entertaining others. "Though, I should mention, I'm not actually a—" The whistle of the kettle overpowers my confession.

It smells distinctly like dog food, yet I don't see any bowls out, which is curious. Normally people with pets live with the incessant jangling of ID tags banging against collars, little paws scampering around rooms. Here, you could hear a pin drop if she weren't boiling water.

"I'd give you the tour, but I think you get the gist." She gestures at the rubble around us. "You're welcome to see yourself around when we finish chatting. I assume you've looked at the property profile. It's not much, but it's mine, and I don't want it to be any longer. That's where you come in." I have no idea how to come clean now. "Do you think you can sell it?"

I grasp for the right words, but all that comes out is the single wrong one. "No."

"No? Then why are you here?"

"No, sorry, I didn't mean no."

"Then what *did* you mean?" she asks, growing agitated with me. This woman means business. I slip the blazer off my shoulders to air out my neck. There's clearly no AC in here (*How is she comfortable in that sweater?*), and my internal temperature keeps rising. I've never been good under pressure.

"I meant I'm not a real estate agent." That feels good to say. I'm certainly no actor. I couldn't have given an award-worthy performance even if I wanted to.

"You mean you're not a *licensed* real estate agent?"

"No, I mean I'm not a real estate agent at all."

Her eyes narrow gradually like slatted blinds. "Then why are you dressed like that?"

"I wanted to look nice," I admit.

"For who?"

"For you."

"For me?" she exclaims. "I appreciate the effort, but you're a little young for me."

"What?" It's seconds before I realize she's making a joke. "Oh, no. I didn't mean like that. I'm sorry. Can we start over? I think we got off on the wrong foot." I go to stand and extend my hand to her, but she fiercely slams the table and starts away.

In three brisk steps, she's at the sink, which hasn't stopped dripping since she filled the teakettle. The *plunk, plunk* of the faucet speeds up with the hammering of my heart. "You think I'm an idiot then, huh? Thought you could pull the wool over my eyes?" Her voice has grown loud and booming.

"No, Ms. Kelly. I'm terribly sorry."

"Thought you could prey on a poor, little old lady?" She reaches up onto a high shelf. This is the movie moment where she grabs for the gun from her secret hiding spot and pulls a Clint Eastwood "Get off my lawn!" Protects her property. I knew this was a bad idea. Hopefully, she's kind enough to fire a warning shot. Though with her eyes, I wouldn't trust her aim.

"I didn't mean to cause any trouble."

Her movements grow more frantic.

I stand. "I'll be out of your hair!"

A box clamors onto the counter. She opens it but I can't see its contents. The heat rises, and I begin urgently backing away. Nobody would hear my screams or cries for help all the way out here.

"Sorry, again!"

Hiss. Crack. Crunch.

Huh?

She turns and I realize she's snacking on a dark-chocolate-covered almond biscotto. Crumbs collect on the shawl of her cardigan, getting wedged into the hunter-green cable knit. I'm not sure whether to laugh or cry. God, I've seen too many movies.

The tension diffuses, and the self-satisfied grin on her thin, pale lips lets me know she was messing with me the whole time. You can take the woman out of Hollywood, but apparently, you can't take the Hollywood dramatics out of the woman.

"I'd offer you a snack but I'm suddenly not feeling so hospitable." Every *s* in that sentence sends cookie cascading across the room in a hailstorm of spit.

Heart still hammering, I can't even look at her as I say, "I hope I didn't upset you."

She snaps. "Don't give yourself that much credit. It's this house, this town that upsets me. You? I don't even know you. How could you have the power to upset me?" She crosses back to the table.

"I can still go if..."

"No. Sit." I fumble into my chair again. "I'm very interested to know what you want from me since you went through all the trouble of lying your way into my home." Never breaking eye contact, she takes a long sip of her tea. Mine burns my tongue. "Who are you and what do you want with me? If you're here to rob me, I've got nothing of value, and if you're here to kill me, well, I won't put up much of a fight, so I'm sure that will suck some of the fun out of it."

"Oh, no! Neither. I'm not here to do either of those things." I straighten like Earl does when he talks to other professionals. "I'm, um, sorry. My name is Wren Roland. I'm an assistant manager—actually, now I'm a manager-manager—at Wiley's Drive-In, and I'm here to see about gaining permission to re-create the 1978 premiere of your movie *Chompin' at the Bit.*"

She doesn't just laugh. She wolfishly howls. "I'm not one for jokes, but you crack me up."

"Oh, it's not a joke. I'm serious."

One last laugh honks out from her before she stills. "Oh, well, then in that case...no."

She gets up to leave the room, saucer in hand. Is she not even going to hear me out? Is she seriously going to leave a stranger sitting in her kitchen? I'm not giving up that easily. I follow her but not too closely. I don't want to seem like a threat.

"Why did you used to love movies?" I ask, hoping to appeal to some dormant fanatic deep inside her.

She slows, but doesn't look back. "Why does anyone love movies? The escape, the fantasy, the emotion, the catharsis. Surely you're not here to interview me on a bygone phase of mine. You want my permission? It's not going to happen."

"You're not even a little open to the idea?" Raindrops begin to splash against the windows behind her; small ones, with little sound, but the clouds they fall from are enough to make the interior of the house grayer than it already was.

"Not in the slightest. I don't even remember that clear-eyed girl who made that movie. I don't know what I was thinking when I did."

A wave of nostalgia ripples through her features, remolding her cheeks into sunken valleys. She glides into the living room, the source of the TV noise.

"Haven't you ever been to Wiley's?" I ask. Like a vampire, I don't dare step over the threshold until she invites me to do so, which means I could be waiting forever. I hover in the foyer to be safe.

"Of course. It's a Willow Valley landmark. I've lived here long enough to have popped in a time or two hundred."

"What if I told you that landmark was at risk of dying? I want to resurrect your work to bring attention to the drive-in and help save it."

Her petite nostrils flare. "'Resurrect'? Why would you use that word?"

"I read it in an interview you did with the *Film Geek Gazette*. That's how you described your movie—a resurrection of an old wound manifested in the zombie character. I did a college paper on it. I'm not some kid asking for a favor. I'm genuinely interested in rewriting a little piece of film history for this town to save one of its best spots. You ran away before another audience even got to see it. You pulled the movie from distribution and canceled the Willow Valley premiere, the first premiere this town would've ever seen. If I can make that happen, then…"

"Enough!" she orders.

I close my trap.

Her house shoes squeak on the wooden floor as she crosses to the mantel. There, she grabs a box and turns back to me with an apologetic expression. What's in her hands has the appearance of an ornate jewelry holder, yet inside there are paper clippings, all carefully preserved and labeled. She hands me the *Film Geek Gazette* print edition.

"I haven't thought about this in ages," she says. Tears prick up at the edges of her dark eyes. The first hint of vulnerability beneath her jagged exterior. Her bags tell a story of struggle I'm keen to hear about.

Mistaking her gesture as an offer, I go to reach for the box. She snaps it shut so fast, she nearly catches my fingers.

"You want this information and my movie? You're going to have to work for it. I've been trying to sell this blasted farmhouse for ages. I can't work the land. Nobody wants to do the hard labor. Every—*real*—real estate agent says this place is a money pit. Not that I blame them." She cradles the box, clutching it close to her chest. "If you come here a few times a week and spruce up the place to help me sell, I will strongly consider allowing you to screen my film."

"Oh, wow. Um, I don't know much about home renovation." Does watching *Love It or List It* reruns with Mom and Claire count as practice?

She gives me a once-over. "I assumed as much, but I trust you're young enough to figure it out. Yes?"

"Yes," I say immediately. There's too much riding on this. I can't risk her taking her *strong consideration* back because of my wishy-washy indecision. My anxiety is not getting in the way of this opportunity. I'll show up next time in coveralls and steel-toed boots if that's what she needs. "Yes, whatever I can do to help. Yes."

Alice appears unamused by my smile. "It's not a *yes*, though. Do you hear me? It's a *maybe*. It's a maybe contingent on your performance."

Optimism cracks open inside me like a fizzy can of Coke. *Maybe* is better than a straight-up *no*. That's more than I could've hoped for a week ago. She shows me out the way I came in, and the excitement makes certain I can't keep my mouth shut. "Thank you, Ms. Kelly. Thank you. You won't regret this."

A cynical smirk grows on her face. "Maybe not." She cackles once. "But you might."

The door slams shut in my face.

Chapter 8

The admission booth at Wiley's stands between two lanes of traffic. A lineup of blinding headlights spills out into the street. I slip off my hoodie, hang it up on the hook by my station, and roll my short sleeves up to the peaks of my shoulders.

I'm determined to make my second weekend as manager better than that despicable day one.

Everyone was still snickering at me when I clocked in tonight. The rumors of what went down in that storage closet last Friday are out of control and greatly exacerbated by Mateo's overreaction. If only they knew I was still a kissless catastrophe. One that refuses to get wrapped up in Derick's charms. *Again.*

I commit to doing better. There's no other option. Not now that Alice is possibly on my side.

"Have a great night," I say to the family of four who drove in all the way from New Jersey just to experience the magic of our lot. The kids in the back seat were squealing with excitement, this being their first time. I shut the cash till and check on Mateo, who's working across from me.

From his overexaggerated posture, I can tell he's faking assurance in everything I've shown him. A car peels away from his side. He blunders with the cash stack and ends up drenching us both in a shower of singles. It's like we're the world's least-deserving Chippendales dancers.

As I'm making sure we've collected everything, another car pulls up to my side. I recognize it straightaway by the swanky tires with black rims, and I realize there's no escaping this inevitable interaction.

"What are you doing down there?" Derick asks. He's a paragon of temerity in the red leather driver's seat. His hair is held in place by mousse, and he sports another classic white T-shirt. It must be easy to organize his closet. "Hope you're not hiding from me." His half joke lands with a resounding thud.

My smile snaps back into a straight line. "You don't need to stop since you don't need to pay. And, for the future, if you hook the second left instead of the first, you can come through to the staff spots." I pause for effect. "You just need to show up on time."

I know he doesn't deserve the third degree, but I can't help it. He's partially to blame for the storage closet incident. If he hadn't insisted on hashing out our past in the middle of my workday, right there in the busy snack shack, maybe I wouldn't have gotten in so much trouble with Earl. Later that day, he marked down one strike on my employee index card, the dated, impartial way he keeps his staff in check.

Earl has a hard and fast three-strike rule. If I get two more infractions, I can kiss my new name tag and position goodbye. Shoving some of the blame off onto Derick is easier than admitting that maybe I *wanted* to talk it through with him.

"Noted. Just lost track of time," Derick says.

"Here's a program with a snack-shack menu, if you're interested." I throw the folded piece of paper through his open window with nervous force.

He catches it but flinches. "Dammit. Paper cut." A droplet of blood forms on his index finger, glistening in the dashboard light.

Wincing in apology—I didn't actually mean to *hurt* him—I dig under the counter for the first aid kit. When I pop it open, I notice it's filled with single-dose packets of ibuprofen and antibacterial ointment, but detrimentally devoid of Band-Aids. "We're... Uh, I don't have any bandages. There are some in the office. I can run and grab one if Mateo can cover for me."

Mateo's false certainty has transformed into straightforward terror. His quivering hands can't even sort the change into its proper slots. This must be why his parents never let him have any major responsibility at their restaurant. Is offstage stage fright a thing? He seems to be breaking under pressure without a proscenium to protect him.

I'm trying to be patient, but I realize his performance is a direct reflection of mine.

I do my best to reassure him with my eyes, but he lets out a whimper that reminds me of those "In the Arms of an Angel" animal ads, so leaving is not an option.

Pivoting back, I spot Derick sucking his finger the way he did when he pricked himself on thorny foliage during our woodsy peer-leadership retreat at a campground back in the day.

"All good." He holds up his finger like I need proof. He's always been adaptable. "We should probably digitize these, though. Not only are they a waste of paper, but they're dangerous."

His casual assessment sits wrong with me. Digitizing? Building a brand? Wiley's isn't some trendy fad company. It's a homegrown institution with eighty-six years of experience. It's one of the oldest operating drive-ins in the country.

I scoff. "People love the paper programs."

"I think people would love them just as much if they didn't have to have these littering their floor mats for the next two weeks." He flashes me a smile, as if I hadn't been avoiding his texts all week. Does he not care? Did he even notice? Or (benefit of the doubt) is this still him offering an olive branch? "We could make a link on the website through our socials. They could be printable. Best of both worlds." He pauses, hesitating over his words as if trying to choose them carefully. I brace for impact.

"You've been ignoring my texts," Derick finally says, a cloud of disappointment hanging around his words.

The lie's already on my tongue. "I've been busy."

"Busy listening to our old collaborative Spotify playlist," he counters. "You know we're still friends on there, right? You may have shut me out of all your other social media, but I can still see what you're listening to in the updating activity feed."

My face goes blotchy. I always forget to set myself to private. Now he knows that after he brought it up, I've been reacquainting myself with all the old me's that live between the notes of those songs—the good, the bad, and the late-puberty ugly.

That's when I hear it. The playlist is cranking out from his state-of-the-art car speakers, turned down low but still audible if I strain. It's Barbra Streisand. One of my picks. *Her cover of the pivotal jazz song from Casablanca.*

"I didn't unfriend you. I deleted the apps. I don't really do social media anymore."

A lone crease of contemplation appears on his forehead. "Hmm. You went dark? How did I miss this?"

"Not like you were paying very close attention over the last few years." I hate how pert I sound, but he brings out my defensive side. "Or any attention at all, for that matter."

"Wrenji," he says with damnable earnestness, "I've been trying to—"

Honk! The man in the car behind Derick's is leaning on his horn, waiting impatiently for the line to move.

"God, it's like the universe is hell-bent on interrupting us."

"Can you move it along? I have guests to serve," I plead.

His jaw tightens. "Not until you agree to talk to me. To finish our conversation from last weekend."

"Now is not the right—"

Honk! Honk! Honk! I beg Derick with my eyes but he won't give in. Just like I don't settle, he doesn't give up.

"Tonight, after the second showing," he hedges.

Vexation rolls through me. "That's too late."

"Fine. I can sit here all night. No problem." He fastens his hands behind his head and leans back in his seat.

The honk from behind becomes a steady, relentless trill, tightening me to the point of snapping.

"Fine! A quick talk. Somewhere quiet." The words have to fight their way through my gritted teeth.

The man swerves out from behind Derick and flies into Mateo's lane. I don't even wait for Mateo's frantic tap out. I instruct him to switch with me immediately. He's not ready to handle a berating patron just yet. At this rate, maybe not ever.

"I'll find you after," Derick calls before closing his window and cruising off.

I take care of the burly, agitated man and his pregnant wife. I apologize with a free voucher for a return visit, which seems to satisfy them. The line tapers off as the dancing-popcorn-bucket video begins to loop on the screen. The old, familiar *Let's all go to the lobby! song plays.*

Mateo lets out a deep, dramatic sigh and slumps against the wall. "That was stressful as hell."

"You'll get used to it," I assure him.

We'll need to wait a while before we head back to the snack shack since there are always a few late stragglers who need assistance. I give myself a second to catch my breath, too.

"Sounds like somebody has a hot date tonight."

"It's not a date. It's not even a hang. It's a quick conversation before I come home, curl up in my sheets, and sleep forever." I decide right now that I'm setting a timer on my phone. If we don't finish hashing it out in the first thirty minutes, I'm hightailing it back to the apartment and not looking back.

"On your birthday, you said you were hoping to meet someone at the drive-in. Doesn't it seem like fate that he just happens to be here?"

"The key word there was 'meet.' I was hoping to meet someone new. Not get reacquainted with someone old who hurt me."

Ouch. Admitting the hurt out loud makes it fresh. To mitigate the sting and redirect my thoughts, I count the novelty paper tickets people love to keep as souvenirs that I stacked up for Mateo earlier. There's a surprising number still left.

"Mateo, did you not hand these out?" It's not like we did terrible business tonight. If he forgot to issue them but took the money, no harm done. I can always do a quick walk-through to see if any of the families missed out.

"I did. One per car. Just like you said." He's half talking to me and half posing for a Snapchat he's going to send to Brandon. They are joined at the hip these days. I'd be happier for him if it wasn't interfering with his work.

"Mateo, I said one per *person*. Not per car. Everyone needs a ticket."

"I...don't remember you saying that." His voice rises.

"Mateo!" I yell. "There were SUVs full up with six people in them tonight. Are you telling me you let them in for $10 total?"

"Maybe I misheard you? I don't know, babe. It was a little hard to focus when a love connection was happening inches from where I was standing!"

"It wasn't a love connection! And, *ugh*, we're not running a buy-one, get-five-free promotion!" We need that money. Even though concessions is where the big bucks are, Earl had to raise the admission prices right before I started here to offset the astronomical costs associated with going fully digital.

I snatch up the stack of tickets and head out. I don't know what the policy is for a mistake like this, but the drawer can't be that light when I count it out and report it back to Earl. He's going to think I'm embezzling or something.

"Should I come with you?" Mateo calls timidly to my backside.

All I do is shake my head and begin my *Please, sir, can I have some more?* tour.

$$\heartsuit$$

Around thirty minutes post-closing, I hear a gentle knock on the open door of the office. After an evening of canvassing cars, asking for the missing admission costs, and comforting Mateo for an honest (albeit concerning) mistake, I'm elbow deep in an incident report, writing quickly in red pen.

Being manager is already far more work than I assumed it would be.

"I'm almost finished, Earl. Sorry," I call over my shoulder.

The office is tucked away in the back of the projection room at the front of the snack shack. This is where Earl hides out, in the shadows of the movie-magic machines and the radio equipment. It's a bit dark and dreary, given its only window is the tiny square one through which the movie shoots out and onto the screen.

"Uh, it's not Earl." Derick is ducking into the space. I hop out from behind the L-shaped, antique desk. "I was waiting by my car and you never showed. Avery said you were up here."

I scramble to put my papers away. "I'm sorry. I totally forgot. I'm still getting used to my new position and my brain is everywhere and Mateo undercharged all the cars in his line."

"Ha," Derick laughs. "That would explain this comment then."

Beneath one of the photos Derick posted, someone named 420BlazinBoii wrote:

Was it 1960s throwback-pricing night already? The cheap tickets weren't the only way I was celebrating the decade ;) A real puff-puff-pass party at Wiley's!

Obviously, I missed them in my count. They were likely in their car with the windows up, hotboxing in the back somewhere. Though, now that I think of it, I do remember seeing a "Go Green" bumper sticker that may have been advertising cannabis and not recycling. I groan. "Can we get that taken down?"

"Already deleted. I just took a screenshot. Thought it was kind of funny."

"Send him a DM and offer him a voucher to assuage the comment deletion. Apologize again for the pricing mistake, and maybe mention the use of recreational drugs is…prohibited on the property?" Those vouchers are supposed to sustain us through a whole season and be a last resort. I collect my keys, my hoodie, and my satchel. "Oh, and don't tell Earl. The less he knows about this until he reads the report, the better."

"The report about what?" Earl asks, sneaking up on us. He is playing with his impressive ring of keys, blocking our exit. I'm about to tell him the truth when Derick steps up and explains away the situation, taking full responsibility for holding up the admission line and praising me for managing to save the day. He even adds the Instagram comedy as a punch line to bring some levity.

Earl looks as angry as he did when found us playing footsie in the closet, but then he breaks into a hearty laugh that fills the room. It's uncharacteristic and infectious. My own laugh lightens my load; the stress of this job doesn't feel so laborious.

"That's certainly a new one." Earl tells me to put Mateo on concessions where Avery can keep her iron fist wrapped tightly around him. He motions with his thumb for us to get out of here so he can lock up.

When Derick is halfway gone, Earl's hand stops me in my tracks. He warns, "It may be funny, but consider this strike two. Don't get to three, kid. As manager, when one of your employees messes up, it's on you. Don't make me regret giving you more responsibility. I can count on you, can't I?"

His words whip at me. "You can," I croak.

"Don't let D… *Distractions* get in the way of doing a good job." I know he was about to say Derick. I don't know how to feel about that. He smiles ruefully. "Now, get some rest."

Back outside in the fresh air, walking toward our cars, I exhale hard, yet the exhaustion sets in. It starts in my temples and makes its way down to my toes. I'm trudging, unseen weights tied around my ankles.

"You seem tired. Sure you don't want to call it a night?"

As much as I'd love to fall into bed and emerge well rested sometime around noon tomorrow, I know I won't be able to sleep until I get this torturous conversation wiped from my mental agenda. Once we clear the air, we can call a cease-fire and keep our summers separate. I can do what Earl demands and not let Derick distract me.

"No, no. I'm fine. Really. I had more than one Mountain Dew tonight. I'm going to be wired for a while." I roll out my neck. "Thanks for owning up to Earl back there."

He stops and looks at me. His expression is shrouded in nighttime shadow. For half a heartbeat, we're four years younger, and he's taking the fall with Coach Clarke for one of our missed peer-leadership assignments. He charmed her into giving us an extension.

"I wanted to say something last week about the closet fiasco, but there wasn't a right moment. And while I was working tonight, I realized that holding up the line was a shitty thing to do. I'm seriously not trying to make more mess for you, but I really want to clear the air."

His honesty is a welcome surprise that reinvigorates me. Even though Earl's admonishments are burrowing themselves into my subconscious, I'll turn this around. I'm sure of it. I didn't work that hard to strike out this early.

Despite everything, I'm thankful Derick was here tonight.

"You're good." I pull my keys out of my bag, mulling it over. "You're all good."

He brightens. "I'm starved. Any chance you want to grab some grub? I know a spot with killer chicken wings."

Overlooking the fact that I'll be dead for tomorrow night's shift, I agree.

Chapter 9

An orange, light-up sign blinks above my head:

The Lonely Lass-O.

Drinks. Billiards. Girls. Fun.

This is the last place I expected to see tonight and the exact opposite of what I imagined when Derick suggested a quiet place to talk. There's conspiratorial glee growing in Derick's eyes. I've already got a bad feeling about this.

The Lonely Lass-O is one of the seediest storied joints in Willow Valley, known for its scantily clad waitresses, its brusque clientele, and its back-alley brawls over girls or bar tabs or both.

Derick seems unfazed as he flashes his ID to the bouncer who has a graying beard right down to his stubby, exposed knees.

"This is a joke, right?" My uncertainty magnifies when we're waved inside.

He says deadpan, "I don't joke about chicken wings."

Flabbergasted, I covertly set the timer on my phone. He's got thirty minutes.

I expect the inside to be hazier, smoke-filled and deafeningly loud, but the music is crackly and the air is lemon zesty. The bar is circular, light wood and spacious. Servers wearing Daisy Dukes and flannels tied into midriffs rove about their sections taking orders as Luke Bryan plays.

It's honky-tonk rustic with a slapdash urban flair. Think Hooters if you threw leather chaps and spurs on it. The walls are wood-paneled, covered in wagon wheels and whips.

A white, stocky man with a buzz cut comes over to us, recognition in his countenance. "Derick, buddy boy, didn't think you'd be back here until we hired some male servers," he says, the borderline offensive humor not landing the way he intends it to.

"Wouldn't kill you to diversify your staff a bit," Derick replies. Underneath the clean scent, there is the pervasive stench of patriarchal bullshit. My skin crawls.

"We're shortchanged as it is. We take who we can get. Either of you looking for a gig? I think I've got a few pairs of booty shorts in your sizes." He doesn't sound like he's joking. I don't even have a booty to show off in a pair of booty shorts. My ass is one long extension of my back. I could stand do a squat or two, but that's too much effort for my busy schedule.

"We're both gainfully employed, thanks," Derick says.

"Working with your dad still? I know he's making headway on that big bus-line expansion."

"Uh, no, not exactly," Derick says, a bit flustered. "I'm helping out over at Wiley's Drive-In. Wren is the manager there. That's why we're out so late. We're here for the wings."

The man nods as if he, too, takes his football-game-day poultry dishes super seriously. "You want a high top, or should I seat you two toward the back?"

"The back, please," I say, noticing the inquiring looks from those around us. They aren't the types I'd want to have overhear our conversation.

The man takes us into a roped-off section near the kitchen doors. We pass scraggly men and women scooping mixed nuts out of wooden bowls. Guess I didn't get the memo about this being a "Boots Only" establishment because everyone, even the waitresses, are wearing calf-high leather with custom stitching.

"Two orders of the dry rub," Derick says when we sit. "And all the celery you got."

"Anything to drink?" the man asks.

"Can I have a Coke?" My earlier Mountain Dew wave of awareness is faltering, even though Avery plied me with a steady IV stream of it. A heady caffeine crash is coming for me if I don't act fast.

"Is Pepsi okay?" he asks. I internally cringe, but externally say, "Water will be fine. Thanks." I'd rather crash than drink the devil's syrup.

Derick orders water, too. "Thanks, Uncle Leon."

When the man disappears through the swinging doors beside us, I ask, "Uncle Leon?"

"My mom's older brother. The one who was getting married when Damien was born."

"How did this never come up in high school?"

He shrugs. "You think my dad would ever soil our family image by advertising our association with a place like this? Nah. But he's more than happy to make a profit off it. He actually owns the property. My uncle just manages the joint." Derick shakes his head at the extent of his father's power in this town. "Anyway, this place has a strict eighteen-and-over policy."

"But it seems like you can still get service without shoes and a shirt." I incline my chin toward the redheaded waitress who's on her break at the bar. She's still wearing her uniform, but her boots are kicked off beneath her seat. A man in a Led Zeppelin shirt captivates her with talk of his home garden.

Derick's leisurely grin falters. "If this is awkward, we can take the wings to-go."

"No, I'm fine. Really." I'm surprised to find a semblance of truth in this. Overall, the place seems chill, not entirely living up to its infamous name.

"Good, good. I knew Uncle Leon ran a business when I was little, but my parents always referred to it as an 'adult eatery,' so naturally I begged to be taken any chance we went out for dinner to prove I was an adult. I just assumed by an 'adult eatery,' they meant the place only served, like, salads and Brussels sprouts and other stuff kids hate. Being a middle child is such a burden." His eye roll is fantastically over the top. "On my eighteenth birthday, my older brothers, David and Dale, brought me here for the first time to ogle the waitresses and fill in the family-business blanks I'd been missing." He hesitates, then adds, "Obviously that's when I was still letting people assume I was straight."

"I know that feeling. Always being on the defensive. Thinking it's easier to just let people project onto you rather than make any hasty declarations of your own." I don't even know where this is coming from. Maybe it's my current insecurities over my sexuality, but Derick's vigorous nod tells me he knows exactly what I mean.

The wings arrive in steaming paper-lined baskets. Leon sets down silverware, a pitcher of water, and wet wipes for when we're done. Lastly, he places before us a wooden platter with the largest stalk of celery I've ever seen and what appears to be a freshly sharpened butcher's knife on it.

"Eat up, champs." Leon gives us a wink before leaving.

I'm certain my mouth is hanging open, but I can't quite find the hinges to hike it up. Derick has his phone out and is snapping a pic. He sends it in a group chat with his brothers, chuckling all the while. The goofy GIFs roll in right away.

"Classic, Uncle Leon," Derick mumbles before getting his hands down and dirty in the dry rub. He picks up the plumpest wing in the mix. It's animalistic the way he devours it down to the bone in four bites.

Hunger overtaking me, I claim one with my fork and use the nearby knife to start cutting it up.

Derick places a hand on mine to stop me. "What are you doing?"

"I don't like eating certain foods with my hands. Too messy," I say, evidenced by how he's got wing juice all over his fingers and lips. As if he can hear my thoughts, he runs his tongue across his prominent, pink Cupid's bow.

"Oh, right. I forgot that about you." He puzzles over it. "What about pizza?"

I hold up the knife and fork in answer.

"Tacos?"

I do jazz hands, the utensils like mini disco balls in the red-tinted light.

He shakes his head, grabs another wing, and decimates it in three bites this time. A new record. I busy my mouth to avoid the inescapable. There's a reason we're here, and we're circling it like the gorgeous bartender around her section, making sure no drink is ever empty. I wipe my mouth with a scratchy napkin before taking a big breath.

"You wanted to talk," I say, getting us back on a more comfortable track.

We've been so easy, breezy casual so far tonight that it almost feels like senior year again. I can't go back to that mental place.

"Hold up a finger field-goal first."

Confused, I do what I'm asked and connect the tips of my thumbs. He closes one eye, lines up his shot, and flicks a paper football through my hands. The pointed corner hits my chin, slight pain cropping up at the site.

"Whoops! My bad." The tops of his cheeks turn Swedish Fish red. "See? I told you paper was dangerous."

I glower at him. He takes the hint and softens into something resembling sweetness. "Okay." Two cats are quarreling inside my stomach, while I wait for him to say more.

"I fucked up. Those We Love Leo movie-marathon plans—the ones to watch *Inception* for me, *Romeo + Juliet* for you, and *Titanic* for us were…a lot for me back then."

"A lot for you? You weren't the one trying to find *Inception* on VHS to keep with the vintage theme. It was one of the final films to ever be released in that format and only in South Korea. It's basically a collector's item at this point." I'm surprised my computer didn't get overrun by a virus due to how many sketchy websites I had to sort through to procure one.

"Wait, we were going to watch the movie in Korean? Neither of us speaks Korean."

"Whatever. You've seen the movie, like, six hundred times. You probably know the lines by heart. We would've gotten the gist." Also, my commitment to a unified viewing aesthetic was more important than the logistics. We could've just pretended it was a foreign film sans subtitles for all I cared. All I wanted was to be with him for one perfectly planned night.

Then, it all blew up in my face.

"Okay," he says, stretching the A out for way too long. "Let me rephrase then. It was emotionally a lot for me. Not logistically a lot. If that makes sense."

Not any more sense than us watching *Inception* in Korean now that I'm really considering it. The things we do for our secret crushes…

"I knew you liked me."

My chest tightens. "What? You knew I liked you?" Guess it wasn't such a secret after all.

He nods thoughtfully and lets out a gentle "I had a pretty strong gut feeling, yeah."

That's the thing about queer longing. In high school, you think you're hiding it so well, until you come out and everyone says they saw you slogging through it, but didn't think it was their place to bring it up. If only he'd let me down easy then, maybe I wouldn't have kept these feelings so close.

"And standing me up was your way of telling me you didn't like me back?" I ask, incredulous.

"Not exactly. I wasn't out. You weren't out. My feelings were all jumbled up. All I knew is that those plans *felt* like a date. A date I was in no way ready for. I had literally only kissed a guy for the first time a few weeks before, and I was reeling from it." His elbows are spread apart on the table and his hands are clasped, almost in prayer. "You know how my family is." His forehead smacks into his knuckles.

He says *family*, but I'm almost certain he means his dad. That harried whisper in the restaurant returns to me. Derick being commanded back into his chair. It wasn't that it was a family meal and getting up without excusing himself was rude. It was that he was coming over to see *me*.

"I hate myself for doing that, but avoiding you was easier than facing any of those feelings." On a sigh, he meets my gaze again. "One kiss can cause a whole lot of trouble. You know what I mean?"

"Actually, I don't. I've never *been* kissed." The admission flies out of my mouth before I get a chance to gobble it back up.

I know I shouldn't feel inhibited by this. Everyone evolves at their own rate. Some people never kiss anyone, and they don't want to and that's normal. So why, oh why, do I feel bottom-of-the-barrel rotten and bruised?

Oh, right. Because the boy I wanted to kiss more than anything is sitting across from me asking me to be vulnerable with his probing eyes.

Derick looks at me for what feels like a long time. Then, "You mean you've never had *the kiss*, right? The big one with the butterflies and the swelling score you loved in all those famous movies?"

I'm not sure why I tell him the truth. Maybe because, despite what happened four years ago, he's always been so easy to be myself with. "No, I mean, not at all. Not ever." I shake my head. "I had four almost-kisses. You included. You weren't the only one who got an email."

His interest ignites. "What? Who were the others? Do I know them?"

"Do I owe you that answer?"

He's silent for a long beat. "No, I guess you don't."

Needing somewhere to channel these unexpected feelings, I line up the gritty paper football. Noticing, Derick does his own finger field-goal. With a harder hit than I intend, the triangle goes soaring up and over Derick's hands, angling dangerously close to his upper face. He swerves just in time for the paper to land in the tray of a nearby busboy who looks up, befuddled.

"You almost took out my eye." In the years since high school, I'd forgotten how elastic his features are; expressions instantaneously grow and shrink like a Slinky. Always so legible, always so *him*.

I apologize for my bad aim.

"I'll accept your apology if you consider accepting mine." He catches my eyes, his own serious. Earnest. "I'm sorry I hurt you. I'm sorry I avoided you. I'm sorry I didn't…" Derick hesitates, then shakes his head, sad almost. "I'm just sorry, Wren."

Just as I'm about to answer, the vibrating timer goes off in my pocket.

Then, abruptly, the mood in the bar shifts. "I'm Gonna Getcha Good!" by Shania Twain begins playing so loud that the table is shaking.

Every waitress from the back struts out onto the floor, grabbing the patrons' hands and lifting them to their feet.

Oh no. They're about to do a line dance. I've heard about these before. They do them every half hour.

Even though our section isn't being attended to by one of the women, Uncle Leon comes out and starts a clap to the beat. Derick, moving like the slippery embodiment of mischief, reaches an open hand across the table. My two left feet quake inside my shoes.

"I don't think so."

"Come on! It'll be fun!" Those are his famous last words.

Before I know it, I'm thrown between two flannel-clad women dancing with more energy than you'd expect at 2:00 a.m. The brunette breaks down the footwork with Derick and me. It's simple, but I still get turned around a few times.

When the chorus kicks in, adrenaline kicks me in the ass. I shift into high gear, forgetting about my long night of cleaning up messes and excruciating paperwork. I even let the anxiety about being here with Derick spring away. Each heel dig is another shot of dopamine.

It doesn't even bother me that some of the more macho men in the room are looking on and laughing at the two young guys making absolute fools of themselves.

I glance sideways at Derick, who's already looking at me. Mischief has been replaced with maddening charm. "You're a natural," he shouts over the music.

"Hardly," I tut back. But still, his compliment catalyzes me to go all in. I *yee* my best *haw* without a cowboy care in the world.

When the song ends, something has shifted in me. The brunette and blond escort us back to our table by the hands. Before they part, they plant blood-red kisses on our cheeks, mementos of the night and a hallmark of this torrid, kitschy establishment.

Derick glances up at me, the apology still tagged on the tip of his tongue, sweat dotting his brow. I swear I blush so hard the lip stain on my face disappears into my complexion.

There's a part of me that wants to hang on to that old hurt and anger, but there's a bigger part that's more than ready to let it go like I just did out on the dance floor.

"So, what do you say?" he asks. "Can you forgive me?"

Slowly, I begin to smile. "Okay," I say. And, because he seems to need to hear it outright: "I forgive you."

A good chunk of the weight of our past, that heavy load I've been carrying with me, evaporates. We smile at each other for a little infinity, and I hear that ringing in my ears again. Those blasted bells only I can hear, signaling a new beginning.

We sit for a while longer, chatting and laughing like the old friends we might just get to be again. When I finally look up from him and scan the room, I realize we're some of the last patrons left. The waitresses have traded in their uniforms for track suits and flip-flops; they're counting their tips and calling it a night. Leon lurks near the bar, shooting glances our way. It's clear he knows we're having a moment and doesn't want to intrude.

"We should probably pay."

"I'll grab it. Family discount. No sweat," Derick says, even though I can see his palms are slick with the stuff. Was he as nervous as I was? He's always been somewhat reserved with his feelings. But, I guess all closeted people kind of have to be when they're burdened with their true selves underneath the performance.

He thanks his uncle for the service and the wings. I notice a plaque on the wall crowning the Lonely Lass-O BEST WING SLINGERS IN WILLOW VALLEY by a local publication. You've got to celebrate even the small stuff, I guess.

Derick bumps my shoulder in the narrow hallway on the way out, something we used to do all the time when we were hanging with our friends. The sense memory clings to me like static socks straight out of the dryer.

We both stop by our respective cars. "What was the project Earl mentioned you were working on last weekend?" He leans back against the driver's side door, kicking one leg over the other. A good lean goes a long way.

"I did some of my undergraduate research on a retired director from Willow Valley named Alice Kelly. She was supposed to have a film premiere here back in 1978 for this awesome indie zombie movie she made on a tiny budget, but it fell through. I want to make it happen now."

He straightens. "That sounds pretty awesome. Why'd it fall apart?"

"Everyone says it's because it got panned by critics, but there are theories floating around on the message boards that her husband, another hotshot director at the time, paid off the press to kill her movie."

"What the fuck? That's messed up. Why would someone's husband do that to them? Jealousy?"

"Maybe." I press my back into my car. My lean isn't nearly as alluring as Derick's. "It's possible he was afraid her rumored bisexuality would be too apparent in the movie or that it would finally prove to everyone that she was the real visionary behind their collaborations. Whatever the reason, he served her papers, sent her packing, and Hollywood blacklisted her."

"That's bullshit. You definitely have to make that happen." There's a distinct, sudden fervor emanating from Derick.

"I really want to, but I'm afraid I can't. She wants me to do manual labor around her house in exchange for her permission. The only time I've even worked with power tools was when we did those peer-leadership Habitat for Humanity projects. Do you remember that one horrendous one in Baskersville? My glasses fogged up while we were building that deck. I missed the nail and ended up hammering my hand. They had to send me to the ER. My parents were not happy."

Voicing my fears has always been hard for me. I work overtime to ensure people see me as the confident leader I want to be after so many years of being background actor invisible. That's why the storage closet and the ticket incident were so insufferable. They set the tone for me to be a bumbling idiot rather than someone to look to for guidance and support.

"I know my way around a toolbox," Derick says, because of course he does. "I could help out if you want. To make up for the, well, everything."

"I don't know. Alice is really particular. She didn't even seem pleased that I'd be invading her space."

He crosses the white-painted parking line on the pavement between us with one confident step. My breath snags. "Okay. I won't press you. If you change your mind, you know where to find me." He's one of those tall guys who doesn't know how much space he takes up, how blissfully suffocating his nearness can be.

"I'll think about it," I gasp. I'm staring up at his face, charting his left-leaning, freckled nose and his boyish cheeks. There's a millisecond where it seems like he might crane his neck down toward me, make it up to me, create a moment where he *thinks of me like that*.

But instead, he waggles his eyebrows and asks, "So, we really can be friends again?"

My preservation shell snaps over me.

Ghosted. Stood up. Rejected. My evolution to unrequited cliché has come to its climax. Behold the Boy Wonder. Watch as he repels every person he's ever pined after.

But, in the end, it's not Derick's fault he doesn't feel the same way I do.

He can't control the way his heart works. If it doesn't beat for me, it doesn't beat for me. He's not the mighty suitor sent to slay the kiss quest, which I've abandoned anyway.

He's never been *mine*. He's just Derick. I guess I'll have to learn to be okay with that.

And since I've already forgiven him for the past: "Uh, yes, friends. For sure."

He smiles, all warmth, before he says, "Good night, Wrenji."

"Good night, Derick." His helpful proposal and platonic proposition trail me into my car and all the way back to my apartment complex.

Twenty minutes later, I slip my phone from my pocket. Idling in park, I notice a text from Derick already waiting for me. He's typed:

Done thinking about it yet?

My heart hitches at just how much he wants to help me, and I find myself smiling at the phone screen long after I should have gone to sleep.

WileysDriveInWV Nothing better than a double rainbow over the screen to welcome you back for another amazing season at Wiley's Drive-In. WANT TO JOIN US FOR FREE NEXT WEEKEND?

CONTEST—
LIKE this post and FOLLOW this account. For an extra entry, TAG one friend you want to bring along in the comments. For two extra entries, SHARE this post in your IG STORY and don't forget to tag us. Max 4 entries per account.
ENTRIES ACCEPTED UNTIL 6/10 @ 11:59PM EST.

DylPickle2700 Date night? @AngelaDaviesLuvsU 🖤
Fishin4Life44 @TswiftStan13131313 We haven't been in so long!! This would be so fun if it's nice on Friday!!
Billy.Wilson.Films Anyone know what they're playing next weekend?
WileysDriveInWV Stay tuned for our schedule later this week. Set post notifications for our account to be the first to know! 🍿 🎬
420BlazinBoii *comment deleted*

420BlazinBoii Comment deleted?! Don't play me like that, Wiley's! 👀
420BlazinBoii Jk, we good. They r givin me a free voucher... 😳
Let's get that paper!!!!

Chapter 10

Avery, Mateo, and Brandon are all hovering over my bed when I open my eyes. Instead of questioning the concerning situation, I sleepily say, "But it wasn't a dream. It was a place. And you and you…and you were there!" I flop headfirst back into my pillow.

"Breakfast time, Dorothy Gale," Mateo instructs. That's when I get a whiff of smoked turkey bacon. I sit up and notice Mateo's holding a lap table covered in a smorgasbord of eggs and other foods cooked to perfection. There's a glass of fresh-squeezed orange juice, probably made from the expensive press we chipped in for a year ago but never took out of the box. Bubbles float to the top.

"Did you make me a mimosa from our spare champagne?" We always keep prosecco in the fridge with a label on it reading: Pop in Case of Emergency. It's been a running joke since sophomore year when Avery's FWB put a full stop on both the friendship and the benefits. All she wanted was fancy wine for the emotional wind-down. We were fresh out, and all the stores were closed. Now, we're always prepared. If we pop a bottle, we buy a bottle. It's a flawless system.

"Nope, we're still in stock. Brandon brought this one over to congratulate us on graduating," Mateo says. He pecks Brandon's chubby cheek. "He may have also made the eggs."

"And the toast," Avery chimes in.

"I poured the mimosa, too," he says, pushing his glasses up the bridge of his nose. I reach for my own pair on the bedside table. My previously blurry world comes into focus, and I cringe at their plastered-on smiles. Something is up.

"What's going on?" They set the tray down over my lap. Mateo takes special care to unfold my napkin and stuff it into the collar of my niche sleep shirt that reads: *G is for Gerwig*.

"Nothing, babe. Can't we treat you?" Mateo asks. Avery moves to open the blinds. I check the time on my phone, wiping the crusties from my eyes. It's already eleven thirty.

It's then that I remember where I was last night, how late I came home, and how inebriating being around Derick can feel. This is like my post-birthday hangover, except it's only affecting my heart. It took me forever to find a deep breathing pattern that slowed my thoughts down enough to let me fall asleep. Some nights, and some guys, are just like that.

"Okay. Seriously. What is going on?" They simulate surprise over my skepticism. They're acting like bringing me breakfast in bed is a Sunday tradition that somehow slipped my mind. Maybe I did hit my head while running from a twister, and this is my sepia-toned reality now.

Avery nudges Mateo with her elbow. Her eyes are prompting. He clears his throat and says, "Boss babe, I wanted to apologize for the ticket incident. I'm going to be better about putting my listening ears on when you're giving instructions."

"And?" Avery flicks him.

"And I'm sorry for getting you stuck in the storage closet." He sounds like a bratty child having his arm twisted into apology by his mom.

I bite into the buttery, half-charred toast. It's exactly how I like it. "Apology accepted," I say with my mouth full.

The three of them take seats around my room—Brandon on my desk chair, Mateo on his lap, and Avery by my side on the bed. She steals a tater tot from the small bowl they made for me, reheated leftovers from a bougie brunch spot we hit up earlier in the week.

I scroll through my morning notifications and notice a new text from Derick in the lineup. The first part of the thread is a selfie of him eating sour gummy worms. A pink and blue one dangles over his open mouth like he's a fish about to latch onto the bait.

When you say you don't like to eat with your hands, does that include candy? If, let's say, someone were to offer you a cherry-lime gummy worm, would you break out the utensils? If so, how have you survived so long working at a drive-in where your options for break foods are hot dogs, soft pretzels, funnel cakes with strawberry sauce, etc.?

BTW I'm currently salivating over the snack shack menu that you attacked me with.

Underneath is another photo of his healing paper cut with the caption:

Hope I get a cool scar from this.

"Where were you after work last night? Heard you come in late," Avery says, clocking my uninhibited smile over the new photos on my phone.

Derick and I went from zero to friendship real fast. I'll need to learn to quiet the unfriend-like fluttering behind my rib cage before it gets out of control.

"Sorry if I woke you." I lock my phone and set it down.

"You're good. I had an alarm set for 2:30 a.m. so I could be up to catch the first episode of Season 2 of that feminist superhero show on Disney+. It's so worth the hype. I hate being behind the game and getting it spoiled on Twitter." She's Exhibit A in the case for Wiley's closing. Our drive-in can't compete with 3:00 a.m. drops of buzzed-about shows.

That's why I think an event like Alice's could capitalize on FOMO. If you're not there, you're not in on the conversation.

Four sips of mimosa later, I say, "I went to the Lonely Lass-O for wings."

Mateo launches off Brandon's lap and onto my bed. The tray rocks. Avery heroically salvages the last of my toast tower.

"You went to heterosexual hell? With who?"

"With whom!" Avery corrects. Her creative writing minor is both a blessing and a curse.

"Thank you, Merriam-Webster." He rolls his eyes and then stares me down. "Now, dish." A siren wails inside my head. I don't need to give them more ammunition in the plot for Wren-Dies-of-Embarrassment domination. I've given them enough material to last a lifetime. They'll be telling the closet story at my wedding. I'm sure of it.

Wait. Scratch that. That would only be relevant if I married Derick and… Geez, that's not a thought I needed this morning.

"Nobody important." I finish off the mimosa, sop up the rest of the runny yolk with rye, and set the tray down on my nearby desk, making sure not to knock over the fake Academy Award statue Mateo bought me four years ago engraved with "Best Roommate in a Freshman Dorm."

Avery doesn't let me off that easily. She pulls me back and pins me to the bed. Sheathed in the vines of her hair, I can barely see her possessed eyes as she shouts, "OMG! You were there with Derick! I told him you were in the office, and you went to the Lonely Lass-O together. WTH! This is why we have the group chat, Wren! How dare you break the first rule of group chat!"

"I thought the first rule of group chat was you do not talk about group chat," I joke to resounding crickets all around. "It's not a big deal. We ate, he apologized for ghosting me, we did the stupid line dance, and he offered to help me with the Alice Kelly situation." They look at me like I have seven heads. "Right. Sorry. I want to remount her premiere. I was going to tell you all, but I know how annoyed you were after my out loud brainstorming sessions for my capstone project, so I kept it to myself."

"Oh, yup, we started that drinking game. Take a sip of hard seltzer each time Wren says the name Alice Kelly. Take two sips every time he brings up *Chompin' at the Bit*. Shotgun the damn thing if he says *second-wave feminism* or *the Hollywood glass ceiling*." Mateo chuckles.

Brandon gives me a pitying look. "How do you put up with these two?"

"An excellent question." I get up, moving swiftly out of Avery's reach. "I got so caught up in the email debacle that I forgot. Dr. Tanson introduced me to Oscar Villanueva and told him about my research. He said if I was able to make the premiere happen, he might consider having me on his podcast." Without decoding their reactions, I begin picking out clothes for the day.

"Wren Roland, a guest on a major podcast? Alert the presses!" Mateo yells. "Should I get your autograph now, babe? I promise I won't sell it." He crosses his heart and bats his eyelashes, then reconsiders. "Unless you go viral, then that shit's going right on eBay."

I roll my eyes and throw a pair of denim shorts on the free end of my bed. "You know I'm terrible at public speaking. Plus, it can only happen if I help Alice get her house in order to sell. She's apparently been trying to lug it off for forever. It's like the ruins of the Roman Forum right now, and I'm not exactly a handy person. At least Derick offered to help."

"It sounds like he's looking for an excuse to be around you," Avery says.

Derick's question from last night loops back on me: "*We really can be friends again?*"

"There's nothing there," I admit forlornly. "Last night only confirmed he never felt that way about me and that he just wants to be friends now."

My prospects are delicate. I can't be hearing nonsense, allowing them to fill me further with fantasy. Putting stock in what very well could be a mindless offer he won't even make good on seems stupid. High School Me would've jumped at the chance to play what-if with my best friends, but currently, I can't conceive of a world where this works out for me.

"I'm sorry, babe. That sucks," Mateo says, losing his last ounce of excitement.

Their pitying eyes plague me. "It's fine. Really. I should focus on Wiley's and Alice and Earl and, yeah, it's fine."

It's a far cry from fine, but it will be one day—someday soon, I hope. So, today I'm going to embrace rekindling the friendship. The kiss quest can wait. What's another twenty-two years?

I grab my towels, signaling everyone that they should leave so I can get on with my day. I'm not about to be derailed with delusions of grandeur. I need to email Oscar back about Alice. I also promised my mom I'd stop by before my night shift to help her pack up some of Bella's Bottles, the painted, light-up wine bottles she makes and sells on Etsy. It's her side hustle when she's not the front-desk receptionist at an eye doctor—the one I go to and the reason I can afford my semi-stylish frames, and not have to wear the tragic bargain-bin ones I used to buy.

Avery gives me one last look. "There's nothing wrong with focusing on you for a change. You know that, right?"

Ignoring her inconvenient wisdom, I turn to Mateo. "Thanks for breakfast."

"Thanks for not firing me," he says.

The amateur chefs scuttle out of my room.

Before I step all the way into the bathroom, I call into the living room, "Oh, by the way, Mateo's your responsibility now, Aves. Concessions duty as punishment for his first strike!" Avery's groan echoes through the whole apartment, while Mateo's happy shriek rings in sharp contrast.

I turn on the shower with actual intention of getting in. No emotional water wasting today. I need to wash off the Lonely Lass-O. As I wait for it to warm up, which could take forever since this is an old building, I open Derick's text again and draft a reply:

Too much grainy sugar on a sour gummy worm, too much sauce and powdered sugar on a funnel cake, too much salt on a pretzel (and that's not even counting the dips!). I make exceptions for unbuttered, unsalted popcorn, Starbursts, Swedish Fish, and my all-time favorite: Twizzlers. ESPECIALLY the cherry Pull'n'Peels.

As usual, I select a Spotify playlist to listen to while washing up before setting my phone on top of the toilet to get the best acoustics. I choose Derick's and my old collaborative playlist. What's a rousing collection of songs among friends, anyway?

Still waiting, I stare at my scrawny frame in the streaky mirror. My mediocre muscles make it clear I'm not equipped to renovate a spooky house all alone. Sure, I can handle the small stuff, but the heavy lifting? My body's not the powerhouse I wish it were.

I don't have the money to pay for a crew, and I can't rope Mateo and Avery into any more of my shenanigans. Which leaves me to wonder: Who am I to turn my nose up at a strapping volunteer?

Because of this, I rush out another reply before I can think too hard about it:

If you were serious about the offer, meet me at Dunkin' Donuts at 7AM sharp on Wednesday. Bring your toolbox. We ride to Alice's for 8.

@WileysDriveInWV

Don't mind messy foods? Like eating with your hands? Don't forget to stop by our snack shack on your next visit to Wiley's Drive-In! Our updated menu features film-going favorites. Napkins needed! See full details in the photos below. 🍿 🌭 🍦 🍦

3 replies. 2 Retweets. 13 Likes.

@MovieFanatic198 Dang! Wish I lived closer. I'd kill for a funnel cake right about now!!!

@420BlazinBoii Perfect food for a case of the munchies 👀

@RolandOnTheRiver14 I feel personally attacked by this tweet. 😶

Chapter 11

Dunkin' Donuts at 7:00 a.m. on a Wednesday is a war zone. Undercaffeinated people grip and grab for whatever sugary, syrupy drink in the largest size they can get their hands on. This is why I avoid mornings like they're the plague.

Today, I have no choice.

I arrive early to make sure I snag a table. I have an iced oat-milk chai at my side. Picking at my hash browns with a fork, I brush off my nerves.

The nerves, however, come crawling back when Derick pushes through the glass front doors. The mere sight of him is like a thousand little bites.

He's wearing a purple tank top that I remember from high school, probably plucked from the bottom of a rarely opened drawer. When he spots me, he comes over and dives in for a hug. He's always been a hugger. He smells like papaya-scented sunscreen and sweat. There's already a dark triangular stain pointing down from the loose collar.

"Sorry I'm damp. I had to get in my run a lot earlier this morning. I figured there was no point in showering just to work up a sweat again."

"Makes sense since we'll be painting and hammering and screwing all day."

"Screwing all day?" His devious smile sparkles. A very unfriend-like blush blazes across my face. "Shit. Sorry. Was that okay?"

Derick developed a flirtatious side in high school, and we practiced it together all the time. Surely, it's one of the pillars of being part of a well-to-do family: perfecting the art of flirtation, even on people you don't plan on getting with, as a means to get ahead. At least that's what I told myself back then.

"You're good."

He shrugs. "I don't smell too bad, do I?" He unsubtly checks his pits.

See, he's *definitely* not trying to get with me.

"Again, you're good."

This is good. This is fine. The more I berate myself with the word: *FRIENDS!* stylized in my mind like the nineties sitcom, the more I'll default to it. The more I'll start hearing the iconic theme song in my head every time he appears.

He sets his bag down at the table and joins the ever-growing line. I fiddle with my phone for a distraction. I notice a red "1" hovering over my email app. Tapping in, I find a response from Oscar to my note about my progress with Alice:

Dear Wren,

This is fantastic news! I'm delighted to hear you're making moves with Alice Kelly. I've had the chance to read over your capstone paper, and I have to say, I'm more than impressed. This level of detail weaved into personal narrative is both informative and affecting. I think you have a real way with words and research.

Do you have any idea when you might be able to hold the screening of *Chompin' at the Bit* at Wiley's? I may have briefly mentioned it to a few of my fellow film lovers and they are clamoring to know more. Of course, I'm warding them off. I want the first exclusive scoop!

I'd love to coordinate a time for you to come into Manhattan. We can watch the movie together, discuss, and hop into my studio for a recording session. Then, I can see about sending off the original 35mm film to my connection at a lab in Maryland who can restore and digitize for the big screening.

Let me know when you know more.

All my best,
Oscar

Elation elongates my spine, clears my acne, harvests my bounty. This is huge. I need to make sure our day at Alice's is as productive as possible. Getting in her good graces could seal me the deal before I even know what the deal is. In my wildest dreams, it's a *book* deal.

My hands hold the phantom weight of my future bestselling hardcover.

"Why do you look like you just won a game show?" Derick asks when he sits across from me. There's an entire box of doughnuts in his hand.

"Are those all for you?"

"No, they're for Alice. We can't show up empty-handed. What kind of guests would we be if we did?" I suppose he's right. He sips from his unsweetened iced tea. "Two glazed, two strawberry sprinkled, and two Boston creams. But, don't touch those. Those are for me."

"I wouldn't dream of it."

"I realized, the more I thought about your aversion to finger foods, that my favorites are all foods you exclusively eat with your hands." He does a showgirl presentation of the box. "Case in point."

"How very caveman-make-fire of you."

He stops his pleased smile by chewing on his orange and pink straw. "Sorry, I probably should've done some research of my own, but who is this Alice Kelly again and why is she so important?"

I run through a mini film-studies presentation before a lecture hall of one, and I'm surprised when I don't shut down from the stress and the sheer intensity of Derick's unwavering gaze. "What Alice made wasn't really an art-house movie, like what Barbara Loden was doing, and it wasn't quite a studio film, like what Elaine May did or what Barbra Streisand would do."

"Art-house? Studio? It's like you're speaking another language."

Frustration momentarily riles me. How could he help rebrand a drive-in movie theater if he doesn't even know basic film jargon? He'd be a bad trivia partner at the Cat's Pajamas' Hollywood Her-story Night, which I've won every single time I've attended. I have an impressive collection of feathery boas to prove it.

"Is Barbra Streisand the *Meet the Fockers* lady?" I'm not giving him a gold star for that one.

I push my glasses farther up the bridge of my nose. "Sorry. I forget you're not a film nerd like me." I know not everyone grows up to be a cinephile. Though the world would be a better, more empathetic place if they did.

"If anyone could convert me, it would be you," Derick jokes with a wink, but then backtracks, making a face like he stubbed his toe. "God. Even I know that was too much."

"Yeah, that was even worse than your coming-out-of-the-closet joke."

"Oh, so you *did* read those texts and choose to ignore them?" He scolds me with a wicked smolder. Then, he shakes his head. "I don't mean to. Sometimes I make jokes about being gay to shield myself from the hard parts. I did it for so long with friends and family before I was out, and now, even a few years later, I'm still working on it."

It's nice to hear him so self-aware. To know that the seismic waves of coming out are still rippling through him, too. I thought I was alone in that. Everyone makes it seem like coming out is crossing the finish line and now you just get to parade around while wearing your medal. For me, it feels more like I'm still winded midmarathon.

"When exactly did you come out?" We've missed so much over the years. "If that's too personal, you don't need to answer."

"First semester sophomore year and then again over winter break at home," he says. The winter break after he abandoned our movie marathon plans. A whole year to come to terms with what he couldn't wrap his head around. What he felt he couldn't share with me. "My brothers pretty much knew and my parents took it as well as two Pennsylvanian, tax-obsessed Republicans could."

"What do you mean?"

"I mean they smiled, nodded, and then never brought it up again." He laughs, but I know it's to cover up something more insidious. "How about you?"

I tell him the tale. This past January, I sent a timed coming-out email to my family and scampered back to campus for the start of my final semester, into the waiting arms of Mateo and Avery, who already knew. They were my soft launch into my identity a year prior when I was still figuring it all out.

I say that as if I'm not still "figuring it all out." Some days, it feels like I don't even know what "it all" is.

"It would've been nice if we could've been there for each other," Derick says in a way that suggests he doesn't have a Mateo and Avery of his own. That his frat brothers probably treat his sexuality as a diversity checkbox rather than an integral part of his identity.

"Yeah, it would've been."

While I'm contemplating what that alternate reality would've looked like, he lifts the lens of the camera I didn't even see him pull out, and he snaps a sneaky shot of me.

"What was that for?" I'm not used to being on this side of the shutter.

"The light was good." He inspects the image on the screen. "The subject was good, too. Just the right amount of red in the cheeks..."

He's teasing me, play-flirting at a level 10, the way we always used to. And he's damn good at it. I'm alight with a thousand twirling, twinkling thoughts.

Friends, I remind myself. *Just friends...*

"Anyway," he recalibrates, "you were saying about Alice Kelly."

"As I was saying," I echo, flustered and trying not to show it, "her movie *Chompin' at the Bit* was a one-night-only love story between a zombie boy and a local girl. It's supposedly swoony and campy and melodramatic and more than a little bit queer. From what I've read, we never quite know if the protagonist, Robin, develops feelings for the zombie, named James, because he's her only tether back to her dead friend and possible queer crush, Tammy, or if she really wants to kiss him, which she definitely can't do or she'll turn undead as well." My voice pitches up a few octaves with my rising excitement. "So, Alice gets this grant money and finds private investors through her LA connections to fund the film she wrote based on a proof of concept she shot without her husband's knowledge during one holiday season in the Willow Valley cemetery by our Catholic church." Before he asks, I add, "Yes, the one where kids go to smoke weed."

"I'm guessing it never took off considering I've never heard of it."

"I mean, yes, but you've never heard of Elaine May, so I'm not sure you're the best barometer for movie popularity." He seems half-hurt by my words. "Sorry, that was a little harsh."

"No worries. So, what happened?"

I tell him the whole story, basically an overview of my entire Rosevale research project. He listens and nods at all the appropriate places. I end by explaining how Peter Borellio went on to direct his own indie-budget film with a supernatural bent right after exorcising Alice from Hollywood. His would be taught in film courses, while hers would not even be a footnote.

"At some point, she donated her copy of the film negative to the archives of the Willow Valley library, but it's impossible to get your hands on it without her express permission. There were talks that around 2008, they might bring it out of the vault to see if it could amass a cult following, since supernatural romances were big again and the internet can make anything cool, but Alice shot the idea down."

Derick steals the last bit of hash brown from my bag without asking. Flinging it into his mouth, he asks between chews, "So, how bad is the house we're working on really?"

I sigh. "Almost as bad as her attitude."

♡

"Oh perfect. Make my blood sugar skyrocket and send me into shock so you don't have to do work. Good plan," Alice says as soon as she opens the door and spies the Dunkin' Donuts box.

I shoot Derick a see-what-I-mean look. He laughs under his breath, passing it off as a series of coughs.

"Who's this infected person? Is he sick? If he's sick, he's not stepping foot in here," Alice says to me after snatching the doughnuts out of Derick's hands.

"He's not sick," I promise.

"He's coughing like he's sick."

"I'm Derick Haverford, and I assure you, I'm as healthy as a horse."

"We used to have horses on this farm," Alice says.

"How lovely. I bet they were fit as—"

"Most of them died of colic."

"Oh."

Her eyes narrow at him. "Can you work a paintbrush?"

"Yes, ma'am," he says.

That's all she needs to hear before she pulls him across the threshold.

In the kitchen, Alice decimates one-and-a-half strawberry doughnuts iced with sprinkles while she tells us about the repairs that need to be done. Upon closer inspection, the house really is a dump. The cumbersome buckets of paint she drops in our waiting hands can't cover up all the cosmetic faults. This is more than our rookie skills can correct. This isn't months of neglect. This is years of damage. I'm surprised she hasn't taken a nasty tumble down the decrepit staircase at this point.

As we move all the furniture into the center of the living room and cover it all with plastic, it's clear we're not here to play *Property Brothers*. Our goal is to give the place a facelift. Just enough to entice a potential buyer.

Despite the inhospitable welcome, Derick and I are joking and laughing while we lay out newspaper all over the floor so the blush-colored paint doesn't drip everywhere. Alice packed up the picture frames from the mantel over the wood-burning fireplace all by herself, making certain neither of us snuck a look at what was in them. Cryptic.

The Mary Tyler Moore Show theme song, with lyrics about *making it after all*, pipes in from the other room when Alice finally lugs her box of knickknacks out and away. I've learned they're not frequent reruns. Alice has one subscription service—to Hulu so she can binge-watch her old favorite show for comfort.

Even *she's* into streaming!

Derick's exposed biceps bulge and stretch each time he runs the roller across the wall in front of us. The more I look, the more that purple tank top reminds me of our history, of nights spent around backyard firepits and chasing fireflies, night swims and boardwalk games.

I force myself to look away.

The house is drafty, and the June weather is brutal. With no AC, the temperature will only continue to climb and the more sauna-like this room will become. I take a swig of cool, ice water to trick my body into stasis.

"So when you said you've never been kissed," Derick says out of nowhere sometime later, "does that mean you've never dated anyone either?"

I dab my brush into the bucket. "Not really. I've been on dates before.

Most of them bad. I guess I was sort of dating Alfie, one of the other guys who got an email, during the summer between eighth grade and freshman year, but that doesn't really count. I don't think either of us knew what being queer was. We just knew we liked spending time with each other. We held hands on the dock after curfew one night and he showed me where different constellations were. Honestly, I think he made most of them up, but I was gullible and, frankly, couldn't stop thinking about how warm his palm was. I didn't care if Strega Nona was in the stars or not."

"We read *Strega Nona* in school story time. What, did you think some pasta-cooking grandma was part of Greek mythology?" He gawks at me.

"Okay, whatever. I was a little more focused on whether we were going to kiss or not. I wasn't caught up in the semantics. Plus, it would've been rude to interrupt. Some of them were factual—like the Medium Dipper."

"Wrenji, there's only a Big Dipper and a Little..."

"Gotcha!" I swat my brush at him. There's a line of pale-pink paint across the bridge of his nose when I yank away. The imperfection makes the symmetry of his face even more striking. "That was a test and the paint is your punishment!"

"Don't make me roller you." He holds the instrument up as a threat. "I know how to use it."

I laughingly back down and together we zero in on the second wall. Two more to go and then a second coat all around. "To answer your question," I finally add after a long stretch of focused work, "no I've never dated anybody officially. You?"

"When I got to college, I started seeing this cute guy, Charlie, around all the DTD interest events I was attending. Long story short, we crossed paths at a lacrosse party freshman year. We kissed. I freaked. Classic crisis of conscience." He laughs at himself.

"Ah, so Charlie is to blame for you missing our movie marathon?" I ask facetiously, attempting to mask my latent jealously.

"I mean, not exactly." Derick grows flustered, looking away. "No, actually not at all. That's on me. I take full responsibility for that." It's strange to wonder what right now would look like without our complicated coming-out experiences. What if the world were a place where being queer didn't necessitate a *crisis of conscience*, as he put it, but rather was just accepted as part of the norm? Would we have gotten together back then if we didn't have to cobble together our identities first?

Derick moves on. "Sophomore year, during rush, we ended up hooking up. He wanted to be exclusive. I wanted more hooking up. At the time, it seemed like committing to him was the easiest and safest way to do that, but it ended up hurting me more in the long run. When I called it off junior year, he didn't take it well." He steps back to get his bearings.

I'm cautious when I ask, "How so?"

"He started snooping around in my phone. A red flag I should've seen coming. He saw some of these pictures of us from prom. I still had them saved on my phone, and he remembered that one of you I have up on my business website, in the portfolio section. He got really cagey and started asking all these questions about you. What we were like in high school, if we still talked. Honestly, he was possessive and intense and jealous, and he kind of messed me up. Especially when it came to my family."

It's sad how this is starting to sound like a Peter/Alice situation. A toxic relationship disguised as something sweet.

"He threatened to out me to some of my dad's business partners," Derick says after some time. My whole body tenses at that. "I know it's ass-backwards, but the circle my dad runs in isn't exactly open-minded and my dad is mum about my identity as is. If they knew Daniel P. Haverford had a gay son, they might choose to put their money elsewhere. My dad made that very clear."

"Crap." I pause, placing a comforting hand on his shoulder, even though I know it's not nearly enough. "I'm really sorry that happened to you."

Derick nods appreciatively. "I thought about reaching out to you after Charlie and I broke up. I had mostly forgotten about those pictures until he cross-examined me about them. I remember I spent this one whole night scrolling through all the old high school albums, majorly stuck in my feels, and there were so many pictures I wanted to send to you. But then I remembered what I'd done and how much time had passed and, well, I felt like shit. I thought you'd blocked me on all social media because I couldn't see your profiles."

"I didn't," I'm quick to qualify. "Again, I set the accounts to private when I deleted the apps. It was easier that way."

"I know that now, but I figured you didn't want to hear from me." He sets his paintbrush down in the tray. "So, you can imagine my surprise when I got your email."

It all comes back to the whopping electronic elephant. And yet, I'm surprised that this time around it doesn't feel all that much like an elephant. It feels more like a house cat. An orange tabby strolling around somewhere. It only makes itself known when it needs food or wants a cuddle. Strange to think that maybe I've tamed it.

"I wish you had reached out," I say at last.

"Me too."

We complete the third wall in silence. There's not much more to say. It's not until we take a breather during number four that Derick reopens the dialogue.

"Are you going to get back to that Oscar guy about the podcast?"

I nod. If Dr. Tanson drilled one lesson into me, it's that I need to build and maintain my contact network. Whatever happens with Alice, I need to ensure this line of communication stays open. Even if the idea of speaking on his podcast makes my skin seem like it's melting off.

"What's this talk about a podcast?" Alice asks, appearing out of thin air, ghostly in her all-white outfit. She moves with such silent agility. Her mouth is full. She's scarfing down that leftover half of a doughnut. She better not crash from all that sugar. I can handle painting, but I can't handle lifesaving resuscitation. "What even is a podcast? Is it like radio on demand?"

"Sort of," I say. "It's like long-form storytelling. The hosts are usually specialists in a field or actors playing characters. You can subscribe, stream, and download the episodes based on their release schedule. Lots of people listen to them on commutes or to unwind at the end of the day."

"And what does the long-form storyteller want with you?" Her tone suggests I don't have anything interesting to offer.

"Well, it's not so much with me as it is with you."

She brushes her hands clean of crumbs. I pull the paint tray out from under her so she doesn't destroy the glops I've poured out for a second coat. "If you think I'm doing an interview, you're deranged."

"You don't have to do anything you don't want to do. They just showed general interest in doing an episode on *Chompin' at the Bit* is all," I say, sitting a spell on the edge of the step stool. "If you let us do the premiere, of course. It would really help boost sales at the drive-in. Exposure on a popular podcast could draw in revenue Earl really needs." I shoot her my best pleading eyes.

"It seems stupid he's struggling. I thought you youths were all about bringing back trends of the past. Bell bottoms and Polaroid cameras and TV shows that should've stayed dead and buried." I have a suspicion she could gripe forever over how our generation has destroyed this country by being unoriginal consumers.

I shrug with the fate of the drive-in like an albatross around my shoulders. "Earl would never say it, but everyone has at least one streaming service now." I'm about to add *even you*, but think better of it. She'll contort it into me calling her an old bat or something. "Everything is digital, even our equipment now. Those black-box projectors anybody with half a brain could turn on and control cost a lot. The expense to make those improvements was at least in the five digits, if not six. I'm still unsure how Earl managed that. As far as I can tell, we've been in the red for a while. I think he thought we could compete with IMAX and 3-D and all the other newfangled technology, and we did for a few seasons. But that's just it: we operate in just one season. It's hard to see a return on an investment when you can't be open year-round."

"How hurt do you think the lot is?" Derick asks. "Ballpark."

"Earl mentioned being down significantly in attendance from last season. He's secretive about his books, but I've snuck a few peeks at his handwritten ledger in the office before. He's not good about keeping it in a secure location. Not that he's worried about anyone stealing money he doesn't have." I grab Derick's roller and finish the section of wall I was working on.

"There's nothing good to see in theaters these days anyway. Superheroes and remakes? I see all the trailers. No thank you." Alice's distaste causes her lips to gather and her eyes to squint like she's just eaten the world's tartest lemon square.

"Still, it's a fixture."

"Even fixtures have to close shop sometimes," Derick says. I glare at him. "What? I'm just being real. My social-media savvy can only do so much."

"That's why the podcast could be a major boon!"

"Podcast schmodcast." Alice riffles through her box and pulls a photo from it. I'm just close enough to peer over her shoulder.

I'm not trying to be nosy, but she makes a big show of looking at it, bringing it increasingly closer to her face. It must be terrible to have your eyes betray you the way hers have. The engraved frame is weathered, yet the photo is clear, three girls smiling, shoulder-length hair curling up at the edges, wearing houndstooth skirts and floral blouses.

"Is that Annie?" I ask. Alice had one younger sister and five older brothers. It must've been a busy farm. Annie had a brief career in the movies as well, but never made it big.

"Yes." Alice's hands are shaky, partly from age and partly from emotion. She strokes a spotted thumb over her own face.

"And who's the other girl?"

She's silent for a long time. "Tammy."

I don't know if she's misremembering or if she's serious. Tammy was the name of the protagonist's dead friend, and possible queer crush, from *Chompin' at the Bit.* The story goes that every year on Halloween night one zombie rises from the cemetery beside the protagonist, Robin's, church to get a final night to take care of their unfinished business. It really subverted the preconceived notion from other exploitation films that zombies were mindless flesh-eaters. Instead of hunting for brains, James was searching for closure.

Despite not knowing if she buys into the town lore, Robin camps out there because that year Tammy passed away in a car accident, so she thinks Tammy might be the one to emerge from the earth. If that's true, she wants to be there to see her one last time.

From the few reviews that were published and still accessible, I remember the actress's name was Anya. Was Tammy a real person? Did the movie have some basis in the Kelly sisters' real lives? That didn't come up in my research. I want to ask, but Alice sets down the photo with such force that I'm thrown from my speeding train of thought.

"That's good for today," she says.

"We've only done one coat," Derick says.

"I said, 'That's good for today.' Don't make me kick you out." She wrings her hands as she walks toward the door. "I'll sic the dogs on you." Today, I noticed a ton of untouched bowls of kibble lying around on the floor.

Something tells me the dogs aren't real and the BEWARE OF signs outside are false illusions of protection. I don't test her claim, though. Derick and I collect our belongings and see ourselves out.

"That was weird," Derick mumbles when the door slams shut behind us.

I just nod, already setting a reminder to do some research: Tammy, car accident, obituary, 1960s.

Derick is smiling widely when we reach the edge of the porch.

"Did I miss something?" I ask, gesturing to his general expression.

"Just...that was fun," he says. "This is fun. It's interesting. I'm excited. Alice seems cool and her movie seems cooler and you..."

"Please, please, please don't say I'm the *coolest*."

"Aye, aye, boss."

"Aye, aye is for captains."

"Alright then. Aye, aye, *Captain* Wrenji," he says. I unlock my car and step toward it, but then he calls after me, "Permission to deboard, Captain?" He's standing in a yoga pose, foot to knee, on the edge of the last loose step. His right hand is raised in salute.

I salute back. "Permission granted, sailor."

As I get into my car, I swear I hear him murmur to himself, "Ha, sailor, love it."

♡

Around 8:00 p.m., after a dinner of pad thai in the living room with Mateo and Avery, I close the door to my room and launch an internet search. I put my sleuthing cap on. If only I had a kick-ass monocle to match.

I sift through digitized newspaper prints with different obituaries circled in red. I'm surprised that there were five total county-area crashes involving a young girl named Tammy around that time. It was a popular name, I know, and it seems drunk-driving accidents were far too common. I hate how macabre my evening has become, but this feels important to unlocking Alice's overall frame of mind around the movie. Something Oscar would have to uncover for a special podcast episode.

What she won't tell me, I'll need to find out for myself.

The more I think about maybe being on Oscar's podcast, the more nervous I become. I'm not used to being in the public eye in the way that would entail. I'm largely an introvert. I like my small group of friends, my safe spaces, my insular life. I get my fill of adventure from the movies. Safe, and at a distance. I much prefer my synthesis to be in writing, read from afar, critiqued without my knowledge.

An hour into my hunt, I read about Tammy Wilson, a senior at Willow Valley High, two years behind Alice. As I learn more about the accident that ultimately led to her death—on impact, no pain, thankfully—I'm shocked when I read the name of the surviving passenger: Annie Kelly.

Alice's sister.

The new information locks in like the missing number in a secret code. The safe of Alice's life swings open in front of me. Alice wrote the screenplay about her deceased best friend.

I'm even less shocked when I see where Tammy was buried: Saint Thomas, right off Broad Street, a side road diverting from the Willow Valley main strip and not far from Wiley's. It's the white, tucked-away building with a tall steeple and cross-shaped layout. Behind it is the small Catholic cemetery that was the set of Alice's movie.

The connections run deep but the pain runs deeper. How had I missed this in my capstone work? I'd seen Tammy in one of those old yearbooks I'd looked through in the Willow Valley Public Library.

Annie passed away a few years ago from a stroke. She continued to work in New York until she, like Alice, returned to the out-of-service Kelly farm to take care of their ailing mother who was battling cancer.

When it rains, it really does pour.

Alice is the only surviving member of the original Kelly family. She might have an estranged niece or nephew out there somewhere but no one close, which explains why she's holing up inside that house, living off disability checks, letting the wood rot around her.

To wake up every day in the home that used to be filled with life and laughter but is now devoid of either must be terrible. Her sorrow is a boiling pot without a lid, dangerously close to overflowing.

Alice may be curt and demanding, hard to read and even a little mean, but maybe it's all a defense mechanism. I feel for her in a way I didn't expect to. My preconceived idea of her, the one I developed alongside my collegiate thesis, is shattered.

I decide to be more tender with her. If she sees me as an ally, she might be more open. She's a well of lived experience in my chosen field. She needs a friend. I might not be her first choice, but oh well.

Nobody knows what happened to her when she ran away from it all. Who's going to survive those stories when she succumbs to old age? No children. A deceased ex-husband. Nobody's story deserves to die with them, just like no film deserves to be suppressed after its first showings.

Death makes the air in my room heavy and hard to breathe. I start to spiral, thinking about the people I love in my life and how horrible it would be if I ever lost one of them too soon. Especially someone who I had more to say to, more to experience with. Mateo. Avery. Mom. Dad. Claire. Earl.

Now, I'm even including Derick.

What if he had died before coming home this summer? I can't even imagine the never-ending pain of our unfinished business.

I pull my favorite (stolen from Claire) purple blanket up onto my bed and pick out a Penny Marshall movie from my VHS collection. I need a feel-good hit to lift my spirits. As the *Coming soon to home video* trailers play, I realize this is the blanket from the night of the almost-kiss that I mentioned in my original email to Derick. That trigger sets off a domino chain, and during the opening credits, I end up pushing aside the neatly hung clothes in my overly organized closet—color, cut, size, etc.

In the back corner, there's a box filled with a hodgepodge of old vestiges including those Polaroids starring High School Derick that Mateo mentioned a few weeks back. There's even the lei I wore to the party where Mateo and I almost-kissed. It still feels sandy somehow.

My hand clamps around a soft strip of fabric in the depths. From the clutter, I find Derick's scarf, the one I wore in Baskersville on Halloween night. The pièce de résistance of his Ken doll costume. It still smells faintly like him. Even after all these years. Even as it's fraying at the edges.

I thought about dumping it, but maybe it's time to give it back, let loose the feelings I clutched onto that night. A friendship is better than a summer fraught with unresolved tension.

I lay it out on my bed and snap a picture.

In a text to Derick, I write:

Ahoy! This look familiar? Thought you might want it back. I'll bring it to the lot this weekend. See you soon, sailor.

Instagram

WileysDriveInWV MEET THE STAFF SPOTLIGHT. Wren Roland is the newest manager at Wiley's Drive-In, but this will be his EIGHTH summer with the establishment. With years of experience and a film studies degree, he's the perfect person to spearhead a very special screening at the end of the season. Here's a hint: A premiere that almost was. Want to know more about what that means? Say hi to Wren next time you see him around the lot!

.

.

IMAGE DESCRIPTION: A white, medium-height, handsome, shaggy-brown-haired boy with facial scruff sits at Dunkin' Donuts wearing a niche movie reference T-shirt.

.

.

#drivein #moviesPA #WileysDriveIn #comingsoon #moviepremiere

NessaRoseKnowsBest A Willow Valley premiere sounds 🔥 💯
MovieMagic_Mike Wait, is this going to be a movie made in the area?! @DontYouForgetAboutPod aren't you obsessed with a movie made in Willow Valley?
DontYouForgetAboutPod Chompin' at the Bit??? Yes! I'm in conversations with Wren to make this happen. Keep your eye on this space.
MovieMagic_Mike @DontYouForgetAboutPod Can't wait!
420BlazinBoii Did a business account just call an employee handsome?! Y'all definitely hiding some good good in that snack shack…smh 😵

Chapter 12

Derick called me *handsome*.

On social media.

Technically, @WileysDriveInWV called me handsome, but I'm privy to the mastermind behind the handle.

It takes twenty minutes for this to process, and even then, I have a hard time believing it.

Avery sent me a screenshot in the group chat followed by a series of indecipherable emojis.

Do male friends call other male friends handsome? Avery's called me a cutie before, and whenever I put in extra effort and slick back my unruly hair, Mateo says I'm give off "leading man realness," but their confidence boosts are categorically platonic. Calling someone handsome in such a public forum seems loaded in a way I'm not ready to unpack. It goes beyond the harmless semi-flirting that had always been part of our deal *because* it's so public.

Unfortunately, Derick did so alongside a photo he should've asked my permission for before posting, but that slight oversight is being drowned in a whirlpool of other woozier emotions. Confusion, happiness, and maybe a pinch of guilt? I'm sure this is not the kind of attention Earl was looking for when he agreed to bring Derick into the online fold.

Though I'm sure he's not keeping tabs on the feeds. His cell phone is a fossil from the Stone Age.

I should force myself to shrug it all off—I try!—but I keep getting pulled back to stare. The light hits me at a flattering angle. My hair looks messy, but in a fashionable, grungy way matched with my slight facial stubble I've been too busy to shave. I actually like it? It's a weird sensation, yet it's exciting to see what I look like on the other side of Derick's lens.

Maybe this is way *he* sees me. That's the most exhilarating part. And the most confusing.

The obsessing stops short when I hit the snack shack.

Avery greets me aghast, pale and panting.

"It's bad," she says, clutching my hand and tugging me behind the counter. There goes my good vibes. "It's Mateo. He's locked himself in the break room and he won't come out."

I should've known. "What? Why? What happened this time?" I buttress myself for what she's about to tell me. I thought concessions was Earl's safe spot. Avery is good about keeping everyone in line.

"I showed him how to start the popcorn machine, fresh batch, coconut oil, how many kernels, special Wiley's seasoning salt, what have you. I told him to wait until the machine beeped and then to dump the steel bucket twice to make sure it's empty. We don't need anything burnt and causing the alarms to go off."

"Good, good." I'm sensing it only gets worse from here.

"I ran to check our candy stock for, like, fifteen minutes, and when I came back he was pouring the *sugar* canister over the kernels on a *second batch*. The *sugar for the coffee*. It's white! The salt is yellow! He was really going to town with it." She shoves her hand into her hair in exasperation. "So, maybe I yelled a bit."

I give her a discerning look.

"Okay, I FASed"—*flipped a shit*, I know this one well—"but can you blame me? Stacia's coming here with her friends tonight. I wanted everything to be perfect, and he ruined two whole batches of popcorn. I had to throw the whole reservoir out and restart. He shouted something about not being able to take the heat and that he needed to get out of the kitchen—this is hardly a kitchen—and now he's locked in there talking on the phone with Brandon."

I shake my head, disbelief tightening all my knotted parts. I run through a list of emergency employees we could probably call, but it's already last minute. We're showing a superhero movie tonight, one in our last weekend before we're open five days a week instead of three, thanks to school letting out, so there's no doubt we'll be mobbed. Nobody with experience is going to be available. Nobody with no experience would be able to handle it.

Except maybe—

As if he saw the Bat-Signal, Derick enters. He hits his mark with aplomb. I can tell he let his hair dry naturally today as it's begun to curl in on the ends, making him look like a surfer-cool West Coast transplant, his quiff its own breaking wave.

"Derick?"

"Huh?" he asks, standing up from photographing the cute candy display Avery had been curating in the glass case while Mateo wrecked perfectly good, undeserving popcorn.

"Any chance you want to have a real Wiley's employee experience?"

"You know I love a challenge." He flashes me his winning smile.

He follows me over to the office. Youssef isn't at his post at the projector yet, and Earl is out on the lot. I pull a duct-taped cardboard box out from below the desk and rummage around for the right-sized shirt. We order in bulk since Earl likes the uniformity of the bright yellow, even if it's unflattering on virtually all skin tones. The more I dig, the more I realize we're out of mediums and larges, the popular sizes and the ones that would fit Derick the best.

I wriggle free a small from the stash. "Do you think this will do?"

He holds it up to his torso. "We'll have to make it work."

Speedily, he's stripping in front of me. I didn't expect this, and I'm woefully unprepared for what I see as he peels his shirt up and over his head.

He's toned, but not cut. Built, but not jacked. Hairy, but only on his chest and a tantalizing treasure trail. My eyes take a trip down the dusty strip that starts between his pecs and bisects his belly button, disappearing into the hemline of his exposed white Calvin Klein waistband.

The word "hot" has never had much meaning to me until now. If I looked up its definition in the dictionary, I'm certain it would be accompanied by a snapshot of *him* like *this*.

I experience a soft stir below my belt. A tingle I haven't had in a while. *Weird.*

Too soon, he wriggles into the one-size-too-small T-shirt. It covers his stomach, yet cinches his shoulders. His muscles are prominent against the straining fabric.

"How do I look?" he asks.

No matter how badly I want to say "hot," I can't and I won't, because that would be entirely unfriend-like, not to mention unprofessional, so I say "fine," and he doesn't question me any further. He's not one of those needy guys who wants praise for his looks. He knows he's got them—the body of a runner and the face of an influencer. I just hope the customers can look past his perky nipples while ordering their hot dogs.

Back on the floor, I plan to leave him in Avery's capable hands, certain he knows the difference between salt and sugar. I need to coax a cowering Mateo out of the break room. Poor guy can't catch a break. Can't use his common sense, either, but that's a conversation for another time.

I'm about to knock on the bolted door when Earl comes charging inside. "Josh just called out sick, stomach flu. You're another short in the shack it seems, missy." Avery turns an even ghostlier white. We can't handle a Friday night crowd with two servers. Doing what a go-getting manager would do, I slip on an apron, willing and prepared to help. I hope it shows Earl how I've turned a corner after our last conversation. I'm taking initiative in every way I can.

Avery gives Derick a rundown of the sizes. She doesn't dare show him how to operate the register because it's old and complicated and slow. We should update its operating system, but at this point it's so low on the totem pole of priorities that we've learned to make do. In some ways, we've come to love it, its finicky controls both frustrating and funny.

This is the first time I've seen Derick appear frazzled. Avery talks fast on the reg, and today, she's hurrying through the instructions. I make myself useful by getting the drawer ready with proper change and singles for the onslaught of hungry customers.

With minutes to spare, I saddle over to the break room. Mateo's still on the phone inside. I call loudly to him. "Go away!" he cries.

"It's Wren. Can you come out here?"

"No."

"Can I come in there?"

"No!"

"I promise you're not in trouble. I just want to talk." This is my eighth summer. It's Avery's sixth. It's Mateo's first, and he only took the job after a heated argument with the artistic director of Rosevale summer stock. Transitions can be hard. I want to understand where he's coming from.

I mean, some of the other newbies are taking to the responsibilities much easier, but that doesn't diminish Mateo's need for extra attention. I only wish we had enough hands to help him out.

"I'm not coming out until Avery apologizes for calling me a VIK!"

"Very important knockout?" I ask hopefully.

"Very incompetent klutz!" He's using his pouty voice, the baby talk he turns on when he wants validation, but both of us know it's not going to do any good. Avery is adamant about many things. Apologies take some time when she feels she's done nothing wrong.

"Give her a bit to cool off. She'll come around." I check my watch. I don't have much time to put a cap on this. "Would it help if I told you Derick is covering for you? You can take as long as you need. We'll be out here when you're ready."

"Derick's covering?" His voice is closer now.

"Yeah." I glance back over my shoulder. For a laugh, Avery has made Derick wear one of the old Wiley's visors, the bright-pink ones with embroidered lettering. I overhear her telling him that his "hair is too lush and tall so it might fall in the food." I'm certain it's to make him suffer a bit.

Considering Mateo a lost cause, I notice Derick's DSLR camera bag sitting on one of the flat fridges. I slip the camera out and tinker with the controls a little. The lens pops out and the screen comes on. Right when he's about to turn to me, a happy smile stretching across his lips, I take a candid shot of him, partly payback for the one he posted of me on Instagram and partly because he looks ridiculous and hot.

Okay, fine. *Ridiculously hot.*

Even. In. The. Visor.

When he notices what I've done, he races over to inspect the damage. Afraid he might delete it, I lead a game of keep-away, even though my height is no match for his. Our bodies press up against each other's. The tight fabric of his shirt rides up, and the back of my forearm skims the exposed, fuzzy skin of his stomach. He's laughing in my ear, hot and immediate, and swiftly, I feel electric. Aglow. Buzzing.

And wrong for even entertaining those joyful bursts.

I give up the game. That's when I hear the break-room door unlock. Mateo steps out, tearstained and sullen.

Our laughs stifle as we all take him in.

"Brandon's coming to pick me up." He tosses his apron onto the pile behind him. "Thanks for covering, Derick." He won't make eye contact with me or Avery.

"Wait, you're leaving?" I ask.

He huffs. "I've got coverage. What does it matter? I'm 'incapable of doing menial tasks' anyway." I wish Avery would be better about hiding her sassy eye roll. Mateo clocks it and storms out the open door.

The heated moment hugs me like a trash compactor. The friend in me wants to run after him. The manager in me is thankful he's out of my hair. Thinking back on Earl's strikes policy, I can't let the friend win out.

"Incoming!" Avery shouts as the hordes of early arrivers cram themselves into the shack.

"All hands on deck, sailor," I say to Derick, shaking off the worrisome feelings.

"Aye, aye, Captain." He salutes again. It makes me snort, but by the grace of God, nobody hears it.

We batten down the hatches and brace for impact.

♡

At the end of the shift, Avery rewards Derick and me with ice cream Popsicles shaped like SpongeBob. They have gumballs for eyes, and I can't wait to cool myself off.

Even at night, mid-June is blazing into July. Derick, standing in the glow of the neon lights, still stuffed into that tiny T-shirt, does nothing to stop me from sweating.

Earl thanks me for a job well done tonight, which means I'm floating on a cotton candy cloud for once. He even seems excited about the Alice Kelly event and lets me put up a Post-it note on the large calendar, a tentative space holder. August 14, here we come. I neglect to mention that we're refurbishing her farmhouse in our spare time because what he doesn't know he can't be angry about.

He slips me two twenty-dollar bills from his wallet. "For the Haverford kid. If he's as good as Avery says he is, we should make him a permanent fixture." He thinks a moment, scratching his dimpled chin. "Eh, maybe. Depends. I'm already paying him for those TweetToks." He huffs. "Good help is hard to find, but harder to finance."

"How are we doing so far?" I try to cover up my concern. I do a bad job of it.

He swats at a mosquito and says, "We've done better and we've done worse. We can't make any price cuts or we're kaput. The projections I wrote up were less promising, so Derick's social media must be doing something. Though I'm afraid Mateo might raze the place to the ground if we let him keep working here."

"It's only strike two," I remind him.

"You're right. Rules are rules." Aggressively, he claps the mosquito between the palms of his greasy hands. Here's wishing Mateo doesn't suffer a similar fate before the summer is out. I don't want the unfortunate displeasure of having to fire him.

"The Alice Kelly premiere could really give us a boost."

"You're really turning the tide, kid. Keep it up." Earl saunters back into the shack.

Derick waves his ice cream stick in the air as I approach. "We survived!"

"Did you doubt we would?"

"There was a moment there, wrestling with the soft serve machine, where I thought I was done for. Who knew swirling an ice cream cone could be so complicated?" he asks, shaking out his overworked hands. His muscles came in handy when we needed him to keep refilling the ice bin in the soda fountain. We were flying through Cherry Cokes.

I pat his shoulder. "It's all in the wrist."

"Can we go sit on the swings in your backyard and eat these?" He tosses his pop up in the air. It flips and lands softly back in his palms. The crinkle of the paper hitting squishy flesh is satisfying. "For old times' sake. Remember the Summer of Free Ice Cream?"

"Of course. How could I not? We almost got T-boned by the teenager driving the ice cream truck." It was a total life-flashes-before-your-eyes moment.

"She looked about sixteen and scared shitless to be behind the wheel of that monster."

"I was haunted by that jingle for months. *Do-do-duh-do-do-do-duh-do*." My singing is nails-on-a-chalkboard bad. The owner of the truck called me that night and offered us free ice cream for the rest of the summer if we promised not to report the incident. We had so, *so* much ice cream squirreled away in my freezer.

"It was really hot that summer, so it worked out. That was the same summer that…" Derick's voice trails off, but he doesn't have to finish for me to know what he's thinking about. That summer. *Our* summer.

"I know," I say quietly, and we both let the memories fall away.

One at a time, we hop the chain-link fence at the back of the lot, the most direct route to my backyard play set. The house is dark, the windows lifeless. Everyone is asleep, and I tell him we need to keep quiet. If my family knew I was out here, they'd insist I stay the night. Something I don't want to do.

Life is easier when you cut off childhood like an annoying tag on your favorite sweater. At the apartment, I'm an adult with a chosen family and a laundry list that includes *Do your own laundry, you procrastinator*. At home, I'm a kid with a biological family of four and a hamper that never stays filled thanks to Mom's love of her water-saving, top-loading washing machine.

I've got to hold tight to my independence.

The swings are creaky and the flags have all since blown away in various storms. When Claire and I grew out of it, my parents decided it wasn't worth the upkeep. We tried to sell it on Facebook Marketplace when I left for college, but the damage to the wood was too great and even lugging it off for free wasn't worth the time or energy needed to break it all down.

Maybe Derick and I, with our pending power-tool know-how, could make this our next improvement project. I can picture us in tool belts with hard hats, sanders, and hammers. Labor doesn't seem so languishing when I'm with him. Even tonight, I was surprised how effortless it felt in the snack shack. We were slammed with customers, but he kept me laughing, smiling, light on my feet. The time flew by.

Derick and I settle into those weathered blue and red swings. We face away from the house, looking back into the lot. The physical distance from our hectic pace of work is soothing. The wrapping on my ice cream skins off easily. I cloak four napkins around the wooden stick, covering the tips of my hands so melty goop won't get all over me. Derick doesn't comment this time. Kindness incarnate.

We eat in silence for a few minutes. The night is filled with a surging sense of chance and the discordant song of male cicadas, out on a hot night, making noise to find a mate. If only humans did that. I know we're attracted to voices and pheromones and a plethora of other biological phenomena completely out of our control, but, wouldn't it be nice if we heard a 90-decibel noise once and knew we were matched for life?

"It's gorgeous out," Derick says between licks. It may not be 90 decibels, but, damn, that voice could do it for me.

Fuck.

This sort of thing is not my forte, so I don't know what to do with this information other than lock it away in the attic of my heart. No sense drudging out old feelings just to play dress up in my hurt. We're friends now.

"Thanks for all your help tonight. Actually, your help, period. You've been there for me. I really appreciate it," I say.

"No worries." He pops a gumball into his mouth. He chews loudly and slowly, cow-like but still charming. "I hope Mateo's okay."

"Same." I sent two texts to him earlier, both read and unanswered.

"You don't have to keep thanking me, by the way. I like what we're doing. My family moved out to our Myrtle Beach house pretty permanently for the summer last week, and being stuck here doesn't sting so hard when we're together."

Together. What a dreamy word.

I start pumping my legs, setting the swing into motion, allowing myself to slice through the air. Derick joins me, keeping tempo.

I change the subject, so he doesn't have to doggy paddle in his pain. "If you could be anywhere in the world right now, where would you be? You know, if you weren't interning at Wiley's and money wasn't an obstacle..." I pause. "I mean, I know money isn't really an obstacle for your family, but you're not making much this summer."

"I'm making memories. That's currency, too." It's oddly profound. "Can you go first? I need a minute. I want to hear your answer."

"Walt Disney World."

"Really? Walt Disney World? You could go to Europe or Asia or Canada..."

"You can go to *all* of those places at the World's Showcase at Epcot." He opens and closes his mouth quickly, knowing his rebuttal won't weaken my argument. "Though, to be fair, Disney did me dirty when they closed the Great Movie Ride, so I'm not sure I'm willing to shell out that kind of money for a company that slighted me so."

"Slighted you so, huh? Sounds serious. But, uh, what's the Great Movie Ride?"

I let my legs go limp. My swing stills as I dig my heels into the wood chips. "Are you serious? Have you never been to Disney before? It's only the greatest ride ever invented. Hence the 'great' in its name."

"I went a few times when I was young, but unless it was a ride where I could raise my arms up at the big drop or shoot stuff with a laser gun, I wasn't really interested." That checks out. Judging by his car, his love of The Fast and the Furious, and his willingness to work with power tools he's never touched before, he's something of an adrenaline junkie.

"Come on." I stand and offer him my hand. He takes it, no questions asked. There's even a gentle squeeze that makes my heart skitter. "Be quiet and take off your shoes."

I lead him through the sliding glass door into the kitchen of my childhood home. We traipse through the hallway with our shoes in hand, our socked feet slipping only slightly on the hardwood floor. I open the door down to the basement slowly so the hinges don't screech the way they usually do and turn the lights on in the lounge. It's not fully finished or furnished, but one corner of the basement has carpeting, a love seat, and a TV.

Derick makes himself comfortable on the couch. I open the YouTube app on my TV and launch a search for the Great Movie Ride POV. It's weird, I know, but it's one of the many ways I de-stress. Watching videos others take while riding rides at theme parks I love or dream of exploring one day is like therapy to me. I mean, therapy is therapy to me, and I do that, too, with Dr. Hatcher. Mostly virtually. But, I'm never calmer than when I'm getting lost in the wonders of what an Imagineer can make.

"Are we about to watch someone else ride a ride?"

"Shhhh," I demand. "Just pretend like you're there."

The camera is shaky, but the quality is 4K, so I relax into it.

The ride debuted in 1989. It takes you into a replica of the Chinese Theatre where you board a roving car with an actor aboard, ready to guide you through the sights and sounds of great moments in cinema from Sigourney Weaver in *Alien*'s greatest jump scare to Gene Kelly singing in the rain. The *Casablanca* moment, showcasing the animatronic lovers in their last embrace, jolts my heart awake.

They'll always have Paris. Will Derick and I always have Wiley's?

I forgot how tight a squeeze this love seat was. It's been a while since someone's been down here with me. Derick and I are shoulder to shoulder. We both sink sideways into the walloping dip between the cushions. It's uncomfortable, yet comforting.

I tune back in right at my favorite part; Munchkinland lights up in vibrant glory. "Ding Dong! The Witch is Dead" rings out from the sound bar in front of my TV.

"Did you know that back in the day asking someone if they were a friend of Dorothy was a euphemism for being LGBTQ?" It's a tidbit Mateo loves to tout anytime someone brings up Judy Garland. And, let's face it, our college had a big performing-arts department, so people were always (*always*) bringing up Judy Garland.

Derick holds out a hand to me. "Nice to meet you, friend of Dorothy."

"Same to you, fellow friend of Dorothy." We shake hands once, twice, the gesture lingering for seconds longer than it should. Lightning zaps up from my palm, surges through my forearm, and strikes my heart.

I have to force myself to pull away, and even then, it's like he's left behind a phantom hand I never want to let go of.

When the video ends and the next in the playlist from this user begins to buffer, I go to switch the TV off. It's late. We should go.

But Derick asks, "Can we watch another?" He's enlivened somehow, no longer beat from being on his feet all night. "I'm enjoying these. It's still a little weird, but it's…soothing. I see why you like them."

I smile. "Sure." Anything to spend more time with him, to not let our little late-night bubble burst just yet.

I allow the Peter Pan video to load, and a cozy feeling to take up residence in my chest.

That's how we fall down a rabbit hole of ride POVs and how we end up falling asleep, nuzzled into each other, on the couch in my family's basement.

Chapter 13

Derick isn't anywhere to be found when I wake up.

Thank God. That's not a situation I wanted to explain to my parents. Claire would turn it into something it wasn't, doing that classic younger sibling act. I've barely been home since graduation. If they even so much as catch a glimpse of me, they're going to want to catch up. With so much going on, I don't have the energy to withstand that conversation.

This isn't some sordid romance movie, so Derick doesn't leave a note or a clue or a token of his affection. The only vestige is the shape of him slowly fading from the couch cushions. I trace the outline with my finger. It's still warm. He couldn't have been gone long, and it's sweet that he didn't wake me. Instead, he draped me in a blanket and left me to dream.

That's what last night felt like, a dream. A fabrication, faraway and nonsensical. That handshake, the videos, all of it. Except, the YouTube playlist is still looping on silent, so I know it happened. I shut the TV off. If I don't see it, I don't have to come to terms with the residual emotions.

When I find my phone, fallen under the couch, I notice a new email from Oscar waiting:

Dear Wren,

Fabulous news about August 14th! That means we should get a move on. Any chance you can make it into Manhattan for a two-day stay? Let's say around July 14th. That gives us plenty

of time to watch the movie, discuss, come up with questions,
and hop into the studio for a session. My editor will then be
able to finesse the episode. We can build some buzz leading up
to a release date and then supply a good lead-in to your event.
Let me know if this is good for you.

I hug my phone to my chest, not knowing what else to do with these
cheerful feelings.

Without too much thought, I shoot off a text to Derick, wherever he
may be right now:

Any chance you're down for a trip to NYC soon?

There's no one else I could take with me. No one that would understand
the heft of it anyway. Derick's as entrenched in this Alice project as I am.
Even if he's not as entrenched in his ooey-gooey romantic feelings as I am.

If Derick agrees to the trip, maybe I'll listen to "You've Got a Friend in
Me" by Randy Newman while staring at Derick's yearbook photo as psycho-
logical conditioning before we go. Anything to make the heart palpitations
stop and ensure a successful excursion.

Upstairs, I hear a notification ding from down the hall. I pause before
heading toward our second story. It's probably just Claire on her phone in
the family room. Derick has to be on his way home by now, right?

If I'm quiet, maybe I can disappear into my bedroom without being
spotted. There's nothing worse than a walk of shame when you've done
nothing to be shamed for.

Then, I hear the honeyed, husky notes of Derick's voice float out from
the kitchen.

Oh no.

Four steps and I'm staring at Mom and Derick laughing over a fired-up
griddle, a bowl of batter at Mom's right elbow.

"Good morning?" I call to them.

They turn. Neither looks surprised.

"Just in time," Mom says. She's still in her sleep shorts with an apron over top, brown hair pulled back in a ponytail. When Derick turns fully, he's wearing a checkered, full apron as well. Underneath, he sports one of my old film-club T-shirts. "Set the table and text Dad and Claire to come down. We made blueberry pancakes."

Mom is notorious for delineating duties and playing the generous host. She never lets a guest go unfed, even if they aren't hungry. Though, in fairness, she usually does the cooking herself. When she excuses herself to the garage, on a hunt for more paper towels, I sweep over to the cupboard and pull down a heap of plates.

"If she's holding you hostage, blink twice," I say to Derick. His face morphs into a question mark, but his eyes never close.

"I offered." He adds another blue-speckled disk to the growing stack. They smell delicious and look cooking-show flawless, fluffy and brown. I begin placing the plates down around the ovular kitchen table. For the extra setting, I grab a folding chair from the dining room.

I stop to inspect his work again. "How do you get them so perfect?"

"When I was little, I used to play sous-chef to my mom. I had the tall white hat and everything. She'd make Sunday brunch for my family, so I picked up a few things here and there. The trick is to beat the egg white separately. Then it's all in the air bubbles." He ladles fresh batter onto the sizzling surface. "Notice the air bubbles? Once you see those, that's when you flip."

I don't hint at how adorable it is to see him doing a domestic task like this, and I try not to mourn a future I might've had if only the almost-kiss had gone my way. "I thought you had left."

"I was about to when your mom and I bumped into each other. She seemed confused, but happy to see me. I didn't want to be rude." He kills the stove and takes the stack of flapjacks to the table. "She seemed weirded out by my Wiley's shirt and offered me one of yours. I hope you don't mind."

How could I mind when he looks this good? There's an unspoken intimacy to sharing clothing. My tee doesn't fit him any better than the Wiley's one did. The shoulder seams are begging to bust open. Just like my heart into a cloud of confetti.

"I hope I'm not overstepping by staying for breakfast. If you want, I can go."

"No, stay. Eat. Enjoy your bounty." My awkwardness knows no bounds.

He makes a funny face. "Did you know you talk in your sleep?"

"What?" Embarrassment bubbles in my stomach like that pancake batter. "What did I say? Sorry if it was weird. I can't even remember what I was dreaming about." I hope it's not the one where I'm starring in the famous *Psycho* shower scene, but instead of the killer butchering me like Janet Leigh, I see his knife shadow before the curtain opens, scare myself, slip on a dropped bar of soap, and crack my own head open. It's one of those shoot-up-in-bed, gasping-for-air dreams I get every now and then when I'm stressed.

What a mortifying way to go. At least there's some dignity in being slaughtered.

"You don't need to be sorry." He laughs. "It was mostly gibberish. Like you'd made up your own language. I caught a few phrases before I came upstairs, though."

"Such as?" How quickly can I haul it over the Canadian border and subsume a new identity? My mortification magnifies when he unlocks his phone. "Please tell me you didn't write this down."

"Oh, no. I did you one better." He turns the speaker toward me. "I recorded it. I thought you might be interested."

The recording is scratchy, and the TV is still playing in the background. The twinkling notes of "It's a Small World," a song that could use seven less refrains, only makes matters worse.

My voice is gurgly: "Should we? No. Harumph. Hardly. Maybe. Flabberdoo. Check...check one, two. Let me see script. Again, again!" My dream comes back to me. I usually don't remember them, but I can tell this is another reoccurring one. I'm on the set of a movie and the lead actor needs me to stand in and show him how to do the big kiss scene, except I keep forgetting the lines. Probably on purpose. "Clapper. Quiet. Set. Please. Harumph."

"You made that sound a lot." I can tell he's enjoying this.

"Okay. Again...harumph. Rolling. On action..." It's an instruction to the costar. Every time it's someone different. Sometimes, it's Humphrey Bogart. Sometimes, it's Harry Styles. Freshman year, it was often Mateo. "Lean in, *Derick*."

His name is followed by the sickening sound of air smooches—slick, wet, and all around wrong. I press Stop. The force of my finger nearly causes his phone to go flying into the breakfast spread. My body is alight like a losing move in a game of Operation.

"It was a different Derick," I blurt out.

"I thought you said you didn't remember your dreams." He's grinning down at me.

"No, yeah, but it was probably a Derick with an *ek* instead of an *ick*. Like Derek Jeter or Derek Hough."

"Didn't know you were a fan of baseball or ballroom or…both?"

Claire appears at the island in her pink Victoria's Secret pajama set. Her brown frizzy hair, almost matching mine, is down. "Weren't you the one who told Dad baseball was far too slow and boring for your tastes? It's why you never come to my softball games."

Her timing is impeccable when it comes to blowing my cover.

"I changed my mind."

Dad barrels in from upstairs. "What have you changed your mind about?" His eyes land on Derick, confused but not unhappy. "Derick, good to see you. It's been a while since you've been around these parts. How's your dad and the rest of the family?" He notices that Derick is wearing one of my T-shirts but doesn't say anything, which I'm going to call a gigantic win for me. Hearing his birds-and-the-bees spiel—which he repurposed into a colorful bids-and-the-birds soliloquy over spring break—again would be the last thing I need.

"They're good. Thanks for asking, Mr. Roland."

"Please, call me Frank," Dad says. "And how's that big bus-line expansion going? I saw they're taking over part of the public library lot for more commuter pickups." Dad's township utilities job keeps him in the know around Willow Valley.

"Uh, fine. I think." Derick looks uncomfortable and quickly changes the subject. "Wren was just telling us how he changed his mind about baseball. He's apparently quite the Derek Jeter fan now."

"A Yankees Hall of Famer?" Dad crows. "You know this is a Phillies-only household. Are you sure you're my son?"

Mom finally returns with four rolls of paper towels. What did she have to do, go on a scavenger hunt for them? "Is Wren coming around to the idea of a family baseball outing? You know your dad and I used to go on dates to Phillies games all the time. That's how we became close. When I moved back here after college, we had a group of friends who chipped in for season tickets. We'd get the nosebleed seats and gorge ourselves on hot dogs and beers."

"Who says romance is dead?" Claire jokes.

"Baseball games can be very romantic," Dad says, serving himself some pancakes with a healthy dose of maple syrup. "Your mom and I ended up on the kiss cam more than once! We always got the loudest cheers."

Nothing like picturing your parents making out in front thousands upon thousands of people. My appetite has packed up its bags and vacated my body.

"Your father proposed to me at a Phillies game!" Mom opens her Instagram account. Even she's social-media literate and loving it. For their last anniversary, she posted a photo of Dad on one knee in the aisle of Citizens Bank Park, the field fanning out behind him. The players look like action figures from the distance. Mom has two hands clasped over her mouth. Her eyes are wide with surprise and happiness.

"I did it during the seventh-inning stretch! The whole crowd was singing 'Take Me Out to the Ball Game.'" It might not be my idea of cinematic grandiosity, but it is endearing.

Mom starts singing the famous American pastime jingle and soon we're all joining in. During the sing-along silliness, Derick and I lock eyes. His gaze is loaded.

When he smiles that I've-got-a-secret-and-it's-only-for-you smile, I can't help but think *Derek Jeter, who?*

Chapter 14

Derick is wearing the purple tank top again, washed of course, and I can't quite keep my eyes off his lats as he wields a screwdriver, fixing an unsecure cabinet door.

We finished painting Alice's living room last week, so she corralled us into the kitchen.

We brought bagels this time, which Alice was thrilled by, though she moaned that New York bagels were "soooooo much better." On a list of Alice's favorite activities, complaining would take the top spot.

I've been put on floor duty—sweeping, mopping, and scrubbing. I'm still on phase one since Derick keeps tracking in dirt on the bottoms of his multicolored, pricey sneakers. Alice is sorting old dishes and china pieces into three piles: keep, donate, and trash. Whenever her eyes wander away, she's sure to point out a spot I missed in the recesses of a corner, though I know she can't see that well so she's just messing with me for the hell of it.

I move to the back door with the heavy gallon bucket. Heaving from the knees, I dump the excess water-vinegar-dish soap mixture out into the yard. I instruct everyone to strip off their shoes while the floor dries. Derick hops up onto the counter to do so. Mercifully, it doesn't snap from his weight.

Even though she's not watching it, *The Mary Tyler Moore Show* still loops in the other room.

Finally, I ask, "Do you ever watch anything else?"

She frowns, deep folds dragging down her face. "What? Do you have problem with seventies sitcoms? Too cool for comedy?" She places a chipped cup, one of the ones from the first day I was here, in the trash pile. I grab the battered tennis ball Alice set out for me and begin going at the black scuff marks. Doubtful at first, I've come around to seeing how effective everyday objects can be for cleaning. Here's one way Alice uses her creativity now: inventive solutions to everyday problems.

"No, it just seems like it's the only thing that's on when we're here. Don't you watch any movies?"

"I don't watch movies anymore."

I stop what I'm doing and gape at her. My heart almost stops. "Wait, seriously?"

"That's wild," Derick chimes in after a grunt that snaps the cabinet door right into place, no squeaks, no wobbles. Two instructional videos and he's an HGTV pro.

"Movies are unpredictable. You never know what you're going to get. I can't handle that in my life anymore. I need simple sitcom prediction— comfort, laughs, Rhoda walking into Mary's apartment without knocking. Mary mothering the newsroom."

Ditching the tennis ball back where I found it, I collect the plastic brush and rubbing alcohol. It took forever getting the funnel into the spray bottle and pouring in the foul-smelling liquid. At least that part's done, though I fear the burning scent has singed my nostrils for eternity.

"I read, too. Well, I read with my ears. Audiobooks that Candice, my home aide, downloads for me when she comes. My eyes aren't what they used to be, and even the large-print editions are difficult, but sometimes doable. Even after the surgeries for the cataracts. I didn't catch the macular degeneration soon enough. Too stubborn to see the right doctor." She snaps her head in our direction. "Don't go saying anything about my stubbornness, you hear me? I know I'm stubborn. I'm difficult. I heard it my whole life. I heard it on every set before I was running my own and even sometimes after. She's a *monster*. She's a *lunatic*. She's a *bitch*." She licks her thin lips. "Heard that last one from my ex-husband, too."

I did a lot of research at Rosevale on female directors in the 1970s, pioneers in a push for gender equality in a bro-y field. The pay gap is still gross, and opportunities for female directors (not even considering trans female directors or nonbinary directors) are still slim. At the time, many men wrote off female directors as too emotional or too "bitchy" to oversee an entire production. Plus, they thought there were too many other men in line already, waiting their turn for opportunities so they couldn't let women "cut."

"I'm sorry you had to deal with that." I know it doesn't wipe away her bad memories or her bad eyesight, yet it feels like the right thing to say. Not that I speak on behalf of the universe, or anything. I just want her to know that I'm on her team.

"It was what it was. Men cower at women like me. Peter's movies wouldn't have been half of what they were without me, even though he never gave me the credit I deserved. He drank himself into oblivion in his trailer during half of them, while I oversaw everything," she says. "'Bitch' is only a word. Young people seem very comfortable with it now. It can't hurt you, but I will say, it hurt me back then. I was juvenile. Now? *Psh*. Now, call me whatever you want, just don't let me hear it or I'll show you what this bitch can do."

With a playful smile, she smashes the first of the "trash" dishes on the floor. Shards of pewter ceramic spill across the linoleum.

"Hey, I just—"

"Don't be a stinker!" Alice shouts, smashing another and then passing one to Derick. Relishing this too much, Derick smashes three cracked plates in quick succession, the floor becoming a mosaic of destroyed dinnerware.

Not wanting to be left out, I take the smallest cup and hurtle it at the floor. It doesn't even break. It just skitters away and lands by Derick's socked feet.

We really didn't think this through. We're three people nearly barefoot, trapped in place by pointy shards ready to slice us open.

"Damn, Ms. K," Derick says, "you're cool as hell." He tosses me the cup again. "Give it another go."

I sigh, swing back with force, and smash it to smithereens. It feels good. Almost great.

"That's it!" Alice says. "Now, someone throw me my shoes and you boys clean this up." She pauses and then adds, "Oh and you'll need to sweep and mop again. Oops." She snickers slightly before disappearing.

At least our clutter is contained to one corner of the kitchen, the one we didn't need to wade through to get to our shoes. I slip my feet into them and waddle back to my seat, the lace tips tapping on the linoleum the whole way. My hands are coated in dust and vinegar, and I can't make it to the sink to wash them without crunching through the wreckage. Apparently reading my thoughts, Derick pops my right foot onto his lap. At the table, in an oddly sweet gesture, he starts tying the laces for me. I'm happy to note he uses the bunny ears method, not the popular around-the-loop bow. It's a peculiar quirk of his, maximum cuteness.

It makes me want to ask about the Instagram post where he called me handsome. To clear the air about the basement cuddle. But what good would that do? I don't want him to think I'm reading into anything. If this is our new normal, I kind of like it. I don't want things to change.

He grabs his backpack before letting me go. With a playful grin, he gifts me a bag of cherry Pull'n'Peel Twizzlers and a bottle of hand sanitizer from its main pouch. "Screwing all day works up an appetite."

I swallow a laugh as I clean off my hands and then accept a Twizzler, thanking him before biting into the sweet, stringy candy.

"Whoa, whoa, whoa," he clamors, looking horrified. "Did you just eat a Pull'n'Peel Twizzler without pulling *or* peeling?"

"So what? You get more bang for your bite this way. More flavor."

"You're a monster. You wouldn't eat string cheese without stringing it! You wouldn't eat a Kit Kat without breaking off a piece! The instructions are right there in the jingle!"

"Kit Kats are too messy. Chocolate gets melty." I'm wiggling my digits to emphasize my adverse feelings.

"Weirdo." He leans back in that infuriatingly unflappable way, spreading his legs apart and letting his arms go limp. "By the way, I'm in for the Manhattan trip you texted me about. I'll use my dad's account to get us bus tickets and my mom's rewards points at one of the Midtown chain hotels. I can book us their usual room. As long as Alice gives us the all clear."

"Really? Are you sure? I don't want to put anybody out." Not that I have the money to finance this trip, and Oscar didn't make any mention of reimbursement.

"Way more than sure." He gives me a soft bro-punch to the bicep, completely negating the shoe-tying and candy-gifting. "I finished the cabinets. Let me help you with the floor."

He grabs the mop, while I grab the broom. Halfway through, Alice returns with the box from my first day here. Setting it down, she looks at us both long and hard. When I cross to her, she nods twice and then leaves the room.

An olive branch for the mess she made.

Derick smiles as he wrings out the mop. I know he's curious, too, but he's willing to let me have a moment to geek out over whatever golden goodies she's stashed in here. I open the box and devour each notebook, paper clipping, review, and photo. It's a shadow box that belongs in an exhibition.

At the bottom, I get the confirmation I was looking for. One, weathered, seafoam notebook is made up entirely of unsendable letters written to Tammy, dated after her death. In a convoluted way, this exercise is kind of like my almost-kiss emails. Toward the end, missives from 1978 taper off into blank white pages, but before they do, she's written:

I loved you from the day I met you. I only wish you were here to see this.

To the side, she added:

Glad you weren't here to witness that after all.

A pit opens inside me. It's not until Derick rushes to my side that I realize I'm crying. I show him the notebook, though I know he doesn't have all the info. He gets it, anyway. Somehow, his nearness makes the hot and salty tears flow freer. I'm a blubbering mess by the time Alice gets back; her eyes are dewy as well.

She takes one prolonged look at me and says, "I may be a bitch, but life's a bigger one, ain't it?"

We all laugh, which cushions the pain, but only so much. It's clear Alice, like Derick, has found humor a helpful coping mechanism against life's injustices. The words, cross-outs, and ink smudges in this book prove that Alice has been living in pain for so long, but I think our presence here has been helping lift that. At least a little bit. Not that she'd ever admit it.

"I'm giving you the all clear," she says suddenly, echoing Derick's words from earlier.

"Pardon?" Are those floor-cleaner fumes finally causing me to hallucinate? I need to be sure I've heard her correctly.

"Don't make me repeat myself." She twiddles her clubbed thumbs, unable to look at us. "Go talk to your podperson. Show my movie. You've more than proven yourselves worthy."

A second round of tears comes on as I register this. "Th-thank you, Alice."

"Don't thank me yet," she says, grabbing her keepsakes back as speedily as she offered them. "Onward!" When we don't move right away, still shocked by her generous about-face, she barks with her usual cranky cadence, "Back to work!"

And, like a couple of fake dogs, we obey.

Twitter

@WileysDriveInWV Break out the sparklers! Let the Fourth of July celebrations commence. When you're done grilling and swimming, don't forget to head over to Wiley's Drive-In for prime Willow Valley Fireworks Spectacular viewing spots. Reduced rates for groups over four. Bring your lawn chairs and your children! You won't want to miss this epic display of patriotism! 🎆 🇺🇸

5 replies. 10 Retweets. 45 Likes.

@StayAtHomeSteph25 Is this a per car or per person event?
@WileysDriveInWV $5 per person! But discounts given to any carload over four. It's our carpool discount! Want as many people as possible in our lot tonight to celebrate! Please tell your friends.
@RolandOnTheRiver14 I'll be there! 😊
@WileysDriveInWV Can't wait to see you! 👍 We'll save you a good spot! 😊
@420BlazinBoii Y'all flirting on here still?! Shameless. 😒 You think if I slide into the Burger Joint's mentions with this cute shit they might hook me up with free fries?!

Chapter 15

Mom is a Pinterest fanatic. Sometimes, she stumbles upon spectacular ideas—see the mason jar of "Keys to Success" she made for my high-school graduation party where guests wrote words of wisdom on tags attached to ornamental, antique keys. Sometimes, she strikes out. Like, right now, with this American flag made from hamburger buns.

She's dyed the rolls red and blue. They look even more unappetizing than I anticipated. The food coloring is off and the flag looks sickly. Like a good son, I do my part and discard the atrocious ones before anyone notices so I can finish the staging and move on.

Mom is in the dining room strategically organizing her Bella's Bottles into a covert display. While her crafty side hustle is mostly an online enterprise, she does bust out the back stock whenever she gets the chance to attend a craft show or roving market. Our annual Fourth of July backyard bash, at least for the last seven years, has moonlighted as a sneaky marketing strategy.

"Do these look conspicuous enough?" Mom asks, pushing her summer selections to the front of the bunch in the china cabinet. Not sure why we even have a china cabinet when we've never had any priceless, fancy china to display in it. Now, it's full of her crafts. "I want people to notice, but not notice too much, you know?"

I do know. "Seven is too many for one spot. Put the sunset beach one on the stand in the bathroom, plugged in. It goes well with the seashell decor. Spread four out in the cabinet, and then add the lemon grove to the kitchen—it'll complement the backsplash—and the summer sports one in the den so the men can see it."

"That's my smart, little manager. Always thinking ahead." She bumps my hip as she passes by me to get to the den, her hands full of her highly breakable creations. "Be sure that Avery and Mateo know that the seltzers and beers go in one cooler with the laminated Adults Only sign taped on it. We don't need a repeat of last year when the Wongs' little girl ended up shaking all those sparkling ciders and cracking them open in a twenty-one can salute."

Avery and Mateo know the drill by now. Mom is a planner by nature (likely where I get it from) with full-blown checklists that need to be precisely followed. Their help is integral to the success of our party. Together they fill the cooler with ice and various canned beverages out on the back patio.

"Is Derick on his way?" Mom asks. She insisted I invite him after his exceptional breakfast skills went over so well only a few weeks ago. All I do is nod to avoid any further probing questions. She was more than a tad inquisitive when he left that morning, even after I did the "We're just friends" song and dance for her.

Claire is keeping company with Alice in the living room. She's probably telling her all about the all-girls school she'll be attending next year for chemical engineering—a field no one in my family can comprehend where she got the smarts for.

I ferried Alice over this morning, trying my best to ignore her back-seat driving. "You know you can make a right on red here. No need to make a full stop. Keep it rolling, jittery Jack."

"We're not in a hurry," I reminded her.

"I could drop dead at any second. I want a cheeseburger before I do."

Having seen a sneak peek of the buns, I told her she might want to stick to the hot dogs instead.

I put on a short-sleeved blue button-down and my nicest pair of shorts, cuffed at the hem. I even dug out an old pair of boat shoes I never wear because they're impractical for navigating the Wiley's lot. Cologne, from a bottle I've never opened, got spritzed on my "seduction points" as per Mateo's vehement instructions.

Dad's finding the best adult-rock radio station to set the mood, which will surely play "Born in the USA" an exorbitant number of times. When he's satisfied, he throws on the *Netflix and Grill* apron Mom bought him two Christmases ago and holds his spatula at the ready. I'd make a snarky comment except *Drive-In and Grill* doesn't exactly make sense, due to insurance liability issues, nor does it have a nice ring to it.

All the cul-de-sac neighbors descend upon our backyard in droves. Being one of the corner properties and with Wiley's right there, we have the most space for mingling and Wiffle ball games. When I was a kid, even though social situations largely frightened me, this one didn't faze me. I knew everyone coming. I knew I wouldn't be left on the sideline for any team games and that I wouldn't be left standing alone by the spinach dip.

I always say I was born in the wrong decade. In-person socialization is hard enough for me. Adding an online component makes it downright unmanageable sometimes. But, it seems Derick is showing me how social media can be used for purposes greater than status updates and mindless scrolling.

I join my friends by the swings. A group of kids have begun a game of freeze tag nearby. I'm almost tempted to join them and unleash the child inside me I've been missing since going to college. This is the final summer under the guise of comfort, until I'm thrust into adult life—bills, budgeting, and finally learning how tax software works.

Leaving Wiley's seems impossible. Not seeing Mateo and Avery every day is depressing.

Across the way, the gated fence glides open. Derick steps into the yard, and the future worries fade to black. He looks like a less built but more stunning Captain America, dressed in an American flag–patterned Henley, a pair of shorts, and trainers.

Heads turn in his direction, making it clear to everyone he's not a usual guest at this event.

Since his eyes are focused on mine, he nearly stumbles over a stray Wiffle ball bat. With ease, he kicks it up from the grass and catches it. "Oh, man. Are we playing or what?" he asks, looking around for the bases that are hidden in the grass.

"Looking to get your ass handed to you?" Claire challenges. She loves to talk shit. They built a good rapport over pancakes the other morning, talking RBIs and Damien Haverford's MLB aspirations. Derick kept asking for my input, any opportunity to playfully throw my lousy excuse for sleep-talking back in my face. My baseball knowledge, unsurprisingly, does not extend beyond *A League of Their Own*.

"You're on." Derick gives us a snarl. He begins setting up the diamond. Life of the party, already taking the lead. I like it.

"I'll sit this one out," Mateo says.

"Oh, no you won't," Avery replies.

"Ugh! I don't do baseball."

"It's Wiffle ball," I offer. "It's different."

"It still involves running." He glares at us. "The only running I do is running lines!"

Derick insists that I can be captain, keeping with the banter we've partaken in since the start of this absurd situation. At least in this scenario it truly makes sense. Mateo and Avery lead the opposing side, opting to be cocaptains since neither wants to let their ego take a vacation today.

"I'm not very good at this. I don't even know all the rules," I say to Derick softly, so he knows in advance that my poor hand-eye coordination, exacerbated by my glasses, is not going to be an asset to our team.

He looks at me sideways, one brow playfully cocked. "Come on, Jeter fan. This is the perfect chance to show me your stuff. Make me believe all those major-leaguer dreams you've been having."

"That's, well, I just… You know, we can't—"

Unbelievably satisfied, he jogs into the outfield without another word.

Around the fourth inning, Derick and I are waiting for our turns to bat. We're down by two with no saving grace in sight. Surprising to no one, I'm bad at both pitching and catching. The only MVP on our team is Claire who's scored all our measly three points. Athletic prowess will never be my superpower. Even though that one is feasible for human beings. Just not this human being, apparently.

"I'm super stoked for our trip," Derick says as we shuffle about on the sidelines.

We are officially booked to leave for Manhattan on July 13. Derick sent me a full itinerary.

I've been to Manhattan a few times before. My parents aren't the city type, though. They don't like the traffic or the crowds. We didn't do a lot of tourist-trap activities growing up. We spent weekends at sunflower patches and Claire's rec softball games, where I handed out CapriSuns and clementines to grabby girls in New Balance cleats.

I'm excited to see what's in store for us, maybe do some sightseeing, but also nervous about spending so much alone time with Derick. Are we at that friendship level yet? What does that mean if we are? Questions constrict my heart until I feel faint from the lack of circulation.

"Alice and I made a list of approved questions and topics for the podcast." I glance over at her on the porch, talking with my parents while eating a cheeseburger. Of course, she ignored my recommendation.

"I can tell she likes you."

She sometimes had a funny way of showing it, but I could tell that, too.

"You're up," Claire says to me, placing the plastic orange bat in my hands.

"Go get 'em, Captain," Derick says. "Remember, plant your feet, square your hips, follow through. You got this." Derick's faith in me is adorable, if entirely misplaced.

I step up to bat. Avery's eyeing me from the pitcher's mound. She spits like a serious sports pro from the fifties who would have a wad of chewing tobacco lodged in her bottom lip. I love her commitment.

Strike one whizzes by, while strike two is a clear miss from me.

No strike three comes because the third ball sails and hits me right in the upper arm. Avery looks entirely unapologetic as she yells, "Walk!" and I scuttle to first base on a technicality. Could've been worse.

Right around dusk, Derick peels off and hops the fence. He needs to report to Earl before the gates open for the fireworks guests.

We got creamed in Wiffle ball. Despite Claire's impressive batting average, we lost 10 to 6. Mateo is a lot speedier than he looks, and who knew you could throw a curve ball with a holey orb of plastic. Avery's wheelhouse of tricks defies logic.

"How does it feel to be the *Wicked* to our *Avenue Q* at the 2004 Tonys, babe?" Mateo asks, gloating about their shocking win. I laugh and finish my pasta salad in peace.

An hour later, in the middle of a rousing discussion about which patriotic anthem is the queerest (top contenders: "Kids in America" by Kim Wilde or Whitney Houston's rendition of the National Anthem), I get a text from Derick:

Jump the fence and come meet me. Earl says it's okay if we all come up here.

I type back:

What do you mean "come up here"?

His reply:

You'll see

As we trek over the fence one by one, Avery gets her dress caught in one of the wires, crying out for help like she's being attacked by rabid animals, so we all pitch in to save the fabric of her vintage thrift-store find. And here I thought Mateo was the drama queen in our friend group.

The day is fading into night, and the lot is almost filled. Earl appears happy, standing in the shade of the screen, thumbs hooked in his belt loops. I expect Derick to be at his side. I scour the lot but don't see him.

Avery wants to pop into the snack shack to grab the Rosevale sweatshirt she left here last weekend. That's when I hear Derick whisper, "*Psst. Up here!*"

When I tilt my gaze upward, Derick's head is peering over the edge of the roof.

"What are you doing up there?"

"Earl says if we're careful, we can watch from up here! There's a ladder propped up over by the bathrooms." I'm not a huge fan of heights. Even still, I'm up for this—watching fireworks on the roof of my favorite place in the world. Brandon holds the base of the ladder chivalrously while the rest of us navigate the rungs until we're all on the very dirty landing.

Derick's set up on the edge. He points his camera lens skyward, capturing the swirling sunset over Willow Valley, almost as beautiful as the impending display. The clouds have parted and the night looks clear. The view should be unblemished from this spot.

I settle down next to Derick, sitting crisscross so my legs don't hang, fear percolating only slightly. He smiles at me beneath a draping of golden locks that spill across his eyes. He got sweaty during our Wiffle ball game, and his usual poof has deflated into a delightful, damp mess. He smells like two fresh swipes of Mountain Spring deodorant.

"Come close," he says, holding up his phone for a selfie. He's activated the interactive filter he made for the evening. There's a superimposed exploding firework effect, a bit of facial softening, and the Wiley's logo roving beneath our chins. "Smile," he chirps before taking the shot.

"How'd you do that? It's so cool."

"I do it on Spark AR Studio." Tech dork is a different role for him. It suits him nonetheless. "Anyway, it's all about making a fun branded, interactive element that the consumer can keep. Once they try the filter once, it saves into their preloaded options when making a new story. It's the hope that after Fourth of July, they'll see the Wiley's logo and remember to come back and visit us again."

Us. My ribs crack open and rainbow light spills out when I hear that he considers himself a part of the Wiley's family. Sure, I was hesitant at first, but he really does mesh well with our mishmash of recruits. Unlike Mateo who, on the pyramid of stellar employees, has solidified himself as a staple in the bottom row. But today is not the day to dwell on that.

"Do you mind if I post this?" Derick asks, tilting the screen toward me to show me the shot. It's a winner, for sure. We're both happy, smiling from ear to ear. When I look back up at him, he's wearing the same expression, but the tips of his ears have turned Dubble Bubble pink.

"On the Wiley's account?" I ask, secretly hoping that's not what he meant.

"No, I was thinking on my personal one. If that's okay."

Judging by the sounds my heart is making, you'd think the fireworks had started early. "Sure, yeah, that's okay." Which is a blatant lie because it's more than okay. It's wonderful that he wants to share with the world (okay, his couple hundred followers) that we're friends again. That I *mean something* to him.

As darkness descends on the lot, the chatter stops and the anticipation rises. The cranking tunes turn off.

"This is my favorite part of summer," I say, ignoring the vibration of a you've-been-tagged-in-a-photo notification from my phone in my pocket.

"This is my favorite part of summer, too," Derick echoes.

And just like that, the first explosion crests across the sky evoking oohs and ahhs from the crowd below. Awe blankets the lot as colors careen over the tree line. My chest swells with each crash, bang, and boom.

Derick slides in closer to me, our bare thighs touching. The heat of his body radiates and the heat of the moment elevates. I'm lost in a haze of holiday excitement and hormonal overdrive. Fitful inside me, my heart becomes an entire drum line, playing a song I don't recognize.

Twenty minutes later, internal percussion section still going strong, the show is set to come to its satisfying close. Derick turns to me gradually, catching me off guard. But when our eyes meet, it's senior year in the bed of Dad's pickup truck all over again.

Is this it?

He begins to lean in, eyes dropping to my parted lips.

It occurs to me that by attempting to ignore the kiss quest, I may have made my will to complete it stronger. I've been dauntless. I've been daring. I've been defying the odds of friendship.

But, wait. That's right. I thought he just wanted to be friends. I thought he didn't *think of me like that*. So many mixed signals and no time to decode any of them.

I don't care, I decide. I'll *think of us* like that enough for the both of us. I tip forward in encouragement, ready for my very first kiss as blooms of color explode above us.

Just as I'm about to let those perfect lips collide with mine, I...

I...

I whip my head away.

Instinct forces the kiss to come to a record-scratching halt.

I'm back in the Cat's Pajamas, sweating under a wilting look from Goldie Prawn. The boos in my memory mix with the rapturous applause from the spectators beneath us. The fireworks have ended and so has our moment.

"Oh," he says. "Oh, um, sorry."

"No," I croak without looking at him. But that's all I get out before I'm on my feet and crossing the roof. I descend the ladder without thinking about its stability. With the grass under my shoes again, tickling my ankles, I break out into a run, swerving around families and cars. My run becomes a sprint ending in a leap back over the shoddy fence. I nearly lose a boat shoe in the process.

It's stupid, but some part of me thinks I can outpace my feelings.

I learn how untrue that is when I face-plant onto my childhood bed and come completely undone, crying into my pillow, wondering over and over: *What's wrong with me? What's wrong with me? What's wrong with me?*

Chapter 16

Thump. Thump. Tha-thump.

Hiking uphill three days after thwarting your perfect first kiss is excruciating. Even more excruciating when you haven't left your bed in those three days except to go to work and hide from the guy you almost kissed at every turn. Who knew avoiding people took so much energy? Every close encounter killed my glucose levels.

The incline up the side of the hill at the Willow Valley Nature Preserve is steeper than I remember. I haven't walked it since I was in high school. Either I was in better shape then or the ground has moved. I'm choosing to believe my shortness of breath is a product of sediment shifting. The moment I think that, I nearly trip over a treacherous tree root.

I swear the universe is out to get me.

There's a lookout at the top of the trail with a buffalo sanctuary and a spot to sit. We're still twenty minutes out. I glug from my water bottle and trudge on. My hiking boots are heavy and slow me down. I'm seven steps behind Mateo and Brandon and four behind Avery. She keeps stopping to retie her shoe laces. It's annoying how the act makes me think of Derick tying mine in Alice's kitchen, how cared for and connected to him I was.

"The great outdoors!" Mateo cries. "I am one with nature!"

This was Brandon's idea of a fun outing, so Mateo is pretending to be all Bear Grylls to impress him. "Hold on, Mateo, I think you just stepped in deer poop," Brandon says.

"Ew, fuck nature!" Mateo looks down horrified. He begins scraping the bottom of his baby-blue Adidas on a nearby tree trunk.

I slip my water bottle back into the side pocket of my backpack as we continue our uphill trek. A myriad of monarch butterflies have come out today, dancing on the breeze and playing hide-and-go-seek in the milkweed. I wish I could float through life like that.

Avery tries a new walking pattern that she thinks won't loosen her laces, but really just makes her look like a gazelle with a bum ankle. She catches up to Brandon as I fall in beside Mateo.

"This must be what it's like to be on *I'm a Celebrity, Get Me Out of Here!*" he whispers. A real whisper. Not the usual stage whisper he uses when he doesn't actually care. I love that Mateo projects himself into the person he wants to be. He sees fame and fortune (and perhaps dubious reality-show appearances) in his future, and I've always admired that ability to manifest confidence in the present.

"At least nobody's going to be able to make a meme out of your deer-poop moment."

"There's no such thing as bad press, babe."

I try to smile, but it comes off a little wobbly. I've missed this. Not only have I been avoiding Derick for days, but I've also been tiptoeing around Mateo. As my best friend, I want his comfort, but as a receiver of one of my emails, I want to pretend he doesn't exist after my big scene on the rooftop.

That's stupid, I remind myself. Mateo will always be my friend before anything else. I can talk to him about anything, *ask* him anything. Which is why I finally let myself take a deep breath and say the words that had been on the tip of my tongue for a long time now. "Why didn't you ask more about your email?"

Mateo glances over at me, unsurprised. It's like he knew I'd been stewing over that. "I'm a drama king, babe, but I'm not a narcissist." He flips his imaginary long hair in faux offense. "Besides, I know those feelings are in the past, and even if they existed in the present, I'd destroy you."

"Destroy me?"

"Emotionally speaking," he says. "Also, there were some"—he clears his throat for dramatic effect—"narrative inconsistencies wedged in there."

"Care to enlighten me?"

He stops and squares our shoulders into one another, so I can't dodge his eyes. "You pulled away from that kiss, Wren, in that basement of the Pride House. Nobody spilled their drink on you. Nobody cursed you out. You pulled away so hard and so fast, you spilled your own drink on yourself. I felt terrible for weeks that I'd misread the moment, but you seemed unfazed by it, so I just let it go. Little did I know you were harboring some fanfic version of the events in your mind and your email."

Part of me knew this all along, but wasn't ready to confront it.

The first thought that came to me on July 5th was: *You rewrote the stories.* I thought those emails were a way to preserve the memories of what almost was, but instead I was retooling them to shirk the blame. Onto the other person. Onto the situation. Onto fate and the universe and the higher powers that be. I thought the Great Screenwriter in the Sky was getting a good laugh out of messing up every perfect moment, but instead, I was reacting in earnest to a gut instinct I haven't yet sorted out.

The situation with Goldie should've showed me that.

"You did it again with Derick, didn't you?"

Brandon peers back at us. We're the only four on the trail, given that it's ungodly early and a weekday, so he can hear everything Mateo is saying.

It's weird thinking about it now. Every box on my kiss-before-the-credits checklist was marked. On paper, the Fourth of July had the winning cinematic formula, and yet the rolling camera captured a considerable misfire. I hope all that metaphorical footage gets left on the cutting room floor to be swept away and forgotten about.

I nod with the full weight of realization.

Some invisible security system I didn't know I had was tripped when Derick leaned in to kiss me. I haven't admitted this, even to myself, but now I know I keep my heart heavily guarded in a glass case. My body's a whole damn museum.

"Hey," Mateo says, squeezing my shoulders and setting us back on our path. "Everything's gonna be okay. You know that, right?"

"Yeah," I reassure him. "I do." I'm just not sure when.

The trees break at the top of our trail. Dozens of buffalo graze in a lush, light-green field behind serious fencing. They're tagged, but happy, healthy, roaming in a place away from hunters. Some are lying and basking in the sun. Others are standing and munching. Mateo and Avery race over to begin their selfie spree.

I spy a bench on the opposite side of the road. My calves are killing me and my head is throbbing, so I go take a seat and look out over Willow Valley. My exposed sunburned shoulder blade presses into something cold. I jerk around to read it. It's a small, silver plaque that reads: *Donated by the Haverford family.* I roll my eyes.

Of course. No matter how fast I run or how far I hike, I can't get away from him.

Brandon approaches, running a tan rag over the top of his head with one hand while holding his hat in the other. "Can I join you?"

I scoot over.

The view is breathtaking. My hometown may be blink-and-you-miss-it small, but it's still a conglomeration of gorgeous rolling hills and houses, cornfields and riding stables. I take out my phone to snap a picture. As I squat on the seat of the bench, I think like Derick would, worried about the right framing, how to tell a visual story within the composition.

"How are you feeling since the Fourth?" Brandon asks when I'm finished. "Mateo said you were pretty shaken up."

I shrug. "I've been better. You saw the whole thing, right?"

I mean, I wasn't subtle about my exit. I was practically hyperventilating. He nods, looking almost guilty for having witnessed my breakdown. "Have you spoken to Derick since?"

I shake my head. "I wouldn't even know what to say if I did."

"Do you mind if I ask why you didn't kiss him?" That's the plaguing question. I shared a couch with him no problem. I shared memories and secrets and hurts and dreams with him even easier. Why was kissing him, *kissing anyone*, such an insurmountable hurdle? Aren't I ready to cross this coming-of-age moment off my list? Lord knows there are many, *many* more left to complete.

The bitter taste of uncomfortable truth tingles in my mouth. "I wasn't ready."

He nods thoughtfully. "Why do you think that is?"

"Part of me feels like I only want a first kiss because that's how relationships start in the movies. That's what those two expect of me." I glance back over my shoulder. Mateo and Avery are still circling the buffalo enclosure, laughing with each other. I know they mean well, yet it's still so much easier to talk to Brandon, to anyone else really, about all of this. Distance and fresh perspective are what I need right now. "It's not that I don't like him. I do. Really." Geez, that's the first time I've admitted that out loud. It sounds right, *feels* right. So, what's wrong?

Other than the fact that he asked me to be friends and then tried to kiss me. But, mixed signals aside...

"Is it a connection thing?" Brandon asks.

I ponder for a moment. "Maybe? Yeah, probably. I'm not sure we've connected on the level where I feel comfortable initiating something like that. I'm attracted to him, but...It's like, I know him, but I don't *know* him, if that makes sense. Mostly, I don't know where High School Him ends and Current Him begins. I need to feel certain in who I'm kissing. I mean, a kiss isn't just a kiss to me." I realize how ironic that is considering the theme from *Casablanca*, one of my favorite songs of all time, has a line that says the exact opposite.

It's even worse that I sound so self-serious, but this is who I've always been. Hiding it hasn't done me much good. I feel deep, love hard, and can't fight it.

Brandon taps his chin and posits, "Maybe you're demi."

I blink in confusion. "Like, Lovato?"

He breaks into uproarious laughter. "No, not like Lovato. Like the romantic and sexual identity." At my blank look, he adds, "It falls under the ace umbrella. It's a spectrum, of course, but that's where the community situates it." His women and gender studies expertise is showing.

These aren't words I'm familiar with.

"Let me guess, you didn't know sexual and romantic attraction were separate?" He takes stock of my panic-stricken eyes. "Don't worry. You aren't alone in that."

I catch my erratic breath before I ask, "What exactly does 'demi' mean?"

"It can mean a lot of things for a lot of different people, but the textbook definition is about establishing a strong emotional connection with someone before feeling sexual or romantic attraction to that person."

That would explain why I never find guys "hot" before I become close friends with them. But...

"Friendship is a form of intimacy," he recites.

I can barely believe what I'm hearing—the connections that are clicking into place inside me. It's not that I'm utterly unkissable, or weird, or a self-saboteur. It's that all the guys I've crushed on before have rushed to use physical closeness to seal the deal when, maybe, I don't work that way.

The other night, Derick barged in through the front door of my museum after hours instead of spidering in like a spy over the laser-beam grid. He set off the alarm. I need some *Ocean's 12*-level acrobatics and extensive heist planning before I can even consider completing the mission.

"And maybe," Brandon continues, "kissing for you is part of your sexual attraction, or your sensual attraction..."

"Wait, I have a *sensual* identity too?"

He clamps his lips closed so as not to laugh right in my face, a kindness when I'm clearly falling apart. Or coming together? "It's a lot to process at once. There aren't easy answers, and you don't need to make any definitive decisions."

"But I came out as gay. I can't just walk it back."

"Who says you can't be both? You *can* be both." He wipes his sweat rag across the bridge of his nose. "Think of it as a bonus. That third camera lens on your iPhone. An added feature that helps you view your experiences more clearly. I can send you some online resources and podcasts about it if you want. Might be helpful. Even if it's not you, it could help you understand better how you approach attraction."

"I'd like that. Thanks." I sit back on the bench. "Demi," I whisper to myself. The syllables swirl around in the air. It lingers like I've sung an incantation that's evoked a sexuality sprite who's here to coat me in magical dust and whisk me off to the demi dimension.

Avery and Mateo rush over with their phones, interrupting my thoughts. "OMG, this view! I forgot how stunning it is! Let's get a picture of all of us."

Brandon says he's got it. He sets his phone down, tilted upward on the bench, and uses the functionality on his Apple Watch to set the timer. We all squeeze in, the sun hanging low in the sky, perfect natural lighting.

"Say 'deer poop'!" Brandon jokes.

"Fuck, where?" Mateo shouts right as the camera goes off.

The shutter sound draws me back to what Brandon said. How demi could be the missing lens for me to see my life and my relationships in fuller detail and color.

I don't know if it'll stick. I don't know if it's *me*. But I know it's a possibility, and isn't that what I was hoping to gain from sending those emails in the first place: possibility?

 *Instagram*

WileysDriveInWV The Fourth is finished. If you missed the fireworks from our lot, better luck next year.

IMAGE DESCRIPTION: a firework exploding.

#drivein #moviesPA #WileysDriveIn

J.M.Mendelson Loved watching the fireworks with my family! So pretty! Great shot! 👍

NessaRoseKnowsBest Better luck next year??? That's a little passive-aggressive.

420BlazinBoii Bro, you good? Who hurt you?

420BlazinBoii Hit me up if you want to talk. Or…not talk. 🍁 🌀

Chapter 17

Armed with only a bottle of Windex, I do my best to wipe years' worth of grime and gook from Alice's front windows.

Outside, Derick is mending the porch steps. It's sweltering today with temperatures rising into the midnineties. Rivulets of sweat run like rivers down his back muscles. I tear my eyes away, wishing that fixing our problems were as easy as running a rag over them.

I wasn't sure Derick would show up to Alice's after my stealth-level avoidance. I was pleasantly surprised when I noticed his Dodge Camaro with its rear-window louver parked out front. He was already hard at work replacing the boards. We didn't exchange hellos, and he didn't ask for help.

With the ability and space to reset since the second almost-kiss, I feel like a person again. Brandon's guidance and suggestions have been helpful. Who knew podcasts weren't just for film history?

Behind me, Alice watches an episode of *The Mary Tyler Moore Show* guest starring Betty White as host of *The Happy Homemaker*, the fictitious TV station's women's show. I get flashes of that bedazzled phone case Derick found at the boardwalk once. I long for the carefree ease of our expectation-less friendship. Though, I guess that's not true when I'm harboring something way more for him right this very minute.

It seems Alice isn't ready to take the hop into film just yet. I've come to understand the simple syrupiness of this sitcom that soothes her in her lonely hours. I wonder if Tammy was the Rhoda to her Mary. I mean, from the photo I found at the bottom of her memory box, I know they were more, but I can't help but imagine what their dynamic was like. How deep their romantic love ran.

During a commercial for auto insurance, Alice asks, "All set for your trip to the city?"

Spray, swipe, sigh. "I'm not sure I want to go anymore." Oscar is jazzed about the whole endeavor. I got the movie print from the Willow Valley Public Library archives on film. He has a projector setup in his office we can use and a blank wall to show it on. Everything is lining up, except for the fact that Derick and I are traveling together and going to have to share a room. On this side of a revelation, it's overwhelming. "Maybe it's for the best if we don't go. Right now, I can keep my world contained. The thought of guest hosting a podcast makes me queasy."

"You're chickening out now?" she asks. "You lie your way into my home, you work your way into my permission, and now you're going to croak when the going gets tough. What happened?"

For someone who has a hard time seeing, she has no trouble seeing right through my bullshit.

"Derick tried to kiss me." It's strange knowing he's right on the other side of the window. He could hear me. He could walk in at any second and find out we're discussing this when I haven't even had the guts to bring it up to him directly.

"I don't see the problem. He's got Ryan O'Neal's hair, Cary Grant's smile, and Gene Kelly's charisma. You could do much worse." I roll my eyes and end up laughing. His heartthrob looks are far from the issue here. "What's the deal?"

"I wasn't ready." Saying it aloud for the second time only solidifies it for me. Reminds me that there's nothing wrong with it. There's nothing wrong with *me*.

"You may never be ready, but love is fleeting and so is life. Grab it by the lapel while you got it or"—she inhales sharply—"it might not be there when you are."

While I can't expect her to understand my position completely, I'm still aching to understand hers. How she lived and navigated the world back then. I decide it's time to tackle the tough topic. "*Chompin' at the Bit* is a love letter to Tammy, isn't it? Everything you didn't get to say to her before she passed away?"

Some directors pride themselves on an aesthetic distance, telling their stories with a sense of detachment. We're looking in on the action, judging a character through the lens. Even from the most horrendous reviews of *Chompin' at the Bit*, I could tell that the movie was shot and made with heart, a spirit people couldn't yet appreciate. Bad zombie makeup and probably too-dark lighting don't discredit any of that.

She only gives me a nod. It says everything I need to know, and when I ask if I can hug her, I'm surprised when she nods again. We both need it. I'm even more surprised when it's not a joke. Shakily, she stands, and I embrace her. This cactus-like woman doesn't prick me, forcing me to shoot away stuck with thousands of needles. Instead, she softens and lets me wrap my arms around her.

"Did anyone know?" I ask.

"Only my sister, Annie. It's the reason she fought for me to direct the picture. She wanted me to imbue a film and a fictional character with the arc of my young life. The screenplay was an exorcism for me. One my ex-husband despised from the moment he saw me writing it."

It's sad how a toxic business burned an avid film lover. It's even sadder how she's had to abandon the medium as both a form of expression and a means of entertainment. If I lost my love of movies, I think I'd lose my sense of self.

"Does that mean you're bisexual then?"

"I never used that word. I lost Tammy while I was at film school. I ran away to New York after graduation with the intention of never looking back—the farm life was not for me—but I was in love. It does something to the brain. I found myself coming home to her, not telling my parents, and hiding out in her attic bedroom. She had a neglectful family who didn't care what she did. Annie was always covering for us." Melancholy pinches the sides of her mouth. "Then, I lost her and it was heartbreaking, and I swore off Willow Valley with every fiber of my being. I think that's why I fell into Peter's arms so easily. He made it simple to forget. He had a magnetism, a power, hard to pull from, harder to process…but he knew. Deep down, he knew when he introduced me to Betsy, years later, that something shifted."

Alice moves to grab her box off the mantel. From it, she produces a photo of her and Betsy, ripped at the edges and slightly out of focus. They're sitting in directors' chairs, peering over the backs with open scripts in their laps.

"I'll have you know, I never cheated. I loved Peter. I was faithful. That was that. But, I will say that Betsy and I grew close, something straddling the line between friends and emotional lovers. She was the only woman I'd had real attraction to after Tammy, and I counted that a blessing that I'd never act upon." I hand the photo back to her, afraid the glass cleaner on my fingertips might tarnish the image more than it already is.

"In short, yes, but it wasn't until the seventies when that word was hitting the mainstream and my career was hitting its stride that I even formulated that. Then, everything happened all at once. I got the idea for the movie and I ran with it. Peter stole the script one night out of my locked desk drawer and threatened to torch it. My mother had her first run-in with cancer around that time, so I lied and said I had to fly home to be with her. I did that, but really Annie and I got a small crew of old New York friends together to shoot my proof of concept."

Before she sits, she brushes her shirt clean of crumbs. There's a border collie embroidered in the center, and I wonder for a split second if that's the breed of dog she used to have, the kind she still advertises as guarding the property. Her loneliness becomes more and more apparent the closer we get. I want to hug her again, but don't press my luck.

"You must've really loved her," I say, and then clarify, "Both of them, but I'm talking about Tammy."

"What we had was special." A fresh tenderness crops up in her voice. "Something like what you boys have."

I blink hard and swallow harder. "How do you mean?"

"Don't play dumb. Go on the trip. Apologize as best you can for hurting his feelings, and explain your situation. Make it happen while it's here or you'll regret it."

From my vantage point, Derick is framed by the windowpane. He lifts the bottom of his tank top to sop up the sweat on his upper lip. His farmer's tan is prominent in the afternoon sun. My heart swells.

"I came up with a demand for my premiere, by the way," she says, unpausing her show. "I want an exclusive screening spot. Somewhere private for me to watch where I won't be bothered or gawked at or asked of. I want to lay low." She smacks her lips. "But I want snacks. Lots of snacks. Those strawberry doughnuts!" So much for her blood sugar.

I can understand why she'd want to stay incognito, after what she went through. "We can make that happen."

The door opens behind us. Derick stands in the foyer holding the ornament from the fallen weather vane. The bronze rooster hovers in the air on its back.

"Think it might be time we set this back?" he asks Alice.

She nods briskly. "You can head upstairs and out through my bedroom window. First door on the left. Be careful on the roof." She juts her chin in my direction. "Take this one with you for balance."

It sounds as if Derick is about to protest so I chime in first. "I'm happy to."

I'm unhappy to, actually. My fear of heights hasn't magically disappeared. But I guess if I'm about to go out on an emotional limb for him, it makes sense I should go out on a physical limb, too. This is how I show him I'm serious about moving on from what happened.

At the top of the rickety stairs, we enter Alice's bedroom. It's the only untouched place in the whole house. The frilly, cream-colored curtains are spread open, spilling sunlight into the space. There's no dust in the air or off-putting smells. No unnecessary dog food bowls.

The wardrobe is closed and neat. The desk is stacked and clean. The bed is made so crisply you could bounce a quarter off it. This is where she holds her control. There's so much story in here, from a stunning hand-carved vanity by the window to a crocheted pink baby blanket slung over a rocking chair.

Derick opens the window and hands me the ornament without asking. He dips out, then turns back, plunging his hands through the pane to grab it back. I think, for a second, he might not help me, but he sets the rooster down on its side and then offers me a hand. I take it.

The slope down is scary. Shingles are loose beneath my sneakers. My flight urges kick in, but I fight back. Derick's grip on me never falters as we climb up to the summit. My foot slips once, and I don't dare look down when it does.

Sticky summer air lashes at my face. A bird, confused by our presence up this high, squawks before taking off. Derick jerks me toward the cupola, a white box with a copper top. The base is attached to the roof. Without the weather-vane ornament, it looks like a miniature house on top of a bigger house, one where an athletic elf could live undisturbed.

When he offers me the rooster end of the pole, I ask before I lose my nerve, "Why did you try to kiss me?"

He's stunned into stopping. "That's a complicated question."

"I'm okay with a complicated answer."

We tentatively move toward the cupola where his end of the pole slides precisely into the hole at the top. The unset ornament slips down so fast it lets out a brassy *clang*. From his tool belt, Derick pulls out a screwdriver.

As per his instructions, which are starting to feel like stall tactics, I crouch down to tug the rooster up to the top. He takes out his phone to find out which direction is true north. Once we figure that out and line the ornament up with the proper openings, he screws the final nails into place.

"Back in high school—I don't know if you remember this—but you had this list of perfect-first-kiss elements. Right place, right time, right person, or whatever? I caught you writing it in peer leadership in that bullet journal you carried everywhere. I remember joking about it, laughing, busting your chops a bit," he says wistfully. "You looked so hurt. I regretted it immediately. I didn't realize how serious you were about it. It always stuck with me for some reason. I hated making you feel that way." He takes a deep reset of a breath. "One of the things on that list was—"

"The Fourth of July fireworks," I finish for him.

He rakes a hand through his deflated mane. "Yup."

"But, you said you didn't think of me like that. You asked if we could be friends."

"In my first email back, I was trying to say I didn't think about anyone that way in high school because everything about my sexuality was still so mixed up. And later, you told me that email meant nothing to you. That it was an accident. That you didn't feel that way either," he says. "I guess I was just trying to protect myself." All the hurt words I'd speared him with in the gazebo were full-scale deflection. How did I expect him to see through my swords and suit of armor?

"Wow," I mutter. "We are really bad communicators."

"We're out of practice," he says. He's right. Those three and a half years of silence have taken their toll on us. Finding our footing among all this change hasn't been easy. "I'm willing to practice now if you're up for it."

I gesture for him to sit. On opposite sides of the cupola, we look out on the untouched land. Everything the eye can see could use a trim or a cut but, even overgrown, it has a humble peacefulness, a painting come to life.

"You're different this summer. Seeing you take charge around the lot and interact with Alice around here, I just, I don't know, started to catch full-on feelings for you," he admits. "After that night in your basement, I didn't know how to backtrack, what to say to let you know, so when the fireworks opportunity presented itself, I thought, *You better take this, Derick. This is your shot.* Clearly, I misjudged the moment."

"No," I jump in. I stand without holding on, feeling steady on my own two feet for once. "I have feelings for you, too." He looks up at me, cheeks reddening. "I think we just…"

"Moved too fast?" he asks. It's not exactly wrong, and I'm not sure I'm ready to share my demi-ness just yet. Not until I feel certain or set about how that puzzle piece lodges into the image of me—is it a corner or is it one of the many unsorted pieces that make up the middle?

"Yeah," I breathe. Because that's fine for now.

"Does that mean our trip is still on?" he asks. "I really want to go to the city with you, Wren."

Wren. Not Captain. Not Wrenji. Just my name, short and sweet sliding off his tongue in the shining sunlight.

"The concrete jungle better make way for us." I let loose a stupid laugh.

Like Cupid's sending us a message, a gust of wind sends the weather vane spinning, and when it stops, the arrow points right at me, aimed straight through my heart.

Chapter 18

"Babe, why do you own these?" Mateo asks, picking up my boxer shorts with cartoon clapper boards on them.

Avery oversees folding my shirts while Mateo rifles through my underwear drawer. I'm happy to have help packing for this trip. Otherwise I'd be blasting some swoony Rachel Portman (my favorite female composer) and waltzing around my bedroom in an embarrassing, grandiose fashion. I'm still buzzing on high from Derick's and my declarations earlier in the week.

"They're novelty loungewear. They're comfy," I retort.

"They're tragic." He slingshots them across the room with expert aim. They land in the trash can. "Have I *mentioned* you're in desperate need of new *unmentionables*?" He tugs at a tearing waistband on a threadbare pair of Hanes.

I zip up my cosmetic case, now stuffed with toothpaste, floss, and other oral care must-haves so my mouth is always minty fresh. I may have curbed the Fourth of July kiss, but who knows what this trip might bring. I like to be prepared. "That's not really a priority right now."

"Is this, like, a couple's trip?" Avery asks. She secures the straps over my clothes in the main body of my suitcase, pulling tightly so they don't slide around.

"After we get the Alice event situated, I do have a big, flashy date planned for us, but nothing is official right now. We're feeling it out," I say.

"Can you even believe we're discussing Wren Roland's love life? It's felt like a taboo for so long, and now suddenly this summer he's the one with all the juicy drama."

"Uh, babe, excuse me. What about me and Brandon?" Mateo sasses.

"Please, you two are practically wearing Jonas Brothers-era promise rings at this point. Catch me when you finalize your registry." Mateo blushes harder than I've ever seen him blush before. "Let Wren have this one. We've been waiting forever for this."

If they've been waiting forever, then I've been waiting forever and a day.

Avery grabs the second zipper and meets mine in the middle so we can stand the brimming bag up on its wheels. "I need your advice on something," I say, pushing the suitcase over toward the door. "Brandon brought up a good point on our hike the other day about how I, uh, experience attraction and why I pulled away from Derick's kiss." I pause, failing to make fire from my last two emotional flints. When I finally feel a spark, I say, "I think I might be demi."

"Romantic or sexual?" Avery asks without missing a beat like she's been anticipating this moment.

"I don't know. Does it matter right now? I'm still learning about it, but a lot of these experiences I'm reading and hearing about are ones I've had as well. I think a big part of why I'm hesitant around Derick is because there's the relationship timeline I've internalized from the movies and then there's the one I feel comfortable with, which is why all this pressure to get a kiss or have sex or define the relationship is really messing with me."

"Ugh, our baby queer is growing up," Mateo says, sounding tearful.

Avery adds, "We've always wondered, but it took you so long to settle on gay and get comfortable coming out to everyone that we didn't want to push the nuances. We quietly celebrated the small victory."

"Quietly? You threw a surprise Baby Gay Shower in my honor. You made everyone call you Mama and Papa all night. It was creative, but also kinda creepy." I shudder at the memory. I still have more *Love is Love* T-shirts than I know what to reasonably do with.

"Oh, hush. You loved every second of it," Avery snaps.

I roll my eyes. "What I really need to know now is if I should tell Derick. Especially since I'm still working it out."

Avery instantly says, "I think you should. However you feel is valid and however you identify in the moment is right. If you feel like the label of demi is going to help him understand you and what you want from a relationship, then I'd say go for it."

"Easier said than done, obviously, but you said you wanted him to know you, and if this is you, then don't wait for him to read your mind, babe," Mateo adds.

I take all of this in, processing as best I can before I have to leave to meet Derick at the bus station. I'm not usually one to wait until the last minute to pack, but I've been wavering on this trip since the holiday, and now I'm scrambling.

"But what if it makes everything weird? What if he doesn't like me anymore? I'm just wondering what happens halfway through this trip when he finds out and we're stuck together." My breathing quickens. My anxiety whips up a brain tornado. I sit down in my desk chair to keep myself from getting too swept up in it.

Avery's concerned eyes meet mine. "Call us. We'll come get you."

"Babe, if he gives you shit over something like this, then he's a piece of shit. Got it? Your identity is valid and if he makes you feel otherwise, you best believe I'll show up to that Courtyard Marriott with my claws out," Mateo says.

"Easy, tiger," Avery says with a laugh.

They pile on top of me in a group hug so tight and long, I fear I might suffocate from their love. Chosen family or found family? I'm not sure, maybe both, but either way I'm happy to have them always. That is until Mateo says, "Just know I will be throwing out your underwear while you're gone, babe, so either get used to going commando or buy yourself some cute, supportive briefs as soon as possible."

♡

In the small, glistening Any Weather Transportation group bus station in Baskersville, I roll my suitcase back and forth with frenetic energy. I haven't seen Derick yet, but I have a text on my phone letting me know he's on his way.

After my conversation with Mateo and Avery, and a car ride over to the station singing Celine Dion's greatest hits at top volume, I feel at ease and ready for whatever this trip throws at me. Conversations can be tough, feelings can be hard, but I'm willing and able to accept the challenge.

To keep myself distracted, I'm reading a digital poster on the proposed plans for bus expansion. It seems like Willow Valley is the next town to see major shifts and its own pickup schedule. From a news article a few weeks back, I saw they were taking over some of the Lonely Lass-O's spaces for the nine-to-five crowd, since it's mostly an after-10 p.m. establishment.

I question how much Derick's family is making on this deal. It's not like they need the extra capital.

I don't have time to think too hard on it because our bus pulls up early to the boarding lane. The beleaguered woman in the ticket booth, gum snapping and head tilting, makes an announcement over the loudspeaker that Bus 139 to New York Port Authority is now boarding. I check my phone for more word from Derick. Nothing.

The rest of the passengers file onto the maroon metallic vehicle that glints in the broad daylight. This bus appears to be brand-new. Nothing like the old blue ones with the faded fabric seats and peeling ads for now-canceled network cable shows. This whole business seems like it got an upgrade since I left for college.

I tack myself onto the end of the line, willing Derick to show up. If we don't make this bus, the next one doesn't come for another hour and a half. We promised Oscar we'd meet him at his office near the Flatiron Building to view the movie and have a general discussion. I want to be on time, and Earl ensured I know that on time means early.

At the accordion doors, I attempt to heave open the underbelly latch to stow my luggage. The handle is jammed. Hard as I pull, the blasted thing won't budge. My hand cramps and a sinking feeling starts, leaving me wondering if this is an omen for the whole trip.

But right as I'm about to call it quits, Derick's voice calls out from behind me, "Need some help?"

When I turn, I see he's wearing his classic sunglasses. He has a race-car red suitcase behind him and his camera bag strapped on top. I nod, and he opens the hatch without so much as a wince. After he tucks my bag underneath his, he hugs me. It's jarring in public like this, but I mold myself into it.

I let him pick our seats when we board, much to the driver's obvious chagrin over being delayed.

There's a nice spot near the back away from the already snoring man in Row 7 and the lady talking loudly on her phone in Row 10. We get a quiet corner to ourselves. Derick pulls a pair of tangled, wired headphones from his pocket, plugs them into the jack on his phone, and hands me the right bud. He's queued up two hour-long episodes of *Don't You Forget About...* to get us in the right mindset for the next two days.

During the opening piano theme song, I ask, "You packed the box Alice gave us, right? I want to make sure she's happy and that we don't lose anything."

He points to the floor. "In the suitcase in the undercarriage. No worries."

He's always saying that. Never in my life have I had no worries. I sigh, acknowledging my anxiety and trying to let the feeling pass. "What if the movie is...bad?" He tips his head toward me. "I know, I know. It's just I have such high expectations, and I've done all this research and if it's bad, how can I responsibly screen it and be sure she won't get raked over the coals again?"

"I get that you're nervous. I'm a little nervous, too, but just remember that this movie is a piece of Willow Valley history. Alice wouldn't have given you permission if she wasn't ready for her second act."

"Second act? I like that. We should use that in our marketing."

He smiles a knowing smile. "Already ahead of you." He switches away from the podcasts app and opens some mock-ups for Alice's event. Since we have a date and time, he created a social campaign where a zombie hand emerges from the ground, hearts float in the air, and Alice's old, glamorous headshot from the seventies is featured and left-aligned.

It reads:

A Second Chance Story by a Director Ready for Her Second Act...
Chompin' at the Bit (1978) by Alice Kelly
Witness the Premiere That Never Was...
Rising again on August 14

It's so perfect, I tear up. I'm a waterworks factory lately.

"I'm guessing you like it," he says.

"I love it." A deep breath escapes me, relief coursing through my system. "I really need this to go well. Alice's reputation and Wiley's future depend on it. It's a lot of pressure, and you're really helping. There is a lot riding on this for me."

"For me, too," he says. That's music to my ears, even if I'm unsure exactly what it means.

I fiddle with the earbud still dangling between my fingers, debating whether to ask: "Would it be the worst thing in the world if I stayed at Wiley's past this summer?" Well, it's out. Derick bites his lip in answer. "I only ask because Avery says it's not an *adult* job and that I can't expect to be there forever, but what if, well, uh, what if it's the only job I've ever really seen myself at?"

Derick's silence stretches out for longer than I'd hoped. Finally he says, "What about Oscar? Isn't this whole meeting so he can introduce you to new contacts? I think it's probably smart to start thinking about life beyond Willow Valley and Wiley's."

It's strange to even consider how one interview on a long-lost movie could catapult me onto a career path. In all fairness, I didn't have any idea what I'd do with a film studies degree when I declared it as my major in my second semester of freshman year. All I knew is that I liked watching movies, writing about them, and finding new ways to relate them to their historical context. I never imagined Oscar Villanueva would be opening doors for me, let alone be sitting in the same room, at the same table.

But, still, I worry about Alice. I've seen her still-healing wounds, and I want to protect her at all costs.

And, even more, I worry about Earl. He's past retirement age. I know he's not itching to give up the grind, but with no partner, no kids, who's he going to pass the drive-in on to? This isn't the first time I've asked myself this question, and each time I ask it I come to the same logical conclusion: Me. And each time I come to that conclusion, I grow a little fonder of the idea.

But Derick is searing me with his pressurized gaze, so I say, "You're right. I can't stay there forever."

He sighs, nods. Says nothing more on the topic.

He's about to restart the episode when the bus comes to a bout of bumper-to-bumper traffic. "Hey." He pokes me instead. "I saw you posted a picture on your stalled Instagram account the other day. Coming back to the social-media dark side?"

It weighed on me for most of the day. I adore the photo of the 3Bee Gees and Brandon at the top of that hill, Willow Valley laid out behind us, and I wanted to share it. Being around Derick has made me realize that social media has its advantages. It can be a tool. A platform where I can shout about the things and people that are important to me. A digital soapbox of sorts.

"I figure once this episode goes public, people on the internet are going to start looking for me online. I don't want to be one of those people who's unreachable."

"You mean you don't want to be a grandpa at twenty-two?"

I roll my eyes—Avery and Mateo have clearly gotten him to call me that, too—but he's right in a way. And *grandpa* comes across like a term of endearment when he says it.

"Building a brand is important."

"Care to share any wisdom?"

"Hmm, so, it's all about getting your engagement up." I can tell by the way his voice pitches that he's extra excited to be asked about this. "It's about telling a story that marries text with image and targets your key demos in a way that keeps them interested. That makes them feel something." His vocal speed intensifies. "For example, if I held your hand..." He pauses a beat, his voice dipping to this low, sultry place that's still oozing with sweetness. "Can I hold your hand?"

"Yes," I tell him, offering up my palm.

"So, if I held your hand, which I am now. Thanks, by the way." He sports a goofy grin. "You would have an immediate emotional reaction, either good or bad or indifferent, and it would play a major role in whether you'd like to continue engaging in said hand-holding. Whether you liked it. Whether you liked it, just not with me. Whether you felt unmoved by it. Or you just didn't like it at all."

"I like it," I assure him. "With you."

He stops, but only long enough to let his feverish blush pass. "You see, so branding content is about targeting those who like hand-holding and figuring out how they like to do it. Fingers intertwined, loose grip, firm grip, etc., based on engagement data—that's your audience—then creating posts that appeal to their emotions. People will often forget what you say, but not how you make them feel. 'Pathos' is the word Aristotle used to describe motivating a sense of empathy and urgency in your social-media audience, a feeling of belonging."

"Ah, yes. Aristotle, the famous Greek philosopher and avid social-media user."

"Hey now, he did have a lot of *followers*." I shake my head to hide my smile at his nerdy attempt at a joke. "Okay, okay. End rant." He lets out an embarrassed laugh. After he listened so attentively to me when I went on and on about Alice, the least I could do is return the favor. He sounds impassioned, all fired up. It's adorable.

"Oh, and one last thing to remember with social media," he says. "A good hashtag goes a long way."

"Got it." I let go of his hand, reach for my tote bag, and pull out my notebook and pen. I write in large, looping letters at the top of a fresh page:

#HowToBeSocialMediaSavvy as taught by Derick Haverford

He flashes me a thumbs-up, appearing heartened that I'd take his lesson so seriously.

As I make sure to jot down every detail, never knowing when this might come in handy, he puts the episode back on. Our bus continues to barrel toward the Lincoln Tunnel, and I think, *This is going to be an interesting two days*.

Chapter 19

The Flatiron Building reminds me of a massive slice of deep-dish pizza dropped into the wrong city.

My stomach growls, but there's no time to eat.

Since our room wasn't ready yet when we arrived at the hotel, Derick and I checked our bags and left for our meeting downtown. We skipped into the depths of the subway system and then emerged at Madison Square Park as if by magic.

The streets are packed with people. Yellow taxis whizz by, triangular, splashy ads slapped on top. The sidewalk is punctuated with towering stalks of steel, windows and walls creating ginormous, winning games of Tetris.

Just beyond the food-like feat of architecture, Oscar leans against a brick wall wearing pointy-toed shoes with silver buckles and no socks. A vape pen dangles from his fingertips.

"Hello, hello." He extends his hand to both of us. "So good to see you. Glad you could make it."

"Thank you for having us," I say, breathing this in.

Once pleasantries are exchanged, he has us sign in at the security desk and then whisks us up to the eighth floor by elevator. The view from his spacious office is stellar. There is a ton of natural light, and the hardwood floors, I can tell, are original. It's amazing what he's made of himself since starting out as a freelance film critic and working his way up to bestselling author and podcast host. My imposter syndrome comes on strong.

"Anything I can get you folks? Water, seltzer?" He pops open an impressive mini-fridge filled with rows and rows of beverages. I never pass up a LaCroix.

Derick presents Alice's box of memories, while I flip through my notebook for Alice's approved list of topics. Oscar is prepping the projector. Alice shot her movie on 16mm film, the smallest size used for professional films and the biggest money saver, and then it was blown up to 35mm, so Oscar had to call in a few favors to get the proper antique equipment. She told me the 16mm was also an aesthetic choice because older zombie films had used it before to give their movies a gritty, grainy look. Blowing it up made it more easily viewable to a mass audience, albeit one that never got a chance to embrace it anyway.

The tin the film is in smells heavily of vinegar, an apparent sign of aging. Setting the center hole of the take-up reel onto the proper arm, Oscar threads the film through the tabs as if he's performing surgery. It must be precise and exact; otherwise he could risk ruining it, destroying the negative we need to preserve.

As soon as the projector starts up, the noise is cacophonous, something akin to a symphony of snowblowers on a suburban street after a blizzard. I plug my ears.

"You'll get used to it!" Oscar yells over the sound.

My heart starts beating faster and louder.

"And now for the main event…" Oscar says. The cranking sound fades a bit as the opening image appears on the clean, white wall opposite us. It's the cemetery, a moody fog rolling across it. There's the shadow of a girl in the distance, a flashlight flicking past the headstones. Oscar dims the lights so the image becomes sharper, even though the edges are fuzzy with a vignette effect.

When I sit, my leg won't stop jiggling. A lush, frightful score fills the room. Derick places a comforting hand on my thigh. "Is this okay?" he whispers. Oscar is already too enthralled in the film to notice. I nod my approval as the fate of Wiley's future plays out before me.

♡

Silence befalls the room when Oscar stops the projector an hour and forty minutes later. Derick hits the lights. I bite the inside of my cheek.

None of us speak for a long stretch. We couldn't if we tried.

Chompin' at the Bit is…

"That," Oscar says, breaking the tension, "was worth the wait!" His fists hoist up in jubilation.

Everything I hoped it would be and more!

Derick was right. I had no reason to worry.

The pacing is tight, the writing is sharp, and the acting is cohesive and well directed. The editing can be choppy at times and the audio isn't the best and, yes, the zombie makeup is hokey, but as it stands, an homage to lost love and a little Pennsylvania town, it's beautiful.

Derick's hand left my thigh only once to pass me a tissue from his bag. Now, I blot at my eyes, not even embarrassed that I'm crying over a campy romp that turns soapy in the big twist: the zombie boy was the driver of the car that killed Tammy on impact.

When she finds this out, Robin, the protagonist who has begun to develop a soft spot for the bleary-eyed, undead boy in the checkered tie, tries to cruelly stop him from crawling back into his grave before sunrise, essentially dooming his soul to an eternity of never-ending unrest, wandering this plane of existence. Instead, she finds understanding in his impassioned apology and his promise to bring a message back to Tammy, should they both end up in the same afterlife.

Oscar was furiously scrawling comments the entire time, barely touching his Melon Pomelo. In the episode, he's going to have a lot to say. He's known to spar with his guests when it comes to stringent opinions, and even though I have a bachelor's degree, I don't measure up.

What I lack in experience, though, I make up for in personal anecdotes. Surprisingly, Alice wrote on her list of approved topics "The Real Tammy Wilson." Alice isn't only ready to reshare the movie, she's interested in having her story told.

"I'm stunned," I say.

"It has a grindhouse hook, so that B-movie drive-in appeal, but arthouse sensibilities, and yet the camerawork is so commercial. How she blended all those styles is masterful. I'd be remiss if I didn't say thank you for bringing this to me," Oscar says. "This is a big deal for movie lovers. It's not every day a film of this much mystery gets let out of the vault." Pride mixes with nauseating excitement in my belly. Derick grips my forearm as if to say *I knew it.*

"We can get the podcast episode recorded and edited before August 14th, right? We really need this exposure to help keep Wiley's afloat."

Oscar's nod is enthusiastic. "Yes. As I said in my email, I want to help the lot. Drive-ins are so important to the ecosystem and economy of movies. Not to mention their historical significance. Wiley's is one of the oldest continuously operating drive-ins in the country. It'd be a shame to see it go."

"Maybe we could release a week and. a half ahead of time. That should drive enough traffic to our socials, right?" I ask, looking to Derick. He's gone stoic, yet still nods. "I convinced Earl to approve an online preorder window in the last week of July. He hates internet reservations, but it's necessary. Once that sells out, we can advertise a drive-up price." My words are falling out over one another. "We can add all that to your cool campaign posts."

"Sure," Derick murmurs. I didn't run all this by him, but I'm on the fast track to success. I can't stall at a crossroads waiting for the permission gates to go up. Sometimes, when you're in charge, you have to make the hard and fast decision to floor it.

"I love it," Oscar says. "I think it's all very doable. We'll meet back here tomorrow. We have a small soundproofed studio in the office next door where we can record. Tonight, I'll send you my thoughts to help you collect your own. It'll be like a loose script that we follow so we make sure to hit all the important points. My editor, Elissa, can make anything flow, but it's best we have a solid through line to make her job easier and our conversation more fruitful." He taps the end of his pen on his leather iPad case. "I'll also send the film negative out to the lab Priority Mail first thing in the morning, so we can get the digitization process moving. We want a good quality file to show at the screening."

We shake on it all, and I'm stoked beyond belief.

Back out on the simmering pavement, Derick suggests we get some dinner. Twilight is blanketing the city. Businesspeople emerge from buildings, phones in hand, walking home with loosened ties and sneakers swapped in for dress shoes. I grow sheepish as Derick swivels into me, and I stop him from heading back in the direction we came from.

"I had another idea, actually, if you're up for it," I say. A smile climbs up onto his face.

It's showtime for:

Wren Pulls Off a Grand Gesture.

I want Derick to know that I'm serious about making up for the Fourth of July. And about him.

Time is of the essence as we race to catch the 4 Train downtown. A half hour later we emerge near the southernmost tip of Manhattan and snake our way over to the South Street Seaport where the asphalt fades into old-timey cobblestones. Tourists and trendy hipsters are flocking over to Pier 17. Every group and pair clutch rectangular papers, and a growing number of them wear Leonardo DiCaprio merchandise.

The confusion on Derick's face smolders only for a second. Then he reads the large sign that waves overhead:

One Night Only! The South Street Seaport Museum Presents Movies under the Stars: Titanic aboard the Wavertree.

A cinema pop-up company is screening the film on the deck of one of the largest wrought-iron sailing vessels still afloat. Its jutting bow pokes up and out in front of its teardrop-shaped body with dozens of flags flapping in the breeze.

The employees are all dressed in period garb, and our tickets are stamped to look like real *Titanic* passenger tickets. On the deck, there's a screen and a small smattering of chairs. This is an exclusive and expensive event, one I had to get up before 7:00 a.m. to secure admission to. A never-ending virtual queue and one whole paycheck later, I still knew it would be worth it. The ecstatic look on Derick's face is priceless.

Our hands braid together once more as we move to find our designated seats. The evening in my basement felt like a blocking rehearsal, and this feels like the first take on the film of our future relationship.

"I know you're used to drive-ins, but I figured a boat-in would be something different." We shuffle down our row. "And this is one of the movies I had on the docket for our We Love Leo movie marathon. Just enough love story for me, just enough action for you."

Derick's mouth breaks into a gleeful grin. I'm thinking back on our late-night text conversations about James Cameron's directorial choices, the scintillating performances, and the geometric proportions of a certain door that probably could've held two bodies.

A waiter comes over and serves us flutes of sparkling wine as I recall our running argument: whether the "draw me like one of your French girls" scene or the hand-on-foggy-car-window scene was steamier.

It dawns on me that I've orchestrated our official first date. The more that sinks in (pun intended), the more I realize that this is the right time to tell Derick about my blossoming demi-ness before anything goes too far. Give him an out if he wants it.

"Hey, I wanted to explain about the night of the fireworks," I say in a small voice.

"What else is there to explain?" He chokes on the bubbles of his champagne. Even his chokes are charming.

"Well," I start, "you were right when you said it was too soon, too fast, but there's another part of this, of *me*, really, that I've...uh, well, I haven't fully talked about or figured out for myself."

"Okay." His hand cups my knee. That hand acts like an anchor holding me tight to his dock, which is exactly what I need since I feel as adrift as Kate Winslet will be in three and a quarter hours. "You can tell me anything."

He planned a perfect trip, comforted me through Alice's movie, and forgave me for publicly shirking his advance. I owe him—no, scratch that—I owe myself this moment of honesty. If I don't, I might sit on this secret forever, never letting my true self see the light.

"I think I might be demisexual." The words feel even more right, which assuages most of my anxiety, until his brows crease. My stomach circles in on itself.

"You gotta help me out here. I'm not sure I know what that means." There's no trace of disgust or disdain in his voice. Instead, he's properly engaged in listening, like he did dutifully when I geeked out over female filmmakers from the seventies.

When I finish explaining as best I can, he puzzles through it. "So, basically you're saying, before you feel attracted to me, you need to feel close to me?"

"Yes!" I shout too loudly. Curious gazes come our way. I mouth an open apology to anyone willing to accept it. "Yes, and I had just started to develop that attraction for you before the Fourth of July, starting that night you helped in the snack shack, but when you went to kiss me, a Code Red fired off in my brain. I felt like I was in danger, which is maybe because I didn't know this about myself yet. It helps explain why I've never been in a rush to fly through my firsts. I was in sexuality limbo, thinking some wires inside me were crossed, but now I'm pretty sure that I equate physical affection with my sexuality, and before I feel sexual attraction, I need to feel emotionally safe."

His face goes crestfallen. "You don't feel safe with me?"

"No!" I shout again, even louder. Our seat neighbors are seriously annoyed with me. I hold a finger to my mouth, promising to whisper this time. "No, I do. Or, I do now, anyway. I'm romantically attracted to you. I know that for sure. I want to hold your hand and do couple-y things like this with you, if that's what you want, too. But kissing, making out, sex? I'm not sure when I'll be ready for those things. Maybe in a month, or a year, or tomorrow, or an hour from now. I can't predict it. I thought all these firsts came in a predetermined timeline, but relationships can't chart a course over three acts like a screenplay. Life is so much messier than a story arc."

He laughs. "I like the way you see the world through the movies." Calmly, he squeezes my shaky hand. "I was just happy we had a second chance to be friends again this summer. I'll be happy with the chance to be more than that, too, even if it doesn't include kissing or touching or sweaty hands on car windows. I don't need that stuff right now." He sets his flute down and takes my other hand in his. "In the future, I can't promise I won't want it, but I can promise that I'm happy with what we have. I like being around you and getting to know you. You make me feel good about myself in a way nobody else does. You challenge me. I learned how to regrout tile because of you!"

"Because of those blog hacks, really." I nudge him playfully, and he nudges me back, until our constant nudging turns into a full-fledged nuzzle. "Thank you for saying all that. Just please be sure to tell me if you're ever not good with what we have. I don't think this can work if we don't communicate openly and honestly."

He raises his hand in salute. "Aye, aye, Captain." He gesticulates around us. "See? We're on a boat. It really works in so many ways."

My heart swells to impossible proportions. I lean in and peck his cheek with the utmost reverence. He's a once-in-a-lifetime 56-carat blue diamond, and I'm not about to let him slip from my hand and sink to the bottom of the ocean.

This time, I'll hold on tight.

Chapter 20

"I think I see your point finally," Derick says, settling down at a bar not far from the seaport. It's filled to the brim with finance bros, and a stuffed stag is mounted on the wall above the plentiful liquor bottles that line the long, mirrored shelf. "The 'I want you to draw me like one of your French girls' scene is significantly hotter than the hand on the window."

It's well past midnight. Loose and not wanting the night to end prematurely, we decided another round was in order.

"Right?" I ask. "It's more seductive and teasing. 'Wearing this. Wearing *only* this.' She knows she's got him. She knows she'll have him. She's so confident when she takes off the robe. I wish I had that kind of confidence." My drunken alter ego has taken the reins, and I'm spouting embarrassing truths, overserved and speaking out of my ass.

"You've got confidence," Derick says, poking me right in the center of my chest. A starburst of pleasure fans out from the site. "You just keep it locked in here. I had to look long and hard, but I see it. Especially at Wiley's. Someday, you'll see it, too, and let it out." He makes an explosive noise, his hand flying away like a spellbinding supernova.

Even though we're already light-headed, Derick flags down the bartender. He orders a vodka cran for me and a whiskey sour for himself. It's strange to down the drink that decimated my decision-making skills on the night of the email blast. The familiar bitter-tart combo scorches my stomach.

"Tonight was perfect," he says, snatching a pretzel nugget from the nearby bowl.

"I thought you might think so." His Adam's apple bobs as he drinks. Up and down like a metronome. Hypnotic.

"It was…"

His reverie is interrupted by his phone vibrating on the bar top. "Dad" blinks below a photo of Daniel P. Haverford, the airbrushed one from the bus line ads, not even a casual family shot. This was a usual occurrence back in high school. His father disrupting any outing to learn of his son's whereabouts, who he was with, why he wasn't home. But, this late? I'm surprised Mr. Haverford's even still awake at this hour.

"I should take this," Derick says, all the color draining from his face. He slips away from the bar, and when he doesn't find a pocket of quiet, he shoves out the exit, leaving me alone with two half-full drinks.

A woman offers me her seat before she goes to grab a table in the back, and I take it.

Time becomes fuzzy as I reminisce on the night. Fantasy flurries around me. Derick and I are New Yorkers blowing off steam after a hard day at work—me writing my Alice Kelly biography and teaching film studies courses at a city college before returning to Willow Valley in the summers for another season as the owner of Wiley's, Derick working as a brand manager during the week and doing photography for the lot on the weekends. Adoptive dog dads to a Jack Russell named Jack (we're not that creative and it's a *Titanic* reference, okay?) with a wiry personality and a lazy eye and an underbite. Derick makes his famous pancakes every Sunday morning, and I slip Jack the leftovers when we're done. Life is good.

This liminal two-day trip is a reprieve from summer, the lot, figuring out what lies beyond August. The dream isn't a reality yet, but the longer I drink and contemplate the possible success of this podcast episode, it feels like it could be.

I get worried after about fifteen minutes, lost in my own head. Derick hasn't returned. His glass has gone warm. I settle the tab and turn to go.

It takes three frantic scans of the street before I spot him, hunched against a wall, speaking in hushed, harsh tones. The phone is still stuck to his ear. I approach him tentatively, not wanting to alarm him.

"Because," he bites back. "I'm an adult. You don't need to know where I am all the time." A long pause. "I understand I should've told you, but what is it you always say: ask forgiveness, not permission? You can't have it both ways."

I stand back awkwardly, folding my arms across my chest. It's all I can do to stop myself from reaching out and hanging up the phone for him.

"We can discuss this tomorrow when I'm home."

When he pivots into me, he startles. It's clear I wasn't meant to overhear that, and I try to stay as neutral as possible. "Everything okay?" I ask.

My question breaks him. He flops back into the brick wall and hangs his head. "My dad's angry. What else is new?"

"Do you want to talk about why?" My voice registers barely above a whisper. I've never seen Derick distraught before. Happy-go-lucky always hangs around him like the cloud of his cologne.

"I didn't tell him we were here. That we were coming here at all, actually." He doesn't sound remorseful, but he does sound a tad bitter.

"I thought you were using your dad's account for our bus tickets and your mom's rewards points for the hotel and…"

His gaze bores through me, and I immediately understand. He planned this behind their backs, and he did so for us. Maybe even more so for me. And if our conversation about Charlie taught me anything, it's that his dad's preoccupation with appearances would've hindered this whole trip.

My heart aches for him. "I'm sorry."

"Don't be. I assumed they were slamming margaritas and fishing and wouldn't even notice, but apparently they're back in Willow Valley and breathing down my neck again."

"Have you talked to your brothers about any of this?"

"They're chill, but they're not around much anymore. Nobody's there to run interference when my dad blames a failed interview on me screwing too many guys." He lets out a sarcastic, pinched laugh. "The real screwing. Not the kind we do on Alice's cabinets." I give him a flirty shove, happy to hear him sounding more like himself again. "My brothers are reformed textbook players, and my dad has to rag on me for being gay? He doesn't even know the half of it."

"You've graduated. You can get a job in marketing and move out now. Things can be different."

"No," he says quickly, rapping his knuckle on his thigh, like the sound might summon some answers. "My older brothers got to move away. They got to forge their own paths. My younger brother got the sports genes and gets to play the baby-of-the-family card whenever he wants. Me? Doesn't matter that I have my own photography business. Doesn't matter that I graduated with honors. I'm chained to the family business. Dale should've been the one to take it on. He's the one my dad loves best, but no. He moved to Silicon Valley for some start-up I'm ninety-five percent sure never really *started up.*"

"Can't you just tell him you want to work somewhere else?"

"Not an option. Not even a conversation." His jaw clenches. A bulbous blood vessel I haven't seen before pronounces itself along the side of his neck.

In high school, his dad was demanding. That much couldn't be covered up. If he talked about his family on our coleader dates, he was talking about his brothers, his cousins, sometimes his mom, but never his dad. Which was weird considering every time his phone buzzed or dinged or beeped, it was his dad, checking in on him or checking up on something.

His stormy eyes grow cloudier by the second. "We made a deal that if I got an internship, apprenticeship, or job right out of undergrad then I'd be let off the leash for good. He'd see my major as a real field. I could pursue opportunities there and work my way to full time. And, well, yeah."

He doesn't need to tell me the rest. I'm part of the rest. Wiley's is where Mr. Haverford pulled strings to make the puppet dance.

What Derick said in the storage closet makes more sense: *Didn't exactly have a choice.*

The Haverfords' wealth has always seemed like a freeing agent to me, slapping down a credit card whenever you want and not having to worry, but maybe all that money is the kryptonite Mr. Haverford uses to keep his sons in line. To fast-track them on his predetermined routes to success.

I'd take my weird family over that any day.

"I'm just so tired, Wren," Derick says.

I hold him then. Tight and close. Hoping he feels my rapidly beating heart that's working overtime to soothe him. He's emotionally shown up for me so many times this summer. Anything he needs from me in this moment, I'll give it to him.

"Would sleep help?" I ask. He nods into my shoulder, so I take his hand and lead him out into the crosswalk. Away from the site of the phone conversation that stuck a knife in our evening. Sometimes, you only need a change of scenery to reset.

Upon our return to the hotel, the lobby is quiet and empty. A lone security guard sits playing solitaire on his phone. He tips his hat to us as we pass.

On the eighth floor, Derick rummages around for the key cards. A swipe, a green light, and a lengthy beep later, we're inside the room. It's fancy. There are two bedside tables, two huge windows looking out onto the rooftop garden, two suitcases set beside the dark wooded wardrobe, two of us standing in the doorway, but there's one problem: there's only one bed.

A single California king sits up against the chestnut accent wall.

"Shit." Derick's face falls. "When I called to book under my parents' account, they asked if I wanted to request their usual room, and I didn't really think about what that meant. I just assumed they asked for something nice."

"It's okay." We endured a platonic couch cuddle. This isn't that different. At least we'll be comfier.

"No, it's not. I messed this up. Jesus, I can't even disobey my parents right." He clasps his hands behind his neck. The strain in his arm muscles is enough to let me know that the earlier feelings are resurfacing tenfold. "I can call down to see if they have a cot. That's what I'll do." He surveys the room as he moves to the phone. There's no way a cot would fit in this slender space even if they did have one. He must realize this too, because he says, "You know what? I can sleep in the desk chair. I'm sure they can send up an extra blanket."

"That sounds unnecessarily uncomfortable."

"I'll be fine. No worries. I don't want to crowd you." In frustration, he unzips his suitcase to find his shaving bag, only it's buried under a bunch of shirts. He digs until I gently catch his hand. I stroke the back of it. Once. Twice. His fingers uncurl.

"Can you look at me for a sec?" He meets my eyes. "You won't crowd me. There's more than enough room for both of us." His strained expression softens into gratitude.

"You're sure?" he asks with sweet hesitation that sends my soul to outer space and back.

"I'm more than sure."

We brush our teeth side by side at the sink. He spits. I spit. I break him off a piece of floss. It's choreography we already know by heart. How? I haven't figured that out yet. But the comfort of it seems to do wonders for his state of mind.

He lets me change in the bedroom, while he remains in the bathroom. I draw back the velvety duvet and sink myself into the softest sheets I've ever slept on. I take a moment to check my inpouring of texts from earlier.

The 3Bee Gees group chain blew up to ask for my input on their going-out outfits, and I missed them. They must've been getting ready to head to the club since they weren't on shift. The most recent texts read:

> WREN! Avery asked Stacia about the stamps FINALLY and is now buying her a drink. 👀
> WREN!! Avery is dancing with Stacia to Robyn 💃 💃
> WREN!!! AVERY AND STACIA ARE KISSING.
> WITH THEIR MOUTHS.
> YOU ARE MISSING THIS

The thread stopped until Avery wrote:

> Hope you enjoyed the show 😊

Mateo types:

@Wren what's the status in NYC?

I write:

It's had its ups and downs, but overall, it's…kind of perfect??? 😈

Mateo
HOLY SHIT. Brandon and I are already planning a menu for the Queer
Triple Date Deluxe dinner we're going to throw.
We'll make pasta!
We'll get cannolis!
We'll crack the emergency champagne!!!

I laugh and send:

What's the emergency?

Avery
@Mateo setting the apartment on fire if he tries to cook 😂

Mateo
☝️

Derick returns; he's a vision in navy basketball shorts. *Only* navy basketball shorts.

I set my phone down on the charger. All too quickly, he crawls under the covers. I miss the sight of his solid torso already. The heft of him ripples my side of the mattress. Just the sound of his head hitting the pillow next to mine causes my whole body to unwind.

I could get used to this—sleeping next to my *someone*.

It's early, so no labels, but if tonight was any indication, this isn't a cool-for-the-summer situation. This is something so much more, and I can't wait to explore what it could be.

I reach over to turn out my light, and he does the same. The sheer curtains make it impossible for the room to go completely dark, so it feels like we're in a movie, subsumed in the illusion of bedtime, so the audience at home can still see our faces.

I pinch myself for real, under the sheets since he can't see, to remind myself this isn't a movie. This. Is. Happening.

Flopping over in an offer, Derick's right hand lands smack in the center of the bed. I pull my own hand, the one I just pinched myself with, out from beneath the white comforter and place it rightfully in his.

Fingers interlocked, he brings the back of my hand up to his face, and using the tip of his nose, he draws a languid heart over my knuckle before pressing a kiss into the center like he's an artist signing his work.

"Good night, Wren," he whispers, his breath ghosting up my forearm.

"Good night, Derick."

First names shouldn't be allowed to sound this intimate.

The air conditioner turns over. I lie there and listen as his breathing goes deep, becomes measured. There's a beat to it that intermingles with the swirling woodwinds warming up in my mind. He drifts into sleep, letting out little soft snores that underscore the luscious flutes.

I'm no longer concerned about what he might hear if I talk in my sleep again. The music only I can hear lets me know I'm right where I'm meant to be. I flip onto my back and smile up at the ceiling, thanking whatever lucky star sent me here tonight because this, *this*, is what I've been waiting for.

♡

My eyes flutter open when it's still dark out. Derick's sitting on the edge of the bed putting on a pair of sneakers.

Panic overtakes me. Maybe I should've been concerned. I must've divulged something scandalous in my sleep that scared him off. Is he reconsidering us?

I relax only when he glimpses over at me and smiles with so much warmth he might as well be the Human Torch.

Sleep still holding on to me, I whisper, "Where are you going?" I check the clock. "It's barely 5:00 a.m."

"I woke up and couldn't fall back to sleep. I'm too wired." That makes me feel fuzzy inside and out. "You're not recording until noon, so sleep as long as you want. I figured I'd go for a sunrise run in Central Park." When he stands, I notice he's sporting skintight, black spandex leggings. His calves remind me of the elf tights from the Christmas charity event that somehow feels like just yesterday and a lifetime ago. "I've always wanted to."

"How much longer till sunrise? I'll come with you." I'm awake now and throwing my legs off the side of the bed, even though they feel woozy beneath me from all that alcohol. "It'll be good for me to sweat out these toxins."

He stares at me, stunned almost. "Really? You'd want to go on a run with me?"

"What?" I ask as I sort through my belongings. I didn't bring anything to work out in. Everything I have is nice-casual. "I don't look like someone who would be up for a sunrise run through the park?"

"No, it's not that." He rummages through his own suitcase, sounding animated. "It's just, nobody ever wants to go on runs with me. I'm pleasantly surprised, that's all."

Derick lends me a loose-fitting pair of shorts. I keep on my sleep T-shirt, put on sneakers, and grab the key cards before we go.

The subway gets us to the Museum of Natural History. Its storied stone facade is covered in bold advertisements about upcoming exhibitions and dinosaurs. It's peaceful right now, not yet overrun with families. Kind of like the drive-in at midday.

At the edge of the park, we find a bench. Dawn is approaching. You can almost feel it in the breeze, in the numbers of people that start appearing on every street corner. The pretzel vendors gear up for another day of hawking water bottles under the sweltering sun.

"We should warm up." Derick leads me through a series of stretches, jumping jacks, the works. I'm sweating from the moment we start and my energy is lagging from being up this early, but I'm going to power through. This is important to him. Plus, I want to be fresh and alert for the recording.

When our heart rates are rip-roaring and ready to go, he rubs my shoulders in preparation. "Thanks for doing this. We'll just jog, okay? Ease you into it. Whatever speed you want. You set the pace." I know he's referring to the run, but it feels like he's talking about us. Gratitude washes over me.

The park envelops us. Trees and grass mask the asphalt and chrome of the city. We could be anywhere right now, our feet rising and falling beneath us at a regular rhythm.

Derick hooks a left into the Shakespeare garden where the stone pathways narrow. We slow a bit to take in the whimsical wooden benches. The tranquility is striking, even though my insides are charging up. Flowers in pinks and purples appear like outliers among the blanketing blue-green shrubbery.

"How are you feeling about recording today?" Derick asks, breathing evenly.

I huff, attempting to keep up. "I'm afraid I'm going to sound like a bumbling idiot. I don't do well in front of big crowds."

"It's not a big crowd. It's just you and Oscar."

"What about the thousands of people that will end up listening to it silently, judging me from behind their phones?"

"You can't control their reactions. Don't let them infiltrate something good."

"You're right. This"—I motion with my free hand to the trail—"is definitely helping keep my mind off things."

"Good." He grins at me with a side glance. "I'm glad."

Feeling daring, I pick up the pace.

The first licks of sunlight break through the leaves. They hit the black iron lampposts, creating the illusion that they're lit during daytime, a scenic oxymoron. Nature starts waking up along with my body; my lungs expand and contract with pressing ease.

Derick decides we should do a loop around the Great Lawn. It's clear he doesn't care how free-form this run will be, whether I'm slowing him down or not, whether he's hitting his usual calorie burn. He's just letting us enjoy our time together.

Women power walk with strollers in front of them. Baby hands fly out to wave as we pass. I catch Derick's smile as we round the empty softball diamonds. I could stare at that smile forever.

The skyscrapers begin to glint in the distance like squared-off, snowy mountain peaks doused in early morning blue. It's absolute bliss, until I stop dead in my tracks because there in front of us is a slate-gray stone miniature castle with a turret that appears to have been plucked from a fairy tale.

"What? Are you okay? Did you pull a muscle, get a cramp?" Derick asks, stopping beside me. All I can do is point at the castle. "It's beautiful, right? That's Belvedere Castle. It quite literally means beautiful view in Italian. Do you want to go up?"

"Can we?"

He takes my hand and leads the way. The castle isn't massive by any means, but from every angle it exudes an idyllic regality that fascinates me. It oozes romanticism, right up until we get stopped at the door. The green sign reads: *Open Hours 9 a.m.–7 p.m.*

"Damn," Derick says, looking around at the others who mill about the low-area lookout.

"Can we come back later?" I ask.

He shakes his head. "Bus is at four, right after you're done with Oscar. We wouldn't make it."

Disappointment drips like the sweat off my brow.

"We'll just have to come back another time."

Another time. Another trip. A promise of future togetherness.

That's when we spy a fussy photographer, an uptight wedding planner, and two women in all white traipsing up the steps. Behind the pack there's a park officer with a set of keys. It's clear they're about to take their engagement photos.

Derick and I share the same thought. We hang casually by the door until they've unlocked it and disappeared up the steps. Swiftly, Derick catches the closing door with his foot, and when we're certain they're out of sight, we slip inside, sticking to the shadowy corners of the main floor.

The tight-squeeze circular stairwell is a viper pit of echoes, and we try our best not to be heard, but our plan only gets us so far. As the cameraperson sets up their tripod, the wedding planner's face curdles as she zeroes in on us.

"Excuse me, this is a closed session. You're not supposed to be up here," she growls. "Where is security on these shoots? It's like we prep for nothing!" Clearly, she hasn't had her morning coffee yet.

I start to stammer out an excuse but nothing comes to me.

The shorter of the two brides-to-be—a petite woman with short black hair shaved at the sides—catches how frantic I look, how defensive Derick gets, grabbing my hand in protection. Something sweet smooths out her baffled expression when she overhears.

"They're with us," she says, shooting a tiny thumbs-up to us behind the planner's back. "Jeanine, don't worry. They're, uh"—she fumbles—"distant cousins. Forgot they were visiting. They're just here to watch. They won't bother us."

The other fiancée pushes off the railing and comes over: "Suz, who are these—"

"Becs," Shaved-Sides says, "You remember my cousins…Hugh and, uh, Grant."

Derick does his classic laugh into a cough that sounds like a burp. Then, I'm laugh-cough-burping. And so is Shaved-Sides—Suz. Even her soon-to-be is doing it, too, playing along with whatever is going on here. I like them immediately. The only person who isn't doing it is Jeanine, who's stabbing something into her iPad with an Apple Pencil while rolling her eyes into oblivion.

"Guests needed to be registered with the park and the planning agency in advance but I suppose it's fine," she gripes. As she's walking away, under her breath, I hear her mutter, "Do a lesbian wedding, they said! It'll be fun, they said!"

"Don't mind her. She's not a homophobe. She hates everyone equally," Suz says, rolling her eyes and running a hand through her longer hairs.

"Stop!" Becs says. "You don't want any stick-ups during the shoot. I worked so hard on that this morning."

Suz looks at me as Becs licks her palm to flatten down her fly-aways. "This is what I have to look forward to for the rest of my life. Aren't I a lucky lady?"

"Shut up! You'd be a mess without me." Becs giggles. "And I'm not just referring to your hair."

"How long have you two been together?" Suz asks, glancing between our bashful faces.

Derick pipes up, "This is actually really new..." His hand slips into mine again.

Becs paws at the white pussy bow on her blouse and says, "Sneaking around, breaking in, crashing private events... Ah, the honeymoon phase... I remember it well."

"I guess you'll have the Honeymoon Phase 2.0 soon," I say, eyeing their matching engagement bands, both with gargantuan diamonds. They must be quite wealthy to afford bling like that and private access to a photo location like this one.

"We haven't planned anything yet. We're a one-day-at-a-time kind of couple," Suz says.

"Yeah," Becs chimes in. "Why plan a tropical getaway cruise a year in advance when you might be big into theater and want to hit up the West End by the time you tie the knot?"

"You would never!" cries Suz. "She once asked if Chekhov's *The Seagull* was about Skuttle from *The Little Mermaid*."

"*The Little Mermaid*'s a musical. She must like that stage show," I offer.

"*Psh*. She's just got the hots for mermaids. One time, she made me buy this tail so we could—"

"Okay! That's enough," Becs cuts in. "Let's not scar the children." She smiles warmly. "Stay as long as you want. We paid enough for it. Enjoy the sunrise."

"They're ready for you! We can't lose the light!" Jeanine snaps, one cell phone stuffed between her shoulder and her ear, another in between her clacking fingernails.

"We will. Thanks," Derick says.

When we cross to the ledge to take in the panorama, I'm floored with the way the light brings new dimensions to the landscape. Derick moves in closer to me so our elbows are knocking. His oops-did-I-make-you-blush smile might just be my favorite smile of all.

Even though we're perspiring and in need of showers, I turn in to him, letting him wrap his arms around me the way I know he wants to. When I tilt my head to look up at him, body electric, he whispers sensitively, "Would it be okay if I kissed your forehead?"

Without hesitation, I sweep my sweaty bangs out of the way, and tenderly, his lips tattoo themselves to the spot.

At once, it's like the sunrise is inside of me.

 *Transcript*

Transcript Excerpt of Episode 407 Don't You Forget About..._Chompin'_
At The Bit (1978) director Alice Kelly. Guest: Wren Roland, Wiley's Drive-In

WR: As you know, Alice's film was originally supposed to have a local
premiere at Wiley's Drive-In in summer of 1978. Unfortunately, after the
disastrous New York and LA premieres, she disowned the film and went
into hiding. The owner of Wiley's at the time, Chet Wiley—Earl Wiley's
father—knew the Kelly family and didn't want to dishonor Alice's wishes by
going forward with the event after the production company pulled the film
from distribution.

OV: You're remounting a missed opportunity?

WR: Exactly. It had exploitation film sensibilities, so it would've
appealed to that late-seventies drive-in crowd who wanted to see zombies,
the undead, all that, but it had an emotional core that would've resonated
with more character-driven indie fans. Probably hard to market without
being misleading. Additionally, I think Ms. Kelly is more comfortable and
confident in her work. She's also open to the queer reading of the film that
an audience then might not have been ready to accept even if bisexuality was
starting to be talked about in publications like *TIME* magazine.

OV: Do you think a remake could be in the future? Another film for
Ms. Kelly?

WR: Well, Ms. Kelly is suffering from aggressive macular degeneration. I don't think she'd be in good enough health to step behind the camera again, but stranger things have happened. I do think she might open herself up to more interviews. Let us into the world of an independent female filmmaker, discuss the challenges she faced in the business more openly. I mean, she was one of about sixteen women working as major directors at the time, all white, all well-to-do, all pretty highly regarded, yet they faced backlash and sometimes disgusting harassment from the suits in power.

OV: Yes, I mean, we're still in a world where parity is far from the norm. Look at major studio email leaks that show gross wage inequality. Look at assault-

survivor social movements that are holding men accountable for their repulsive actions, even as most are still getting away with it. Hollywood has not reckoned with the ways in which it fails the women it claims to uphold.

WR: Knowing Alice, I know she would never want to be painted as a victim of circumstance, but you're not wrong that the hierarchy chewed her up and spit her out. There are a lot of theories about why and how this happened that I can't wait to dive into later in this pod.

OV: I agree, and we'll get to those within the hour. Maybe we'll have to do a two-parter. Since I posted about this episode, there has been an outpouring from young female directors tweeting their support of Alice Kelly and shaming the misogynistic industry for brushing her seemingly bright career under the rug. Has Alice seen this?

WR: No, no. She's not on social media. Honestly, she barely watches TV besides the news and *The Mary Tyler Moore Show*. I will be sure to let her know, though. That's wonderful.

OV: So, let's start by talking about Willow Valley, Alice's birthplace and current home. Can you tell us a little about Alice's time there and how it inspired the movie?

WR: Sure. Before I begin, I know Alice is keen on selling her Willow Valley property, so as you're listening, if anyone out there wants a historically significant farmhouse, I know a woman I can connect you with!

OV: *Don't You Forget About...* part podcast, part Zillow ad, all fun! I love it. Let's get down to it...

Chapter 21

Derick's house is a McMansion screen-grabbed from a dream homes TV show. The kind of house that began as a modest two-story, but after years of accumulated wealth and extensions has become a jig-sawed structure with six bedrooms, four-and-a-half baths, and an in-ground pool with a built-in Bluetooth speaker system. From the outside, it's a behemoth, and from the inside, it feels like it's digesting me.

When Derick texted to say I'd been invited to dinner by his parents, I had to read the message three times through to be sure I understood. Only days ago, he'd deceived them into spending money on what essentially ended up being a couples' trip for us. Now, I'm sitting in the formal dining room, white carpet beneath my feet like they expect no one to ever spill or drip.

A painted portrait of the Haverford family hangs on the wall opposite me. Derick looks young, uncertain, and out of sorts in a scratchy-looking sweater and collared shirt combo. They're a beautiful family, to say the least.

Derick rode on the coattails of his two older brothers through the halls of Willow Valley High—a robotics club wizard turned not-yet-launched app designer, and the debate team's secret weapon turned lawyer. The Haverford legacy loomed large, like the painting in front of me does, and Derick always struck me as the outlier—the goofy, artsy one. Despite that, his last name left him at the top of the food chain. His laurels were so stupendous that he charmingly didn't even know he was resting on them.

I've been here a handful of times for pool parties in elementary school before the cliques became constants and everyone stopped being invited to everything. Derick and his brothers weren't the type to throw mythic parties when they came of age, though. Their parents were helicopters with top-of-the-line security cameras and no tolerance for the repercussions an underaged rager might bring upon them.

I popped by on rare occasions when Derick needed to pick up something before one of our co-dates, but for the most part he avoided bringing me here. For a while, I thought maybe he was embarrassed of me. Now, that seems less likely.

Mrs. Haverford enlisted Derick's help in the kitchen, putting the finishing touches on the roast she's made. The scent wafts in as Mr. Haverford saunters by with David, the lawyer and the second oldest of the Haverford brood, and his wife, Preeti, a gynecologist from Philadelphia. She has rich brown skin with a long, tight braid running down her back.

"Mr. Roland, delighted you could join us." Mr. Haverford extends a well-kept hand toward me. He wears a gaudy gold watch with an encrusted face that appears to weigh down his wrist.

"Thank you for the invitation."

"I trust you and my son enjoyed your stay in the city," he says with slithery subtext, settling himself into the high-backed chair at the head of the cherrywood table.

"Yes, sir." I should probably feel guilty about the situation but I don't. Derick remained steadfast in his defiance, telling me it had blown over. If they've moved past it, then I'm not about to reverse matters by saying anything out of turn. "It was lovely."

My voice is much stronger than I expect it to be. I prickle, nevertheless, wondering what's taking Derick so long. Idle chatter has always made me uncomfortable. The weather is standard for this time of year, hot but not too humid, and I don't have any opinions on the latest Tesla model, so my mind is blank.

"Glad to hear it was partially for business and not just for pleasure." The way he says *pleasure* sits poorly with me. David shoots his dad a deadly we've-been-over-this look. "If only my son had that kind of drive." Mr. Haverford unfolds his linen napkin.

"Derick's doing great at the drive-in," I say, coming to his defense.

"I've been following his social media accounts," Preeti says. "The pictures of the drive-in make it look so quaint and cute. I've never been to a drive-in before."

"You should come by," I say. "I'm happy to comp you in any time. Derick really has an eye for what makes the lot special. He even got firsthand experience when he helped us in the concessions stand."

"He did what?" Mr. Haverford asks, turning his ear to me like he misheard.

"We were short-

staffed a few weeks back, and he pitched in slinging hot dogs and scooping Polish water ice—the whole nine yards."

"It wasn't a big deal, Dad," Derick says, entering from the kitchen with a platter of sides. He's wearing ironed slacks and a shirt with a starched collar. He looks like a buttoned-up, cardboard-cutout version of himself. That's until he smiles at me and he melds back into flesh and bone, tender and attractive.

"Clear the way," Mrs. Haverford says, oven mitts on, a steaming roast on a serving platter in her hands. Derick swerves to the side, and she sets the cut beef down as a centerpiece. It's topped with frizzled onions over a bed of arugula with roasted carrots all around.

"New York Strip roast. Brought a little city back to the country." Mrs. Haverford calls for Alexa to play her easy-listening Linda Ronstadt playlist. Derick gives a not-this-again eye roll. "Wren, darling, it's been far too long since we've seen you. Look at you. You're all grown up!"

"I suppose I am," I say, laughing. I'm not the ten-year-old boy who dropped ice cream cake on his lap at Derick's half-birthday party (yes, they had half-birthday parties, too) and had to be changed into a spare pair of his shorts because Mom was at work and Dad wasn't picking up the phone.

The sides get passed around. I load my plate with vegetables and mashed potatoes. Mr. Haverford's eyes never leave our side of the table. What is he watching for?

"Derick, how *has* your time at the drive-in been? Aside from your stint in the snack shack." Mr. Haverford makes the snack shack sound like it's a lurid hotbed of sin.

"It's been nice. It's a good place to work. Thanks for setting it up." He's so submissive, head bowed, fork scraping over his plate. I squeeze his hand to buoy him. "I like it there."

"Well, that's good, but it is a temporary position." Mr. Haverford chews his medium-rare steak with razor-sharp incisors. I see now where Derick gets his carnivorous ways. "You'd do well to remember that."

Derick slumps even lower in his seat. It's rude of his father to be reprimanding him in front of company, making him feel worse about having to transition over to the family business when the season ends. This further explains why Derick kept me out of this house when we were in high school. I change the subject to save him from further passive-aggressive flogging. "How was South Carolina?"

"Oh, lovely, thanks," Mrs. Haverford says, dabbing the corners of her peach-tinted mouth. "It's nice to be home for a bit, though. We spend a lot of our time biking and walking the beach there, and my back is not what it used to be. I'm accustomed to my nightly soaks in the hot tub here, but we don't have one down there just yet." Her eyes fly to Mr. Haverford's face. It's a source of dispute, I can tell.

"That sounds nice," I say and then stuff my mouth with glazed carrots.

"Doesn't it? You boys should take a dip in the pool this evening after dinner and then sit for a spell. If you shut the lights out on the back patio and tilt your head back, you can see so many stars. It's peaceful," she says wistfully. Maybe she's a romantic like me.

"We'll join you," David adds of him and Preeti.

"Derick tells us you recorded a podcast episode while you were away," Preeti says.

The recording feels like a little lifetime ago, the puffy headphones hugging my ears and a spit-shielded microphone in my face. It went well. The banter and passion came easily. Oscar put me at ease even as the morning-run endorphins surged within me.

"When can we hear the finished product?" she asks. "I love podcasts. It's like eavesdropping on a million interesting conversations. The hosts start to feel like your friends."

"Hopefully, the beginning of August. We're coordinating the drop with the Alice Kelly event we're throwing at Wiley's."

"What event is this?" Mrs. Haverford asks.

Has Derick not even mentioned Alice once? We've spent the last month and a half redoing her house. Mateo and Avery get earfuls of her wild antics every time I come home drenched, tired, and starving. I don't shut up about her.

"It's—"

Derick cuts in. "A special screening. That's all. The roast is fantastic, Mom."

Mrs. Haverford beams.

When everyone returns to their plates, Derick mouths to me, "They just won't get it," and then shrugs. I offer a half smile and slice off another hunk of steak.

♡

Later, I'm up in Derick's bedroom. I'm supposed to be changing into one of his old swimsuits, but I'm struck. This space is nothing like I remember from the ice cream cake incident of old. When we stopped here in high school, I never made it up the stairs. In and out. Quick stops that never necessitated a hello or a goodbye.

It's austere now, gallery-like, clean lines and little color. The walls are bright white and covered in rows and rows of black picture frames with pebbled white matting.

Each frame showcases a different one of Derick's photos.

I ignore the blue shorts with a crashing wave pattern across the front and give myself a full tour of his space, the place he can be alone and himself at any time. The room smells like his signature cologne, and the floors have a zigzag pattern to them.

On the far side, beyond a modern-looking black metallic desk with a small collection of books on top—*Paul Strand: Sixty Years of Photographs* pushed up against a textbook about branded storytelling—is a new addition to the collection of pictures. It's the photo of me from Dunkin' Donuts, the one he posted on the Wiley's Instagram, redone in gray scale. The shadows add a hint of mystery.

Just below, on the hook attached to the desk, he's slung the scarf from his high school Halloween costume.

Something old. Something new.

My heart races. I've always wanted commitment, yet I've never imagined it would be this scary. Handing your heart to someone else is an act of frightening defiance. Tom Hanks and Meg Ryan should've warned me about that.

Out the back window, down below, Derick is standing at the edge of the pool, a skimmer pole in his hands. The color-changing lights below the surface of the water reflect onto his face, his features changing from hazy orange to mossy green. When he looks up and catches me peering at him from the window, my body begins to flutter. He waves and yells for me to come out.

I stuff myself into the slim trunks and hightail it back downstairs, until I'm intercepted by David. He's in a pair of board shorts and expensive-looking flip-flops. "Wren, may I borrow you for a minute?" There's something in his tone that lets me know it's not a request. My stomach clenches as he ushers me into an office, which has the same modern stylings as Derick's room. It's as if an interior designer came through the entire house, threw out all personal effects, and went with the first idea that popped into their head: monochrome.

"Have a seat," he says, gesturing to a geometric chair in front of the impressive desk. This must be where Mr. Haverford works from home.

The scratchy, thin bathing-suit fabric slides wrong against the pristine black leather. It's like I'm about to reprimanded by a headmaster at a boarding school exclusively for Apple geniuses. "So, what are your intentions with my brother?"

I stifle a laugh. That's what this is? The classic big-brother shakedown when meeting a new partner—or whatever we're calling ourselves since New York. It's new for me, but not uncalled for. "I promise my intentions are good."

"I'm glad to hear you say that." He toys with a decorative glass orb resting in a silver bowl. "As I'm sure you know, my brother went through some shit with his last boyfriend, and I kicked myself for not stepping up for him. Derick's special. He's sensitive. He needs a boyfriend he can count on."

I choke on my own saliva. *Boyfriend?* Has Derick been referring to me as his boyfriend? A word has never made my heart fully stop before. In a good way, I mean. Overcoming the immediate shock, I reassure David, "He can count on me."

Silence falls over us. I wait a beat, wondering if that's all he called me in here for. To ascertain my true feelings and be sure they were pure enough for his baby brother. It's sweet, if somewhat old-fashioned. But I don't mind old-fashioned. That's the kind of romance I've always craved.

He eventually breaks the intense eye contact. "Good. I always could tell you were a good one, Wren." The hard-guy act falls away to reveal a friendly smile. He pats my shoulder as I stand.

Right before we step out back, David adds, "I'm glad you two could work it out despite everything that's going on with my dad. It's not personal."

Before I can ask for further clarification, he zooms over to Preeti. They shed their extra layers by the lounge chairs and race each other into the pool. Father John Misty's discography plays at a low volume—Derick's request. Something about *real love, baby*. You can tell the two in the water have it by the way they try to reenact the *Dirty Dancing* lift halfway toward the deep end. It's a spectacular, flailing fail, but it doesn't stop them from trying again almost immediately, laughing all the while.

"What took you so long?" Derick asks.

"David roped me into a quick conversation." Derick shuffles his feet. "He shared something very interesting," I say, a teasing lilt to my voice. Derick must not pick up on it, because he appears aghast.

"I can explain, Wren. I was going to tell you. Actually, I've been trying to tell you all night that…"

I cut him off. "That you called me your *boyfriend*?" It's funny to no longer be play flirting. This is the main event, real-deal flirting, and it's deliciously fun after all that practice.

"Oh. That." He sets the long, blue net up against the cabana where they keep their pool supplies. "I sort of let that word slip out in conversation a day or so ago, and when I tried to take it back, he kept mocking me about it, and I know we haven't had that conversation, so I told him not to say anything, but he's my older brother and he loves to troll me so of course he did." He throws a fiery glare in his brother's direction. Too bad David's too busy kissing Preeti to take notice.

"It's okay. Family is family. Claire would've totally done the same thing."

I want to ask if he meant it, if he wants to make this official, but...

"Hey, lovebirds!" Preeti calls from the waterfall. "Up for a game of chicken?"

Derick is all too down for fun and games. Daring me with his eyes and abandoning our conversation, he throws off his shirt, and cannonballs into the pool. Thankfully, I've been wearing my contacts instead of my glasses, so I chase right after him. I hold my breath and pinch my nose as I vault off the edge.

"Wren's cannonball takes the prize," Preeti cries when I come up for air, adrenaline coursing through me.

David splashes her. "Nuh-uh. No way. Derick's had more air time."

"Wren's had more pizzazz!"

"Pizzazz? We're giving points for pizzazz?" David asks like they aren't two late-twenties adults arguing over a cannonball competition they just made up on the spot.

"We doing this or what?" Derick asks of the game.

As Preeti mounts David's shoulders, Derick swims up underneath me and taps my legs apart. His shoulders lock below my knees, and right away I'm weightless, straddling his skull.

Derick and David find equal footing close enough to the center of the pool that if either of us falls, we won't crack out heads open. My jittery heart hiccups each time Derick readjusts his grip on my shins.

"3...2...1!" Derick cries.

Preeti and I engage in hand-to-hand combat. I push and shove, while she pulls and prods. She's a worthy sparring partner, and my meager upper body strength is severely tested. Derick's encouraging cheers spur me on.

One bad move happens, though, a sneaky twist of the wrist, and I miss Preeti's final blow for dominance. The thrust sends both me and Derick falling back into the deep end. I slide from my perch, and the world goes lavender.

I open my eyes underwater, even though it's terrible for my contacts.

Derick is staring back at me with wonderment. Time stops here in our own personal fishbowl. I could swim in circles by his side forever.

As he comes up for air, Derick's eyes find mine again. It's as if they're trying to send me a message, but I don't have the proper tools to decode it just yet. I need more time to study him. I hope he'll give me that. *Time.*

Preeti sashaying out of the pool pulls me from the moment. David is waiting with a victory towel to wrap around her shivering body. "No hot tub?" Derick calls after them.

"No way, the real adults have work in the morning." Preeti sticks her tongue out at us. "Don't get into too much trouble."

"Yeah, don't do anything I wouldn't do," David calls with a devilish glint of his teeth.

Preeti smacks him. "Don't encourage him."

Derick flushes as the two of them cross back into the kitchen, barefoot and damp.

"Should we hot tub it out?" he asks me.

The temperature is already set at 101 degrees Fahrenheit, and the jets are on full blast, making the water frothy, white, and bubbly. The steam rises into the air and swirls around my face. It's almost mystical.

Derick moves to the switch near the door, dims all the lights like his mom said to.

When I get into the water, allowing my muscles to unclench, I look up. It's as if the gods are practicing pointillism with white paint and the bruised Pennsylvania sky is their canvas. New sparkling specks appear each time I turn my head, a hypnotic optical illusion.

I sense Derick beside me before I see him. I'm too mesmerized, too grateful, too wrapped up in this moment to even think to overthink. The fumbling conversation from earlier gets struck from the record, and I embolden myself to rewrite it in real time. "If you meant it, really meant it, like I think you did, it's okay to call me your boyfriend. I mean, I want to *be* your boyfriend. If that's what you want, too."

His audible exhale registers like a long-held sigh of ecstasy. "That's exactly what I want, Wren." His careful earnestness makes my heart sing.

"Can I kiss you?" I ask.

Hunger is laced into his whispery growl. "Absolutely you can."

With his permission, I pull myself up to his level, grabbing the sturdy, smooth mounds of his shoulders. And just like that, I kiss his lips so tenderly that I might cry. Not from sadness. Not from happiness. From…I don't even know what. And I don't really care.

I lean back to take in his astonished face, memorize the passion in his eyes and the slight wrinkle of his forehead. Every nerve ending in my body is at full attention, making sure not to miss a single moment of this.

With only the stars as my witness, I kiss him again, deeper, and to my surprise, it doesn't feel like scratching an act off a list or completing a quest: it feels like coming home.

Chapter 22

"Who are you? Whattaya want? How'd you get in here?" Alice jumps out of her chair, and her hands fly up in defense. "Don't make me sic my dogs on you! They're ruthless! Vicious! They'll tear you to shreds!"

I knocked a bunch of times on Alice's front door when I arrived, but she couldn't hear me over the booming TV. We're friends now, or at least I'd like to think so, and when I jiggled the knob and noticed it was unlocked, I let myself in.

"Alice! Alice! It's me. It's Wren," I say, raising my hands to let her know I come in peace.

She squints with apprehension. "What's wrong with your face?"

I reach up to feel for what she's talking about. "Oh," I breathe out. "I put in my contacts today. I'm not wearing my glasses." Ever since New York, I've felt compelled to keep up this streak. I don't see better without my frames per se, but I have more peripheral vision, which is helpful when working the lot.

"Jesus, warn an old woman next time you burst into her home without knocking." She fixes her fussy hair.

"I did knock. Four times. You just had the TV too loud to hear me." I venture farther into the room. Barbra Streisand stands before a lecture hall of college students in round glasses and a dowdy outfit. She's speaking about the fictional idealization of romance. "You're watching *The Mirror Has Two Faces*?" I gape. "Wait, you're watching a *movie*?"

After all this time, she's breaching her film ban for my favorite

Streisand-directed feature. "Don't get your panties twisted into a bunch! I decided I would give them a try since I'll soon have to watch my own. Break my forty-year streak."

"Forty years? Alice, that's an excessively long time."

"There were plenty of times I was tempted to walk into a Cineplex and sit down in the back row. There were times I flipped channels and caught the end of a feature and thought, hmm, maybe just one. But, I couldn't do that to myself because if I fell back on old habits.... I'm a tough broad, but even tough broads have their limits."

There's a murky layer of understanding coated like soy candle wax over her words. "I get it. Have you watched anything else?"

"I've already binged through *Yentl* and *The Prince of Tides* while you were away. Figured it was time to see her final directorial work."

"Final? She's not gone yet! She's got time." I'm speaking about Barbra, yet I'm really planting a thought seed in Alice's head. After Oscar and my recorded conversation, I want to water that seed, nourish her emaciated career until it's in full bloom again.

"Your boyish optimism is deeply irritating."

Ignoring her remark, I say, "Baffling to think Barbra's still one of only two women to ever win a Best Director Golden Globe." Alice invites me to sit in the chair on the opposite side of her circular end table. There are a lamp, a cup of tea, and two biscotti between us. "How did the meeting with the real estate agent go?"

"She's coming in a week and a half. The initial call went well. I had Candice email photos over. She said it looked enticing." She shrugs, downplaying the importance. "How did it go with the podperson?"

"You make him sound like some Black Lagoon creature." I roll my eyes at her. "Everything with Oscar went well. He let me know over the weekend that his editor and producers were thrilled. He'd done an episode on one of Peter's films a few years ago, so they're pulling some audio clips from the archives to cross-reference."

"Good thing that man died young. Hearing his name up against mine all these years later, well, that would've given him a third heart attack." She lets out a sadistic laugh. "I don't mean to speak ill of the dead."

"Of course." I can tell she loved him in a unique way I'll never quite understand based on how he treated her and discarded her like useless set dressing.

"More importantly, how did your trip go?" she asks.

My blush broadcasts our *official* status loud and clear.

She demands details by pounding her fist on the table in triumph. I'm far too giddy to get it all out. I weave in the meeting, the movie, the bar, and the singular bed. "You didn't give it all up, did you?" she asks.

"No." I decide not to go into detail about my demisexuality. Bisexuality was a tough enough talking point for her. This explanation would be extra draining. I've decided when people ask how I identify, if I feel comfortable, I'll say "queer." An encompassing word that encapsulates my demisexuality and my homoromantic nature, without needing to feel like a dissection frog in an anatomy class. "But, we did finally kiss."

Her mouth opens so wide I'm afraid her dentures might fall out. "Who kissed who?"

"Who kissed *whom*," I correct. Avery is really rubbing off on me. "I kissed him. And he kissed me back."

"Where'd you do it? At the top of the Empire State Building like what almost was in *An Affair to Remember*?" All this time I've been itching to know more about her, and this is the first moment it seems the feeling might be mutual.

"No, but we should watch that one together since you're back on movies. I've never seen it. Though, I feel like I have after Rita Wilson's iconic monologue in *Sleepless in Seattle*." Alice's expression is blank. "Right. That one released in 1993. You have four decades of female-directed films to work through. You have no idea what you're in for. Anyway, we kissed at his house." I leave out the hot-tub part. I don't want to scandalize her. Though she was a woman-of-a-certain age in the seventies. Probably nothing could scandalize her.

"I love saying I told you so… I told you so!" Alice is bright-eyed, happy, and enjoying movies again. She's done a complete one-eighty since those initial days in early June. "Alright. Enough about real romance. I want to find out what happens between the calculus professor and the literature professor who take sex out of the $x + y$ equation." She picks up the remote then asks, "You staying?"

For most, this wouldn't be a welcoming invitation, but right now, I'd be stupid to say no. She offers me the second biscotto as the flick starts back up. We sit in silence and laugh, cry, and squeal together through the amusing rom-com dramedy.

♡

Mateo's belt could shatter glass.

It's game night in 3B—a monthly tradition we forgot all about during June due to life being life—and now we're midway through a rousing game of Be a Broadway Star!

Obviously, it was Mateo's turn in the rotation to pick the game. He keeps this one stashed safely in his closet and breaks it out every three months. While Avery and I will hem and haw over Monopoly or Parcheesi, Mateo will run to his room and grab this one every time. My Fosse walks have gotten much better since freshman year. At one point, Avery and I even started listening to original Broadway cast recordings in the car just so we could stand a chance.

Right now, I'm being crushed, so I'm not sure it helped any.

The movie earlier was longer than I remembered, though I forgot how much I loved the ending credits where the leads dance to a sweeping duet around a vacant New York City street, so I was in a rush to get back to the apartment. The board was already set up in the living room along with a few bottles of cheap wine and snacking chocolates. It's our night off from the lot, so we have the whole evening to ourselves. No partners allowed.

Mateo finishes a snippet as the Witch from *Into the Woods*, then says: "We're all set for Queer Date Night Deluxe next Monday. Brandon wants to do a Bolognese. Wren, you can grab cannolis from the bakery, since I know you'd pout without them. And, Aves, babe, do you think you or Stacia could do a salad? Oh, wait, maybe fresh mozzarella and tomatoes? Make the theme When in Rome!"

Stacia's name makes Avery light up. "Sure, I'll ask. If she can't, I can. I know she's busy. She's planning a trip to Greece at the end of August to visit her extended family for the first time."

"How very *Mamma Mia!*" Mateo says.

I pop a piece of chocolate and ask, "Is this another FWB scenario, or something else?"

"We haven't talked about it. She agreed to come to the triple date next week, so I'm thinking that's a good sign?" Avery tepidly plays with her curls. That's when I spot something new just below her ear.

"Um, excuse me, what is that?"

When she tucks her hair back, we get a full view of the sketch: It's a llama with butterfly wings and a lizard tail. "She said this is how she sees me." I don't make a snide comment about how her hookup sees her as a spitting pack animal because I'm a good friend. The wings, however, are really detailed and lovely.

"Is it permanent?" I ask.

She grimaces. "No, she did this last night with a temporary tattoo marker. We were lying in her bed and she asked if she could draw something on me, so I said sure. You know those stamps I'm obsessed with?"

"Noooooo, what stamps?" Mateo and I say in near unison. "Stamps? I don't know her," Mateo adds. She throws a pillow in our direction.

"You guys suck! She makes those! Like, she sketches and has a friend who works in the rubber-stamp business. She sends off her designs, and the friend does all the manufacturing. When she came to Wiley's a few weeks back, she told me how much she loved the vibe of the place, so I mentioned she should make a special zombie stamp for Alice's movie."

"I wouldn't say no to that." I laugh, circumventing Avery's attempt to change the subject. "Would you ever get that done for real?" I crawl over for a closer look.

She runs her pointer finger down the design. "Maybe. Let's see how the triple date goes before I make any permanent body modifications. I don't want to end up the cliché queer girl with a tattoo from her ex on her mastoid." She sets her hair back in its rightful place. "I told myself I'm not jumping the gun this time. I will not rush to DTR before we FSO."

"Fight some ostriches?" Mateo asks.

"Figure shit out," she says, chugging the last of the wine straight from the bottle.

"But you're happy?" I ask.

She battles off a smile, but she doesn't win. "Yeah. Yup. I am."

"Can you believe it—all of us, happy at one time?" It feels weird. Shouldn't someone be in turmoil? This is the first instance we've all been "seeing someone" at the same time. No major drama to unpack in our apartment for a change. "It's nice."

As soon as I speak it, I notice it's my turn. I roll the dice, hoping to catch up to Mateo, and instead land on a spot that reads: "Ego trip. Demand more money. Lose three fan cards." I groan and hand over my losses.

"That's showbiz, folks!" Mateo announces in a Porky Pig voice, before kick-lining his way to the fridge for more wine.

God, I love these idiots.

Chapter 23

There's something fresh about the lot tonight.

The popcorn smells butterier. The kids running around sound happier. Even sundown is more colorful and luminescent than it usually is. A Creamsicle caked across the sky.

Is the world changing course, or am I just stopping to smell the roses? It's like I'm living inside a kaleidoscope. Every moment with Derick is like a twist of the viewfinder, dazzling and incandescent.

I greet everyone by name on my way through the snack shack and into the office. Derick texted to let me know he'd be a little late. He wanted to get some mock-ups of the posters for Alice's event printed at an office supply store to show Earl. He's proud of his design, as he should be, and I think he craves Earl's approval as much as I do at this point. Earl has that grandfatherly energy that makes you feel like if you impress him he'll reward you with a hard candy from his secret stash and a quarter for your troubles.

Avery is already making her rounds through the snack-shack displays, ensuring everything is organized and presented to perfection. Mateo, as usual, is slacking off, but not in an egregious way, so I let it slide. He still has a hard time seeing me as his friend and his boss, so it doesn't even register that he shouldn't be on his phone when I pass.

The booth is quiet, which is good. I have logistics emails to send—updates on the wet-gate restoration and digitization of the film, finalizing our online reservation platform, and making sure the schedule for that evening is air-tight. There's a lot left to be accomplished before August 14 and not a lot of time to do it.

Earl is stingy with the Wi-Fi password. He doesn't want us employees hogging up the bandwidth, so I have to log in to his fossilized desktop computer. The mouse barely connects, but I finally get the screen to load and the internet browser to launch.

Usually, I'm the last one logged in since Earl doesn't use Gmail (since he thinks Google is keeping too many tabs on him), but I'm surprised to see his own sketchy email browser opened. The inbox is mostly ads for multivitamins, hair regrowth treatments, big-box stores, and, inexplicably, a multitude of Bath & Bodyworks special offers. He must really enjoy his foaming, floral hand soaps.

It's beyond the coupons and deals that I spy an email address I don't expect to see:

FROM: DHaverford@AnyWeatherTransport.com
TO: Owner@WileysDriveIn.com
SUBJECT: Review Board Meeting

Dear Earl Wiley,

Thank you for meeting with me to discuss the demolition of your drive-in. I understand how long this business has been in your family, and sympathize with the struggles of management and upkeep of a small business such as yours. Any Weather was nothing more than a single bus and a dream when it started.

As discussed, I am prepared to go before the Historic Review Board on Tuesday to get our certificate of appropriateness for full demolition. Any Weather will, in turn, make the drive-in a paid commuter parking lot for a new, commercial Willow Valley bus line pickup hub. This is crucial to the livelihood of our community, so we assure you: this is the right thing to do.

You, being an upstanding Willow Valleyian, see the value and immense opportunity this can bring to a small town such as ours. We honor the history of what you, your father, and your grandfather built, but know that today, everything is accessible by phone and on the go. There is simply no need for a drive-in nor a want for the novelty of one.

You are welcome to attend the meeting as our application provides certainty that we intend to fund a historic marker commemorating your lot to be displayed by the pay machines. A prime location of remembrance.

Again, thank you for your understanding. This was a difficult decision for me as well.

Your fellow townies will be forever grateful to you for your sacrifice.

Only my best,
Daniel P. Haverford

Qualified rage flames out from my gut. While I was off in New York City, giving my best go at creating an event that could help resuscitate this place, Earl was off solidifying its demise? Sure, we're hurting. Sure, we're a non-necessity. Hell, we may even be a relic like Earl said earlier this summer, but we're also nostalgia, love, joy. A place to make memories.

Novelty? What does Daniel P. Haverford know about novelty? We provide summer delight in the night! Earl says it every year, and I witness it on the faces of those that leave our lot happy with salty fingers and plenty to discuss. How could this be happening when everything seemed to be going so well?

Emails continue to be my undoing. I wish the whole pesky platform would destruct, but, yeah right, the internet is forever. I thought Wiley's was, too. How naive I'd been.

My impulse is to go searching for Earl, but when I whip around, he's already there, looking at me with folded arms and anguish threaded into his brow. I go to yell, finger pointed and trembling, but nothing comes out. My voice is stuck in my throat, blocked up by too many garbled words.

"I'm sorry, kid." He starts to sweat under his mustache, a telltale sign that what I just read wasn't a fabrication.

"You're sorry?" I croak. "You sold the drive-in for what, a parking lot? Why would you do that?"

He closes the door so nobody can hear us. "I didn't sell recently, Wren. Mr. Haverford already owned the lot. It's his decision what to do with it."

"Wh-what?" I stammer.

"A while back, when studios stopped printing films of their features, I had a choice to make: pawn the 35mm 1949 projectors and go digital or stop showing new releases. I knew we couldn't compete in the market if we went the retro route." His hands dig so deep into the pockets of his threadbare jeans that I fear his fingers might pop out the other side. "The decision was simple: secure the money or shutter. No bank was willing to front a loan that big. You know I don't do the internet-asking-for-handouts thing. I went to the only man I knew who would have the capital to keep us afloat. His family has had roots in Willow Valley for as long as mine has. We go way back. He grew up here. He saw movies here. I knew he would help."

"Help? You call this *helping*?"

"Keep your voice down," Earl demands. "I've been leasing the land under a handshake agreement with him for years now. If I met the annual deadlines in full, I got to keep the drive-in operating on my own terms. But things have been slipping, kid. I've been struggling with the financing."

"That's why I did all this Alice Kelly stuff! To save this place! To bring buzz! You're just going to stand there and take it?" The welling, waiting tears threaten to fall, but I won't let them.

I know I'm throwing a tantrum. I can't stop it. The bratty little boy inside me—the one that begged to stay up past his bedtime to watch the second feature from our backyard—is standing in this room, stomping his feet. I'm red-faced, overcome with more conflicting emotions than ever before.

"That's unfair!" I've never heard him shout before. "I've worked my whole life to keep this place open! I met with him. I pled my case. His mind was already made up… It wasn't a meeting. It was a formality. He fed me a steak dinner, told me the drive-in was being paved over, and handed me an expensive cigar as a parting gift." His stern gaze bores through me, his eyes never-ending black holes. "And, don't kid yourself. Your work was for you! I wanted you to have this as your final memory of working here. I was giving you the chance you've always wanted, knowing this might be our last go-around."

Anger makes way for soul-crushing sadness. It's like I'm standing on a fault line waiting for the earthquake to come. "But, what about hiring Derick?"

My head spins. His name in my mouth turns from tasting like peppermint to tasting like puke. Realization hits me lighting fast; he had to have known. This must've been what David was alluding to, what Derick was about to tell me before we jumped into the pool less than a week ago. But, "about to" doesn't cut it when he probably knew this whole time, this whole summer, since the email.

Suddenly, I'm as nauseous as I was the morning after my birthday. As the stream of tears weasels its way down my cheek, I yank open the door and dart away for fresh air. Nobody stops me, but everybody in the snack shack pauses and turns to stare.

Nothing to see here, just your manager breaking down into a heap of spare parts.

The night air washing over me does nothing to stop my chest from caving in. When Derick walks into my field of vision, everything goes red.

He's holding up one of the finished event posters as if he's a kid showing his parents a perfect grade on a spelling quiz. The only thing he's getting an A+ on is his deception this summer.

"Derick," I seethe.

"Don't they look amazing? I went for matte instead of glossy so that if local businesses hang them in the windows they won't be too reflective." He registers my squished expression. "You think I should've gone with glossy? I wasn't..."

I snatch the poster from his hands. In a single, swift motion, I tear it down the middle and then once more for good measure. His horrified look only makes my fury feel more justified. I throw it back in his face, a sad shower of confetti.

"Did you know your dad was planning to demolish Wiley's?" I ask, even though I'm certain I know the answer. When he's quiet for too long, I ask again with more bite, "Did...you...know?"

"I did," he says, ashamed. "But I didn't know for sure that he'd go through with it."

"Was the internship ever real? Was any of this real?"

"The internship was real, I swear. After a while, it became apparent that my job here wasn't to boost sales, though. It was to dig into the drive-in's finances."

My fists ball up. "Is that even legal?"

"I didn't report anything back that I wasn't told outright." The dread rises into my throat. *I told him?* Shit. I realize in being open with him, I may have advertised Earl's money woes to the man with the means to lock the gates for good. How stupid can I be?

"What was the plan?" I need to hear it. To know this isn't some talking-in-my-sleep stress dream.

In a low voice, he says, "I was ordered to see if the investment was still lucrative, to help decide if this could be a prime spot for the new station. It's all a numbers game. My dad determined he could make more on parking than he can from Earl's lease." And then, sounding suspiciously like his father, he adds, "It's business. It's nothing personal."

"What is with you people? Why do you keep saying that?" Exasperation makes it hard to speak. "Business is between people. Interactions between people are inherently personal." Part of me wants to mention *our* personal interactions, our slow build from former friends to friends to something more. Was that all business, too?

Derick immediately sobers, fully himself again. "Wren...I swear I tried to talk him out of it. You know I have no power with him. It's completely out of my control. And anyway, I thought this whole Alice Kelly thing was to move past this place. You said it yourself. You can't stay here forever." His seriousness is upsetting. He really believed that. Wow, I almost believed it, too.

"That wasn't the truth and it definitely didn't mean I wanted to see this place close."

The lot continues to fill up. Cars box me in on all sides. My stomach tightens, knowing there's nowhere to run.

"If I could do something, I would. Please, let me explain."

"Nothing you can say will make this better," I hiss. I wipe the tears from my eyes. I'm blubbering too badly to see. "This is my life, my job, my home you're ruining." All those times I concluded that Earl should logically pass the drive-in on to me were signs of something I wasn't ready to accept. It seemed foolish, a nonstarter. But just as I hadn't been aware of my demisexuality because I hadn't let myself explore the identities beyond the ones presented to me, I hadn't let myself consider that the answer to my future had been right in front of me this whole time. Of course, I'd realize it right as it's being ripped out from under me.

"Just because you and your father think everyone needs to chase the urban quotidian dream doesn't mean we want to. Some of us are happy here. Some of us don't need Fortune 500 internships or fancy colleges or sports cars with stupid grated windows." I close my eyes so I don't have to see his Silly Putty expressions of distress. "We promised in the city that we would communicate, and this whole time you were keeping the worst imaginable thing from me. How do you think that makes me feel?"

On the inside of my eyelids, a montage of us flickers at top speed through every frame. All the clues I missed because I was too busy wasting time on boyish whims and Hollywood romanticism.

"Listen. I swear, I didn't know the whole time, and when I found out my dad was moving forward with the application, there was never a right time to tell you." My eyes snap open at that blatant lie. He had every opportunity to be real with me. He let me kiss him while sitting atop this Jenga tower of lies, or half-truths, or whatever.

Across the way, Mateo twirls the traffic wand in one hand and taps his lit-up phone in the other. I know I should march over there and pry that device from his grasp, insist he focus on his job. What he's doing is dangerous. But I'm stuck in this horrendous scene, playing out heartbreak in real time.

"I hate myself for upsetting you, but I promise my intentions are good," Derick pleads, snapping me right back. Those are the exact words I said to David in the office the other night. It's like they're pranking me. Bring out the hidden cameras!

"*Wrenji*." His voice is pleading and that nickname means nothing now, drowned out by engines and laughing. A car, going faster than it should, is swerving down Mateo's aisle.

"Your intentions mean nothing to me," I say.

Behind Mateo, a car is backing out of its space, trying to straighten out to face the screen, tires spinning in a sticky patch of mud. They rev and rev. Those spinning wheels speed up with the thumping of my heart.

"You don't mean that."

It doesn't matter what I mean once I realize what I'm witnessing: *a clear collision course.*

"Watch out!" I call in the nick of time.

Mateo looks up right as he's about to be sandwiched between the two cars. He leaps out of the way as the headlight of one kisses the taillight of the other with a violent crack and a disheartening crunch. The piercing wails of competing car alarms go off.

I don't spare Derick another look as I run away from him, from this useless argument. As the two women yell their heads off about new paint jobs and car insurance, I rush to Mateo's shaking side. Somebody announces over the walkie that they're calling the police. One less thing I have to worry about.

"Are you okay?" I ask. The confusion, anger, sadness and panic overflow and flood my system. I inspect him for scratches or bruises, but he's fine. And he's still on his goddamn fucking phone! He nods without glancing at me, texting Brandon about what just happened. I snatch the phone from him. "Are you kidding me right now?"

"Babe, what are you doing? Give that back!"

"No! Okay, first, we're at work so don't you dare call me *babe*. Second, this phone is the reason this"—I gesture uncontrollably at the fender bender—"happened! How could you be so careless?"

"It was an accident. God. Chill out. Look, nobody was hurt," he says flippantly.

"Go home." My eyes are narrowed and my forehead is beaded with sweat.

"What?"

"After you make your statement to the police," I say as evenly as possible, "go home."

"I'm fine. Look at me. I'm good. I can work."

"No. You're not getting it. You're not good. You're bad…at this job. You're fired!" Yelling is the only thing that releases some of the hurt hacking away at my heart.

"Seriously?"

"Yes, *seriously*. That's three strikes. You're out!" I shout. Now, I'm making even more of a scene. The two women have stopped bickering and are staring at us, but I can't stop myself. "You're fired! Get out!" Control slips out of reach until I'm wild, running entirely on raw emotion. "Not that there would be a job waiting for you if you stayed anyway because this place is being demolished, torn down by some sleazy businessman to make a commuter parking lot, so you know what? I'm honestly doing you a favor. Get out before they crush us. Leave while you still can!"

Mateo's lip quivers. He drops the wand, strips off the safety vest, and shoves both into my chest. I stumble back. He's out of sight before I even have a chance to exhale.

The police sirens can be heard on the horizon. With nothing left to lose, I stand there like a dutiful manager does in the middle of a dying drive-in, not ready to accept my fate, but sure in the knowledge that I'll have to. One way or another.

Chapter 24

The FOR SALE sign is not where Alice said it would be.

Clouds, gray and menacing, roll swiftly over the farmhouse, and I know something bad—something worse—is already brewing.

I had to leave the apartment early this morning before Avery woke up. Mateo went to stay at Brandon's, unhappy even sharing a roof with me, the monster who canned him with no sympathy. The well had run dry way before I got to him. I'm gutted for hurting his feelings, but at the end of the day, he caused an accident on my watch. I don't make the rules. I'm just paid to enforce them. Even when the man who signs the checks has given up.

I was eager to watch another movie with Alice to make myself feel better, fill my hollow spaces with undigested bits of hard biscotti, but that seems less and less likely the closer I get to the house. The dismantled bike has bizarrely reappeared on the porch. One of the rocking chairs has collapsed as if by force. The front door is wide open.

As soon as I stop the car, Alice comes out, lugging garbage bags full of miscellaneous objects. She throws them like they're javelins into the yard, narrowly missing the hood of my car. That's when I notice Derick's stash of tools toppled over on the steps.

"Alice!" I yell, suddenly wishing I'd thought to bring a hard hat. "What are you doing?" I plant myself firmly behind my car as not to end up in her line of fire.

The muttering under her breath grows louder and more frantic. It's as if she's experiencing an Alzheimer's episode, the forgetting filling her with ire. I saw my late grandmother do it once and it's always stuck with me. She'd misplace a photo album and become so enraged over the reality that everything she touched was as good as gone.

I approach, hands spread wide and voice calm, a posture that says I-come-in-peace. "Alice, is everything okay? What happened?"

"Inhospitable! She says this place is still inhospitable! Can you believe that? All that work. All that money. Wasted, gone, done for. If nobody is fit to live here at its best, I might as well leave it at its worst! I'm going to die here anyway. It should feel like a mausoleum. That'll show them!" She carries a framed painting of the farm outside. I don't know whether she plans to kick it or chuck it, but either way, I know she's not in the right frame of mind to decide.

I come up the side steps. Before she builds up the strength to destroy something that's likely a family heirloom, I tug on the edge and snatch it out of her clutches.

"What are you doing? What'd you do that for? That's my property! *This* is my property! You can't waltz up here and decide what to do with my stuff." Her self-righteousness flares out from all sides. She's a woman on the verge. I'm the only one close enough to talk her down.

I set the painting up against the railing Derick and I worked so hard to reattach. It was sturdy only a week ago. It took three how-to videos, two sets of tools, and one very long, cuss-filled day. I'm happy when the weight of the painting doesn't knock over the remaining stakes, even if everything else we've built together has been torn down.

When I follow the distraught, hunched Alice inside, I see that wallpaper has been torn off the walls, molding has been ripped from its rightful place, and food has been toppled from the cabinets. An entire box of brown rice is spilled everywhere I swept, mopped, and waxed only a few weeks ago.

Even the living room, where we coated the walls in a soothing shade fit for a new buyer, has been desecrated. Alice used the brown touch-up paint from the bathroom to streak wavy lines across the drywall.

This act of rebellion only hurt herself. Can't she see that?

"Are you ready to tell me what happened?" I ask, leaning in the kitchen doorframe. The excess gravity of it all is pressing down on me, too much so to stand up straight. I keep a watchful eye trained on her as she puts the teakettle on the burner. The last thing I need is her snapping off the knob and starting a gas leak.

She clears her throat for a long time. Ultimately, she says, "The real estate agent said there would be no prospective buyers willing to put in the money to gut the place completely. I told her I didn't have that kind of cash lying around. She said there was nothing more that she could do." Alice laughs from a wicked place in her stomach. "That woman drank the last of my decaf before telling me, too!" She flings the empty tea canister across the kitchen. It hits the lid of the garbage can with a clang. I swoop in to pick it up, knowing I'm going to be the one to sort through the wreckage she's made.

"Can't you get a second opinion? Aren't there other real estate agencies you can contact?"

"No. I've been in contact with them all multiple times. Pamela Marks at Yardling Real Estate was the only one even remotely interested in representing the place a few years back, saying it had *potential*, and now even she's dismissed it as a rotting monstrosity, a death trap."

It must be difficult to view your childhood home that way. Young Alice must have bounded through these hallways with her siblings, playing tag and getting ready for school. They must've sat around a table in the dining room eating a breakfast feast of eggs from their very own chickens. This is where she cared for her mom when she was sick. Where Annie lived before she passed away.

Alice gives me a haunted look, eyes sunken and hair wild.

Ghosts linger here.

No wonder she stripped the walls of their paintings and photos except the chosen few she'd stuck on the mantel. Even those selections stayed behind her on display. She positioned the craggy chairs to face away, placed the TV on the opposite wall—that way she didn't have to spend time staring at them. Only when she entered the room, prepared, would she have to face the memories she couldn't part with.

That must be why she keeps Tammy, Annie, and her old life in a tin box with an air-tight lid. Some pasts are too painful to keep out in the open.

If I were her, I'd want to feel less alone right now. She may seem like she wants me gone, but there's a need underneath it all. I'm here to look out for her. My tattered world can wait.

"Do you want to go get a drink?" I ask.

The way she looks at me, you'd think horns had sprung out of my head. "I can't just leave!" It dawns on me that she doesn't even do basic errands. The only time she goes out is when Candice takes her to doctors' appointments. Clinically lit waiting rooms and sterile offices don't necessitate the kind of interaction a bar would. "What if someone breaks in? Who's going to look after my dogs?"

I don't mean to give away that I've caught onto the lie. It happens naturally. She's steadfast at first, but then she sighs. "When did you realize?"

"Does it matter?"

She relents, kicking at a nearby box. "I'm allergic to the darned animals anyway." She sneezes twice, defeated, as if to prove her point.

"Even the imaginary ones, it seems." My joke makes her facade crack.

She agrees to the drink on one condition: "You're buying."

♡

It's pouring when we arrive at our destination. Of course, today is the day I would forget an umbrella and a raincoat, two items I always keep in the trunk for occasions like this. I drop Alice off at the door to stand under the awning while I scour for street parking.

The Cat's Pajamas is open late afternoons for lunchtime drinkers and pricey fried foods. I've never been before 11:00 p.m., so the sight that greets me is startling. You don't notice the peeling paint, the chipped floors, or rickety bar stools when you're drunk, dancing, and unscrupulous. Now, every wall looks like a Pollock painting of questionable stains.

"Great. Take me out of one dump and bring me to another," Alice mumbles. I shush her as we approach the bar. There are only a few other patrons seated around. The normal lights, yellow and buzzing, are unflattering at best and headache-inducing at worst.

From the slow-moving overhead fans, the circulating air sends a shiver straight through me. I'm freezing from the cold rain, my hair matted and my shirt soggy.

I help Alice onto her stool. Her short legs don't even reach the runner.

"What can I get you?" the bartender, a curvaceous, going-bald white man with striking eyes asks. Then: "Ugh, it's you."

"Wren, you didn't tell me you had enemies," Alice says with far too much merriment in her voice.

I swear I've never laid eyes on this person in my life. "I–I don't? Have we meet?" I know that's sort of a rude question, but I can't place him. Maybe we bumped into each other here once before or maybe he scolded me sophomore year when I tried to buy drinks without having my over-21 token yet.

He glares at me and then motions to the sign on the opposite wall. The faded poster reads: *Saturday Night Drag Show:* Overboard *starring Goldie Prawn*. In the photo, she's dressed like Goldie Hawn as Joanna Stayton— red, pointy sunglasses and a skimpy zebra-print, French-cut bathing suit— from the 1987 movie of the same name.

When I turn back, I swear a phantom blond wig swirls down from his head. He polishes the glass in his hand with a dirty rag, lips puckered, this time in disdain, not in search of a kiss.

Alice gets up to inspect the image closer. "You make a beautiful woman," she calls over her shoulder. He thanks her. "Do you know that RuPaul character? I'm always seeing ads for her on my Hulu."

"Honey, do you think I'd be here if I did?" he asks. "Are you gonna order something or just stare at me?"

"I'll have a whiskey sour. How about you?" I ask Alice.

"A vodka neat! No, wait. A martini, extra olive! No, no, hold on. A sex on the beach!" I spew laughter. It's the first time I've belly-laughed in twenty-four hours. "Oh, stop being so immature." She slaps me on the arm.

As he makes our drinks, I feel compelled to say, "Sorry I spoiled the fun back in May. I had never been kissed and I wanted my first to be special, and then it was special, but now it's not. I didn't mean to make you look bad in front of the crowd."

"Save it, sweetie. I don't need the *60 Minutes* sob story. It got a laugh. It's all good." He sets the cocktails down. "What are we drinking to?"

"She can't sell her house. My job is disappearing, and my ex is the ass who helped make it happen." How have I gone from never having a boyfriend, never being kissed, to having an ex in a matter of two weeks? "Oh, and it's pouring out in case you didn't notice." The rain continues to pound away on the roof.

"That'll do it," he says, sliding our glasses onto the counter. The last time I was in a bar, I was with Derick, both physically and in the Facebook-status way. Now, I'm here with Alice, drinking the drink he drank in the city and slipping into a comatose state of inaction. What's left for me to do other than sip this shit away?

"What is this about a job and an ex?" Alice asks. Her tone is concerned, but her face is flush thanks to the fruity, sweet drink she seems to be relishing.

"Derick's dad is the rightful owner of the land Wiley's is on. The Any Weather Transportation Group plans to tear it down and turn it into commuter parking. Derick knew the whole time. I feel like an idiot."

"Sounds like that Joni Mitchell song—'paved paradise, put up a parking lot.'" Alice sings a little. Her voice isn't half-bad.

"The soundtrack for depressed gays everywhere," Goldie says with a showgirl laugh, false and echoing. "That sucks major ass. What are you going to do about it?"

I shrug, sliding my glass back and forth between my hands. "I don't know. What is there to do? My boss is resigned to our fate. There's apparently some meeting with some historic board to discuss the demolition next week, but they're on track for approval. At least I think they are. We'll do your event, Alice, but then, I think that's it."

Goldie points at me, still wearing his show nails—huge, clanking, fire-engine-red claws. "Words are cheap. Actions are priceless. If you don't like what's happening, set something else into motion."

Alice looks at me. "I like her."

Goldie winks. "The feeling is mutual, doll."

"That's all good and fine, but I can't stop something already in motion. The drive-in will close. Roll credits."

I don't have the energy or patience for more. What's done is done.

"Roll credits?" Alice slams her empty glass on the counter. I hope she doesn't keel over from the swift alcohol intake. "You got a cigarette?" she asks Goldie. Goldie produces one and lights it up for her. She's probably not supposed to be doing that either with her, I don't know, frail health and all, but we're too far gone at this point.

A satisfying puff floats into the air. "'Roll credits' is basically what I said when you shoved your way into my home asking about my darned movie, wasn't it? You didn't take that from me then, so I'm not taking it from you now either."

"You're spunky, doll," Goldie says.

"You don't know the half of it," I groan.

"Another round, please, and keep them coming. We're going to drink our way into a solution. I'm sure of it." She pulls a pen from her purse and slaps a fresh, square bar napkin down in front of me.

It's the worst plan ever, but it's better than no plan, so I accept the second whiskey sour, crack my knuckles, and begin jotting down whatever comes to mind.

Here's hoping free association will be my superpower.

Chapter 25

3B has always had a no-knock policy.

When I get back from the bar, I burst into Avery's room. I didn't expect her to be topless, lying facedown, while Stacia draws a lion head with a deer's body and a unicorn horn in red BIC BodyMark pen on her back. A notebook is open in front of Avery's face, a poem forming in eye-catching stanzas in familiar sloppy script. She hugs her pillow to her chest and smiles up at me.

"Sorry, I didn't mean to interrupt."

"We're almost done," Stacia says, adding fullness to the mane. The eyes are bold and daring, peering at me from between the slatted breaks of Avery's tan lines. This is a strange yet divine kind of affection. "Cool, right?"

"Very," I say, realizing we've never had any real interactions outside the brief moments on the way in and out of the Cat's Pajamas. In the light of day, she has shaggy blond hair, a slender nose, and cheekbones that are so high and sharp they could be used for cosmetology class demonstrations.

"Is Mateo here?" I ask.

Avery sighs. "He packed up a bigger bag and is permanently staying with Brandon until, and I quote, 'the ogre that lives on the other side of the wall grows a pair and apologizes.'"

I expected as much.

"You could always do what I did—take him out for iced matcha lattes and then let him sing through his entire audition book for you," Avery says.

"The entire thing?"

"We made it to S for Sondheim, 'Being Alive' I think, but he got all weirded out and said his instrument was tired. Granted, I'd heard eighteen letters worth of sixteen-bar cuts already, but that's beside the point."

"'Being Alive' is from *Company*. It's Bobby's big song," I say for Avery's benefit, and for my own waterlogged brain. That's one of the cast albums we attempted to learn to beat Mateo at his board game. I shake my head at my own nearsightedness. "He must still be upset about not getting the part. God, maybe I have been an ogre. I never even asked about it."

Consumed by reviving the lot and falling for Derick, I've let my friends take a back seat when they've always been my copilots, my ride or dies, my grab-the-keys-and-go buddies. I may have been right to let Mateo go, but I shouldn't have blown up about it the way I did—and I really shouldn't have let my own crap get in the way of our friendship.

"I'll make it up to him." Though, I don't have the mental stamina to sort that out right now.

"How are you feeling?" Avery asks. Stacia tosses her the maroon, scoop-neck shirt she was wearing. Without interrupting the conversation, she takes photos of her artistic work on her phone. She readjusts the crisscrossing back straps to make it look like the lion is stalking its prey from behind the brush of fabric. "Derick texted me a few times asking if you were okay, but I wasn't sure what you wanted me to tell him, so I just said you were safe and wanted space."

"What I want is the ability to time travel back to when I told you I wasn't working at Wiley's this summer. I should've taken the film studies office job. At least the only hurt I would've experienced digitizing the archives was the occasional paper cut." I roll my eyes, but a sharp sting hits me. I remember Derick's paper cut from the night he held up the admission line. Every memory of us from this summer is now singed at the edges like I took a lighter to the Polaroids for the sickening pleasure of watching them burn.

Stacia shoves her pen in her pocket and says, "I'm going to give you two some privacy. Mind if I take this?" Avery shakes her head and hands her the journal. She gives me a sweet smile before closing the door behind her.

"What's in the book?"

"Oh, I wrote a poem based on the creature she drew behind my ear and sent it to her on a whim. She gushed over it and asked if I'd do more for others she did. Now, she's thinking she might want to make an artists' account where we post the drawings beside the text of my poems. Or, maybe some videos where she draws on my body while I read the poem aloud? We're not sure exactly what it could be yet, but it could be cool."

I beam at her as I sit down on the bed. "That's awesome." That's all Avery has ever wanted in a partner: someone who takes her art seriously, who doesn't think writing is a wasted pursuit. Even if this is a temporary fling, she'll have something to take with her when it's over.

"Did you need something?" she asks, nodding down toward the crumpled napkin in my hand.

"Your dad knows someone at the Historic Review Board, right?"

"Yeah, I think someone from our synagogue is on it. I can call him and ask. Why? What are you thinking?"

I hand her the napkin and let Alice and my brainstorming do all the talking.

♥

"What are you doing here, kid?" asks Earl, concerned, as soon as he spies Alice and me rushing across the sidewalk outside the Municipal Building. We're already late. Alice gets ready to leave the house like a teenager getting ready for school, begrudgingly and with little urgency.

"You gotta dress for the part you want. Not the part you got," she scoffed when I mentioned this, and then she shooed me out into the car as if I had been holding us up.

"I could ask you the same thing." I stop in front of him. "Shouldn't you be inside assuring that monster gets you your historic marker? That's the least he can do." My will to fight has been amplifying the whole drive over. Even if Earl's called it quits, that doesn't mean I will.

Avery came through on the official time and location of the meeting. On the public agenda was Mr. Haverford's COA request for the demolition of Wiley's. The conversation with Goldie reminded me that Willow Valley has had a historic district for a few decades now. We learned about Act 167 of 1961 in Derick's and my high school honors history class. Wiley's falls within its parameters.

There's still hope the board will refuse Mr. Haverford's plans.

But then, I notice the thin, off-white handkerchief in Earl's hand and his bloodshot eyes. He's been crying. "It was too hard to hear, kid. I thought I could handle it, all that talk of wrecking balls or what have you, but I can't."

Earl's never been one for displays of emotion, preferring the sweep-it-under-the-rug method. "I didn't want to disrupt the meeting with my sniveling." If he thinks his half-dry face is *sniveling*, he should've seen me on the Fourth of July.

"What's happening? Are they siding with him?" I ask, heart sinking.

I know for a fact they're a tough bunch. Avery reminded me that Earl had to get express approval from this overseeing body to make renovations to the snack shack to accommodate the new digital projector the year we started there. Little did we know our boss had sold his pride and joy to the devil in the diamond-encrusted wristwatch to make it happen.

"They're only a review board. Whatever they recommend will go up the chain to Borough Council, and they'll have the final say. Mr. Haverford has too many friends in high places." His sigh is all-encompassing. "Perhaps it's for the best. I'm getting up there in age. It is probably time for me to retire."

"Come on," I jockey. "You've still got a few good years left in you, Earl. That place gives you life and purpose. It gives a lot of people life and purpose."

I whip out my phone and pull up the social-media accounts. Even though Derick made them with murky intentions, their reach is undeniable. I show Earl the follower counts, the voracious emojis. It's all evidence in the case to try to stop this.

"Were you and Derick publicly flirting in the comments section this whole time?" Earl shows me a particularly damning Twitter thread between @WileysDriveInWV and @RolandOnTheRiver14. I snatch the phone back to distract from my reddening face.

"That's..." I stammer. "No, that's nothing. That's not the point."

Though maybe that *is* the point.

The care and craft Derick put into the video and photo edits are enough to make me pause. Would someone with solely devious ulterior motives have been doing such a good job rebranding the place they were helping shut down?

I don't have time to entertain that thought right now.

Earl lights up with a half laugh and a full smile. "Even so, it's not like I have a line of inheritors waiting." Earl never dated, never married, never had kids. I never asked about it. Nobody did. He moved through the world a mysterious boss whose life didn't extend much beyond our fences.

I don't think he regrets any of that, but I do think there's a small guilt that lives inside him, that nags him every now and then. One that makes him wish he could do what his father did and gift the family business. Continue the legacy in this small way.

"We're family," I tell him with immediate certainty. "I've been thinking about it a lot since the promotion and since meeting Alice." She perks up at the mention of her name. "I want to do what you do, Earl. I want to run the drive-in. I want to keep that legacy alive. I know that's not feasible right now. I don't have the money or the credit or the know-how, but I'll find a way. I can't do that if we let that man in there"—I point toward the redbrick building towering over us—"bulldoze it down. I want a proper chance to take over. Help me get that. Please."

Earl's so-called sniveling starts back up. He's crying, but not hiding it this time, and I take that as a good sign. "Do you really mean that, kid? What about your fancy degree?"

"What about it? I got it because I wanted a life focused on the movies. Overseeing the lot would give me that and time in the off-seasons to do research and write or whatever else I plan to do." The drive-in means too much to me and, yeah, I couldn't stay manager forever, but owning a spring-summer small business could be a fulfilling part of my future. Abruptly remembering the time-sensitive meeting, I check my phone. "If you're able, let's get back in there and give that board a piece of our minds."

Earl doesn't hesitate for one second. "Give 'em hell, kid."

"Huzzah!" Alice yells, leading the charge up the *Rocky*-esque steps. I can almost hear the theme song pounding around in my ears, pumping me up for my grand entrance.

Only it's not grand. And it's barely an entrance. The doors to the meeting room are wide open, and nobody seems to notice when we shuffle in.

Ahead of us, there's a dais where name plates and microphones are set up. Behind the nine members—among them a building inspector, a real estate broker, and a licensed architect—are paintings depicting Willow Valley historical scenes, done in ambers and leafy greens with fine brushstrokes. Flags hang on golden poles in the front corners.

Mr. Haverford appears to be finishing up his presentation; the 3D picture of his ugly, proposed parking structure disappears from the screen off to the side. Satisfied, he clicks back into his perfect family unit, and my eyes wander until they land on the last pair of long legs in the lineup: *Derick's.*

The sight of him stops me dead in my tracks. I didn't think he'd show up to this. He's wearing the maroon blazer from the day at the restaurant, his floral tie again slung too low around his neck. Despite the hurt, my whole body still responds to his gravitational pull, this primal urge to be comforted by him when I need him most.

Hard to reconcile when he had a large hand in that hurt.

Carl Goldstein, the architect among the pack, calls the room to order with a gavel and makes a motion for public comments on items included in today's meeting. The others "second" the motion.

My heart jumps into overdrive when I raise my hand.

"Hi, my name is Wren Roland. I am one of the current managers at Wiley's Drive-In." As soon as I speak, Mr. Haverford turns in his chair and grimaces. His disdain radiates off him in almost visible heat waves. The rest of the family is slow to turn, and Derick remains forward facing, my voice obviously already too much for him. "I'm here to say that the Any Weather Transportation proposal should be shot down. The historic significance of the 1934 architecture and the community value of the drive-in can't be overlooked. It's an integral part of our historic district and one of the oldest operating drive-ins in the country. If you help steamroll our summer haven to make way for a parking lot, you're doing a grave disservice to the legacy of the movie business and to the preservation of our great town."

Alice claps loudly for me. It almost covers up Mr. Haverford's groan and

Mrs. Haverford's *tsks*. The board members' faces all seem to shift in agreement. They are staunch preservationists, after all.

They are about to move on to someone else when Earl bolts up. "My name is Earl Wiley, the owner of Wiley's Drive-In, the current lessee of the lot, and I second the motion made by the kid."

"You don't need to do the motion thing. That's just for us," Carl says with a thunderous laugh. The man keeping the minutes makes a big show of jotting down the joke, as if they'll get another laugh out of this later.

"Mr. Wiley, I thought we were in agreement when we spoke last. You said you understood," Mr. Haverford says, getting heated. Whatever goodwill these two shared in the past has gone out the window.

"I'm singing a different tune today. Sorry, Dan," he says, using the shortened nickname to get under Mr. Haverford's skin. From Mr. Haverford's ruddy complexion, it looks like it worked.

"Anyone else from the public care to comment on the record?" asks Mr. Goldstein.

There's a stirring in my stomach willing Derick to stand and state before this small gathering that he loves Wiley's. That he's on my side. That all those posts and long nights and wild snack-shack shenanigans were done with the belief that Wiley's was worth saving.

I need to hear that he cares before my heart breaks into seventeen, eighteen, nineteen more pieces.

But his head is hung, his shoulders are slumped, and I can almost hear the shards in my chest as they crack apart and fall to the base of my sternum.

"I must say, Mr. Haverford, your plans to pour asphalt over a community gem is concerning," says Sal DeFalco, the middle-aged building inspector. "You must understand that the architecture of Wiley's Drive-In, the snack shack, the beloved sign, all can be considered historical resources, which we as a review board have a duty to uphold. The team we sent out to inspect the lot found evidence that backed up that statement."

"I'm not sure how a hut with dancing lollipops on it counts as a resource," Mr. Haverford scoffs.

"There's a giant shoe on the historic registry, Mr. Haverford," says

Sylvia Mueller, the real estate broker who's wearing a fifties-style polka-dot dress. "History is not always in the eye of the beholder."

Carl clears his throat. "Like the plucky preservationist in the Wiley's T-shirt, I, too, believe your parking lot will destroy the character of our historic district and do a great a disservice to the history of a business that is already too hard to find in our country." He nods at me in acknowledgment. "Do I hear a movement to recommend to Borough Council to deny the application?"

"So moved," Sylvia says.

"Second," says Sal.

"All those in favor," Carl announces, "say aye."

A unanimous round of aye's rings out.

The way it hits my ears, it's almost choral. Their overlapping spoken words create beautiful music, vamping to send us into the next stage of our fight.

As Alice would say: Onward! Huzzah!

Text Message

Wiley's Staff Chat

Mateo Trinidad left this chat
Derick Haverford has been removed from this chat
Youssef
Anyone know if the schedule has changed this week
because of the big news?
Wren
Hello all. 👋
First off, I want to apologize for my behavior this
summer, especially, but not limited to, the night
of the accident. I haven't been focused, and I hope
you can forgive me for slacking.
Second, I want you to know that Wiley's needs
us now more than ever. Mr. Haverford's
demolition plans are going before the
Borough Council next week. We need
all the community support we can get to
ensure they aren't approved.
Tell your friends, tell your family, tell

the media, tell anyone who will listen.

Lastly, if you feel so inclined,

join us on Monday for a planning meeting at

my house. We're not going down without a fight.

Chapter 26

It's like the Fourth of July all over again.

My backyard is bustling.

The old lawn chairs from our drive-in viewing days are arranged in a circle in the grass. Alice sits to my left, foot tapping anxiously, and Earl to my right. Across from me, Mom, Dad, and Claire type on various tablets and laptops. There are books and manila folders sprinkled around their feet.

Avery convinced a begrudging Mateo to come pitch in, so they're off to the side, sunglasses on and noses buried in information. The rest of the Wiley's crew keeps company by the swing set.

We've all convened to build my pitch for the Borough Council meeting.

Mr. Goldstein informed me that during the public forum part of their next meeting, I should be prepared to make an impassioned plea for the future of our sacred spot. He told me to rally the troops and prepare to get loud, so that's just what I'm doing.

Earl rubs his mustache, deep in thought, as his eyes scan lines of newspaper text, a yellow highlighter at the ready.

Claire is our organizer, Avery is our writer, Alice is our harsh critic, and Earl is our wealth of firsthand knowledge. Mom and Stacia are using their artistic skills to sketch a visually pleasing timeline of the drive-in's history. This will give the council members a succinct, eye-catching graphic that lays out the community aspect of this long-running business. Brandon agreed to gather a street team. They'll spread the word to the summer study students still on the Rosevale campus, urging them to join the cause.

We need as wide a reach as we can manage.

Since Alice's eyes aren't good enough to read through most of the small printed materials, I read aloud to her, which is an act I'm coming to enjoy. If she nods, I put that source in our "need it" pile and if she scowls, I bring it over to Dad so he can sort, alphabetize, and keep track of what we've deemed unusable. What isn't relevant now might be pertinent later.

At the end of all of this, I'm the one kicking off the open forum. It's as if I'm some underdog defense lawyer preparing closing remarks on a high-profile case. A regular Erin Brockovich. I need to prove my worth.

Even in this circle of special people, Derick's absence is palpable. If he were here, I know he'd force me to go on a run to knock out my stricken panic. He'd hold my hand and help my fear fly away. My lonely, achy heart yearns for what I felt before he imploded everything. Those fleeting weeks were wonderful. It's sad and stupid but true. He's part of the reason we're in this mess, scouring for a lifeline. I can't square how seen and wanted he made me feel all summer with how invisible I felt when he wouldn't even look at me in the Review Board meeting.

I scroll back through his latest text:

Derick

Two truths and a lie, round 3:

1. I'm so sorry I didn't tell you sooner, but I had a good reason. I promise.

2. I'm proud of you for standing up for what you believe in.

3. You can't ice me out forever.

When I got this, I started to type back: *They're all lies!* But decided those kinds of dramatics would only detract from the issue at hand. I need to wrap my focus up in saving Wiley's. I lived without Derick before; I can do without him now, too.

If only my heart could start believing that.

Attempting to shake off the feelings, I take a break and walk over to the drink table Mom set out on the deck. Even an impromptu meeting of the troops called for a full spread. Mateo is pouring himself some of her famous sweet tea. Mom's a tristate area girl who went to college in Georgia. She knows her way around a southern comfort drink. The secret is a pinch of baking soda and simple syrup, which kills the bitter tang of long-steeping tea bags. Mateo can't get enough of it.

Approaching with caution and cultivating empathy, I say quickly to his back, "Before you run away, I want to say I'm sorry. Really, truly sorry."

Mateo turns slowly, charting the distance from here back to his seat, but I've cornered him and he knows it. The silent treatment is his way of inflicting punishment on me. But, honestly, I need my best friend back.

"I treated you terribly the night I fired you. When I found out about the demolition plans and Derick's double-agent status, I don't know, I just snapped. I know it was an accident. I know you didn't mean for it to happen. I know I'm an ogre."

Mateo takes a long sip, clearly enjoying making me sweat. After a commercial-ready, refreshing *ahh*, he says, "You're not an ogre. If anything, you're more like a grouchy bridge troll."

I laugh. "Ouch. At least ogres have layers."

"*Shrek* references will only get you so far," Mateo says. I pick a wedge of watermelon off a stacked tray, realizing I've forgotten to eat all afternoon. "At least you're a troll. I'm a donkey."

"A sassy and lovable sidekick?"

"An ass."

I laugh so hard I almost spew out watermelon seeds. "Why do you say that?"

"It pains me to my core—my very worked-out from Pilates and dance classes core—but I was in the wrong, babe."

"Remember when you said you weren't a narcissist?" I tease.

"Shut up, I'm trying to be serious." He does a very dramatic exhale. "I shouldn't have been on my phone. Brandon helped me see that. You were right. I've been in this funk since I got passed over for the part of Bobby, and I felt like I was above the job and above the work, and that was selfish of me." He bats his eyelashes. "Can you ever forgive me?"

"Of course. Our friendship comes with an accident forgiveness policy. Didn't you read the fine print when you signed up?"

He smirks at me. "I'm glad the random room assignment gods paired us together four years ago. You're a good friend, Wren. At least when you're not blowing up my spot in front of a sold-out drive-in movie theater or sending me lovey-dovey emails."

"That's only *two* friendship strikes!" I counter. He chuckles.

"It may have worked out for the best anyway. Rosevale summer stock called. The dude they cast as Bobby came down with laryngitis after their first weekend of shows, and they didn't hire an understudy, so...I'm in!" His tea spills a little from unbridled excitement.

"Oh my god! Mateo, that's incredible! Congrats! Uh..." I grab for a drink cup. "To laryngitis!"

"To laryngitis!"

A summer of so many toasts, and somehow this is the only one that rings true. The night of my birthday, I acted out of hormonal panic. The day of my graduation, I acted on impulse. Today, I'm finally going with my gut—my steady, sure-of-it gut. I'm ready to start trusting myself for once.

We sip in silence for a few seconds.

"Have you heard from Derick?" he asks.

"I'm ghosting him. Giving him a taste of his own medicine." It sucks that it doesn't feel nearly as satisfying as I hoped it would.

"Babe, I hate to traffic in clichés, but two wrongs don't make a right."

"Says the guy who practically moved out of our apartment so he didn't have to share a wall with me!"

"I was pissed, and you were a wreck, and poor Avery would've been in the middle of it. I did us all a service." He pulls out his phone. "You've said his family is overbearing and demanding. His dad, most of all. If he's still living under their roof and fighting off their expectations, he might not have much of a choice in the matter. I know that's a shitty excuse, but it's not nothing, right?" He taps into the Wiley's Instagram page. "This didn't even exist in May and it already has over 3,000 followers. If he was only here to fuck shit up, don't you think he would've done a bad job like I did?"

"Funny. I had the same thought last week..."

If Derick was pulling incorrigible stunts, he'd have been actively working to destroy the lot, but his social-media engagement numbers went up and up and up. Duplicitous or not, maybe there's more to the story.

"Are you suggesting that this was all an inside job to build Wiley's business so his dad wouldn't tear it down?"

Mateo looks at me like *Duh, how am I the one who thought of this first?*

There is an unsuspecting sense to it. Derick wants out from under his father's thumb. Doing a bad job at Wiley's would look poor to future employers outside of the nepotism sphere, so as a kiss-off to his dad, he went to great lengths to make sure his position did the opposite of what his father intended. It's devious and almost inspired.

That doesn't explain why he didn't tell me, though. He had ample opportunities to come clean.

Mateo shows me the Twitter feed with its well-designed header photo and steady stream of well-loved tweets. His coordinated boost campaigns. His perfectly edited TikToks. It's all the work of someone who had a digital media plan. Someone who knew how to tell a story, engage with his audience, and evoke *pathos*.

Wait. That's it!

This is an absolute Aristotelian turn of events. I scramble back to the circle where I left my tote bag. Inside, I grab my bullet journal and flip frantically through the pages.

"Wait, what's happening right now?" Mateo asks. Everyone stops what they're doing, but I'm too busy unburying the obvious answer to all our problems.

The Borough Council meeting is at the end of the week. There's a big chance they'll see the economic benefit of a commuter parking lot outweighs the historical significance of Wiley's and the upkeep of the historic district. If that's the case, Mr. Haverford will erect the plaque and then bring in the wrecking ball.

All that would stand in the wake of the screen and the snack shack would be a commemorative tombstone that no one would read as they boarded a bus to Philadelphia. Majorly depressing.

Not just to me, though—to legions of film fans everywhere on *social media*.

This online novice is about to take everything Derick taught me and twist it for my own gain.

"We should launch a social-media campaign. A full-scale attack evoking nostalgia and a love of the movies," I announce to the group. Eager murmurs from the Wiley's team erupt almost immediately. "If we appeal to people's emotions, they might want to get loud online with us."

Avery is the first to speak up. "I love it, but we're not influencers. Nobody here has over a couple hundred followers. How do we get the word out?"

"By expanding our core audience. Signal boosting our cause." A longing pang strikes my chest, but I don't let it crush my newfound crusader status.

A new title appears on my mind marquee:

ALL IS FAIR IN LOVE AND HASHTAGS

"You and Stacia started that art and poetry account. It's new but it's starting to take off. I'm sure your followers would be willing to share info about us in their stories." I point over to Youssef. "And you're popular on all those projectionist film forums, do you think you could put out a post about our situation?"

"My online buddies would eat this shit up," he confirms.

"Great! Mateo, your actor friends love movies, and I'm sure I can get Dr. Tanson to shoot out an email blast to the film studies department. Plus, she has tons of…" The key player in all of this suddenly becomes clear to me. "Excuse me for a second." I race up to my room, phone at the ready. Oscar gave me his number before the New York City trip, so I click the contact and connect the call.

After the second ring, he answers, "Hello? I'm about to lose service any second."

The robotic subway voice beeps behind him: "Beware of the closing doors, please."

"Hi. It's Wren. I'll be quick." I'm breathless with anticipation. My mind is submerged in visions of what could be. "Before we drop the podcast episode, I have a huge idea and I need your help."

"Of course," he says, sounding jovial. "Whatever it is. I'm in."

Twitter Thread

@DontYouForgetAboutPod
Our nation's drive-ins are at risk of dying out. Don't let @
WileysDriveInWV be the latest causality of big business.
Join me in supporting #TheLittleDriveInThatCould with
our latest episode discussing #AliceKelly and her lost film
Chompin' at the Bit (1978) with special guest.

37 replies. 256 Retweets. 708 Likes.

Thread

@DontYouForgetAboutPod @RolandOnTheRiver14 is a manager and long-time employee of the drive-in. He's leading the
fight for historical preservation. Please SHARE this message far
and wide. See the links in our bio on how to let the Willow Valley
Borough Council know you DO NOT support demolition.
@DontYouForgetAboutPod Emails, calls, and letters appreciated! Once we've emerged victorious, join us for a special screening of the film on August 14. It's an undead night of film history
not to be missed!

Chapter 27

By Friday, we've gone viral.

#TheLittleDriveInThatCould is everywhere—from Twitter to TikTok to Tumblr. Avery asked Stacia to draw up a logo for our cause. Within hours, we had it slapped on stickers, T-shirts, stamps, of course, and more, all up on for sale on Etsy with Mom's expert help.

Local news picked us up as an unfolding story, dropping updates on their social feeds. Online film bloggers are echoing our call to action, citing developers as the death of cinema. It might be a reach, but I appreciated the gravitas.

We even got a brief ticker byline mention on a national morning news show since one of the hosts grew up going to a drive-in just like ours. It's all moving and gratifying and scarily exciting.

I stand, surrounded by my core people, in the vestibule of the Municipal Building as the Borough Council meeting gets set to begin. There's a podium off to the side of the room Alice, Earl, and I barged into only a week and a half ago. I will give my formal address from there.

My note cards shake in my hands. I donned my best bespoke suit, popped in my contacts, and fastened my popcorn-patterned bow tie to the white collar. Mateo made no mocking mention of my love of novelty attire this time.

Avery makes last-minute adjustments to my hair. Mateo runs a lint brush down my right arm. Even Claire is here, doting on me, dotting a blotting sheet across my nose so I don't look shiny on camera. Or rather, *cameras.*

Yes, cameras. I panicked when I saw the news vans pull up and the primped reporters jump out. The local news and press have been allowed access to the meeting, severely limiting the number of townies that can attend. My parents are already seated up front. Alice and Earl are close by, chatting like long-lost friends. There are kids from my high school scattered throughout. Every Wiley's employee wore their staff T-shirts in a strong show of support.

I know a bunch of people here have my back, but when the council members, mostly in their fifties and sixties, file into their seats, wearing much nicer suits than mine and looking irked beyond belief by the media frenzy, I freak out.

"This is your eleven o'clock number, babe. You got this," Mateo says.

Claire grabs another oil sheet. "Keep your numbered cards in order and make sure to make eye contact."

"But not too much eye contact," Avery warns. "You don't want to come across like a creeper."

"You're giving me a lot to think about." All eyes are on me. I'm a ball of rubber bands wound together too tightly. If one more person plucks at me, I might snap.

"Just go out there and do your best!" Avery says.

"And, geez, try to stop sweating," Claire moans.

As more and more people pack into the smaller than small room, I focus on my breath. Inhale. Seven count. Exhale. If I keep repeating this, maybe I'll trick myself into thinking I'm out on the lot, wind in my face, movie playing. My happy place.

I went for a run by myself this morning, waking up alongside the Willow Valley sunrise this time. Surprising myself, I took a detour past Derick's house. Part of me thought maybe he'd be up, way too restless to sleep a second longer. I was disheartened when I didn't spot his bouncy blond hair up ahead of me at any point.

But even if I had, what would I have done? Sped up ahead of him, so he could gaze longingly after what he lost and, more so, what he's missing? I'm still hurt and angry, but I should hope I'm not *that* petty.

Councilwoman Harper, a short Black woman wearing a violet pantsuit, calls the room to order with an official gavel and welcomes the assembled parties.

My phone vibrates in my pocket. It's from Oscar.

Knock them dead! 💪

Wait. I'm watching online and they look OLD.

Don't knock them too dead. 💀

After his gallant retweet game lifted our hashtag off the ground, we spread like wildfire across all platforms. Even Oscar's publisher, an indie press with a known, glowing reputation in the nonfiction entertainment space, added his tweet to their stories. He's an instrumental part of whatever happens here today. I send him my thanks followed by a series of nervous emojis with a trail of hearts hanging behind it.

Right as I'm setting my phone to silent, I'm called in. My friends give me a gentle shove. All heads turn in my direction as I take the aisle in stride.

Don't trip. Don't look down. Don't choke.

At the podium, I stand taller, harnessing my managerial authority, my podcast guest confidence, and a little bit of Alice's get-what-I-want aggression.

"Thank you for hearing my argument regarding denying the Any Weather Transportation demolition request and upholding the historical significance of Wiley's Drive-In, an 86-year-old Willow Valley institution that has been, and should stay, a vital part of our beautiful community." My sweaty finger pads leave behind smudges on the previous notecard, but I remain strong. "My name is Wren Roland. I am the newest manager at the lot. I've been working at Wiley's for eight summers now—eight of the best summers of my life, actually—but I'm not here to woo you with stories and memories of midnight screenings of your favorite Marvel movies or tales of the numerous couples who got engaged on our grounds, even though I do see one such couple here today." I make a sweeping gesture over to Nisha and Devon, two regulars, who did so during one of our throwback showings of a popular nineties romcom. "I'm here to make a case for why the architectural and historical resources of Wiley's Drive-In need to be kept and cherished."

The speech goes on as planned. There are *ohhs* and polite nods from the council at all the right places. I run down the full timeline with little, dramatic pauses (coached by Mateo, of course). They follow along on Mom and Stacia's printouts. We even slapped together a pleasing PowerPoint for further pictorial appeal. I yield the clicker with aplomb, flipping through portraits of the Wiley men who came before Earl. A lineage of film lovers.

My confidence crescendos to a fever pitch when I step out from behind the podium to drive my point home. "Wiley's isn't just a place of business— it's a tradition. A rite of passage for so many Willow Valley youth, both the ones who work there and the ones who come to visit."

Heads bob with every word. Even if I expected to, I don't crumble under the pressure. For once, I feel like the fearless leader I've always wanted to be.

It occurs to me that my film studies major prepared me for this—oral history, class discussions, cogent arguments. In the back of my mind, I questioned my major for its validity, yet here I am, embodying everything the Rosevale department taught me.

"Thank you for your time, and thank you for your consideration."

Applause rings out and I rejoin my crew. Their squeezes of support lift my spirits.

They can only rise so high, though, before the rest of the public gets a chance to take the stand.

It's surprising how many came out today. A woman with a bob and a Birkin bag complains how her husband needs a closer commuter lot so he can be home for weeknight dinners. She implores the council to "think about her children." A counter comes from Jacob, one of our employees, who warbles about needing this job or else he might not be able to afford his car insurance or the gas needed to get to and from his community college classes.

This whole portion is a tennis match of opinions, the ball volleying across the net so many times I fear we might all leave this room with moral whiplash.

Dread looms larger the longer the Any Weather support outweighs the

Wiley's backing. It feels like the Haverfords hired actors to stage a coup. Yet, I know that's not true. I know these people. I've seen their faces driving through the admission booth. That's what's so devastating. They know the wonder of Wiley's and are still deciding to let it be buried alive.

One of the neighbors from my cul-de-sac gets up, an older man with a salt-and-pepper goatee. I think, finally, someone who'll be on our side. Instead, he says, "I'd rather have commuters clogging up our roadways than not be able to leave my neighborhood on a Friday night between six and eight. Not to mention the noise, noise, noise!"

It's upsetting to the umpteenth degree. He was all too happy drinking our booze, eating our burgers, and lazing around our backyard a month and a half ago. Now, these people are turning their backs on me like they didn't play a part in raising me, like the lot didn't become part of the charm of our district.

Victory slips out the side door.

"Would anyone else care to speak?" Councilwoman Harper asks.

This feels like the moment in a wedding where the officiant asks if anyone has objections to the union. While many have been voiced, few others will speak up. This portion of the meeting is about to be packed up and shut down to move on to more hot-button issues. It's over, and—

The door flings open.

There, backlit by the setting sun, is Derick Haverford.

He's just as tall (genetically), just as handsome (improbably), and here (fortunately?).

He steps into full view and everyone gasps when they see what he's wearing: that too-small Wiley's T-shirt. He rakes a roguish hand through his hair before announcing, "I have something to say."

The cameras swivel around to get a better shot. Reporters raise their recording devices. iPhones shoot up and turn to LIVE mode. Something is about to go down.

"My name is Derick Haverford. I'm the son of Daniel Haverford, partial owner of Any Weather Transportation Group and the man who's overseeing the demolition of Wiley's Drive-In." His voice is straight-line serious. "I'm not proud to admit that as the former social-media marketing intern at

Wiley's Drive-In, I was tasked by my father to gather intel about the financial dealings of the movie establishment to determine whether his property investment was worth maintaining."

Derick can't go back and undo his previous actions, but taking ownership over them in front of a packed room like this means more to me than he could ever know. I'm hanging hopefully on his every word.

"Legal? Yes. Ethical? I don't think so." A deep breath causes feedback in the microphone. "Before I go any further, I'd just like to say that my father is a smart businessman, and I love him, but he doesn't give two shits about this town or the value of and inherent need to preserve our historic district." This evokes a variance of big responses. The reporters, however, are eating this up, encouraging him with their eyes. "This bus-line expansion is about money and bottom lines. It's not about your access to urban jobs. It's not about getting you home to your families for meat-loaf night. Honestly, it's about a hot tub on the back deck at our beach house. Plain and simple."

When I glance down my row, everyone is leaning forward in their chairs, eyes wide, mouths agape. I'm the only one sitting back with satisfaction. Because I know for certain the cardboard version of himself he's been asked for years to display in the storefront of his family life has been incinerated for good. He's flesh and blood right now, flushed with freedom. He's standing up for himself and his own beliefs, and I couldn't be prouder.

"Derick!" Mr. Haverford clamors from his seat. Derick pretends not to hear him.

"I'm sure some of you think that's okay. What do we need a drive-in for anyway? Our town can survive without it." He pivots to address the greater group. "That may be true, but isn't our town better with it? In my time working at Wiley's, I've come to love the lot and"—he breaks for a fragile beat—"the people who work there..." He grows flustered, darts a glance in my direction. "It's a beautiful, wonderful place where movies and magic and memories all come together. I, for one, think preservation of our historic district needs to be upheld. The little drive-in that could can and should rise again. Don't let the credits roll on Wiley's Drive-In. Thank you."

Mr. Haverford jumps to his feet, but his wife pulls him down by the back of his jacket.

Almost as abruptly as he arrived, Derick dashes out the back door. In his wake, he leaves a riotous crowd that has climbed to its feet.

I don't know what to feel right now. For once, I'm too stunned to psychoanalyze myself.

I check my phone for Oscar's updates. The response is overwhelmingly positive. Derick has already been screen-grabbed and deemed the White Knight of Tight Shirts. Apt in so many ways.

This story isn't going away anytime soon.

And, hopefully, neither is the drive-in.

Chapter 28

Derick is sitting on the front porch of Alice's house when I drop her off. Sunset pinks and yellows float beyond the roof, highlighting the colors of his T-shirt that's now a Twitter sensation.

Social media may have made a scene, but the council shut down production.

"I hope you're not here to throw a celebratory house party. We lost," Alice crankily says to Derick as she hobbles past him onto the porch, carefully clutching the railings we repurposed weeks ago, which still look loose. In a four-to-three vote, the council overturned the recommendation to deny the certificate of appropriateness—something about the reasonable rate of return on the investment and the displayed histrionics. Testimonies, apparently, aren't sufficient evidence in matters this great. "Those bastards."

Derick nods glumly. "I was following along on the stream." He's gripping his matte black phone case like it's a grenade that might go off at any moment. Seconds pass, and he still won't meet my eyes.

"I'd invite you boys inside for dinner but the fridge is empty," Alice says, struggling with her shaky hands to find the right key from the bottom of her brown leather purse.

"My stomach couldn't handle food right now anyway."

With a knowing nod, Alice pads inside and shuts the door, though I swear I never hear the knob click back into place. If I know her like I think I do, she's going to be listening to all of this through the crack.

So much left unsaid swirls between Derick and me. The dismay hasn't yet set in, so I'm standing there, staring, still appreciative of how he came to the rescue.

"I didn't know where else to go," he admits, staring at the loose laces of his white high-tops. I nod. Since crash-landing into Alice's life, this place has become a haven for me, too. If I were running away from something, and maybe I was when the season started, this is the first place I'd think to come.

"What you did back there was incredible." I've been dying to say it, and I know he needs to hear it. "That couldn't have been easy."

He pulls his knees in to his chest, squeezing his agile body onto one narrow step. This is the smallest I've ever seen him. "It wasn't, but it needed to be said. Not just for Wiley's, but for me." He hasn't sounded this sure or steady since the night on the *Wavertree* when he told me he was good with what we had. How was I to know that what we had was undercut by a secret so huge it could threaten my livelihood?

I sit down next to him, while unfastening my bow tie, but leave necessary buffer space. Closeness of any kind isn't in store for us. Not yet at least. "Have you heard from your family at all?" I ask, testing the limits of his quietness.

He groans on an exhale. "At the end of the stream, I shut off my location settings and turned my phone off." It sits between us, black screen almost menacing. "That thing is just another way my dad controlled me, kept getting under my skin. I'm done letting him bulldoze me into submission."

I don't dare make a comment about his ironic word choice. Not that I have time to. Derick is winding back his arm and chucking the phone out into the overgrown field. It arcs like a sparrow swooping down for bugs and disappears into the stalks.

"Wren, I hate that I'm going to see Wiley's suffer at the hands of my family. They—*he*—shouldn't get to inflict any more damage." Hurt sucks the last of the light out of his tired eyes. "For so long, I've been told to be a certain way. Join a frat, make the grade, get a good job. Only speak up if you have something smart to say. You can be gay, but don't make a thing of it. And above all else, don't do anything to tarnish the family name or business." He spouts a sardonic laugh. "So much pressure for so long, I'm like,

what parts of me are even *me*, you know? How much of who I am did they…
construct? Today was the first day I've felt like I was acting on my own wants
and needs. Not someone else's."

"I could tell."

"And, of course, it didn't even work. That's what makes this infuriating.
Not that I can't go home. I didn't want to be there anyway. It's infuriating that
this was my last resort. That it even had to come to my last resort!"

I let him go off, releasing the anger that's festered inside him for so long.

"For the better part of this summer, since we started getting close again,
I've been attempting to jump-start Wiley's, just the same as you. I've scoured
the engagement data, built the filters, and run the giveaways." It's strange to
hear him confirm my suspicion. I should've seen it. I *would've* seen it had I
not been so wrapped up in my own insular cocoon. "Anything to boost sales
and give my father a reason not to move ahead with demolition. But I failed."

What he did today took guts, but it also took gall. I wish I could protect
him from the fallout, use a mystical force field to shield him from the inevitable pain.

But I can't. I know that now. Wishing to be superhuman was a waste of
mental space.

"No, hey. You didn't fail. We can't control everything. Believe me, I've
tried. Really. Since forever, I've tried to micromanage my life, to direct it
the way it might play out in a movie. I've waffled between indecision and
bad decision so many times that I've lost count. But, I've realized recently,
sometimes you've gotta let life be life." I never pegged Mateo as a prophet,
yet here I am, spreading his good word like a devout disciple. Maybe he does
have the powers of divine intervention after all.

"You made a very clear statement today that you are your own person.
Not a product of your family or some scapegoat they can push around."
There's a tense, pulsating need in the set of his jaw. It takes all my willpower
not to massage my thumb from the base of his ear to the tip of his chin, to
take on at least some of that burden. "You are so brave and creative and
funny and charming. And, sure, yeah, you were born into more status than
this small town can handle, but you can't change that. You are who you are
because of everything you've been through. Not in spite of it."

His shoulders ease, and slowly the muscles in his face relax. "Thank you. You don't know how much that means to me." His voice is small yet hopeful. "You're good at that."

"Good at what?"

"Big, meaningful speeches. I know you said you were scared and that public speaking made you queasy, but at both of those meetings, you made it seem like it was second nature. It's like you accessed some surprising new part of you. It inspired me to do the same."

"That makes me happy." I pause, letting it sink in that in tiny ways, we make each other better, push each other to strive for more.

"*You* make me happy, Wren."

"You make me happy, too. So happy, in fact, that I can't believe how I treated you the night that everything went to shit. I should've let you explain. I was angry, and I lashed out in a way I never have before. I scared myself."

"I get it."

"I wanted easier, better communication between us, and what did I do when I should've stopped and listened? I shut you down and I ghosted you because some sick part of me thought that made things better." Ghosting, I've learned, is not worth it from either side. "Guess we still need more practice with this whole open-and-honest thing."

"Yeah, I guess so." A beat passes. "I'm not doing anything. Think we could squeeze in some practice now?" Earnest, always so damn earnest.

"I think we could." I unbutton my collar and consider my words carefully, knowing I've only got one chance to get this right. "I'm sorry, Derick. I'm sorry I reacted in the moment without stopping to consider you, your situation, or your feelings. I never want to make you feel that way, and I will work overtime to ensure that doesn't happen again."

He nods, my words uncorking his expression. "I'm sorry, too, Wren. I should've told you everything. Right away. There's no excuse. I can rationalize it all I want, that I was trying to protect you or whatever. My dad always said: Ask for forgiveness, not permission, and that's what I thought I was doing, but really I was just willfully keeping information from you. Important information. I know better now, and I'm really damn sorry."

"We should coin this the Summer of I'm Sorry, huh?" I'm desperately hoping for him to crack at least a small, loose smile at this. No such luck.

Then, right as I think the moment will lapse, he quips, "Not nearly as good as the Summer of Free Ice Cream." There it is. Shiny, white teeth peek out from between his parted lips. I could soar, powered only by that smile.

"I think we still have time to turn this one around." I poke his bicep. "Maybe make this the Summer of Forgiveness instead?"

The buffer space disappears. Derick is close now, and his eyes are glassy. Hope blooms behind my rib cage.

"I'd like that."

"I would, too."

His face becomes a sun-shower. I wrap him in my arms and rub slow, sure circles on his back like he did for me that day at Alice's kitchen table when she showed me her special notebook. His tears eventually cause my own to fall, the reality of the drive-in walloping me all at once.

We shudder into each other's bodies, letting the shoulders of our shirts get soaked through.

Minutes later, the door swings open behind us, and Alice steps out onto the porch in a more casual outfit than the one from earlier. "You two blubbering babies done out here? I found some deli meat and some unmoldy bread. Eat something before you both wither away on my stoop."

With half laughs, we help each other up. Inside, over dry turkey sandwiches, the three of us play games of Go Fish with a deck of bent cards Alice dug out from her bedroom dresser. Something to distract us from the inevitable. The season may chug on, but summer, the carefree state of mind, has slipped away like sand through my fingers.

The gravity of it all zooms back into focus only after nightfall and three full rounds, Alice winning them all. I'm still not certain she wasn't cheating, stuffing sevens up her sleeves. A regular card shark.

"Help me clean up the living room?" Alice asks with angel eyes. She knows we won't say no.

It's the first time Derick fully sees the destruction Alice caused in her chaotic breakdown. Our hard work reduced to shambles. He's taken aback, running a hand over the walls. I can practically hear his teeth grinding.

"It's okay," I tell him. "We'll just have to rebuild." *In more ways than one,* I'm tempted to add.

Halfway through moving the couch back to its rightful place—how she pushed this at all with her bony chicken arms is beyond me—Alice returns with a pile of old blankets and pillows stacked so high we can't see her head.

"What are these for?" Derick asks, helping her before she falls over her favorite chair.

She stands there silently, pulling herself together, and then says, "I'm going to bed now. Stay the night if you want. Go if you want. But please just work it out already. If this has taught you anything, it's that now is the only time you've got for certain. Enjoy what you have while it lasts."

And with that, she scuttles up the steps, making sure we hear her close and lock her door. Derick and I look at each other, trying to read the other's expression. Wordlessly, we come to the same decision. He doesn't want to go home—he *can't* go home—and I know he won't stay if I don't.

We can't both fit on the couch, so we roll out the duvets into a makeshift mattress on the floor in front of it. It's hot in here, so we won't need covering. We shed our extra layers—me stripping down to my T-shirt and boxer shorts, Derick to only his briefs. I fold my blazer and dress slacks onto Alice's recliner, knowing full well they'll be a wrinkly mess by morning.

Our heads touch our pillows at the same time. We lie there, not saying a word, in the hazy glow of a single lamp, staring at each other. The heat of the room bears down on us, but locked in his gaze, nothing else matters to me.

"I'm sorry you're going through all this," I say. "I'm here for you. Through whatever. Even if Alice didn't passive-aggressively insinuate we should spend the night together, I wouldn't have left your side until you told me to."

"Thank you for saying that." His voice is a bashful blip I have to lean in to hear.

"Of course."

We snuggle closer together, even though the temperature's rising. Or maybe that's just a side effect of his nearness. Either way, I'm sweating.

"At least we have until the end of the season. Demolition can't start until the fall. You still get to do Alice's event." He's attempting to soften the blow with a thoughtful consolation prize.

"You're right. I'm grateful I have that." I grab his hand. "And I'm grateful I have this."

He asks with his eyes if he can kiss me, and I nod so emphatically that we nearly knock skulls. When he kisses me this time, with no more lies boiling between us, it feels different, more resolved. Final, in a way that doesn't necessitate an ending. But, rather, final in the sense that this is how kisses between us will always be from now on: tender and truthful.

"I wish it had been you," he says breathlessly when we break apart.

"What?"

"My first queer kiss," he corrects. "I wish it had been you, that night in the truck at the lot from your email." He sighs with so much heady contemplation. "Too bad time travel doesn't exist like it does in the movies, right? Oh well."

He rolls over, signaling me to slide in as the big spoon. I drape my top arm over him and shape my smaller body into the curves of his long back. Our breathing syncs up until we're both falling asleep, and a vivid dream helps me develop a beautiful, *beautiful* plan.

Chapter 29

Maybe time travel does exist.

At least that's how it feels on the night of Alice's event as I look out from the side door of the projection booth. It's packed out there. Decade-specific snack-shack prices. A premiere four decades later. People milling about in seventies-inspired outfits. It's a wholesome throwback because focusing on the future would be too bleak.

If only the council had seen the turnout tonight, could've forecasted our success. Not only did we sell out our advanced reservations, but we sold out the entire lot. We filled the open staff spots and let people sit on the grass down front. Many unfolded old beach towels or made friends with other groups who had extra tailgate chairs. At one point, we even had to turn people away, which is a rarity in my history of working here.

Even though many Willow Valley residents decreed their disinterest in Wiley's and sentenced us to our death, small businesses came out in droves to pitch in. Food trucks reached out asking if they could take space in our overflow lots. We got deliveries of free fancy soap samples and baskets of perfectly aged cheese. The reverberation of our sentencing has rocked Willow Valley.

"Since we're all set here, I'm heading down to the signing table." Oscar is wearing one of the leftover pink #TheLittleDriveInThatCould T-shirts. It's a bittersweet reminder of the effort we made. I guess the Rolling Stones were right: *You can't always get what you want.* "My publicist is having an aneurysm. The line is lengthy, and he can't ward them off much longer. This is incredible. Thank you for including me." He pats me on the shoulder before pushing open the door to the snack-shack lobby.

"Thank you for everything!" I call after him.

"My pleasure!" he yells back.

The social-media storm rages on in my pocket. Vibrate. Chime. Repeat. We may have lost at council, but the internet is still abuzz with our cause. They're calling for other drive-ins to be preserved, for new ones to open. It's gratifying, for sure. If nothing else, at least we'll leave behind that legacy.

I turn off my notifications for tonight. I want to stay in the moment.

"In eighty-six years of service, I think this is the biggest event we've ever thrown," Earl says, stepping out from behind his desk. Mateo, Avery, and I all turn to see him wearing a weathered smile and one of our buttons. "It's almost time to give the big welcome speech. You on the mic or am I?"

"Let the podcast star give it a whirl," Avery says, shoving me toward the table where the mixer sits. I'm still not used to the fresh attention I've garnered since the podcast episode blew up. Sure, I'm not a sex symbol like Derick (and, yes, I *refuse* to call him the White Knight of Tight Shirts, even though he has jokingly asked during more than one make-out session). But, even Oscar was pleasantly shocked by the number of offers I received for features, sponsors, inquiries about starting my own podcast. His publisher even made a passing mention of being interested in Alice's story, should she ever want to share it in book form. With. Me. Attached.

It's flattering, even if they're all more interested in Alice than my expertise. I understand, though, and I welcome it even more. That's the job of a researcher. To unearth the narrative and present it in a compelling way without inserting your own bias into the synthesis. If I wanted the spotlight, I'd have gone into filmmaking forthright.

On Earl's cue, I press the red button. "Welcome everyone to Wiley's Drive-In. Tonight, we present the premiere that never was. Willow Valley history gets made. A second-chance story gets unearthed tonight thanks to director Alice Kelly." I picture her sitting in my mom's SUV in the center of the lot, one of my old baseball caps on her head. The tinted window will protect her, but I have a sneaking suspicion she's going to want the attention after she hears the rapturous response as soon as THE END blinks up on the screen.

"We'd like to say thank you to all who shared their thoughts and support for our #TheLittleDriveInThatCould campaign. This may be our last season, but we're going out with a bang. Sit back, relax, and the feature will begin shortly."

The crowd's enthusiasm cuts through the walls. The rabid film geeks were gearing up, messaging me encouragements all week and asking for Easter eggs and sneak peeks about what to expect. My fingers couldn't reply fast enough.

A countdown clock appears on the bottom right of the screen as the trailers and advertisements begin to play.

"Nice work, kid," Earl says, nostalgia glossing over his expression. I'm not the pimply fifteen-year-old he insisted on hiring anymore. I'm the less-pimply twenty-two-year-old he can count on, who tried to save his family business. He's taking note of it all, finally, and it's bringing tears to his eyes.

"There's no crying in drive-ins," I joke.

"You're thinking of baseball." He produces a hanky from his pocket and dabs the corners of his eyes. "Sorry we couldn't pull a Hail Mary this time."

"Maybe this is how it's meant to end." I've made peace with maybe and almost. Uncertainty isn't so scary when you've got the promise of possibility stretched out ahead of you. I'll save my mourning for tomorrow.

A text pings in from Derick:

You've got a voice for radio,
But you've also got a face for movies.
Is that what they call a double threat?

I blush so hard that Mateo and Avery start mockingly fanning me. I swat them away as I type back.

🙂 I'll meet you at the photo booth in five.

"Everything all set?" I ask Avery, who's got my dad's pickup truck keys with his Harley Davidson commemorative key chain dangling from her ring finger. I enlisted her and Mateo to pull off my dream grand gesture.

"Fluffed, arranged, and executed to perfection. NTB or anything." *Not to brag.*

"And the purple blanket from my room?" I ask Mateo.

"Claire saw me carrying it across the lot when I arrived, and she nearly fought me for it. Said she's been looking for it for months." He shoots me a look. "I had to explain that we needed it for a good cause."

This premiere isn't the only way I intend to turn back the clock tonight.

I smile and laugh. Even in the face of permanent closure, I can't help but feel full of gratitude. Wherever I end up beyond the gates of Wiley's, I'll always have the memories and this fantastic support system.

I wrap my arms around my friends and yank them in close. "I love you both so much. And I know we won't be living together much longer, but please promise me that the 3Bee Gees won't break up."

"Babe," Mateo laughs into my ear. "The 3Bee Gees will never die because we're…'stayin' alive, stayin' alive, ha, ha, ha.'" His falsetto sets us into raucous motion. The three of us end up disco dancing along to his vocals, doing our best John Travolta impressions with goofy grins pressed on our faces.

Youssef appears by the projector. "Do I even want to know?" he asks of the scene we're making. We laugh and then rush out the door.

Avery and Mateo head down front to find Brandon and Stacia.

"Good luck!" Avery calls over her shoulder as they disappear into the fray.

The photo booth is around the side of the snack shack. Derick ordered a drop depicting the graveyard set from Alice's movie and got two plastic tombstones from the clearance section at a local party store. He even got a couple of clip-on schoolboy ties that match the one the zombie wears in the movie. Groups gather round, picking up paper props on sticks. The last gaggle of girls squat together holding up a severed hand.

"All good," Derick calls out after getting the shot. The two youngest girls giggle to themselves, clearly fans of his meme status, and then scamper off. I must admit, he does look extra attractive tonight.

I may have lied and told him we were out of his size when he asked for a #TheLittleDriveInThatCould shirt to wear tonight, so the pink fabric pulls and bulges in all the right places, inspiring all the wrong fantasies.

I swoop in to say hi. Derick plants a kiss on my cheek. PDA with a PYT for little, old me? Groundbreaking, I know. "How'd it go?"

"Great. Let me just break everything down so we can find a spot to watch." He begins demounting his camera when a voice comes from behind.

"Time for one more?" It's Preeti, looking gorgeous in a flowing tie-dye sundress. David is by her side, buttoned up as per usual.

Derick sputters. "What are you doing here?"

"We couldn't miss this," Preeti yelps, enveloping Derick in a hug. Whatever familial tension has been simmering through the Haverford household has not reached Preeti out in Philadelphia. She's elated to see him. "We grabbed the last advance reservation and drove in. Can we grab a pic? I want to post it. All my friends at the practice were so jealous when I told them where we were going tonight."

Derick obliges and sets the camera back. Preeti puts one of the ties on David.

"Quite the turnout," David notes as Preeti fusses over his appearance. He offers a cordial handshake to his brother. The closest to intimacy those men share.

"I've been meaning to reach out," Derick says.

David waves a hand as Derick fiddles with the focus. He counts down from three. I stand back, letting this play out. I'll only step in if he needs me.

After taking a ton as per Preeti's request—she needs *options*—David moves in toward the tripod. "I came over to let you know that I understand why you did what you did. That took balls, Bro. Don't think I coulda done it." He slaps Derick on the back. "Also, don't panic, but…Mom and Dad are here."

Derick's face drains of color. The camera nearly topples to the ground. I dive around to catch it.

David points to the out-of-place white Tesla down front. The windows are tinted and the occupants haven't stepped out once.

"They weren't going to tell you, but I thought you'd want to know."

Preeti pulls on David's arm. "Let's get snacks before the movie starts. I'm craving peanut butter cups." David relents with a smile. "Have a good night, guys." They disappear through the open doors.

"Should I go over?" Derick asks, frozen in place.

"I can't answer that for you." As far as I know, the three of them haven't spoken. He spends most nights at my apartment. Whatever anger I feel toward Mr. Haverford is a pittance compared to what Derick must be experiencing, so I make no mention of how rude it is for his parents to be showing their faces around here right now.

Since I've seen Derick set the camera up more than a few times, I take the liberty of putting his stuff away, carefully transferring the camera back into its case. The tripod folds up easily, and by the time I'm done stashing everything in the storage closet, Derick is coming unglued.

"Will you come with me?"

I grab his hand and tell him to lead the way.

He knocks lightly on the passenger side window. It's not even halfway down when he asks, "Shouldn't you two be back in South Carolina by now?"

"We changed our plans to be here," Mrs. Haverford says. Her pressed, peach lips curl up into an apologetic smile. "The beach isn't going anywhere." I'm about to make a snide remark about global warming (a scientific fact I'm certain they don't believe in), but I zip my lips.

"This was your idea, I assume?" Derick asks his mom. Mr. Haverford hasn't let his gaze leave the screen. It could be the sun dipping below the tree line but I swear I see sweaty remorse glistening on his forehead. Though, that could also just be the boardroom attire he's wearing despite the August humidity.

Mrs. Haverford fumbles for an answer, toying with the gold crucifix hanging from her necklace. "We both agreed to come. We're both here."

Her weak response is drowned out by a sudden bout of booing. Derick and I both jump. When I look up at the screen, an Any Weather Transportation Group ad is playing. Youssef must've forgotten to pull it from the rotation. It runs before every movie we show.

How had I not wondered about this before? What a clear tip-off that Mr. Haverford had our place in the palm of his hand this whole time. I guess everything is easier to see in hindsight.

"We should probably..." Spooked by the turning crowd, Mrs. Haverford reaches for the toggle on the car door.

"Yeah, you should," Derick agrees, gripping my hand tighter. His anger doesn't negate the confusion. There's still love there between the three of them. Strained love, but love nonetheless. He doesn't want them publicly bashed tonight. "Enjoy the show."

The window seals up tight again. We start away. Derick's vise-like grip loosens. "Do you want to talk about it?" I ask, running a supportive hand up the outside of his arm.

"No. Not right now, thanks. Maybe later tonight. I just want to find the perfect spot for us to watch the movie." He weakly smiles down at me. "Is that okay?"

"That's more than okay." I borrow his conspiratorial expression from the night at the Lonely Lass-O. "I have just the spot."

When we reach my dad's cobalt-blue pickup truck in the last row of spaces, I lean against the bumper hoping to exude some of Derick's unflappable ease.

"Why are you making that face?"

"I'm glad you asked." I reach for his hands. "I realized something. Even though true time travel doesn't exist, I have been known to rewrite history." I indicate the crowd around us. "Care to join me on a little journey to the past?"

His nod lets on that he knows where this is going. The element of surprise wasn't on my side to begin with, so I'm unbothered as I pop the back hatch and leap into the bed.

Three flicks and the whole rectangle comes alive with strands of magical fairy lights, battery-powered and illuminating a drove of blankets and pillows. Including the one Mateo had to pry from Claire's materialistic grip.

"Twizzler?" I ask, reaching a half-open pack of Pull'n'Peels down toward him. The interaction with his parents falls away. He accepts one right before I hoist him up to my level.

"You did all this for me?" He does a three-sixty, inspecting days of planning come to fruition. Then, he does another spin, eye line out on the lot, inspecting *months* of planning paying off.

"Half for you, half for *us*. What you said at Alice's the other night gave me the idea." We sit, get comfortable. He reaches for one of the buckets of popcorn. "That one's actually mine." I grab it from him, wiggling my fingers. "No butter or salt. This one's for you." I pass him the second one. "*Extra* butter, *extra* salt. And…*extra* napkins." I drop a stack in his lap.

"You thought of everything, didn't you?"

"What can I say? Anything worth doing is worth doing right." It seems sometimes my affinity for not settling comes in handy. Especially when it comes to him. I slide in closer.

Easing into the moment, I rest my head on his shoulder, the soft cotton and defined muscle making an excellent pillow. I realize it doesn't feel the same as it did senior year. Not even close. Too much has shifted since then. Derick and I are settled into our identities. We know each other on a deeper level. There are no friends here to cockblock our (hopeful, eventual) kissing.

"Remember when you said one kiss can cause a whole lot of trouble?" I ask, recalling that huge stalk of comical celery.

"Yeah?" He's already munching on a handful of popcorn.

"You weren't kidding." I snort. Not on purpose. But thankfully, Derick doesn't cringe. He boops my nose with a salty finger as if it were the cutest thing in the world. An almost-kiss wreaked emotional havoc on my life for so long. A real kiss was the tipping point for complete upheaval. But now, quite a few kisses later, I'm more motivated than ever to rebuild my world the way I want to see it. Even if that world can't include Wiley's.

It dawns on me that this is the last night ever that I'll get to really enjoy the drive-in as an audience member. In the coming weeks, we'll start clearing out, listing equipment for sale, and saying goodbye. I'll be on the clock for all of it. In the end, I couldn't have coordinated a better final experience, nor a better final person to share it with.

Maybe it's the twinkle lights mirroring the stars above us or the buzz building around us, but whatever the impetus, I tilt my head up toward Derick's and whisper what I've been feeling for an eternity. "I hope you know how much you mean to me." His smile shines brighter than the moon. "Doing this was only one small way to show you. If you'll let me, I'd like to keep showing you in a bunch of different ways, in a bunch of different places for a long, long time."

He bites his lip. "I'll strongly consider it," he teases, making a reference to Alice's early hesitation over this exact evening. I give him a playful shove. Setting his popcorn aside, he asks in a low voice, "How else do you plan on showing me?"

"Hmm." I make a grand show of considering his question as if I haven't imagined this specific scenario a million times since that fateful night. "Maybe with a kiss?" I lick my lower lip, anticipating his buttery taste.

"I think I could be persuaded with a kiss."

Just as the countdown clock on the screen times out, I sit up and correct the past with a perfect (*perfect*) kiss. The passion with which he kisses me back tells me I've persuaded him fully, and then some.

"You mean a lot to me, too, Wren," he whispers when we lean back.

His fidgety fist blossoms into an open palm. I lace our fingers together as we prepare to take in the movie and take on the future, whatever that may include, together.

Chapter 30

Alice's house is, for the first time in a long time, full of life.

Light spills out of every window. People sit on every sturdy chair. Food and drinks are splayed out across every available surface.

Good thing Derick and I helped her clean up the wreckage of her riot last week. The impromptu potluck formed immediately after the screening ended, and it's been going on for at least an hour now. I stand in the corner of the porch, empty red Solo cup in my hand, watching as the fireflies dance across the property.

Chompin' at the Bit made massive waves. When the film concluded, as I suspected, Alice walked out from Mom's car to the center of the lot and blew kisses to her adoring public. The cheers could probably be heard for miles.

The pandemonium moved to her farmhouse. Because she doesn't care what destruction ensues here, Alice has allowed the film fanatics, the employees, and the parents to partake in the party however they so choose. The Wiley's gang set up a highly competitive game of flip cup in the kitchen. The adult-adults are chatting over store-bought cupcakes in the dining room. Oscar and his colleagues were allowed supervised access to Alice's special box of memories and are still flipping out over her wealth of files in the living room.

Avery and Mateo are off with Stacia and Brandon respectively. Derick's inside fetching me a refill. I'm soaking it all in. It's been an eternity since I could stop, breathe, and reset. So much has happened this summer, and I haven't processed any of it.

My lease is up in two weeks. Wiley's closes for good in three. After Labor Day, I will be left to my own devices, trying to decide what opportunities to take, where to live, what to fill my days with. It's overwhelming, but, surprisingly, not debilitating.

Alice appears at the front door. She's holding her box of memories close like she did that first day she showed it to me. "What are you doing out here all alone?"

I shrug. "Just needed some quiet. That's all."

She smiles demurely and comes closer. I notice she's holding her ticket from tonight's premiere in her free hand. "I wanted you to be around when I did this." Ceremoniously, she sets the pristine ticket in the box among her most cherished keepsakes, solidifying the event I helped create as an important part of her artistic life. "In case I haven't said it yet…thank you."

"Thank *you* for trusting me with your movie. I mean, this was the most satisfying project I've ever worked on." Impending grief tinges my words. I'm not emotionally ready to say goodbye to Wiley's, just like I'm certain Alice wasn't ready to say goodbye to Tammy. I know it's not the same, but loss, in any capacity, still stings the soul. "I know I didn't know Tammy, and you didn't talk about her all that much, but I think she would've been proud of you right now. I said it in the podcast, but I'll say it again: Your love is lodged in every frame of that movie. It's palpable. Truly."

She nods with the heft of a thousand unspoken words. "Love is the all-mighty inspiration. Distilling it down to one-hundred-and-twenty minutes is hard, but making it work in real life is even harder. Both, in the end, are worth it. Even if they're messy. Even if they end badly." Her slight body shoves into my hip. "I suspect you have that kind of inspiration now, too." Derick and I haven't said those words yet, but I swore I felt them as we sat in the bed of my dad's pickup truck tonight, snacking, crying, and laughing. Upon second watch, *Chompin' at the Bit* is thematically about the lengths we go to for love, but maybe even more so about the sheer power of forgiveness.

"You might be right," I say with a secretive smile.

"When the season at the lot is over," Alice says, dancing around the pain of locking the gates for the last time, "let's get serious about sharing my whole story."

"You'd really be open to me writing your biography?"

She shrugs. "Unless you know of someone better to do it."

"No." I laugh. "No, let me do it. I want to do it. In September, we'll get it right. Start from the beginning. I want to hear it all."

Derick steps out into the cooling mid-August air. He's got two fresh Solo cups in his hands and his camera strapped diagonally across his torso. He smiles a megawatt smile at us. "What are you two talking about?"

"Oh, nothing," Alice intones. "Just Wren writing a bestselling book about me."

"Really? Guess you've got a lot of work ahead of you. Doing the interviews, writing the chapters, picking out a title." He hands me the drinks.

"Oh no! I already have the perfect title." Alice sashays over to the door. She raises her shoulders, tilts her head, and hits a photo-perfect pose. "*Chompin' at the Bitch: The Alice Kelly Story.*"

Laughter spews out of all three of us. Derick snaps a picture of Alice cackling. She shoots him a disapproving look. "For the front cover," he qualifies. This pleases her enough to let it go.

"Enjoy the evening, boys." She dips back through the doorway.

Derick and I are alone. The roar of the party is muffled. Even though our labor wasn't enough to make this place sell, I'm glad it was able to facilitate this. One evening of all-out bliss before it all goes away.

Derick's expression, skewed by the dim overhead light, is inexplicably expectant. There's a twitch in his right eyebrow that won't stop, just like the smile that keeps expanding across his face.

"What's happening right now? Where have you been?"

"I thought you'd never ask." He pulls out his phone—the one he bought himself to replace the one his dad had given him—and shows me the screen. The email I read there makes my heart stop.

FROM: DHaverford@AnyWeatherTransport.com
TO: Derick.Haverford.Photo@gmail.com
SUBJECT: You Were Right

Dear Derick,

After careful consideration, I have decided to cease demolition plans for Wiley's Drive-In.

The social media and in-person uproar I witnessed is a PR nightmare for Any Weather Transportation Group, and as I suspected, it is negatively affecting our sales this quarter. Commercial bus lines need community support, and it seems I've lost the Willow Valley trust. For that I am deeply ashamed, but mostly, I'm ashamed of losing yours.

As a father, I may be harsh and demanding, but it's because I love you and I want what's best for you. As such, once you help me find a new property for our pickup location parking lot, you are free to find your own job, wherever you so choose. *Within reason.*

We can discuss this further when your mother and I return from Myrtle Beach.

Congratulations on your big event. Send our congrats to Wren as well.

All my best,
Dad

Derick is reading the email again over my shoulder. His cheeks are red, and his blue eyes are a dazzling display of burgeoning contentment. My heart is bursting for him. For Wiley's. For the future. It beats and beats and beats with impressive speed and a satisfying rhythm I want to record and turn into a hit song to play over the end credits.

Derick notices my speechlessness and says, "I couldn't believe it either. I had to go stand in the bathroom and collect myself."

Overcome, I set down our drinks on the ledge. "Wow. Your dad's really coming for my title as #1 sender of unexpected emails."

Derick chortles, then grows pragmatic. "Now, I just need to find and sell my dad on another property for his beloved parking lot."

"Seems like a problem for another night." I wink and draw him in to me by the center of his shirt. He doesn't resist as our chests press together. His arm hooks around me, and I want to taste him, wildly, right now, and in all the ways.

"I agree." He cranes his long neck down to me. Our lips meet, satiating my craving, and not even seconds into what should be a lovely private make-out session, I hear Mateo, Avery, and a horde of others whooping behind us. There, watching through the large window frame as if it were a movie screen, is an audience of eight cheering us on.

Their presence startles me, and I lose my balance. My body careens into the railing that Derick and I reattached last month. The force causes the poles to pop off one by one, toppling to the ground. I'm about to go down with them, but then Derick's strong arms wrench me back in. I'm saved from an embarrassing ending to an otherwise enchanting night.

Our audience gasps, and then sighs when they see I'm safe.

"So much for our handiwork," Derick jokes, inspecting the damage over the edge.

I catch my breath. "Thanks for that."

As soon as I'm upright again, the crowd beings to chant "Kiss! Kiss! Kiss!" but I can't hear them. An idea has overtaken me. It was right in front of me this whole time, and weirdly enough, a pile of poles has made it clear.

"Wait, are you thinking what I'm thinking?" I ask Derick.

"That we should give the people what they want?" His quirked eyebrow nearly kills me.

"No," I mumble. "Well, yes, definitely that, but the house, the farm, the…" I'm not making any sense and it shows. "Sorry. What I mean to say is, you should get your dad to buy Alice's property. He can put the parking lot here. Alice can finally move on."

Derick looks at me like I contain the wonders of the universe. "That's"—he pauses to consider it—"actually brilliant."

"Do you think your dad would go for it?"

"It's worth a shot."

"Kiss! Kiss! KISS!" The throng grows louder, and so does my uninhibited heart.

Without putting the show of the century off any longer, Derick and I, entirely elated, kiss right there on Alice's front porch for everyone to see. It's the magical-scene setting for the franchise of us. The first installment might've gotten cut short, bogged down in too much backstory, but the sequel is right on schedule.

It's bigger, bolder, and better than I ever could've imagined.

Epilogue-Instagram

Four Years Later

WileysDriveInWV Join us this Friday for a very special opening night of Wiley's 90th season! We'll be celebrating the launch of new owner @RolandOnTheRiver14's book *Chompin' at the Bitch: The Alice Kelly Story* with a Q&A, a signing, and a screening of the movie that started it all: *Chompin' at the Bit* (1978). Including a special appearance by the director herself…among other surprises. Don't miss out on the fun!

.

.

IMAGE DESCRIPTION: A white, medium-height, handsome, shaggy-brown-haired man with facial scruff stands under the refurbished Wiley's Drive-In sign, smiling while holding up a finished hardcover copy of his brand-new book.

#drivein #moviesPA #WileysDriveIn #booklaunch

420BlazinBoii Best believe I'll be there!

DontYouForgetAboutPod Going to be so fun getting to interview Wren again! Congrats on the new position and book. You and @Derick.Haverford.Photo make such great partners. In both business and in life! 🖤 #TheLittleDriveInThatCould

LifeAccordingToAves @MateoTActor Stacia and I are flying in from California on Thursday. Any chance you can take a night off from your one-man cabaret show to support our baby boys?

MateoTActor @LifeAccordingToAves NEVER! My fans need me! 💅 (jkjkjk, I'll be there!)

Derick.Haverford.Photo @LifeAccordingToAves @MateoTActor You both better be there or you're going to miss something veeeeeeeeeeery special. @RolandOnTheRiver14

RolandOnTheRiver14 @LifeAccordingToAves @MateoTActor @Derick.Haverford.Photo 😉 👏 🖤

The End

♥ *Acknowledgments*

Imagine you're sitting in your car at the drive-in theater and the feature has just finished...

The film fades to black...

Barbra Streisand's cover of "As Time Goes By" croons out from your speakers...

A rolling list of champions and confidants who made this book possible scrolls across the screen...

Never Been Kissed
Listed in Order of Appearance

Supportive, Loving Parents...........................*Theresa Janovsky,*
John Janovsky
Beautiful BFFs...................................*Melanie Magri,*
Tarah Hicks, Kelsey Scanlon, Julie Matrale
Early Mentors.....................................*Charlotte Sheedy,*
Ally Sheedy, and the team at the
Charlotte Sheedy Literary Agency
King of My Heart................................*Robert Stinner*
Secret (Literary) Agent Man...........................*Kevin O'Connor*

Editor Extraordinaire..*Mary Altman*

Assistant Editor Extraordinaire.....................*Christa Soulé Désir*

Marketing Magician...*Stefani Sloma*

Sourcebooks Stars..*Rachel Gilmer,*
Jessica Smith, Stephanie Gafron

Early Reader/Fearless Book Club Leader...........*Sadie Barnett*

Book Buddies..*Kasee Bailey,*
Simone Richter, Jacob Demlow, Laynie Rose Rizer

Amazing Author Pals.......................................*Gina Loveless,*
Alison Cochrun

Incredible Indie Bookstore............................*Let's Play Books!*
Bookstore

Historic Preservation Specialist.....................*Mindy Crawford,*
appearance courtesy of Preservation Pennsylvania

Grammar Wizards..*Diane Dannenfeldt*
and [PROOFREADER TK]

Illustrious Illustrator..*[Illustrator TK]*

Awesome Readers ....YOU!

Thank you to every single person at Sourcebooks Casablanca for shepherding my little, queer rom-com into the hands of readers. From design and production to our sensitivity readers and proofreaders, none of this would be possible without you.

To the #22Debuts and incredible Bookstagramers/BookTok-ers, thank you for your support, community, and rallying.

To the generous authors who agreed to read early versions of this book and offer kind words, my gratitude is infinite.

To all my family and friends, thank you for believing in me no matter what.

And, finally, to any reader out there who's still "figuring it all out" like Wren…like me…I see you. Thank you for being you.

About the Author

©Rebecca Phillips

Timothy Janovsky is a queer, multidisciplinary storyteller from New Jersey. He holds a bachelor's degree from Muhlenberg College and a self-appointed certificate in rom-com studies (accreditation pending). When he's not daydreaming about young Hugh Grant, he's telling jokes, playing characters, and writing books. *Never Been Kissed* is his first novel.

timothyjanovsky.com 📷 @TimothyJanovsky 🐦 @TimothyJanovsky